## Praise for V[...]

'A grimy, tense, crime/gang thril[...] characters; Vendetta *brings drama and realism to a dark story of grudges, revenge and passion.*'
**ALICE OSEMAN, author of SOLITAIRE**

'I stayed up until Late o'clock finishing Vendetta ... It's AWESOME. Great fighting. Great kissing.'
**C.J. DAUGHERTY, author of NIGHT SCHOOL**

'A vibrant new twist on Romeo and Juliet. Full of energy and intrigue!'
**LUCY CHRISTOPHER, author of STOLEN**

'Fan-freaking-tastic ... I honestly can't say enough good things about it! I would read anything Cat Doyle writes after flying through Vendetta!'
**VICTORIA SCOTT, author of FIRE & FLOOD**

## Praise for INFERNO

'It's bloody brilliant, even better than Vendetta if that's possible ... It's exciting and violent and sexy and heartbreaking. Loved it!'
**LOUISE O'NEILL, author of ONLY EVER YOURS**

'Darker, sexier and more dangerous than ever before ...'
**MELINDA SALISBURY, author of THE SIN EATER'S DAUGHTER**

'It's the best, best, best YA romance-slash-Mafia action film that you could ever HOPE FOR ... IT WAS SO GOOD. SO GOOD.'

**W**ow! The explosive climax to Catherine Doyle's brilliant *Blood for Blood* trilogy sees Sophie living the ultimate lie in Mafia-torn Chicago. Love and loyalty collide in an all-action blend of romance, thrills and unexpected twists. Somehow it's the dark humour and the strong friendships that make it feel so much more real: *Mafiosa* is a heartbreaker but with a real sense of the here and now. Steel yourself for a brilliant, shocking end to a fantastic series . . .

**BARRY CUNNINGHAM**
Publisher
Chicken House

# MAFIOSA

*Catherine Doyle*

Chicken
House

2 Palmer Street, Frome, Somerset BA11 1DS
www.chickenhousebooks.com

Text © Catherine Doyle 2017

First published in Great Britain in 2017
Chicken House
2 Palmer Street
Frome, Somerset BA11 1DS
United Kingdom
www.chickenhousebooks.com

Cover and interior design by Helen Crawford-White
Cover photographs: girl © Aleshyn_Andrei/Shutterstock;
boy © Stefano Cavoretto/Shutterstock; rose © rprongjaj/Shutterstock;
bullets © Rueangrit Srisuk/Shutterstock; mask © Zonda/Shutterstock
Typeset by Dorchester Typesetting Group Ltd
Printed and bound in Great Britain by CPI Group (UK) Ltd, Croydon CR0 4YY

The paper used in this Chicken House book is made from wood grown in
sustainable forests.

1 3 5 7 9 10 8 6 4 2

British Library Cataloguing in Publication data available.

ISBN 978-1-909489-84-4
eISBN 978-1-911077-19-0

*For my brothers, Colm and Conor*

# PART I

'Turning and turning in the widening gyre
The falcon cannot hear the falconer;
Things fall apart; the centre cannot hold;
Mere anarchy is loosed upon the world.'

William Butler Yeats, 'The Second Coming'

# CHAPTER ONE
## BLOOD AND FIRE

'Hold your hand out, with your palm facing upwards.' The way Valentino was watching me made my heart beat faster. I raised my arm, conscious of how slowly I was moving.

Felice was leaning back in the chair beside Valentino, one stick-like leg propped over the other. His arms were crossed tightly, like he was made of cardboard and someone had tried to fold him up. 'He's not going to chop it off, Persephone. Try not to let your cowardice show.'

'Felice,' Luca snapped. His jaw was so tight he looked like he could chew glass. He was sitting directly across the table from me, his body half turned away. I wanted him to look at me, to tell me it would be OK, but that wasn't his job. He had gotten me here, at least – I had a foot in the door. It was

3

foolish to hope for any more.

Nic cut his eyes at his uncle. 'The initiation is new to Sophie. Let her go at her own pace.'

Felice raised an eyebrow. 'If you say so . . .'

'Just because she's a Marino doesn't mean she's taken a blood oath before,' he pointed out.

Valentino tugged me towards him. I could feel his ring – thick and cold – pressing against my pulse. 'Let's hope not,' he murmured as he flicked his switchblade open.

I zeroed in on the handle. *Valentino*. The boss.

*It will be easy. It will be quick. It's just a formality.*

The room was nestled in the back of *Evelina*, Felice's gargantuan mansion. It was small, and dark, and way too hot. Everything was a collection of looming shadows and bright Falcone eyes.

Valentino punctured the skin at the top of my index finger and held it over an etching of the Falcone crest – a crimson bird half poised for flight. We watched in silence as the blood fell from my hand.

'At least we know she's human,' Felice muttered.

I threw him a dirty look. 'Try to control yourself, vampire. This is premium-grade initiation blood.'

Felice pointed incriminatingly at me. '*See*, she's already making a mockery of it.'

Luca balled his fists on the table.

'*Stai zitto*, Felice,' Nic hissed. 'Stop goading her.'

Valentino released me, and my hand hovered on its own, the blood still dripping on to the paper. 'Say the words we taught you.'

I cleared my throat. 'I, Persephone Gracewell—'

4

'Marino,' interrupted Felice. 'Identify yourself properly.'

I glared at him.

He glared right back. He didn't want this – a Marino inside his ranks, however ignorant I had been to my own ancestry – but he had been outvoted and it was too late now.

'I, Persephone *Marino*,' I laboured, 'swear by my heart and my blood to uphold the values of the Falcone family so long as I am living. I will demonstrate honour and loyalty at all times, and will not break the sacred vow of *omertà*, on pain of torture or death. Henceforth, I pledge my allegiance to the House of Falcone and denounce all others, from now until my last breath.'

'Withdraw,' Valentino ordered.

I pulled my hand back and clenched my pricked finger inside my fist. He picked up the paper and pulled a box of matches from his pocket. He struck one, and in that instant I felt my world shrink around me. A breath caught inside my throat as it tightened. I could smell smoke – invading my nostrils, clouding my brain.

*I am safe. I am free. It's just an illusion.*

Valentino touched the flame to the paper and it began to burn, blackening and curling at the edges.

In my head, dying screams rang out. I was back in the diner. I was inside the fire again. I saw my mother's white sneakers inside the flames, winking at me. I could taste the ash and dust, I could feel it rushing into my lungs and parching my throat. My arms were sizzling and burning, the healing wounds ripped open again.

*Not here. Not now.*

Luca cleared his throat.

I tried to pull my thoughts from the inferno that had ripped my world away. The fire was over. The pain was all that remained. I tried to ignore my mother's face as it swam behind my eyelids. Those kind eyes, that gentle watery smile. *I'm sorry. I'm so sorry, Mom.*

'And the rest,' Valentino prompted. 'Sophie. Finish it.'

I blinked hard. The paper was nearly gone now. The flames had chewed it up into floating silver flecks.

'Sophie.' Luca's voice, quiet and stern, brought me back. I refocused. I remembered why I was here. What I had to do.

'*La famiglia prima di tutto*,' I finished.

The family above everything.

The family comes first.

My family.

Valentino dropped the last shred of paper. 'Sophie Marino, this ceremony symbolizes your rebirth into the Falcone family. From now on, you will live by the gun and the blade.' He beckoned me closer. I went, like a puppet on a string, jarred by the streaks of similarity between him and Luca as those deep blue eyes loomed larger.

Valentino pressed a hand to either side of my face and brushed his ice-cold lips against each of my cheeks, the movement quick and perfunctory. He was inches from me, our noses almost touching, and a shiver raked up my spine. I stared right into those calculating eyes, as he said, '*Benvenuta nella famiglia, Sophie.*' He dropped his hands and pulled back from me again. 'We are one until death.'

I expelled the breath that had been swelling inside me.

'So, that's it, then?' It was over as quickly as it had begun. There was a strange tingle of warmth blooming in my chest.

'I'm one of you now?'

'Almost,' said Valentino, pushing back from the table and rolling his neck around until it cracked.

Luca answered at the same time: 'Yes.'

They looked at each other, heads tilted in matching displays of confusion.

Valentino twirled his hand in the air, but when he spoke, it was in reply to Luca, not to me. 'She will have to kill a Marino before she can fully commit to the Falcone regime.'

'Ah!' Felice, who had unfolded all his limbs and was on his feet now, lit up like a glow stick. 'Christmas has come early.'

Luca was still staring at his twin. 'You can't be serious.'

Valentino's eyes narrowed. 'How else would we bind her to us?'

Felice's words flashed in my head. *Try not to let your cowardice show.* 'Who?' I asked, hearing the rasp in my voice and hating it. 'Who do I have to kill?'

'A small player,' Valentino replied. 'A test. I'll let you know the target soon.' He was so nonchalant it almost tricked me into a feeling of normality. In place of fear, a sense of duty began to rise. This was my task. Of course I would have to do something to prove myself. Of course it would be this. How else would they know I wasn't a Marino spy? How else could they help me avenge my mother?

'It's fine,' Nic said, the flicker of a smile lifting the hard edge of his cheekbone. 'It's not like she'll have to do it alone, Luca. We'll help her.'

'She'll have to make the killing blow,' Felice warned. 'Make sure she pulls the trigger.'

'Of course,' said Nic, without missing a beat.

'Of course,' I echoed, feeling a million miles away from the girl I had been just a few months ago.

'It's settled.' Valentino's words floated over his shoulder as he moved away from me. 'The next Marino casualty will belong to Sophie. And then Sophie will belong to us.'

I had barely reached the hallway when the distant sound of shouting filtered through the house. I jogged towards it, following Gino's voice as his pitch climbed higher and higher, the sudden wrongness of it echoing around me.

I sprinted past the kitchen, ignoring the laughter of Paulie's three little girls, skidded into the foyer and wrenched the front door open. Outside, Dom and Gino were already trekking towards the end of the driveway.

In the distance, flames were billowing above the entrance to *Evelina*. My heart leapt into my throat as an onslaught of dread careened over me. It prickled in my fingers, slithered up my arms, flashed warmth beneath my cheeks. Memories crowded against my mind, trying to push their way in.

*No.*

I tracked after the boys, my gaze on the back of their heads as they crested the hill halfway down the driveway and approached the flames. Every step pushed me further into my nightmares – into the searing heat of the diner, those final moments with my mother.

*Don't.*

That voice in my head, pulling me back to reality. To the mysterious burning heap at the end of the driveway. How mesmerized I was by the flickering amber streaks, how trapped I felt by all my memories inside it.

The heat of the fire, both real and imagined, was beating against my cheeks. I was close enough to see what was burning, all the shiny bits of metal inside it – a painful, familiar blue – and I knew, several seconds too late, that we were making a huge mistake.

Right in front of the big black gates and blocking the entranceway to Felice's driveway was a battered blue Ford. A Ford that had driven me into the city countless times, that had dropped me off at Millie's house, that had sat in my driveway as I tried to work the stick shift and cursed every time it stalled.

My mother's car was at *Evelina*.

My mother's car was burning at *Evelina*.

'Dom!' I screamed, but he was already circling the fire, trying to investigate it. 'Come back!'

Gino was even further from me. 'Gino! Get away from it!'

My voice railed against the sudden heat, the blinding crackling in my eardrums. Gino heard me, just enough to turn his head and stare, bewildered, at my sudden flare of panic.

I took another step, raised my voice. 'Get away from it!' I flung my hands out to the sides, arcing them as I shouted. 'Move backwards!'

'Sophie!' Luca's voice thundered down the driveway behind me. 'Get back!'

I was still screaming at Gino and Dom when Nic caught up with me, his boots skidding on the gravel as he grabbed me by the waist and swung me around. I barely had time to react before the car exploded and we all went flying backwards under a sky of raining metal and dead rats.

9

The noise thundered all around me as a fireball shot into the air. Heat, white-hot and searing, rolled over me as I scrabbled towards Nic, my fingers clutching the grass. The entire sky turned to smoke and ash, and jagged bits of fur and blood splattered us as we crawled towards each other.

Dom and Gino had gone flying to either side of the driveway, smashing into the blood-streaked gardens, the momentum rolling them over and over into flowerbeds along the periphery. They shouted each other's names as they dragged themselves away from the hungry flames, clawing their way back up to us.

I pulled myself to my feet, barely standing on shaking legs. When I lifted my head, the driveway right in front of the house was full of Falcones, each one consumed by their own unique brand of horror.

Luca jogged over to me, his arms streaked with blood and fur. He was saying something, but I wasn't listening. The reality of what had just happened was sinking in. The ground around us was littered with dead rats, and my body was streaked with their blood. One had landed a yard from my shoe. I stepped over it, moving towards the explosion site.

Yet again, the proof of Marino cruelty was shimmering in front of me. I was watching my mother's blue Ford now burnt black and heaving beneath dying flames. I was fighting the urge to rip their poisoned, savage blood right out of my skin.

Felice and Paulie darted past me, their arms filled with buckets of water. Elena was outside too, trying to keep the children away from the flames. I could hear her screeching at Sal and Aldo behind me. One of Paulie's girls, Greta, was wailing uncontrollably.

I drifted towards the car. At the very end of the driveway, plumes of smoke curled into the sky, turning the air to an unnatural, rancid smog.

A gift of smoke and ash. A hundred bloodied rats. A warning, not a shot. And somehow, that made it all the worse.

I stared as the flames made my eyes water, as the dead rats painted blood at my feet. I stared as Nic and CJ tied rags around their mouths and batted at the dying fire with blankets. I stared as Felice doused four buckets of water over the car, as Paulie inspected the damage. I stared as Elena came charging towards her sons, the younger children now barricaded inside the house.

Gino and Dom were covered in blood, too. It had soaked into their jeans, and criss-crossed their T-shirts, ending in smudges around their necks. Gino had a big crimson splodge on his cheek.

The smell was so achingly familiar. Dom's forehead was mussed with grey, his hair burnt at the tips. Gino's ponytail was like straw, strands broken off at the ends. He looked like he was about to vomit on himself. Dom raised his head to his mother. 'They stuffed the car with dead rats before they detonated it. It nearly blew us into the next life.'

Elena walloped him on the side of his head. '*Non parlare così!*'

'*Mamma!*' he yelped.

'*Imbecilli!*' she snapped, giving Gino a similar clout. 'Have I really raised morons? Do you not understand the danger in unfamiliar gifts? You do not approach what you don't understand! Go inside and get cleaned up before I twist your ears off for not listening to me!'

11

I stayed rooted to the spot as every inch of me turned to rage and ice, as thoughts of revenge surged into my mind and swept me up inside them. I stared and stared, and then I screamed so loud that my voice cracked and my throat felt like it was bleeding. It was a raging cry, a response to their message, so loud and unavoidable now. Because that was when it hit me. They had stood here and looked up at *Evelina*, through the gates, and laughed – I'd bet – *laughed* as they destroyed my mother's car. They had brazenly come to our door and hurled the threat directly at me. *Remember what happened to your mother? Look and see. Remember what we did to her? Here is your reminder. Here is what we do to rats. Here is what we will do to you.*

*You are a rat, Sophie Marino, and we are coming for you.*

'Sophie.' Luca's hand on my arm, holding me back, as though I would leap at the car and burn myself against the scalded metal. 'Come away from it.'

I rounded on him. 'Why should I?'

This message was for me. Why should I hide from it? The immediate world began to fade – the edges of it blurring black and quiet around me. I had never known animosity like this. I had never felt so passionate about anything.

I stared at the car again. I could feel my anger pounding in my ears, heating the tips of my fingers. It was catching in my chest. Pooling underneath my tongue. Prickling up the back of my neck.

*Calm down.*

*Your time will come.*

*You're going to make them pay.*

# CHAPTER TWO

## ALLY

In the library at *Evelina*, I collapsed into an armchair and tried to massage the headache from my temples. Even after three showers, I could still smell the dead rats, the lingering smoke. It was making me sick.

I tried to quell the rush of heat surging through me, pushing my heart rate up, tripping through my breathing. I lay back, counted out a seven-second exhale. Bookshelves lined every wall and climbed right up to the corniced ceiling. Three stained-glass windows peered on to the gardens at the front of the house.

An oil painting of Evelina Falcone, Felice's dead wife, hung over the stately fireplace, her half-lidded gaze turned towards the windows, her lips curving into a small smile. Her dark hair was piled high on her head, coming loose in tendrils around her face. It was like something out of the past – a da Vinci recreation, the makings of a shrine. I had no doubt that Felice had commissioned it, that he had bought her the diamond choker around her neck. And yet, for all the wealth she must have had, her eyes held only sadness.

The library was like a place of worship, with low lighting and an array of sumptuous leather chairs, and yet there was a staleness about it too. In this palace full of game rooms, flat-screen TVs, consoles and acres of land to lose yourself in, there were few Falcones who chose to seek out solace in the library, and so it had become like a time capsule from another era. Dusty and forgotten. Silent.

Silence was exactly what I needed.

A knock at the door roused my thoughts before they could spiral somewhere violent. Nic slipped inside, his hands shoved in his back pockets. 'Hey.'

'Hey.'

His hair was wet, dark strands sticking to his forehead. He smelt like shampoo – not smoke, not like me. He sank into the chair opposite me. 'What are you doing in here?'

'Oh, you know, just seething in a fresh vat of my own vengefulness.'

He offered me a half-smile. 'Sounds productive.'

I shrugged. 'What's up with you?'

He tilted his head, his mouth quirking to one side. 'Just looking for someone to get vengeful with.'

'You sound like you're being serious,' I pointed out.

'I am.'

We looked at each other for a long moment. It was comfortable – the silence between us. It felt nice to have an ally, someone who could see the ugliness inside me and didn't expect me to shy away from it.

I broke the silence. 'So they know where I am.'

'They're an embarrassment to our culture,' he shot back.

'I'm going to make them pay.' My breath hitched, but I smoothed my features. I wanted him to believe me; I needed him to believe me.

'Of course you are.' Nic's features had hardened into a mask of conviction; his jaw set, his eyes blazing. He sat forward, his elbows on his knees. 'It will be a bloodbath, Sophie. Donata won't know what's coming. We're going to take everyone from her. It will get rid of your sadness, when you know she's not out there terrorizing innocent people. We're going to stand over her and show her just how wrong she was to mess with—'

'Nicoli.'

Nic bit the rest of his sentence off. Annoyance clouded his expression as he turned around. Luca was standing in the doorway, his arms folded across his chest.

'*What?*' Nic asked, exasperatedly.

'Can you go upstairs?' Luca said, in what I assumed was his attempt at politeness. It was not remotely polite. 'I want you to check on Dom and Gino.'

'We're in the middle of a conversation.'

'I can see that,' said Luca, nonplussed.

'So?'

'So, now I'm telling you to go upstairs.'

There was a wavering silence. Nic looked at me and then at Luca and then back at me. He paused, deliberating. Luca didn't do anything; he just waited, irritatingly sure of Nic's concession. Nic huffed a sigh, pulled himself to his feet and marched past his brother, leaving a 'Fine, whatever,' behind him.

We watched him go, his shoulders sloping away from us.

Luca stepped inside the library, and I wondered if he could smell the smoke as keenly as I could. It was fused to every part of me, stuck inside my nose and my brain.

'Don't let him get into your head like that,' Luca said, his tone turning reproachful. 'You're smarter than that.'

'So now you want to talk to me?' I said, trying to act casual when I was ten seconds away from imploding.

'What?'

I rolled my eyes. 'You've barely talked to me since I got here,' I said, looking at the collar of his shirt, avoiding his bright blue gaze. 'You leave rooms to avoid me. You don't even *look* at me most of the time.'

'You mean the way you're looking at me right now?' he shot back.

I raised my gaze, cut my eyes at his stupid, perfect face and scowled. 'You know what I mean, Luca. You've been ignoring me.'

He lowered himself on to the arm of the chair across from me. 'I didn't come in here to argue.' I let the silence linger, determined that he would fill it, not me, not when I'd spent the last two weeks trying to get his attention, trying to find out what the hell was going on in his head. I had had to find out about today's initiation from *Gino*.

'Don't let Nicoli paint his intent with false glory. Don't fall for his rhetoric.'

'Says the guy who constantly sounds like he's quoting poetry.'

'I'm giving you advice.'

'Do you want some in return?' I offered. 'Next time you're going to eavesdrop on my conversations . . . don't.'

'What about when I see my brother wrapping you around his little finger? Should I let him finish manipulating you, or should I intervene?'

'Don't, Luca.' I let my voice lag, the weariness seeping through. 'I'm not in the mood.'

'He doesn't have the cure for what you're feeling right now. No one does.'

'That's a message for *me*.' I gestured at the window. Somewhere beyond it, the skeleton of my mother's car was heaving in the driveway. 'And I want to kill Donata for it.'

He shook his head, a frown rippling across his forehead. 'This is exactly the response they want. They want to draw you out, towards them.'

'When do I get to kill my Marino?' I asked.

Luca gaped at me. I studied his chest, his uneven breaths pushing it upwards. The silence grew. I decided to slice into it. 'I'm not really up to date on proper assassin etiquette yet, but judging by this dramatic reaction of yours, I'm getting the sense I've just committed some kind of faux pas?'

He dragged a hand across his cheek. 'Look, I get that you're angry right now. I get—'

'When?' I interrupted him. 'Valentino said I'd get my target soon, so how soon is soon, Luca? *When?*'

The act of having to kill a Marino just to test my loyalty had dropped into my stomach like a block of lead, but with the heat of those flames still burning inside me, I realized I wanted to hit back at Donata. I wanted to show her I wasn't afraid, that she would pay for all that she took from me, that this was only the beginning. I wanted the target. I wanted *my* target. I wanted somewhere to direct all the rage festering inside me.

Luca shot to his feet, and shut the door to the library, sealing us inside. He came towards me, his voice so low I could barely hear it. 'Sophie . . . you don't seriously think I expect you to *kill* someone, do you?'

I kept my voice at level pitch. 'That's what Valentino said at the initiation. We all agreed, remember?'

'I didn't agree,' he said, pointedly.

'Well, he outranks you.'

'I don't care,' he said, unruffled. 'There's no way in this life or any other that you are holding a gun to anyone's head and pulling the trigger.'

How cavalierly he seemed to control my life, how strange he seemed to find it that I would expect to be treated just like the rest of them. 'Oh, really?' I said. 'Well, what do you expect to happen when my uncle and Donata finally crawl back into the world? Do you really think I'm going to stand by and do nothing?'

Luca raked his hands through his hair, pulling the unruly black strands away from his face so he could ensnare me with that hypnotizing azure gaze. It felt almost deliberate, like he knew how paralysing it was. 'Sophie, I think there has been some confusion between us on this matter.'

I tried to keep my voice level. 'And that would be?'

'I didn't let you stay here because you promised to kill your uncle, I let you stay because you had nowhere else to go and I was worried about you.'

'But even Nic said he would help me. He promised we would—'

'I'm not Nicoli,' he cut in.

'I know that,' I said. 'But he—'

'The decision wasn't his. It was mine.'

'And Valentino's.'

'Mine,' he said simply, without elaborating.

All this time I had thought I'd bargained my way in that day I showed up on their doorstep, but here Luca was, telling me the reason I was sitting before him now was out of pity. It twisted inside me – this feeling of uselessness, of weakness, of the idea that my grief had not made me strong or capable, but *pitiable*.

'You expect me to sit tight while they send things to this house that directly threaten me, while they call me out like they did today? What if I *want* to harm them? What if I *want* to actually *contribute* to this family?'

'I said no.'

'Then why have a damn initiation at all?' I snapped. 'Why waste my time?'

'To keep you safe,' he said, like it was the most obvious thing in the world.

I gaped at him, flinging my arm out in the direction of the driveway. 'Do *you* feel safe right now? Does *anyone*?'

A shadow flitted behind his eyes, so quick I might not have noticed if I wasn't searching them so intently. 'Not just from the Marinos,' he said, after a beat.

'From the rest of you, you mean.'

He didn't say anything, but we were both thinking it. *From Felice.*

'Luca, I want to prove myse—'

'I said no,' he cut in.

'Don't pull rank on me,' I fumed.

He took a step towards me, enough that I had to tilt my chin to look up at him. I watched the hardened edge of muscle in his arms, the thick heel of his boots as he ground them into the floorboards. 'Of course I'll pull rank on you. I'm the underboss of this family.'

'I don't care what your role is. I'm not going to bow to you, so you shouldn't expect it.'

'*Dio mi aiuti.*' He shut his eyes tight. 'You, Sophie Marino, are single-handedly aging me before my time.'

Had I really been psyching myself up for nothing? For how much longer was I expected to be a spectator in my own life? How much longer would I feel the squirming, guilt-ridden uselessness of my role in my mother's death? 'It's not up to you. It's up to Valentino. I'm going to prove myself to this family, and then I'm going to avenge my mother.' I got to my feet, cutting the height difference in half, determined to make him understand. 'This is my cause too. This is my vendetta.'

Luca spluttered a laugh – it was hard and sharp. 'Your vendetta,' he repeated. 'Do you know what it feels like to kill another human being? Just because we don't talk about it doesn't mean we don't feel the guilt. Just because the people who die are not good people, does not make it any easier. You don't get used to it. Sophie, the guilt is relentless. It drowns you. It becomes you. It's all you are in the end – a collection of taken lives and the mask you wear to pretend you're OK with it.'

I thought of Jack, of Donata as she flicked the lighter into the diner kitchen and sent my mother to the afterlife. The white-hot edge of rage still burnt inside me. I was already in the darkness, and I couldn't conceive of a feeling worse than the one Jack had bestowed upon me, worse than the sick, creeping feeling of grief that woke me up every morning and rocked me to sleep at night, worse than seeing that car explode in front of me, of letting it throw me backwards, cover me in blood and ash. 'I could handle doing to Donata what she did to me.'

Luca shook his head. 'Every life has value, Sophie. They all leave a stain.'

I was so close to him now – when did that happen? His aftershave hung in the space between us. 'So, when you let me come here, it wasn't to prepare me to face them but to lock me away from them?'

He didn't say anything. He just looked at me.

'You'll have to lie to Valentino,' I said. 'You'll have to trick your own family. How is that going to work?'

He took a step backwards, towards the door, his hands clasped behind his back. 'It will work because it's only temporary.'

'Temporary?' I wanted to bridge the gap he was making, to tug him towards me.

He levelled me with a dark look. 'When we've taken care of Donata and Jack, you're going to leave us. And then it will be over for good. For ever.'

'What will?' I whispered, feeling like the ground was being ripped out from under me.

He swallowed hard – all the things that lingered on his

tongue – and his face re-shuttered, the impenetrable mask coming down once more. 'This. Us. Everything.'

This. *Us.*

# CHAPTER THREE
## COMMON GROUND

I wanted to say something, anything to distract from the feeling of hurt blooming in my chest, but in the next instant, he was gone, and I was alone again. Dwarfed by the sudden, jarring silence, the realization that I had just been dumped by the only person in this house I felt I could rely on. Dumped by someone who probably never felt a shred of what I felt for him. And what did that mean for my future? If I didn't have this family, I had nothing. If I didn't have my cause, then I had nothing to move towards.

I left the library and made my way back into the house. Elena was in the kitchen, soaking tea towels in disinfectant in a basin. She had been tending to Dom and Gino all afternoon. She greeted me by way of a hiss.

'Save it,' I snapped. 'I'm not in the mood.'

She followed me across the room, stood over me as I grabbed a bottle of water from the fridge. I slowed my movements, tried to show her I wasn't intimidated, even though I could feel her gaze in the hairs on my neck. 'Well, maybe *I'm* not in the mood for a Marino living under this roof, girl. Maybe I'm not in the mood for the gifts your *family* sends us.'

I slammed the fridge shut and threw her a withering look. 'Well, maybe you should get over it.'

'You're too close to my sister, girl.'

'And yet it's *you* who share her blood,' I pointed out. 'I'll never be as close to her as you are.'

Her expression changed, her eyes narrowing, and then something weird happened. Her lips quirked up, and she offered me a half-smile. 'You've gotten tougher, little Marino.'

'Trust me,' I said, returning her smile and matching the faint maniacal undertone in it. There was no happiness in this moment. 'This is only the beginning of my strength.' I felt the slow burn of all that rage inside me and kept it there, ready to use as a weapon when the time came. Luca, or no Luca, I would have my revenge. I would finally stand up for myself. 'I am going to kill your sister.'

Elena's smile grew, stretching her cheeks wide. 'Not if I get to her first, Persephone.'

There. My name. Not the ideal version, but still. It was better than 'worm'. It was better than 'Marino'.

'I hate her,' I said simply. 'I hate her, and I want her to pay, and I don't care how or when it happens, but I want to be a part of every second of it.'

'Well,' said Elena, stepping closer until the air between us became a potent mixture of her floral perfume and the faintest scent of smoke. 'There is something, then, that we have in common.'

# CHAPTER FOUR
## BARBARIANS AND LIBRARIANS

'This is literally the scariest thing I've ever had to do.' Millie slammed her locker shut, and the clang of metal reverberated inside my eardrums. She hitched her bag on to her back and expelled a dramatic breath. 'Seriously, Soph. I don't know why I agreed to do this. I can barely live with the anxiety.'

'There there, Millicent.' I patted her on the shoulder. 'I'm sure you'll rise to the occasion.'

She clenched her eyes shut. 'That's easy for you to say, you don't have to deal with all this horrible *pressure*.'

A part of me wanted to burst out laughing – a horrible, screeching, humourless laugh. If only she knew how close I was to committing the most soul-changing act in the world. If only she knew how ragged my soul was now, how much time

I spent replaying all the ways the Marinos had stung me, all the ways I wanted to hurt them. As far as she was concerned, I was just lying low at the Falcone compound. If she really knew what I was going to trade for their acceptance, she'd have my head on a plate.

'I have to organize an *entire* school dance,' Millie wailed. 'Can you even *imagine* that kind of stress?'

I snorted, trying to grasp on to the hint of amusement and not the thick, cloying dread that had taken hold of my insides since yesterday, since the sight of my mother's car burning on the threshold to the Falcone underworld started haunting my every waking thought.

'What was I thinking? I barely have a month to pull this whole thing off and no one has come up with *any* good theme ideas. I am working with a pack of *idiots*.'

'You'll be fine. I have full faith in you.' I linked arms with her as we made our way to English class, pushing my own worries down, down, down. School was for the old Sophie. Not the new one. Not the real one.

We took our seats at the back of the classroom. I slumped into my chair and kept my head down, but I could still feel the gazes drilling into the side of my head, the whispers scuttling around the room like spiders.

*She never smiles any more.*

*I heard it was her uncle who set fire to the place and now they can't find him anywhere.*

*I heard she set the fire. She's a psychopath just like her dad.*

If I had my way I would have dropped out of school the day I showed up on the Falcones' doorstep, but they were adamant about having me continue my studies to retain 'some level of normality' in my life, and Millie . . . well, I had made her a promise. We were going to do senior year together, and only a bad friend would break such a big promise. I was determined to be a good friend. So that meant essays and calculus and dance planning and football games and the slow creeping doom of a future I wasn't sure I had any more.

Millie ripped a page out of her notebook and began furiously scribbling on it as Mr Simmons, our English teacher, swept into the room. He was dressed entirely in tweed, like he had just tumbled out of the early 1900s and couldn't quite figure out where he was.

'What are you doing?' I tried to ignore Erin Reyes, who was one desk over and leering at me. I had already been a source of amusement to her, but now I had graduated to the shelf of 'tragic', and that meant she wanted to stare at me at least twice as much. Without looking at her, I rubbed my cheek with my middle finger. She muttered something under her breath and I let the satisfaction paint the smile across my face.

'For your next assignment, I want you to pick a piece of writing that you can identify with on a deep emotional level, and explain why,' Simmons began cheerfully. 'So with that in mind, today we are going to dive into some poetry.'

*I'd rather dive into a volcano.*

Millie passed me the piece of paper. 'I don't have time to dive into anything,' she whispered. 'We're picking a dance theme.'

'Who is?' I unfolded the paper.

28

'Us,' she hissed. 'By the time this class is over, we'll have nailed it.'

I scanned the list of possibilities. *Pimps and Pirates, Heroes and Villains, Childhood Cartoons, Barbarians and Librarians.*

'That last one is you just rhyming random stuff,' I felt compelled to point out. 'It makes no sense.'

'Shhhhut up.'

At the bottom of the page she had written and then crossed out, *Sexy Fruit?* I side-glanced at her. 'Permission to have absolutely nothing to do with this at any point ever at all?'

'Permission denied.' Millie slid a glitter pen on to my desk. 'Now get creative, Gracewell.'

I glanced warily at the piece of paper. Old Sophie would help with this. Old Sophie was the friend Millie deserved. School was for her. I swallowed my feelings down, and got to work.

What about balloons? People love balloons.

I slipped the note to Millie and watched her face contort. She scribbled back.

Consider me offended by this first attempt.

Mars? Mars is topical.

Against all possible odds, your suggestions have actually gotten worse.

29

*This is why I'm not on the dance committee.*

*If you were, I'd have to fire you immediately.*

*What about Under the Sea?*

*Sophie!! We're not going to a five-year-old's birthday party!*

*I wish we were. At least there'd be cake.*

*You don't even like children. Remember that time you tried to shake a baby's hand?*

*You're underestimating how much I love cake. And I was just trying to be cordial.*

By the end of class, I had twenty-nine rejected dance themes under my belt.

Millie got to her feet. 'Well, that was a bust. I can't believe I thought you'd be good at that.'

'To be honest, neither can I. I mean, as much as I'd like to, I can't just masquerade around here like someone who's expec—'

'Sophie!' Millie's eyes looked like they might fall right out of her head. 'You're a *genius*! I can't believe I didn't think of it before, but of course it makes total sense, especially with it being around Halloween!' She raised her hand above us, unveiling a picture only she could see. 'Sophie, I give you . . . Cedar Hill High's Masquerade Ball. Classy, sexy, mysterious . . .'

'Masks.' I could almost taste the irony. 'You want us to wear masks.'

A memory undusted itself deep in the corner of my mind. The first time I met Valentino at the old Priestly mansion in Cedar Hill. The mask he wore then. The masks he said we all wore for fear of the alternative – being our true selves, risking being rejected for who we are deep in our core, for what we really desire. Even now, I was pretending to my best friend. I was pretending to be happy, I was pretending to get better. Inside, I was twisted and raw.

I was already wearing a mask.

Millie was jumping up and down like an excited puppy and pulling me back into the hallway, where people spread out from me in purposeful arcs, as though I might cry if they brushed against my shoulder, or curse them if they looked me in the eye.

'At least if we have to wear masks, people might start treating me like a normal person again.'

'Bah!' Millie twirled into her locker, throwing me a look over her shoulder as she fiddled with the combination. 'Normal is boring. Weird is where it's at.'

I tried to smile at her but this time it wobbled. I was conscious of where I was going next. Of which Falcone might be outside waiting to collect me. I was brushing off the old Sophie, and stepping outside, back to my new life, where murder and betrayal swirled around me like thunderclouds.

'At least it's Friday.'

'What?' I blinked her back into focus.

'You're looking very pensive and sad,' Millie pointed out. 'I thought maybe you'd forgotten it was Friday. You have all this extra time to make out with Luca now.' She started making elaborate kissing noises.

'Oh my God, shut up!' I swatted her in the arm. I glanced over my shoulder, fearful that a rogue Falcone might be hiding inside a locker, or that Nic might be stuck to the ceiling. 'That's a secret. A *huge* secret.'

Millie wiggled her eyebrows.

'He hasn't kissed me since I moved in. He's barely even spoken to me.' *He's too busy trying to keep me as far away from him as possible, as far away from everything it really means to be a Falcone.* I tried to pretend I didn't care, but a big part of me couldn't shake off the feeling of his arms around me, of his lips on mine, of how comforted he had made me feel. How the badness hadn't seemed so bad when we were facing it together. But now that I was living at *Evelina*, things were different: it was like there was a pane of glass between us.

Everything, according to Luca, was temporary.

*Temporary.*

The word burnt inside me.

'Well, he did make his entire family offer you sanctuary despite the fact that you're . . . you know . . .'

'A Marino,' I supplied. 'It's not a curse. You can say it.'

'Yeah, well, my point is he stuck his neck out for you, and from what I know of him, he doesn't really seem like the type to do something like that so lightly. Maybe he's biding his time . . . or,' she raised her finger, 'maybe he's scared of something . . . or someone. It's probably his twin. The boss-man. Old blue-eyes-creepy-smile. What's his name again?'

'You know his name,' I said. 'And can you keep your voice

down, please? I've taken a vow of secrecy and anyone could be listening to you right now.'

Millie rolled her eyes.

'And no, I doubt Valentino would be thrilled at the idea of me making out with his brother. Especially after everything that happened with Nic.'

'You know,' said Millie who was now narrowing her eyes, 'for someone with such a romantic name, he's a real killjoy, isn't he? He's all, *Ooh look at me, I'm sensitive and kind and I have a beautiful long name and pretty eyes*, and then *BAM! Psyche! I'm going to shoot you.* You know what I call that, Soph? I call that false advertising, and I'm pretty sure it's illegal.'

Dom was sitting in the driver's seat outside school, so I made sure to climb into the back of the SUV.

'Do you really have to be so childish, Marino?' he asked. 'I'm not going to bite you.'

'I just don't want to get any of your hair gel on me. It's *impossible* to wash out.'

'Trust me, this is not what I want to be doing with my afternoons either.'

'I told you I can make my own way back.'

Dom snorted. 'Until you prove your loyalty, Valentino is not going to let you swan around Chicago unwatched. For all we know you could be passing intel back to Bitch Marino and her crew of idiots.'

'After she blew up my mother's car and nearly killed me?' I said. 'Even you couldn't possibly believe that.'

He shrugged, eyes forward. 'I don't know what to believe any more.' Him and me both. 'How's your hot friend doing? I haven't seen her in a while.'

'That's probably because she still hates you.'

He side-glanced at me, a smirk twisting on his lips. 'Good. I like a challenge.'

I shifted forwards so that my fingers trailed the side of his headrest. I tapped them along the leather and studied the silver scar that swiped across his eye. 'Don't take this the wrong way, but if you and Millie were the last two people on earth and the entire future of the human race depended on you two hooking up, she would not even graze you with her pinky finger because she is so deeply, deeply repulsed by your general existence, not to mention your complete selfish disregard for women in general. She would see the world shrivel up and die rather than populate it with any tiny versions of you and your general shittiness.'

He turned his attention to the road. 'How could I possibly not take that offensively?'

I shrugged.

He matched my nonchalance. 'That doesn't offend me as much as you might think it does, Marino.'

I flopped backwards, as the trees in Cedar Hill blurred by me in streaks of autumnal oranges and browns. My thoughts drifted to my old neighbourhood, to my mother's things still locked up in my house. It all felt so unfinished. 'Well, that's because you're an asshole.'

'And when you're pointing a smoking gun at some guy's corpse and screwing over every last bit of your Marino loyalty, what will that make you?'

With my gaze still on my old town and the graveyard it had become, I said, 'I suppose that will make me a Falcone.'

# CHAPTER FIVE

## VILLAIN

I was so not feeling the poetry assignment. The last thing I wanted was to trace someone else's words about grief and pain while my own loss, raw and searing, sat so heavy in my chest. Still, it was a distraction, not to mention a necessary component of graduating, so I was doing my best with it. I had been scanning a giant book of poems for nearly an hour before my attention finally snagged on one. It was practically flashing at me on the page. Plus it *rhymed*, which meant it was a *proper* poem. It was called 'We Wear the Mask', by Paul Laurence Dunbar. I transcribed the first stanza and then started jotting down my reaction to it.

> We wear the mask that grins and lies,
> It hides our cheeks and shades our eyes,—

*This debt we pay to human guile;*
*With torn and bleeding hearts we smile,*
*And mouth with myriad subtleties.*

I used to wear masks so subtle I barely noticed them. A compliment to my mother after a dismal meal, a smile at my best friend when she sang out of tune, a forced laugh at my uncle's bad jokes. I wore small masks that came and went, like fleeting expressions.

I am stuck inside the mask I wear now. I want to rip it off. I want to show my scars to the world, to unveil the ugliness that breathes inside me. I want to be unashamed. I want to be unafraid. But every day the mask gets tighter, and I suffocate a little more.

I stopped writing. This was definitely too much. Simmons would keel over if I kept going. I scratched it out and flipped the book of poems open again. Another poem. Less raw. Less real.

Another mask.

'Very industrious, Persephone. On a Friday night, too. And here I thought you only cared about leading Nicoli on.' He chuckled at his quip. 'Your brain, it seems, is capable of some diversion.'

I put the pen down and sat back in my chair. 'This isn't a documentary, Felice. Can you not narrate me?'

I could feel him coming closer, the sickly scent of honey filling up the study. His shadow fell across the desk, the edges crisp and blackened under the table lamp. He made to lean over me, and instinctively I covered my notebook with my elbow.

'Can you think of nothing else to do than bother me while I'm trying to write this stupid essay?'

He rounded the desk. He was wearing a new suit – dark purple, with a crimson necktie. He arranged himself, with arms folded, against the wall. His smile was indulgent. 'You've had a tough week, so I won't take that to heart, little Persephone.'

'I wasn't aware you had a heart.'

'I don't,' he said, his light eyebrows drawing low over his eyes. He was a skeleton barely fleshed out before me. In certain lighting, I could see the edges of his skull beneath his receding hairline.

'You are literally a villain.'

'I *used* to have a heart.' He didn't betray a flicker of composure at my observation. 'When I was young and foolish and thought the world was a bright, forgiving place. But I've learnt my lessons, Persephone, just as you will.'

There was something in his voice just then that made me quell the insult resting on my lips. I could see it in the careful placement of his smile, the twitch in his right eye. Grief. Grief for the wife who had walked out on him at eight months pregnant and had taken his foolish heart with him. Grief for Evelina, the woman he had built a palace for.

Only Evelina hadn't left him, like he thought. She had been taken from him. He mourned the absence of a woman who was never coming back. A woman my father murdered. Bile rose in my throat at the image of that ruby ring inside the diner safe, of Jack's words to me. The truth of my father's depravity had been wrestling with the pain of my mother's demise, and I wasn't ready to unleash either. I certainly wasn't about to tell Felice what really happened to his wife. I would take that to the grave with me. I hoped Luca would too.

I shut my notebook. 'I assume you've come in here for a reason?'

'Nothing escapes you, does it?' he said mockingly. 'If you must know, I was wondering about the measure of your intent.'

'My intent?'

His eyes darkened. His teeth seemed to grow sharper. 'Do you still wish to experience the feeling of retribution? Do you still thirst for it as you did the day you showed up on our doorstep seeking sanctuary?'

His intensity was more than unnerving. There was no humour or mocking left now. 'Where has all this come from?'

'This week,' he said.

'The week Donata stuffed my mother's car with dead rats and blew it up in front of me, you find yourself wondering whether I still hate her as much as I did? Whether I still want to make her pay for everything she has taken from me? I thought you were supposed to be smart.'

Felice hitched up a brow. 'I would say the same of you, but I've always been under the impression that you're somewhat obtuse.'

I rolled my eyes at him.

He came closer – his breath pushing that cloying smell into the air between us. 'It is my opinion that you give Gianluca too much credence in the matter of your mother's avengement. His words, if you let them, will weaken you, and you will remain as you always have been . . .' he paused, and then elongated the word, as though he could taste it in his mouth and it was almost too delicious to let go, 'powerless.'

*Powerless.* There it was. The button. And he was pressing it.

'Powerless.' I *was* powerless. I felt powerless. Especially after what the Marinos had done with my mother's car. I had stood there, watching the flames devour everything – just like before.

'Let me speak plainly, Persephone. Gianluca has always been broken. His heart and his head are not where they should be. He is certainly not my father's legacy as others contend. He has always given me the deepest impression, beneath his duties and his family loyalty, of being irrevocably . . . *dissatisfied.*' He swirled the word around in his mouth, tasting it, before spitting it out. 'Gianluca is, simply put, *unsatisfactory.*'

I felt an irrational urge to defend Luca, but it would only appear strange, and right now I was trying to fly under the radar. Let Felice think what he wanted; it didn't change the truth of anything.

He poured himself over the table, gripping its edges so hard it looked as though his spindly fingers might snap off. 'I suspect Gianluca sees in you another version of himself. One that is not beyond saving, one that he can actually control. His dealings with you are, in my estimation, a projection of his own failings with himself.'

It felt a little bit like I had been punched in the heart. The idea that Luca saw something of himself in me had never even crossed my mind. I thought he had wanted to help me, maybe even *be* with me, in some kind of alternative universe, but this . . . I had never imagined that I might be some kind

39

of . . . project. A do-over. It hurt. It *hurt.*

I tried to keep my expression placid. 'Wow, Felice. Tell me how you really feel.'

'I am saying this for your own good.'

I cut my eyes at him. 'Oh, I'm sure you are. I'm sure you came in here with the intent of looking out for me. I'm sure you didn't mean it when you raised a gun to my head a few weeks ago and threatened to shoot me in front of your whole family. You care about me. Yeah. That seems really likely. I totally buy that. Oh, I believe you. Whoa, Felice, please stop caring so much about me, you'll give yourself a heart attack. Please, calm down with all that genuine caring.'

He frowned at me. 'Are you done?'

'Yeah.' I shrugged. 'That's all I got.'

'I see how Luca is excluding you from family business. Any attempt he makes to distance you from the glory in revenge is nothing more than a selfish preoccupation with his own shortcomings.'

'Felice' and 'sincere' were not words I would ever put together in a sentence, unless of course the sentence was 'Wow, Felice is not a sincere person.' Yet, there was a disconcerting level of honesty in his expression. He truly believed what he was saying. The idea that Luca might actually like or care about me hadn't even crossed his mind. 'Why are you telling me this?' I asked. 'What does it even matter?'

'We are at war, Persephone. Everything matters now.'

'You really should have majored in theatre, Felice. You would have made an incredible Lady Macbeth.'

He bent his head to my height, his elbows propped across the desk. 'Nicoli will show you the way forward. He knows the path and he walks it, undaunted. Gianluca will shut your eyes until it's too late, and you will, I guarantee, meet the same fate as your mother.'

I sucked in a breath, all dregs of humour evaporating in that instant. 'My mother is not some cautionary tale, and she's definitely not a weapon you can use against me.'

He raised a hand, halting the venom on my tongue. 'The fact remains that we are now all you have, Persephone. If you want to be part of this family and *remain* part of this family, you must choose to whom you are going to listen. *That* is going to make all the difference. Do you understand what I'm saying?'

'I understand,' I said, if only to end the conversation. 'Luca won't help me survive in this world.'

Felice's grey eyes darkened, his lips twisting into a slow smile. 'But Nicoli will.'

# CHAPTER SIX
## PRACTICE

As I tracked across Felice's back garden, the barn rose to meet me – it was tall and broad, and made of concrete. Fall had come and with it the air had grown crisper. There was a biting chill in the wind now, and the trees on Felice's land were turning vibrant shades of orange and yellow. It was pretty, almost like a picture, this assassin's palace. In another time, I might have felt at ease here. I might have grown to love it.

I stalled behind the barn, hidden from the windows of the house, and wrapped my arms around myself. My winter coat was still back in Cedar Hill, stuffed somewhere inside my wardrobe. A million miles away.

I watched my breath fog in the air and tried to imagine how cold it would be here in the middle of December. A blanket of snow and ice – and inside, crackling fires in every hearth to chase away the chill. December brought thoughts of Christmas. Of stockings and candy canes and turkey dinners. Of presents and eggnog and family. Would we all survive until then? How black would my soul be by Christmas morning?

I heard his breath on the wind before he caught up with me. He fell out of his jog and offered me a surprisingly warm smile considering I had harassed him out of bed at such an indecent time. 'Good morning!' he said, beaming at me in all that Colgate splendour.

Of course Nic had had the good sense to wear a winter coat. His hair was messy – ungelled, and flopping across his forehead. He pushed it back. He looked peaky – half warm and half pale, probably from being wrenched out of bed at such an ungodly hour.

'You're late.' I tapped at an imaginary watch. 'I said 7 a.m. sharp.'

'I'm not a morning person,' he said, his grin turning sheepish.

'Is that why your smile is starting to twitch?'

'I just downed two double espressos,' he confided. 'I think my face is vibrating.'

'Well, you could never tell.' I smiled at him. 'Thanks for coming.'

He shrugged, but my smile had brought on his own, and I made a mental note to be very careful about how this meeting progressed. It was business, not pleasure.

Nic cracked his knuckles and rolled his neck around, warming up. 'So, why do we have to be so secretive about this

43

again? Valentino *will* be happy.' He had asked me the same thing last night when I ambushed him in the middle of brushing his teeth.

'I told you I don't want anyone to know until I know what I'm doing.'

Translation: *I don't want Luca to know.*

Even if Luca intended to risk everything to break the promise I made to his twin, I certainly didn't.

'You sure that's it?' Nic edged a little closer, his grin turning wolfish. 'Or is there something else going on here that I don't know about? Because you don't have to make up excuses to spend time with me, you know. There's nowhere else I'd rather be . . .'

'Nic . . .' I pressed my palm against his chest and pushed him back gently. 'We talked about this.'

'So, let's talk about it again, now that things have changed.'

'Nothing's changed,' I said gently. 'We're not good for each other.'

A frown rippled along his forehead. 'For the record, I disagree,' he said. 'I think we are good for each other.'

My smile turned awkward, but I kept my tone light. 'To be in a relationship with someone, both parties kind of need to agree that they're good for each other, Nic . . . it can't just be you. It's not enough.'

Nic shrugged. 'Take as much time as you need, Sophie. I'll change your mind eventually.' His determination puffed him up, made him seem taller.

'You're always so sure of everything,' I said, half-chastising him.

'That's because I always get what I want,' he said, confidently.

*Not this. Not me.*

I decided to flip the subject before the intensity of where this was going steered us off course. 'Do you have the gun?' I whispered.

Nic's laugh shattered the morning silence. He backed up and made a show of looking all around him. 'You really don't have to whisper about guns in this house – you get that, right? This doesn't have to be a secret.'

'I don't want anyone to find out that I'm learning,' I said quickly.

'Of course you're learning. How are you going to drop a Marino if you don't know how to shoot a gun?' He regarded me quizzically. Then he laughed again. 'You are so funny, Sophie.'

Nic pulled a gun from his waistband and my heart did a miniature somersault. I really had to get a grip. 'Can you hold this for a minute?' He handed it to me and I took it on reflex, surprised at the weight. It was sleek and silver, with a black bar of colour running along the top. I was extra, extra careful not to brush the trigger as I studied it at arm's length.

Nic zipped up his coat until it reached just below his chin. Damn, he looked so warm. I was trying not to shiver. I was also trying to look totally nonchalant with a gun dangling by my side.

He gestured at the gun. 'The safety's on, you can relax.'

'I'm totally relaxed,' I said, forcing a laugh that sounded like a dying hyena. 'I've never been more relaxed.'

I passed the gun back to him, the barrel end pointing away from us, laying it flat on the palm of his hand, like it was an ancient artefact.

He laughed again. 'You are so cute.'

'Stop making fun of me!'

'OK, sorry,' he said, smoothing his features into a terrible attempt at seriousness. 'I'll do my best.' He beckoned me around the front of the barn.

I fell into step with him. 'Why are you going in there?'

He unlocked the door and pushed it open, pausing on the threshold to answer me. 'Where did you think we were going to have the target practice?'

'Um . . .'

'Here?' he said, gesturing at the open grounds – at the beehives dotting the back garden, at the clusters of trees in the distance, at the back of the house and all those breakable windows. 'Just out in the open like this?'

'Um, no . . .' I said, looking at my shoes. 'That would be bad?'

Nic snorted. 'Bad is one word for it.'

The barn was a huge open space with concrete floors and a continuous line of windows so high up I couldn't see out of them. Morning sunlight streamed through them, brightening the room. At the opposite end, there were twelve targets lined up in front of the wall – twelve thick wooden bases with black human cut-outs jutting out from them, just like in the movies.

'Oh,' I said, realizing exactly what this barn was here for. 'I get it now.'

Nic was leaning against a long wooden table behind us. 'You didn't think he harvested crops here, did you?'

'I never thought about it.' OK, maybe a small part of me had pictured a barn stacked to the rafters with thousands of honey jars, all black-ribboned and waiting for their recipients. In hindsight, that would have been a bit much, even by Felice's standards.

Nic pulled the drawer from the table and rummaged inside. He handed me a pair of safety goggles. I examined them dubiously. 'Are these necessary?' I rotated them in my hand. 'I didn't think you guys wore safety goggles when you were out doing family business.' *'Doing family business'. That's right, Sophie, act more like a child.*

'Nah,' Nic said, handing me a pair of foam earplugs. 'But maybe for your first time, we'll take some precautions. Just until you get used to the noise.'

I half wished there were knee pads and helmets as well. I was not feeling confident about my skills. I slid the goggles on to my face. They were way too big, balancing precariously on the end of my nose. I pushed them back and they slipped down again. 'Noooo,' I said, colouring my voice with dismay. 'My face is rejecting the glasses.'

Nic pressed the goggle arms towards each other, so they gripped behind my ears better. I stared at his chest, his alpine scent covering me as he fixed them. 'It's because your nose is so small.' He tapped my nose with his finger. 'It's cute,' he murmured, looking at me beneath those thick lashes of his.

It was hard, in moments like this, not to remember the first time we ever spoke, how he looked at me like I was the only person in the world. How he kissed me like it was the first and last kiss he'd ever have. The Nic I thought I knew – the one I thought I needed. There were shades of that desire inside me still, but I had buried them for a reason. I had to remember why.

Nic was distractingly close to me now and my head was exploding with shouts of *Don't you dare touch him! Step away from the enigmatic assassin right now!*

I stepped backwards. 'Nic,' I said, chastising.

He held a hand up in surrender, the corner of his mouth flicking upwards in a lazy half-smile. 'I was just saying.'

'We're here to work, remember?' I slipped the earplugs inside my ears.

'Yes, ma'am.' His smile grew. 'Are you ready?' I could only half hear him. I nodded. 'OK. Watch.'

He took two steps forward, planting his feet. Raising his arm, he aimed the gun at the other end of the room and fired off six shots in quick succession.

Even with the earplugs, the noise was relentless.

A bullet hole appeared in each of the first six target heads – right in the middle. He pulled a magazine from his pocket and reloaded so fast I barely caught the movement. The next six holes appeared in the left side of the chest of each of the remaining dummies. The whole thing took less than ten seconds.

Twelve targets in ten seconds. And he hadn't even broken a sweat. He was relaxed, his expression placid, his breathing slow and natural.

When he was done, he lowered the gun, reloaded it and swivelled to face me.

I gaped at him. If I didn't think too much about the end goal of his shooting, and only focused on the skill, I couldn't help but feel awed. It was all so quick and effortless. 'Your aim is . . .'

'Unparalleled,' he finished, a self-satisfied grin spreading across his features. 'I told you. Your turn.'

I looked at the targets again. They seemed so impossibly far away now; I could barely see the holes he'd made. 'Can I move closer?' I asked. 'Like way, way, way closer.'

He shook his head. 'Don't chicken out before you've started. I'll bet you'll be good at it.'

I narrowed my eyes at him. 'No, you don't.'

He laughed again. It was loud and carefree and giddy this time. The feel of the gun – of shooting – did something to his whole demeanour. It made him happy. Really, truly happy. Beneath all the anger and fear and determination, there was a pinch of something else taking hold of me. It was jarring, that a boy so young could be so maniacally entertained by all of this. Still, this was the boy who was going to help me get what I needed – revenge – and in the moment, that was what mattered to me most.

'OK,' he conceded, 'I don't think you'll be an expert on your first try. But I do think you're very teachable.'

The gun was hot in my hands. I embraced the heat and let the warmth filter up my arm.

'Don't fear it,' Nic said. 'This gun is your ally. It works for you.'

'What if I shoot myself?'

'Have some confidence, Sophie. You're taking back your power. Stand up straighter.' He laid his hands on my shoulders and I leant back into them, raising my chin. 'Good,' he breathed, his voice against my ear. 'You're ready for this.'

He lingered a couple of seconds more than necessary.

'OK.' I squared my jaw and locked eyes with the targets. 'Teach me.'

Nic dropped his hands and came to my side, his attention trained on my stance. 'Plant your feet.' The amusement had drained from his voice. This was the Nic I needed. This was the Nic who was going to teach me what I wanted to know. 'Bend your knees just a little. Good. Now square your shoulders towards the target. Fully extend your strong arm. Now pull the slide back with your other hand.' It clicked into place. There was a sickening thrill in the sound.

'Bring your left arm around and cup the other side of the gun. No – not so loose.' He moved around me, his arms coming over my shoulders against my own, his chin resting against my hair as his hands covered mine. 'Like this,' he said, shifting my left hand so my fingers cupped the gun. His breath was hot on my neck. I tried to ignore it. He moved his right hand over mine, shifting it higher. 'Just one finger on the trigger,' he said, his finger pressing mine into place. 'Three fingers on the grip.' He squeezed the rest of his hand over mine, dwarfing it. 'Keep your feet planted. You need to be able to absorb the recoil.'

I tried to focus. I was not supposed to be feeling this urge to make out with him. He was still morally corrupt – still dangerous, still bad for me. He was still that same boy that had pointed a gun at my head inside the diner. He was still the brother of the guy who was kind and good and smart . . . My brain knew that. Even my heart did. But right now, in these close quarters, my body didn't.

'I've got it,' I said, shuffling out of his grip. 'I can do it.'

He stepped away from me, leaving my back cold and tingly. 'OK,' he said, pointing towards the targets at the other end of the barn. 'Now bring the gun up to eye level, keep your arms straight out in front of you and aim.'

I hunched up my shoulders, my arms bordering both sides of my peripheral vision. I pointed the gun at one of the middle targets at the end of the room.

'Picture someone,' he said. 'It will make it seem more real.'

I let out a breath. 'I see Donata.' I lowered the gun a little, tracing the imaginary lines of her expensive designer suit, her bony neck. 'I'm aiming at her heart.'

'Good,' he murmured. 'She took yours, now you'll take hers.'

My mouth had gone dry. My arms were buzzing, and my breathing was coming more rapidly.

'Let the adrenalin steady you.' He was behind me again, his hands on my shoulders as he turned me just an inch to the left. He squeezed once – a reinforcement – and then withdrew. 'Let it focus you.'

I envisioned Donata's overly made-up face, her sickly grin. I imagined her pallor drained by fear as I aimed my gun at her skeletal frame.

'Fire,' he breathed. 'Kill the bitch.'

I fired.

My hand snapped backwards, the gun veering towards the ceiling on its recoil. 'Shit,' I hissed, releasing the trigger. 'I didn't think it would be so strong.'

'You'll get used to it,' Nic assured me, unfazed by the fail. 'Keep your hand steadier this time. Don't let the recoil push your grip backwards.'

The exhilaration of firing the gun was fast being eclipsed by the fact that I didn't get anywhere on the target. I squinted. 'Where did the bullet go?'

Nic pointed towards the ground on the right of the Donata target. 'It's lodged in the wall.'

'Well, that's embarrassing.'

'Your arm lagged.' Nic stood behind me again. He lifted my hand with his until the gun was in front of me again. 'You have five more bullets in this magazine. Five more chances to hit a target before we reload.'

I focused entirely on the task at hand, not his breath on my cheek or his voice in my ear. Our arms lined up, and I was thankful for his coat and my sweater. Skin-to-skin would not be a good idea right now. 'Line up your sight. Hold steady.'

Donata's features shifted into view. I saw her in my mind's eye, as plainly as if she was there in front of me.

'Again,' he said pulling back. 'Shoot her.'

I fired again.

This time I was expecting the recoil. My arm still flinched, but not much. I missed the target.

'Again,' Nic commanded.

I replanted myself and fired.

Miss.

'Again.'

Miss.

'Higher.'

I held my arm higher. It was starting to get tired.

'Again.'

Miss.

'Again,' he demanded.

That one hit the torso of the target next to the one I was aiming for. The bullets had run out. I dropped my arm, and realized I was panting. Frustration and embarrassment warred inside me.

'Damn it,' I cursed. 'I can't do it, Nic.' I wanted to throw the gun across the room. 'I'm terrible at this.' *I am powerless. I am weak.*

Nic took the gun from me and reloaded it. 'You're a beginner.'

'A bad one.'

Nic frowned at me. 'Stop being so hard on yourself.'

'I want to be good at this,' I said. 'Like, immediately.'

Nic threw his head back and laughed at the ceiling. 'Sophie,' he said, amusement trilling in his voice. 'You can't make yourself an expert marksman in ten minutes. Give yourself the time you need to work on it. I'll help you, but you need to go easier on yourself.'

'I can't,' I huffed, watching the gun in his hands. The ease with which he handled it, the lazy confidence in his stance. Here was something else unexpected: *jealousy.* 'There's too much at stake.'

His face dropped, seriousness returning like a storm cloud across his features. 'I know,' he said. 'But you'll get there. I promise you. You will have your revenge.' He handed me the gun, loaded again. I took it, determination pulling me back into the shooting stance. 'The hardest thing to master is the trigger pull. You flinch when you pull it and it throws your body off-kilter. Your brain is telling you to compensate for the recoil but you need to overrule that part of you.'

I refocused on the Donata target. Those wide black-rimmed eyes. Those thin red-stained lips. *I'm going to make you pay.*

'I'm ready,' I said, before he could ask me.

'Then what are you waiting for?'

I pulled the trigger, this time fighting the recoil. The gun stayed entirely straight, and the bullet, when it hit, sailed right through the target's right shoulder.

'Excellent!' Nic whooped. 'You're a natural!'

I fired again. A miss, but a close one. Then two more misses.

'Focus,' Nic warned. 'Watch the recoil.'

I shot again, and this time the bullet landed right in the middle of Donata's torso.

'A killing blow!' Nic shouted. 'See,' he said, pointing at the two bullet holes in the target. 'You got her!'

I set my teeth, elation rising inside me. Pushing the darker feelings down, down, down, I shot again. This one landed in her breastbone.

'She's dead.' Nic broke into raucous laughter. 'You got her!'

'I got her!' I cried, dropping the emptied gun to my side. 'I can do this!' The feeling of power flooded me, and it was delicious and warm and all-consuming. I was good at this. I was good, and it was only my first time. I would get better. I would be amazing.

'Look,' said Nic, taking the emptied gun from me and using it to point at the target. He put his other arm around my shoulder and pulled me against him. I slid my arm around his back, fighting the urge to jump up and down like an excited child. We stood side by side, examining the target and basking in the glow of my small triumph. My ears were ringing, my arm was buzzing, and I was grinning like a mad person. 'See,' he said, moving the gun-pointer to the three separate holes. 'You did that. All of those.'

We were falling in and out of giddy laughter, still staring at the target with disbelief, when six more shots rang out.

I watched them dent the target – *my* target. Six holes forming a perfectly vertical straight line from the target's collarbone to its navel, like the buttons of a winter coat. Six perfect shots.

I turned towards the shooter, my heart climbing up my throat.

'Maybe she'll be able to do that,' said Luca. He reloaded in a blur and fired off six more. Every single one landed in the middle of the target's forehead. 'Or that,' he said, lowering his gun. 'If she *really* practises.' He turned towards us, shoving his gun back into the waistband of his jeans. 'What do you think, Sophie? Would you like to be able to do that?'

His voice was dangerously even. Nerves swarmed inside me, sucking all the warmth and joy from the moment. I swallowed hard.

Luca gestured at me and Nic. 'You'll probably have to unstick yourself from Nicoli, first. If you really want to hone your skills.'

There. Beneath the anger flashing in his eyes, the hard set of his mouth, there was a flicker of something else. Hurt. Why the hell would he be hurt? Something lurched inside me – hope that he might still care for me that way . . . and then an alarm sounded in my head. Nic still had his arm around me, and it looked like . . . Oh, God.

*Oh no. Oh no no no no.*

I stepped away from Nic. His arm fell with a thump to his side, and I folded mine across my torso. It was *freezing* in here. How had I not noticed that until now? And why couldn't

I think of anything to say? My mouth had gone dry, and my brain was just . . . stagnant.

'She's really good already, Luca.' Pride lit up Nic's voice. He was *so* not getting the undertone of our conversation. A huge part of me was glad about that. 'I think you'll be impressed.'

Luca was still looking at me. 'Will I?'

'Yeah.' Nic turned to me, the gun held out, bridging the big gap I had made between us. His smile was encouraging, his voice full of affection, when he said, 'Do you want to show him?'

I shook my head. 'No, thanks.'

'Go on.' Nic winked at me. 'He'll be impressed.'

I didn't dare look at Luca.

'Go on,' he said, his voice silky. 'Why don't you show me, Sophie? Show me what you've been up to out here all morning.'

'I'm too cold,' I said. 'I don't want to.'

'Come on,' said Nic, bewilderment colouring his tone. 'You were so excited before.'

'Was she?'

'I'm tired,' I said. 'I don't want to right now.'

'I want Luca to see what a good teacher I am. Let's show him what a good team we are.' I knew Nic was teasing me, but that was not the right thing to say in the moment. Not the way he lingered over the word *team*. I could practically feel Luca bristling.

'No,' I said, my answer firm.

'Fine,' said Luca quickly. He was over this. Theatrics weren't his thing, thankfully. 'Some other time, perhaps.' He turned to Nic, his tone clipped. 'Valentino is holding a meeting in ten

56

minutes. Libero Marino is back in Chicago.' He gestured behind him, in the direction of the house. 'He wants to speak to you about doing some recon in the city.'

Nic seemed to grow to twice his size in that moment. 'Whatever he needs.'

He was so . . . *malleable*.

I frowned, scolding myself for thinking less of the boy who had just been helping me. Nic was what he was; there was nothing to be ashamed of. He was a soldier. That was his calling and he was good at it.

Luca simply nodded. 'We'll follow you inside.'

Nic took his leave, grinning at me over his shoulder. 'We'll reconvene this afternoon?' He left the question in the air, and when I didn't respond, he sealed the answer with a wink. 'This was fun.'

And then he was gone, and the door was falling shut behind him, and I was wondering if I could scale the walls of the barn and slither out through a window before Luca gave me the tongue-lashing that was so obviously building up inside him. Would it be worth the drop on the other side?

I raised my chin. I would not be afraid of him or his words. He wasn't my keeper. He didn't control me. I could do what I wanted.

'I wanted to learn,' I said evenly. 'And you wouldn't teach me.'

He didn't even blink. 'So you found someone who would.'

Why the hell did I feel so ashamed of myself? I hadn't done anything wrong. Nic was proud of me. Nic was *helping* me. He was giving me the confidence I needed to walk this new path, and Luca was intent on taking it away. Screw that. 'Nic wants me to be happy.'

Something flitted across Luca's face. 'Nicoli wants you to be like him.'

'Would that be so bad?'

That look again – fleeting. I caught it that time. Betrayal. He thought I had betrayed him.

'Say something,' I said. 'Give out to me if you want, but don't just stand there glaring at me.'

*Show me you still care. Show me something real.*

The silence stretched out.

I just wanted it to make sense.

A muscle feathered in his jaw. 'I don't have anything to say to you, Sophie.'

And then he was gone. But the guilt remained, burrowing deep. I added it to the great, heaving pile already teetering inside me.

# CHAPTER SEVEN
## SNEAKING OUT

On Sunday morning, when everyone at the Falcone compound was getting ready for church, I sneaked out. Millie was parked in the usual spot, half-hidden by shrubbery around a giant bend in the road that dipped into a ditch about half a mile from Felice's house. Her head was bowed, the light from her phone reflecting off her face.

A sense of determination came over me as I drew closer. I imagined a mask absorbing my features, the old bones of my personality clicking into place. I was getting so good at compartmentalizing, it was almost scary. I was learning to be like them. I was learning to be like Valentino.

I swung the passenger door open, and Millie jumped in her seat, her phone sailing across the car. 'HolycrapSophie-youmovelikethewind.'

'Sorry.' I slipped inside. 'Are you ready to make our getaway?'

She raised an eyebrow at me, the engine already purring to life beneath us. 'What else would I be doing on a Sunday morning except smuggling my best friend away from her new home with a bunch of murderers before they notice she's gone and track her down via a chaperone who is most likely the boy I almost fell in love with but as it turns out was only using me for information?'

We pulled out on to the road, and Millie launched into her favourite pastime – unashamed speeding. I put on my seat-belt and gripped the sides of my seat. 'Tunes?' She turned on the radio, and cranked it up until the car was vibrating. 'Now, I don't want you to freak out,' Millie shouted over the music. She always preferred to shout than to turn it down. 'But as of this past month, I think something terrifying is happening to me.'

'Oh?' I said, matching her pitch.

'Yeah.' She nodded solemnly at the road. 'I'm not sure yet, but I think, I *think*, I might be a Belieber now.'

I clutched at my heart. 'Good God.'

'His stuff is just so on point these days, what am I supposed to do? *Not* listen to it? *Not* sing along? I'm only human, Soph. A beautiful, hilarious, intelligent human.'

I fought the urge to hug her lest we both veer off the road and crash. 'I've missed you, Mil.'

Millie snorted. 'Geez, what's it like in that hellish boy-filled mansion? It's only been two days.'

I thought about the ice-cold treatment I had been getting from Luca, Nic's eagerness to continue training me, how

60

stuck in the middle I felt, how badly I burnt for the moment Valentino would give me my target, how guilty I felt for anticipating it. 'Two days too long.'

'Speaking of your somewhat strange living arrangement which I have solemnly promised to stop questioning but secretly always wonder about . . . How *is* your boo?' She threw me a mischievous look.

I deadpanned her.

'What?' she said, innocently. 'Is it "bae" now? Is that what all the cool kids are saying? Or would it be "murder-bae"?'

I shut my eyes. 'Please do not refer to Luca Falcone as my murder-bae ever again.'

'But it's *so* funny,' she protested. 'He would *hate* it.'

*Oh, you have no idea.*

'Yeah, he would hate it. Probably about as much as he hates me right now.'

Millie screwed her face up. 'Why would Luca hate you? He practically escorted you into his family. Is he being an ass to you? Do you want me to get involved? Because I will take him down, Sophie, murder-bae or no murder-bae, I will take him all the way down.'

I smiled at my best friend, a well of love pouring over all of my frustrations. 'He thinks I'm getting with Nic,' I said, after a beat. Half a truth. That was the best I could do.

'Yikes.'

'I'm not getting with Nic,' I thought it pertinent to add.

Millie rolled her eyes. 'Obviously.'

'I don't want to be with Nic.'

'But does Nic know that?'

I weighed the question for a minute. 'You know, I'm

starting to wonder whether there's a difference between me telling Nic that, and Nic actually hearing it.'

'Boys can be so pig-headed sometimes,' Millie sighed. Her phone beeped from where it had fallen on the floor. She glanced towards it – out of reach – with so much longing on her face that she might have just tumbled right out of a war romance novel.

'What's his name?'

Her cheeks turned the most unsubtle shade of pink. 'Hmm?'

'The boy,' I said, picking her phone up for her. I held it between us as she struggled to keep her focus on the road. 'Don't make me invade your privacy, because I'll do it.'

'Oh, please,' she said, undaunted. 'My privacy is your privacy.'

Well, that was definitely a one-way street.

I glanced at the screen. '*Who* is Crispin?' And, as an aside, I thought it best to add, 'And *why* are you dating someone called *Crispin*?'

'Eh, because he's hot, and I'm shallow?'

'Really?'

'No!' She slapped my knee. 'Not really! Because he can't help what his parents named him. And he's actually really kind and sweet, and yes he *is* hot, plus he's perfect for this current phase in my life.'

'Which is?'

'*Which is* the phase of needing an escort for the Halloween Masquerade Ball so I don't look like a huge loo-hoo-ser in front of all my peers.'

'Oh,' I said, suddenly remembering the dance. 'Then I

guess this loo-hoo-ser will be going all by herself then.'

'Cris is on the football team.'

'Oh, *that* Crispin. Cris.' The realization dawned on me. Tall, blond, ripped Crispin. 'He *is* hot. Still, terrible name.'

Millie swirled her hand in the air. 'He sits beside me in chemistry.'

'How convenient . . .'

'We're lab partners . . . I let him cheat off me sometimes.'

I feigned a gasp. 'Millicent!'

'Look, science isn't his strong suit,' she said. 'He is, however, a very accomplished baker. He makes a mean blue-berry pie.'

'Is this . . . is this a euphemism?'

'I kid you not.'

'Huh.'

'Anyway, *anyway*, I was making a point here. If you want, I can get him to set you up with one of his friends and we can all ride in the limo together.'

'The *limo*?'

'Yes,' Millie said. '*The limo.* So you can just go ahead and remove that negative attitude, wrap it up in a bow and hide it away for a rainy day, because you and I are arriving at the dance in a limo.'

'Couldn't I just walk alongside it . . . ?'

Millie cut her eyes at me. 'You're going inside the limo or I'm strapping you to the top of it. Your decision.'

'Fine. I suppose I'll take the luxury.'

'Do you want me to set you up with one of Cris's friends or not?'

The mere idea of adding one more testosterone-fuelled

boy to my life was about as appealing as sawing my little finger off. 'Oh, no thank you, I'd rather die,' I said politely.

Millie reacted like I had just violently yanked her ponytail. 'Sophie! Come on. Let me actually help drag you back into the real world. This could be good for you. And it would definitely be good for me.'

'A minute ago, you were pushing me and Luca together!'

'That was a joke,' said Millie. 'Obviously I'd prefer you to be with someone who doesn't kill people for a living.'

'What about being by myself?' I asked her. 'I'm a pretty cool person. I could be in a very happy relationship with myself. I could also look into acquiring an aloof-yet-stylish cat.'

'And that,' said Millie, with a flurry of old-world drama in her voice, 'is precisely the problem, my dear. Let me get involved.'

I turned my whole body towards her so she would know I was totally serious when I said, 'Millie, do not under any circumstances meddle with my dating life.'

My phone buzzed. I cancelled the call.

Millie blew wisps of chestnut-brown hair from her face, pouting. 'Fine.'

My phone buzzed again. *Cancel.*

'You clearly have enough crap going on,' she said, flicking her gaze to my lap, where Luca's number was blowing up my screen. 'Are you going to answer that?'

I eyed the phone with contempt. 'No.'

'I thought you said he wasn't talking to you.'

'That was before I sneaked out without a chaperone.'

Millie turned the radio down until it was a low hum between us. Her voice changed, tinges of reverence slipping

64

into it now. 'Does he know where you're going today?'

'Of course not.'

A text flashed on screen:

Where have you gone? This is NOT funny.

I flipped the phone over and turned it on silent. 'Why would I invite Luca?'

'Because he was there when it happened,' she said softly. 'I think he would want to be there for you today.'

'Why? To keep an eye on me? Can I not even *grieve* in private?'

Millie flinched. 'No, just to be *there* for you. Like he was . . . after it happened.'

I shut my eyes, the memory of Luca's arms around me rushing in. I remembered how safe I had felt with him, how gentle he was with me, the feel of his lips against my hair, his thumbs wiping tears from my cheeks. I remembered his heartbeat thudding against mine, and how sure I had been, in the dusky quiet of my room all those weeks ago, that it meant something real. I had never felt so close to someone before. I had never felt so *seen*.

How could I have been so wrong?

I shook my head. 'He wouldn't care, Mil. Trust me, his mind is on other things now. And besides, this day isn't about him. It's about my mom.'

'I know,' she said softly. 'We'll give her the goodbye she deserves.'

I looked out the window, at flashes of familiarity – at the open road that was taking me home, back to Cedar Hill.

65

'Are you ready?' she asked.

*No. I'm not ready. I'm never going to be ready.*

I closed my eyes and imagined the mask shifting into place. A smile painted over a frown. Bright eyes to hide the tears. 'Yes,' I lied. 'I'm ready.'

I turned the radio back up. Taylor Swift filled the silence. There were no words for that moment, nothing to take away the sting of where we were going, of what today meant. Millie reached over and clasped my hand in hers.

'Thank you, Mil.'

'Of course,' she said, her voice cracking. I made sure not to turn my head because if I saw the tears streaming down her face, then I'd lose the flicker of composure that was holding me together. I needed that, just for today. Just for goodbye.

# CHAPTER EIGHT
## UNINVITED GUESTS

'Where's your mom's car? Did you take it to the Falcones with you?'

'Maybe it's in the auto shop or something,' I brushed Millie's questions off as we pulled up outside my house. The familiarity was not a welcome one. The empty driveway taunted me: Donata's cronies had been here. 'This is tough.'

'I know,' she said, leaning her head on my shoulder. 'I'll come in with you. We don't have to stay long. Just get what you need.'

I steeled myself: a deep breath, a careful rearrangement of all the memories pressing against my heart. I glanced at my phone. Six more missed calls. Three texts from Luca. Two from Nic. One from Elena. (Girl, get your skinny ass back here now unless you want me to see you into the next life. Classy.) Luca's texts had gone from angry to worried, and I was starting to feel bad. I had thought he would just infer from my absence that I needed some space.

I composed a reply to Luca, ignoring Elena's entirely.

I'll be back later. I'm scattering my mother's ashes today. Please don't call me again.

It even hurt to type it. I tried to rub the pain from my chest, but it was no use. I was just going to have to breathe through it.

I unlocked the front door and we stood there side by side on the threshold, staring at the setting of my old life.

*Welcome home, Sophie. Please enjoy this momentary stab in the heart.*

The house was undisturbed, save for some drops of dried blood on the hall floor. Jack had obviously tracked back through here after I stabbed him in the eye.

How strange that the sight of blood no longer bothered me.

How strange that another's pain would cause me such peace of mind.

How strange that I would wish my uncle, one of the closest people to me in the world, dead, and soon.

And that I would be the one to kill him.

'Let's be quick and careful about this,' I warned Millie. 'Stay by the door and keep it open, just in case there are any Marinos floating around here. If you hear or see anything, don't hesitate to scream.'

'You're joking, right?' Millie snorted. 'I think you've been spending too much time with Felice Falcone, Soph.'

'Well, you're not wrong about that.' I wished I was joking about the warning, but I knew I had to be on my guard. If the Marino family could smuggle my mother's car out of Cedar Hill unnoticed, they could certainly get into my house, and I wasn't dumb enough to stay even a minute longer than was necessary.

'Although,' added Millie, her tone turning sceptical as her attention fell on the bloodied floorboards. 'That does look suspiciously like blood. Or maybe someone was just eating a scone really messily, and the jam got everywhere . . .'

'Yeah, sure. Maybe Jack decided to make himself a random British teatime snack . . . you know, right after I stabbed him in the eye with a switchblade.'

Millie scrunched her eyes shut. 'Oh, I really didn't need that mental image again.'

I took the stairs two at a time. In my bedroom, I shoved the remainder of my clothes into a bag and grabbed a photo of my family – a Christmas shot from three years ago. We were dressed in matching Santa hats and hideously oversized reindeer sweaters, and smiling gleefully at the camera. My father looked at least twenty years younger, his face unlined by worry. My mother was as beautiful as ever, her hair framing her face in a golden halo as she pressed her cheek to mine. I looked at myself in the photo, and saw a stranger staring back. My hair was bright and glossy, my skin tanned. I was smiling so much my cheeks were probably hurting.

Jack had taken the photo. He had downed at least eight glasses of eggnog and kept swaying back and forth, and my father had been chastising him for it, my mother keeping her mouth shut. Swallowing her annoyance, because it was Christmas, and she couldn't kick Jack out at Christmas. I wished she had. I wished she had kicked him to the other side of the world and left him there. At least he wasn't in the photo. There was still the matter of my father and his lying eyes, but it was the best photo I had, and the only one I bothered to take with me. I left the rest – the DVDs and trinkets, notepads, all those prison letters from my father – all those false words.

The scent of lavender was fading from my mother's bedroom. It took every ounce of strength not to lie down in her bed, bury myself in the duvets and never get up. I packed some of her jewellery, a sapphire teardrop necklace and matching earrings – I'd be damned if Donata Marino ever got her spindly fingers on them. I took my mom's favourite sweater, too, pressing my face into it before folding it up.

After calling down to Millie to make sure she was still there – which she was, and obviously texting Crispin too, because she was giggling like a haunted doll from a horror movie – I slipped into a black shift dress and matching ankle boots. I brushed my hair out, swept it away from my face and looked at myself in the mirror. I was giving off a pretty potent Wednesday Addams vibe, but at least I was demure. I was elegant. My mother would have approved.

I looked at my phone. There was a reply from Luca:

Where are you now? Are you by yourself?

I didn't bother texting him back. If he wanted to give out to me, he could save it for later. I wasn't in the mood right now. At the bottom of the stairs, I filled Millie's arms with all the things I was taking from the house, and tried to ignore all the things I was leaving behind. After this, there would be no looking back. Nothing left undone or unsaid. Today was about closure. Today was about moving on.

'You look nice,' she said. 'I like that dress.'

I shrugged. 'My mom always liked me in dresses, even though they make me look about five years old.'

'Ah, Soph, don't be dramatic. You look at least seven and a half in that.'

I stuck my tongue out at her as I slipped into the sitting room, and then found myself standing in front of the urn on the mantelpiece. Stalling.

I stared at it for a minute – this thing that now held the essence of my mother. The urn was dark purple, her favourite colour – I must have told them that. I couldn't remember now. There was a thin gold band around the top, and a banner of floral filigree bordering it. It was beautiful, I supposed, but it made me a little sick inside.

When we got back into the car it was almost one p.m. Millie was adjusting her mirror, frowning. 'You can't be serious.'

'What is it?' I asked.

'Black SUV at the end of the street,' she sighed. 'Can't tell which Falcone it is.'

'Doesn't matter,' I said, refusing to turn around. I was singularly focused. Today was about my mother. Today was about goodbye. 'Let's just go. I don't want to be late.'

*

Beyond the last rows of boxy houses and the dilapidated football field, the town sloped upwards, turning the street narrow as it climbed until the land flattened out unexpectedly and gave rise to a generous spread of cedar trees. It was a peaceful wedge of nature, where everything was crisp and green and pretty, and if you weaved your way through the trees to where the hill sloped down again, you could see the river winding towards the town below.

It was my mother's favourite place. We used to go on walks there together when I was younger. Back when I got bored easily and complained about being too cold or too tired to climb the hill. Back when I didn't know how good I had it.

At the top of the hill, Millie parked along a dirt border beneath a cluster of trees. We got out, my hands clutched tight around the urn. The scent of pine wrapped around me, the light breeze pushing wisps of hair across my face. It smelt like the past.

Ursula, Gracewell's Diner's former assistant manager, bustled towards me, her usual bright clothes replaced by a long black dress and matching coat. She was wrapped up to her nose in a grey scarf, revealing only a hint of her inky black eyes and cropped white hair.

She embraced me awkwardly, the urn still held between us. She cupped my face in her hands, as if she was trying to peer into my soul. 'How have you been? *Where* have you been?' She took a step back, affording me a cursory once-over. 'I've been worried about you. It's been too long since I've seen you.'

I brushed off her questions, like I had been rehearsing. I told her I was staying with friends outside the city, trying to

72

come to terms with everything. She didn't push it, but curiosity burnt in those dark eyes. 'Thanks for coming,' I offered, before she could burrow any deeper into my barefaced lie. I felt glad of her familiarity, even if it did come peppered with suspicion. 'It means a lot to me.'

She squeezed my arm, her brows creasing. 'I wouldn't miss it for the world, Sophie.'

People who make time for the sadness in your life, not just the joy, are worth keeping around. It saddened me to think of my new life now, and how there was no place for Ursula in it.

Almost everyone I had invited was here: Mrs Bailey, who was wearing a netted black veil and a huge fur coat that seemed to say *I'm the chief mourner here and I am also very rich.* Millie's parents had come, and her brother Alex too. He embraced me in an awkward hug, and I tried to remember the time when that would have been the best thing to ever happen to me.

There were some old acquaintances from the diner, too, and my mother's stalwart clients from the city. A few of her closest friends had made it, the ones who had stuck around after my father went to prison.

I recognized most of the faces, and could guess at the ones that didn't immediately register. That's how small her circle had become after my father went to jail. That's how easy it was to corral everyone she cared about into the same space. They parted in a sea of drawn faces, each one offering renewed sympathies as I passed through them. Millie linked arms with me, and I leant against her, finding comfort in the faces of those who had known my mother as I did – as someone who was happy and bright and beautiful. This was how she would be remembered. These were the people she loved most in the world.

I tried not to think about my dad. The last time I had spoken to him I had smashed our house phone against the wall. Michael Gracewell was a lie – Vince Marino Jr was the truth, and he never had the guts to tell me. Above all the other heinous things he had done – the murders and the lies – that was the cherry on top. I could never forgive him for that. For taking away my identity before I had a chance to learn it for myself.

'What a lovely idea this is, Persephone.' Mrs Bailey was in front of me. She removed the netted veil from her face and smoothed it back over her hair. Her eyes were rimmed in black. 'To give your mother this beautiful send-off. It's what she would have wanted after such a tragic . . . well . . .' She trailed off, and I silently dared her to mention my uncle. The fugitive. They all suspected his involvement, but they had no idea.

'Nice coat,' I said, steering the conversation to a safer topic. 'Where did you get it?' *A* Titanic *survivor?*

'Oh, this?' She brushed her hands along the front of it. 'It's just something I had in the back of the closet.'

'Well, it goes very nicely with the veil.' *Speaking of the veil, are you fucking serious right now?*

'I remember when you were younger . . .' She looked past me, to the trees over my shoulder, as though they were whispering to her. 'I would often see you and your mother here. It seems like a lifetime ago now.'

My mind sailed back through those memories. To ham sandwiches and smoothies underneath the trees, to watching the river meander into town, to blowing dandelion wishes over the hill and listening to the sound of my mother laughing. 'This was a happy place for us. For her.'

'I'm sure it always will be.' She touched my arm, her long fingernails pressing grooves into my skin. 'And, well, there's something else.' Mrs Bailey cleared her throat. 'We, as a community – I mean, well, with the short notice, not everyone could make it, but we wanted to do something nice for your mother, to show how much we cared about her, and how wonderful she was. We had a few donations . . .'

Mrs Bailey shuffled backwards, and that's when I saw it properly for the first time. A wooden bench had been set into a new granite slab on the edge of the grassy hill. A bench right where we used to sit when I was younger, where we would search underneath the trees and collect pine cones for Christmas wreaths. I edged forward, the short heels of my boots sticking and unsticking in the grass. I ran my fingers along the wood. I could still smell the varnish. A gold plaque had been set into the middle of the bench:

### *In loving memory of Celine Gracewell.*
### *May she rest in peace.*

'Oh.' My voice was just a squeak in my chest. 'That's lovely.' In truth, it was the loveliest thing I could have imagined.

Someone had even tied a purple ribbon around each arm – an ode to my mother's love of creativity. Here she would be, in nature, remembered for ever in one of her favourite places. Somewhere other mothers could sit with their daughters, and laugh while blowing dandelion wishes over the hill.

'Thank you,' I said, gazing across the small puddle of mourners, wondering just how much they had given from their Christmas funds or their savings to make this happen. 'She would have loved it.'

I stood in front of everyone with the river at my back, and cleared my throat. I wasn't sure how to go about this, and part of me regretted the absence of a formal officiate, but my mother had never really been a fan of organized religion. Or organized anything, in fact.

'Thank you all for coming,' I said, not sure where to rest my gaze. That's the most awkward thing about public speaking – not staring at anyone in particular, but not looking at the ceiling either in case people think you're an idiot. *Focus.* I fixed my eyes on Mrs Bailey's veil. *Too ridiculous.* Ursula's beady eyes. *Too suspicious.* Finally I found Millie's reassuring smile in the small crowd. 'This isn't going to be a formal ceremony because my mom wasn't really a formal person. She loved spontaneity and chaos, she loved nature and being outdoors, but most of all, she loved being around her family and friends – the people who lit up her life. I think it's fair to say she lit up ours too.'

Murmurs of approval filtered through the group, nodding heads and knowing smiles. And then the huddle was moving, just a little, and someone was slipping between the shoulders of Mrs Bailey and Millie. He stopped between them, and they let him stay there, shoulder to shoulder, his head above theirs as he stood directly across from me. And suddenly I knew exactly where to rest my surprised gaze. Luca was standing right there in front of me.

He smiled at me – it was small and fleeting, but I understood. In that moment, we weren't at odds with each other. He had come to honour the memory of my mother. He had come to stand in solidarity with me.

I opened the ceremony up to the others, and Ursula pottered forward to tell a story about my mother. Then Mrs Bailey chimed in with her own and, one by one, people spoke up, just to say something small – a word, a sentence or an anecdote, and they collected in the air around us – the essence of my mother and all the light she had brought to our lives.

And then Millie took a step forward, hands clasped innocently behind her back. 'I've got one,' she said, her smile sloping to one side. A little part of me wanted to take her by the shoulders and whisper, *Know your audience*. 'When Soph and I were younger, there was this store at the very end of Main Street called The Gem that all the cool kids hung out at after school. Naturally it was *the* place to be.'

Luca arched a brow, intrigue cocking his head to one side.

'There was this group of boys who hung out there in the evenings, and I had my eye on one of them. Can't remember his name, but he used to spike his hair in this really cute boy-band-esque way, and he wore high-top shoes which were all the rage.' Alex rolled his eyes at his sister. 'Celine told us we couldn't go on our own because we were too young and it was going to get dark soon. Well, we complained for what felt like hours until, eventually, seeing how much the trip really meant to us, and how important it was for our confidence as young, capable women, Celine finally gave in. It was raining really hard outside but we didn't care. We zipped up our raincoats and set off.'

A ray of warmth tickled my chest. Everyone was enraptured by Millie – that lilting British accent, the elaborate hand gestures, the whirring confidence with which she spoke. Even Luca was listening intently.

'It was winter and it was pretty dark, not to mention the streets were deserted because of the rain. After about five minutes, Soph noticed there was someone trailing behind us. A man in a long trench coat was following us! He'd come out of nowhere, and his hood was up so we couldn't see his face. We upped our pace, and when we looked over our shoulders, the man had sped up too. So we ran, hand in hand, as fast as we could, splashing in and out of puddles until we finally got to the store. I honestly thought I was going to have a heart attack. After all that commotion, and the risking of our lives, the cute boys weren't even there! The place was deserted.

'Well, naturally I was livid. Soph actually thought it was funny, but she always has had a warped sense of humour. So in the end, we bought a couple of milkshakes, drank them way too quickly, and then ran all the way home, the Trench Coat Villain still hot on our heels!'

A laugh bubbled out of me as the memory crystallized, and for the first time, Luca shifted his attention from Millie to me.

'When we got back, we slammed the front door behind us and tumbled into Soph's kitchen. We were panting so hard, we couldn't even speak, and then the door flew open and who should come in but the Trench Coat Stalker!'

Mrs Bailey actually gasped, grabbing Luca's arm in her moment of shock, then releasing it in the same instant with an even bigger and much more dramatic gasp at having actually touched a Falcone. Luca didn't seem to care.

'And then the stalker lowered his hood, and who was it?' Millie's teeth flashed. 'Celine!' Laughter filtered through the crowd. 'She wanted us to have our adventure but she didn't want us to be in any danger, so she tried to follow us to the store in her own stealth-like way to make sure nothing happened to us.'

'Only it didn't work,' I chimed in. 'Because her raincoat was terrifying and the hood covered her whole face and made her look like something from a horror movie.'

'It scared us half to death,' said Millie, shaking her head, a half-smile still playing on her lips. 'But it was so funny.'

I remembered how much we had all laughed after that. How hilarious my mother found it that she had been chasing to keep up with us without realizing we were running from her the whole time.

'But that was Celine,' said Millie. 'Kind and protective, and fierce when she had to be. She would do anything for her family. And even though she's gone now, she's still here.' Millie gestured around her, at the air and the trees and gentle sway of the leaves. 'She's here.' She pressed her hand to her heart, and when she spoke again, her words were watery. 'And most importantly, she's there.' She gestured towards me, trying to smile as we locked eyes. 'She's in you, Sophie. All the goodness in her is in you now, too. You made her so proud, and I know you always will. You are her heart. Her memory will live on in you.'

A ripple of agreement travelled through the huddle. I swallowed the thickness in my throat. Well, damn. If Millie wasn't the queen of speeches, I didn't know who was. She should write for the president. She should *be* the president. Or the prime minister. Whatever.

I did my best to stand straight and not crumple, because if I let myself ponder Millie's last line – of my mother's pride in me, of her place in my life and my future, I would rip my hair out. Today was about saying goodbye. Tomorrow was about revenge. Nothing had changed that. Nothing could change that now.

'Thank you for all those wonderful tributes,' I said, picking up the urn and brushing past the heart-crushing sincerity of my best friend's speech before it demolished me. 'I'm going to scatter her ashes and then I'm going to say goodbye.' I turned from them, the urn heavy in my hand, and walked to the edges of the hill before it sloped downwards again. Silence fell across the clearing, the only sounds the distant rumbling of a car engine and the rustling of leaves overhead. I peered at the river below, the wind sailing across my cheeks, as I unclasped the urn.

*I love you. I'll love you for ever.*

The wind whipped the ashes into the air and pulled them downstream, to where the river flowed freely, and in that moment, I felt nothing but her, around me, within me, and it was a quiet, fleeting second of happiness that I knew I would not feel again for a very long time.

There was a scuffle behind me – a low rumbling intruding on the quiet reverence. I set the now-empty urn at my feet and turned around, ready to glare at whoever had the audacity to talk during such an important moment. I was all puffed up, irritated and heated, the words ready on my tongue . . . but in their place, only one slipped out.

'Dad?'

I froze on the hill over the river, my jaw unhinged, as my father made his way through pockets of mourners. I scanned him, a part of me thinking he wasn't real, that the grief had finally driven me mad.

It was really him.

Scruffy and thin, and dressed in one of his old suits, the sleeves gaping, the collar of his shirt unstarched. A tracking bracelet around his ankle, a prison guard twelve feet to his left, arms folded across his chest as he waited under a tree. And that word – one of the last he'd said to me before I'd smashed the phone – flashed inside my head. *Furlough. I've applied for furlough.*

Well, holy crap. They had let him out. Someone had obviously told him about my mother's ceremony, and the prison had decided to let him come.

Those *idiots.*

I froze as my father dipped his head in reverence, low words exchanged with a couple of my mother's friends, whose eyes were bugging just as crazily as mine. I froze as he smiled and embraced Ursula, as he shook hands with Mrs Bailey, as he stood there, accepting condolences as if they were prizes.

I stayed stock-still, gaping, right up until the moment Millie leapt from her place on the far side of the huddle and pushed herself in front of my father, so that he couldn't come any closer, so that he couldn't see what I could see from my vantage point. Then my brain fissured, and understanding hit me like a lightning bolt.

*Oh, shit.*

Michael Gracewell, aka Vince Marino Jr, heir to the Marino

crime family, was unwittingly hovering ten feet away from Luca Falcone, the active underboss of the entire Falcone dynasty.

Horror roiled in my stomach, my head swivelling to where Luca was standing.

*No. No. No. No.*

Luca was staring right at my father.

His whole body was pressing forwards, leaning across that infinite space between them, and I swear in that moment I could feel the anger rolling off him. If looks could kill, my father – my ignorant, oblivious father – would have dropped dead on the spot.

Luca wasn't moving. He was holding himself together, all his energy bound up in keeping still as he crushed his hands in and out of fists at his sides. His nostrils flared, shallow breaths swelling and falling in his chest. His lips were moving, but there was nothing coming out.

I had seen Luca angry, and I had seen Luca calm, but I had never seen him struggle so hard for composure. I had never seen him so scarily unhinged. He was trying to hold it all inside him, but all it would take was one thing, one tiny thing, to unleash it.

I stared so hard at him my eyes began to hurt.

*Just look at me. Don't look at him. Look at me.*

But he was glaring, unblinking, at my father, assessing him with the deadly quiet of a lion stalking its prey. And why wouldn't he be?

Here was the man who had killed his father. Luca knew the truth – he had seen Evelina's ruby ring. He knew my father's protested innocence had been a farce. Here was the murderer, standing unprotected not ten feet away from him, with a single uninterested prison warden sulking underneath a faraway tree. He wouldn't be quick enough to stop anything, not if Luca pulled a gun.

Not if Luca lunged for my father. It could all be over in a heartbeat. His revenge was there for the taking.

*Please don't,* I implored. *Please don't do anything.*

Millie was embracing my father, inching him back into the circle, away from Luca's glare.

*Do something, Sophie. Do anything.*

Everyone was staring at my father – the great mystery of Michael Gracewell, who was once again walking like a free man among them. No one was looking at me any more. No one was thinking about my mother. The day had been turned on its head.

*Say something. Say anything.*

I had to make my father disappear. I had to pull their focus from him. I had to redirect Luca's thoughts. I had to calm him down, somehow, without drawing attention to any of it.

The words came flying back to me, from the only poem I knew, and the only one that would work just then. *Thank you, Mary Elizabeth Frye.*

'*Do not stand at my grave and weep,*' I said, my voice croaky with fear. I cleared my throat as, one by one, heads turned back to me. '*I am not there. I do not sleep.*'

*Come on, Luca. Come on.*

'*I am a thousand winds that blow.*' My father stopped whispering to Millie and looked up at me. '*I am the diamond glints on snow.*'

*Stay with me. Don't look across the circle. Don't look at Luca.*

'*I am the sunlight on ripened grain.*' Millie nodded at me as if to say *Keep going.* '*I am the gentle autumn rain.*'

Luca was pulling his gaze from my father, slowly, slowly, like the weight of it was a great, hulking thing. '*When you awaken in the morning's hush,*' I said, my voice cracking, '*I am the swift uplifting rush.*'

*Please don't hurt him.* '*Of quiet birds in circled flight.*' *Please don't take this day from her.* '*I am the soft stars that shine at night.*'

Luca was looking at me again. His features had clouded over. '*Do not stand at my grave and weep.*' My eyes were swimming with unshed tears. '*I am not there, I do not sleep.*' And then my dad was breaking rank, crossing the grassy mound, coming towards me with arms outstretched. '*Do not stand at my grave and cry.*' Everyone was watching us. A father reuniting with his daughter, and I realized I couldn't push him away, no matter how much I wanted to. '*I am not there.*' I blinked and the tears streamed down my face. '*I did not die.*'

'Oh, Sophie, sweetheart.' My father flung his arms around me. He pulled me into his chest, and I collapsed into him, staining his shirt with my tears. I hated him with a passion so fierce it burnt inside me, but I needed that hug – that embrace – and all the lies that went with it, because beneath all the anger, beneath every shred of betrayal, I still loved him. I still wanted him to be OK. I needed that hug because it was keeping him from Luca. It was keeping my dad safe.

We stood like that for a long time, my back to the others, my body a shield between the murderer who had lied to me my whole life, and the assassin who had been watching over me in his absence.

When my father pulled back from me, and the cold air rushed into the space between us, drying icy tears on our cheeks, everyone else was crying too, and Luca Falcone was gone.

That was the greatest gift he could have given me. The willingness to walk away. And I knew, had I been faced with the same dilemma, I would have failed.

# CHAPTER NINE
## WARNING

'Who told you?' I was trying very hard to keep my voice under control, conscious of the prison guard hovering nearby.

My father patted the empty seat beside him. 'Can you sit down and we can talk about this properly?'

I kept my arms folded across my chest, my feet planted in the grass in front of the granite slab. 'Who told you?' I repeated.

He tilted his chin so he could see my whole face, the entirety of my disgust. His eyes were impossibly large from this angle. 'Ursula wrote to me,' he admitted. 'She was afraid you had forgotten to tell me about it.'

'If I wanted you here, I would have told you.'

'I know.' He had knitted his hands together on his lap, and

was digging his fingernails into his knuckles.

'And yet you came. You came and you made a scene out of it.'

'She was my *wife*,' he said, as if I needed to be reminded. 'I love her and I grieve her. And you are my daughter, and I have every right to be here with you.'

'No,' I said, leaning closer and dropping my voice to barely more than a whisper. 'I'm the daughter of Michael Gracewell, and Michael Gracewell is gone. I am not your daughter, *Vince*.'

My father jerked backwards. 'Don't act like this, Sophie. This isn't like you.'

'You don't know me,' I snapped. 'And evidently, I don't know you. All I know is a collection of lies you told me, and all those horrible things you did. All those lives you took!'

'Keep your voice down!' Colour rose to his cheeks; his eyes, just like mine, grew dark with warning. 'Are you trying to get me locked up for the rest of my life?'

I could have punched him. Right then, I could have punched him, but I didn't because some stupid, vulnerable, childish part of me was still seeing my dad in front of me. The one who used to read me Dr. Seuss before bed, the one who would lift me on to his shoulders and spin me around when I needed cheering up. 'Do you realize just how much you've hurt me? How much you've betrayed me?'

He slumped in his seat, the black suit seeming to swallow him up. 'Yes,' he said. 'I understand what I've done. What I've lost.'

No. Not this conversation. I was already teetering on the verge of tears, every last emotion from the day lining up inside me, pressing tiny hands against my heart. I stood back, widening the gap between us. 'Where's Jack?'

He looked up at me, something sparking in his gaze. He knew. *He knew*.

'Do not lie to me one more time.'

He raised his chin, defiance meeting my own. 'Sophie—'

'He killed Mom.'

'I know what happened, Sophie.'

'He's the reason she's dead!'

He flicked a nervous glance towards the prison guard.

'I know what happened, Sophie. Your uncle—'

I bent at the waist, bringing my face close to his. 'You weren't there!' I hissed. 'You *don't* know. You have no idea. Now tell me where he is so he can pay for what he did!'

And then I saw it. A smoothening of his brow, his eyes dulling, his lips resetting into a thin line. Commander mode. Here was Vince Marino, the skilled assassin. Finally. He was showing himself to me. He was showing me his steeliness, because he had no intention of ratting his brother out.

'Sophie,' he said, emotionless now. Calm when he should have been immersed in rage, like I was. 'Where have you been staying? I know you haven't been at home.'

'How do you know that?' I challenged. 'Because your scumbag family killed Mom and then came back for her car to burn it out at the entrance to Felice's driveway?'

Something flickered across his face – a chink in his armour. 'So you are at the Falcones',' he said, distaste curling his lip.

'I'm not *at* the Falcones',' I returned evenly. 'I *am* a Falcone.'

He dropped his head into his hands. I watched him fold over on himself, and tried to quench the tiny flame of anxiety that sprang up at the sight of his anguish. 'Oh, Sophie,' he said, raising his head and dragging his palms along his cheeks. 'What have you done?'

'Now, there's the question of the hour. I'll tell you my answer if you tell me yours.'

'They're going to hurt you,' he said, leaning towards me. 'Don't you understand that, Soph? They're going to *hurt* you.'

'They can't hurt me as much as the Marinos already have.'

'Why?' he asked, crestfallen. His voice was weak, his commander facade seeping away like water. This was my father, the man I knew. 'Why did you go to them?'

I dropped my shoulders, my anger petering into resignation. 'Where else would I have gone?'

His silence was answer enough.

*Nowhere. There was nowhere else to go.*

A furtive glance over my shoulder showed me the prison guard was more interested in his phone than in us. Millie was waiting by the car. Everyone else had gone home.

My father buried his face in his hands again. I spoke to the crown of his head, where grey hairs mingled amongst the mousy brown. 'If you don't tell me where Jack is, and what he's doing, I'm going to turn around and walk away, and this conversation will be over for good. I know you know. I don't know why you're hiding it after his involvement in Mom's death, but if you refuse to tell me, then I'll consider it a betrayal to her as well as me.' I could hear the cruelty in my voice, but I pushed on, knowing this was the only way forward. He had been cruel, too, only he was too afraid to show it. I would be transparent at least.

'I loved your mom, Soph.' He was speaking to his feet as I glowered at his head. 'She was the best thing that ever happened to me. Her and you.'

'You lied to her. She had no idea about all the people you had killed . . . about your quest for retribution. She didn't see what was in the safe. The Falcone switchblades. The ring. The names. But I did.'

He snapped his head up. 'The Falcones took everything from Jack and me. Sophie, they murdered our parents. They shot my mother. My *mother*. Can you not understand how I'd be angry about that? Can you not understand why I would want to avenge her?'

I wavered, just for a split second. This was dangerous. This was resonance, and I couldn't afford to feel any empathy with my father. I couldn't afford to let him draw a link between what he had done and what I wanted to do . . . unless I could use it to my advantage.

I hunkered down until we were at eye level. 'Can *you* not understand why *I* would want to do the same to the people who killed Mom? Can you not understand why I'm looking for Jack? For Donata?'

He shut his eyes. 'This isn't the right path for you, Sophie.'

'And yet it was for you?'

He flicked his gaze over my shoulder, towards his prison chaperone. 'Look where it got me, Soph.'

'Where is he?' I pressed.

'Leave them,' he said at the same time as me. 'Get away from the Falcones before they hurt you, Sophie. Because they *will* hurt you. Felice Falcone is mentally unhinged. You won't

90

survive under the same roof as him. And Angelo's boys . . . they have it in for me, Sophie. They'll have it in for you too.'

'And go where? The Marinos'? Should I have Thanksgiving dinner at Donata's house? Sit shoulder to shoulder with Jack? Jack who did nothing as Mom lay unconscious at his feet in the diner?'

My father sucked in a breath. 'Of course not. I don't want you anywhere near the underworld, period. It makes corpses of good people, and survivors of the worst. There's no justice there, Soph. If you trust nothing else I've ever said, trust that. It will destroy you.'

I shook my head. 'It's too late, Dad.'

'It's *not* too late, Sophie.' He reached into his pocket and pulled out a folded piece of paper. 'This is not your world. It's not your path. I made damn sure to keep it from you for this long, I won't falter now.'

'He killed her.' I was beginning to sound like a parrot, but I needed to be heard, and my father was refusing to listen. 'He had a hand in her death, no matter what he told you.'

'This is not your fight.' He held the paper out. It hovered between us, a small white flag. 'Take it.'

I eyed it with suspicion. 'What is it?'

'An address,' he said. 'Someone who will help you. Go to them, and they will hide you. Take your life and run with it. If not for me, then for your mother. She would have hated to see you turning to darkness. It would have broken her heart in two.'

I snatched the paper from his hands and opened it, reading the top of the address. 'Who the hell is M Flores?'

'Someone who will help you,' he said simply.

91

I read the address. '*Colorado?*' I looked up at him. 'Are you serious? You want me to go to Colorado to stay with some guy I've never met?'

'That's exactly what I want you to do.'

'Well, that is ridiculous.' I brandished the paper between us. 'You have seriously lost your mind.'

He raised a hand. 'Put that away. Don't show it to anyone else. When you go, you have to disappear. Don't tell another soul the address on that piece of paper.'

I narrowed my eyes at the hurried script. 'Who is this? And why would they owe you anything?'

He pursed his lips together. Another secret he would not relinquish. He was a fool to give this to me. As if I would ever listen to him. As if I still cared for any of his stupid, reckless advice. My fight was here, in Chicago. My fight was in the underworld, just as his was.

'I'm not a monster, Sophie.'

I blew out a sigh. I had reached my threshold for this particular genre of conversation. All assassins were the same – deluded – and I was done being the resident counsellor. I was done with second chances, *third* chances. I could make up my own mind about who to trust from now on; that much had become very clear. 'How long are you out for?' I said, eyeing the prison guard.

'They granted me furlough for the ceremony.'

'Well, it's over now. You can take off again.'

I was still inching away, trying to distance myself from the love I used to have for this man, from all the admiration and respect that was now smouldering inside me – a wasteland of childhood affection. 'Soph, will you do what I said?'

I looked down at the note. I looked at his face.

'If you prove your loyalty.' I kept my gaze as steely as his own. 'Show me that after everything, you're on our side. Mine and Mom's. Tell me where Jack is hiding.'

He drew in a loaded breath, his chest puffing out. 'I won't do that.'

I crumpled the note and threw it at his feet. 'Then I can't trust you.'

# CHAPTER TEN

## TARGET

'Sophie.' Valentino's voice cut through my mental assessment of his office. The velvet drapes, the mahogany desk, the expensive leather chairs, the dark wood cabinets. 'Are you ready to pay attention to me now?'

I turned back to him, dragging my gaze from a particularly opulent lamp in the corner of the room. 'I was just . . . taking it all in.' I tried to get comfortable in my chair, but I couldn't. The leather squeaked under my attempts, drowning out Bach or Vivaldi or Beethoven or whoever was needlessly upping the dramatics.

I settled under his gaze, and wished he had asked one of the others to come in with me. A one-on-one meeting with the Falcone boss was not high on my bucket list.

He tapped his fingers along the desk, a careful drumming,

perfectly in time with the music.

'How was school?' he asked blithely.

'Do you really care?' I asked. Valentino didn't do small talk.

He was leaning back in his chair. He picked up a pencil and twirled it around, catching and releasing it between his fingers. 'No, not especially.'

The pencil was quite captivating. 'Your dexterity is commendable.'

'How are you settling in?' he said, the pencil still moving round and round. It was like he was trying to distract me. A test. I kept my gaze forward.

'Fine,' I said. 'Felice notwithstanding.'

'Unfortunately, Felice's presence here cannot be helped.' So Valentino didn't think too highly of Felice either. *Interesting. See also: unsurprising.* 'Nic says you're a natural shooter.'

'Yeah, I'm OK,' I said, trying to sound modest. Luca hadn't come home the night before, so Nic and I had managed to squeeze in another session out in the barn. 'I'm a quick learner.'

'It's obviously in your blood,' Valentino said.

'Must be.' *Dimples and marksmanship. Thanks, Dad.*

Valentino flipped the subject. 'You went walkabout yesterday.'

'I was having a ceremony for my mother.'

He clamped the pencil in his fist. 'Don't do that again.'

'In my experience you can only scatter ashes to the wind once. They're very hard to collect after that.'

'Do you think you're funny?'

'With the right audience.' My heart was hammering in my chest.

'I don't enjoy sarcasm,' he said pointedly. 'Just so you're aware.'

*Well, then, you are not going to enjoy me very much.* 'Right,' I said, shifting again in my seat. The leather was cold on my hands. I tucked them under my legs to keep them warm. 'Is that why I'm here? Because of yesterday?' I studied his reaction – that stony impassivity. Did he know that my dad had been there? That we had spoken? How much had Luca said to him?

Valentino shook his head. 'I thought it would be best to get that little matter of housekeeping out of the way first. Don't go walkabout again without telling us first. It's a drastic waste of time and manpower, and given that we're in the middle of a blood war, I'm sure you can see how unfathomably stupid it was.' He pinned me with those sapphire eyes, and then pulled his lips back a fraction, so I could see a hint of his canines. 'Can't you?'

Relief flittered like a bird inside me. So Luca hadn't said a thing. Man, that guy was a vault. A vault I would have to thank whenever he resurfaced. 'It won't happen again.'

Valentino pulled the drawer of his desk open and took out a single sheet of paper. 'Now we can proceed to more important matters.' He dropped the sheet between us, and slid it across his desk so that it was facing me. I pulled my hands from underneath me and scooted forward.

Oh.

It wasn't a slip of paper, it was a photograph.

An eerily familiar photograph.

*Oh.*

'This,' he said, pressing his index finger across it, 'is Libero

Marino, the son of Donata Marino.'

I stared at the photograph of Libero Marino. He had those wide, dark eyes. His head was shaved in the photo, but he had a thick black goatee, and an unsightly scar right across the bridge of his nose. He didn't seem like someone who was used to smiling. I imagined all his teeth, if he bared them, would be gold.

My throat felt like it was about to close up.

'That's Sara's brother,' I said, without taking my eyes off the photo. Underneath, a few details had been scribbled in. His height: *5'8"*, his age: *22 years old*. His skills: *knife and hand-to-hand combat*, and his ranking: *Marino Capo, son of Donata Marino*.

Valentino nodded. 'He's back in the city now, trading with clients on Donata's behalf.'

I lifted my gaze, and tried to swallow the waver in my voice that was about to give away my sudden onslaught of nerves. 'Is he . . . is he my target?'

Valentino had steepled his hands in front of him, fingers touching against his lips, hiding his mouth. 'Yes,' he said. 'Libero Marino is your target.'

I tried to ignore the sudden roaring in my ears. Libero Marino was Sara's brother. One of Jack's right-hand men. Why had I thought it would be someone I didn't know? Why had I thought it would be easier than this? The Marinos were my blood – well, most of them – so of course I would likely know my target. 'When?' I asked, the faintest flutter in my lashes.

'Saturday night.'

Five days. I had five days to prepare.

Did Luca know? Would he try to stop it? Had he finally given in to the idea of me taking control of my own destiny?

I forced myself to answer, ignoring the desert in my throat. 'OK.'

'Nic will have all the necessary details when the time comes.'

I smiled weakly. 'Good.'

'He's keen to be the one to do it with you,' he added, something else creeping into his voice – discomfort, disapproval? 'He wants the opportunity to . . . mend old wounds.'

I felt myself go pale. Nic wanted to win me back, and he thought this was the way to do it. I swallowed hard, unwilling to deal with that part of the equation – not while I had a life to take, my own character to prove. I was done putting boys first.

Valentino misread my hesitation. He dropped his hands. 'You don't need to take Libero down, Sophie, you just have to deal the killing blow. You can use a knife if you prefer.'

'No,' I said, forcing my lips into something that didn't resemble a horrified grimace. 'I'll use a gun. I like . . . I like guns.'

*I like guns? Really, Sophie?*

Amusement swept across his features. 'That makes two of us.' He sat back in his chair, those canines glinting at me. 'If you do this, the next time you have a gun pointed at someone, it will be your uncle.'

'Good,' I said, baring my teeth right back. I didn't have to force that one.

He opened another drawer and withdrew a wooden box. The lid, when it came up, was made of cherry wood, the outline of a falcon etched into it. The Falcones really did like to keep everything on-brand. He flipped the lid over and it landed on the desk with a dull thud. 'This is for you, Sophie. This is for Saturday.'

He lifted a gun out of the box and slid it across the table. It was black and silver, like Nic's, but it was smaller and the handle was curved. I picked it up, rotating it in front of my face. In such a short time, I had come to handle a gun with ease, the fear that I might accidentally shoot myself no longer holding me back.

I studied the sleek lines, the feel of the handle on the pad of my hands. 'It's nice.'

'It is.'

'It's light.'

'It's empty.'

I glanced at the box. 'Where are the bullets?'

Valentino offered me a half-smile. 'You overestimate my trust in you.'

I frowned at him. 'You think I'd shoot you? And in this house, of all places?'

*Probably shouldn't have added that last part.*

Another glint of those canines. The more time I spent in his presence, the less like Luca he appeared. They used their features completely differently. Valentino didn't wear empathy, or sympathy, or understanding. He wore astute- ness and wry amusement. 'I don't take chances,' he said. 'Even in *this* house.' He tapped the photograph of Libero Marino. 'Maybe after Saturday, I'll think differently.'

'You will,' I said, focusing on Libero's dark eyes. 'After Saturday, everything will be different.'

# CHAPTER ELEVEN
## MARINO BLOOD

**F**ear is a relative thing.

'Don't hang up whatever you do. Don't you dare hang up on me during my hour of need, Sophie.'

It was 9.15 p.m. on Monday night, and I was in my bedroom on the third floor of the Falcone mansion. I was sitting cross-legged on my bed, my unfinished poetry assignment in my lap, my cell phone pressed against my ear. I had just finished two hours of shooting practice with Nic, and even though my trigger finger hurt like hell and my arm was aching, it was worth it.

'I'm here,' I assured Millie. 'I wouldn't miss this for the world.'

'Stop laughing at me!' she whined.

'I'm not laughing at you.'

'I can hear the amusement in your voice!' she said, before descending into another bout of shrieking. It sounded like she was on a rollercoaster. 'Oh my God, he's coming right at me! Oh my God, OH MY GOD. HELP ME SOPHIE!'

Millie had been trying to kill a daddy-long-legs for the last fourteen minutes. 'Run!' I said, faux panic raising my pitch. 'Run before he turns you into one too!'

'Oh Jesus, I think there's two of them, Soph!' She fell deadly quiet, and then a gasp dragged in her throat. 'I think they're having sex mid-air! Oh, that is *so* gross.'

'You insect voyeur, give them some privacy!'

There was a very audible thump on the other end. I imagined her throwing her chemistry book at the wall. 'Damn,' she cursed. 'Missed them.'

I flopped back against my pillows and closed my eyes. I took myself out of *Evelina*, away from the homework and the guns and the threats and the boys, and imagined I was sitting on Millie's floral bedspread beside her, watching her nearly twist an ankle as she tried to tackle a couple of harmless insects. 'Calm down,' I soothed. 'They're more scared of you than you are of them.'

'Somehow I doubt that, Soph. If they were the least bit scared, they'd stop having sex, but they're just floating around here, *copulating in my face*.'

Another thump. Another curse.

I tutted. 'The *nerve*.'

'I don't think my heart rate has ever been this high,' Millie panted. 'I can feel it in my throat. Does that make sense? I can actually feel my pulse choking me.'

'Why don't you just learn to coexist peacefully with them?'

'Oh, shut up, you're not here,' she hissed. 'You don't know the trauma I'm enduring right now.'

I opened my eyes – the stark white walls seemed to loom inwards, boxing me in. I could hear the distant sound of Elena arguing with someone downstairs. Two rooms over, CJ was playing obnoxiously loud rock music. Little Sal had woken up screaming every night this week. My gaze flicked to the side table, where the photograph of Libero Marino was staring up at me, daring me to look at him. 'Yeah,' I said, dispassionately. 'I can't possibly imagine it.'

'You know, I think this is probably the most scared I've ever been,' Millie panted.

'Really?'

'Not counting Eden,' she added as an afterthought. 'But it's close.'

Millie was the queen of compartmentalization. Once a thing was over, it was over, in a neat little box in a filing cabinet in the back of her head, never to be disturbed again. I envied that in her. I would need that skill soon.

'Should I just start vacuuming the air until they get sucked in?'

'Sure.' I was looking into Libero's dark eyes, and wondering what Sara would say to me now. But Sara was dead. The blood war made corpses of good people.

Was Libero a good person?

Did it matter?

Another loud thump, and this time, the accompanying sound of triumph. 'Yes!' she whooped. 'Yes! I got him and his lover! Oh, my God! It's over. I finally did it!' Millie was an entirely different version of herself now, all the good cheer returning to her voice. 'I feel so accomplished.'

What would I feel like when it was done? Would it change me for ever, or would it invigorate me, the way it seemed to invigorate Nic?

'Soph?'

I was still staring at Libero, tracing that silver scar, studying the quirk of his mouth underneath his facial hair. 'Huh?'

'I just want to thank you for your support. It can't have been easy for you, hearing me in such peril.'

'No,' I said, pulling my attention from the photograph. 'No, it wasn't.'

'Well, I'm fine now, so I'm going to hang up and watch *Grey's Anatomy*.'

'Sure, Mil, just use me and then discard me.'

She made kissy noises down the phone. 'Much love, Soph. I'll see you at school tomorrow!'

When she hung up, I tried to return to my assignment, but my brain had been wiped blank. I was so not in the mood for this. A yawn bubbled up in my chest, and I contemplated forcing myself to sleep. It wasn't like there was anything else to do, unless I wanted to stay up and further humanize Libero Marino. Maybe he liked chocolate. Maybe he had a dog. Maybe he used to buy his sister a Christmas present every year. Maybe he had cried the hardest at her funeral.

Maybe he murdered innocent people, like his mother did. Maybe he distributed drugs that ended up killing people. Maybe he was coming for me too.

The less I thought about it the better. I could drive myself crazy with all these what-ifs.

There was a knock at my bedroom door. I snapped my

head up, then checked my phone. No messages. No missed calls. Usually they called me if they wanted me.

'Who is it?'

'Nic.'

I was in teddy bear pyjama pants and an oversized hoodie. A part of me wished I looked better. The other part of me told me to shut up and stop being so superficial. I smoothed my hair back from my face and tugged my hoodie down.

'Come in,' I said, brushing the homework aside until it fell on to the floor in a heap.

Nic shut the door behind him. He swept his gaze across the floor, an eyebrow arching at the little bundle of notes, at the big fat poetry book squishing half of them. 'Yeah, I don't envy you right now, Soph.' He stepped over them like they were toxic and plonked himself on the end of my bed. 'I never was one for poetry.'

I gestured at the discarded poem. 'So, I guess you can't help me pick a deeply emotional poem to identity with for this stupid assignment?'

He pulled a face, his features growing almost cartoon-like with faux horror. 'Absolutely not.'

'Oh well. At least I tried.'

'I'll ask Luca for you when he gets home. He's a real nerd for shit like this.'

I tried not to react to the mention of Luca's name. The truth was, I hadn't seen him since he had almost come to blows with my father at my mother's ceremony. He had just disappeared, and had been gone all day. I guessed he needed some time to cool off, but that didn't do much to soothe the squirmy guilty feeling in my stomach.

Nic arranged himself model-like on the end of my bed, like I was about to draw him à la Rose in *Titanic*. He was dressed casually in a black T-shirt and dark blue jeans, his hair swept away from his face in finely gelled waves, a gold cross around his neck. Strictly speaking, Nic probably should not have been in my room, but I had bigger things to worry about right now. 'What's going on?' I asked him. 'Are you looking for a bedtime story?'

'I'd usually request a lullaby, but I heard you singing in the kitchen the other day and I saw the milk curdling.'

I slammed my pillow into his face. 'You rude man-pig. How dare you.'

His hands shot up in surrender. I rearranged the pillow behind me and lay back against it. 'What's really up?'

Nic grinned at me. 'Well, my excitement levels for one.' At my confused expression, he gestured to the nightstand, where Libero Marino's face was staring at the ceiling. 'Valentino just gave me the good news. You got your target. Finally!'

'Oh. Yeah.' I tried to smile but my cheeks were twitching. 'I did.'

'Libero Marino.' Nic laughed his name. 'He was a real piece of shit when we were younger but he's a joke now. He's always high on something. You could pick him off with your little finger.'

I swallowed hard, tried to ignore the ten thousand butterflies taking flight in my stomach. 'Great.'

Nic edged towards me, crumpling the duvet into little peaks and valleys between us. Concern swept across his face. 'You OK, Soph?'

'Yeah, I'm fine,' I said, in the least convincing attempt at a lie ever.

'I thought this was what you wanted?'

I looked at my hands, knotted my fingers together. 'I do. I'm just getting used to it. I didn't think—I didn't expect it to be Sara's brother, that's all.'

'Oh,' he said softly. 'You thought it would be someone you didn't know.'

I nodded at the bedspread. 'Yeah. I guess I did. It just feels a bit more personal than I was expecting . . .'

'The Marinos are your family,' Nic said.

'Well, when you put it like that, I sound pretty dumb right now.'

'I know what you mean,' he added. 'Really, I do. It's natural to have doubts, Soph.'

I stared at all that honeyed warmth swimming in his dark eyes, and felt the knot in my chest loosen. He was silent for a minute. I soaked it up, waited for my breathing to return to normal. He moved his hands a little closer. Instinctively, I pulled away, not wanting to fan the embers of desire still inside me, not wanting to complicate an already complicated situation. 'Nic . . .'

'I heard about your mother's ceremony yesterday,' he cut in. Maybe I had imagined his nearness, the way his body seemed to be inching closer. 'I'm sorry I wasn't there. I would have gone if I had known.'

I studied his face for clues of what Luca might have told him. Did he know about my father? His placid expression suggested otherwise. Another secret Luca had kept, then . . . another reason to feel grateful to him and guilty all at the same time.

'How was it?' Nic asked, his fingers still close to mine, a line of fresh bruises colouring the knuckles on his right hand. City work.

'It was depressing,' I told him.

He nodded knowingly, and just like that, my mood migrated from resigned to angry, my thoughts turning to everything Donata had taken from me. She had reduced my mother to a vase of ashes, a trail of memories that most people would soon forget. That was the truth of it. The cold, harsh truth.

I balled my hands into fists, released the fire inside me. 'I want to hurt her so badly. I can't even put it into words, Nic. I want her to suffer the way she's made me suffer.'

'Good,' he murmured, sitting up and squaring his body up to mine. 'That's the spirit, Sophie.' He put his hands on my shoulders, dug them in until they started to sting. I ignored it, using the pain as fuel as he poured his strength into me. 'You need to get fired up about this, Sophie. You need to feel determined and angry, and, most of all, you should feel excited. This is your time to fight back. Don't you want to fight back?' That smile again, full and white and dazzling. 'Don't you want to take from her what she took from you?'

'Yes. Of course I do.' I nodded, siphoning off some of that unbridled optimism, keeping it for myself. 'I want her to pay, Nic. I'm going to *make* her pay.'

'And I'm going to help you.' He was nodding along with me, his fingers digging harder into my shoulders, but I didn't care. We were in this together. I didn't have to do it alone. 'I'll stand by your side until there's no one left. Until Donata begs for mercy at your feet. I'll be there right until the end.'

A well of gratitude sprung up inside me. This was what I needed: strength, belief, support.

'Thank you,' I told him in earnest. 'Thank you for helping me. I really needed this.'

'You really want to thank me?' He cocked his head, a slow smile curling on his lips. For a second I thought he was going to lean in and kiss me, but instead, he dropped his hands, made the shape of a gun with his fingers and pressed it against my forehead. 'Thank me by putting a bullet in Libero Marino's head this weekend.' He winked at me. 'Thank me in Marino blood.'

# CHAPTER TWELVE
## MY SOUL

When I got home from school the following afternoon and made my way to the library, there was a piece of paper with my name on it waiting for me on the coffee table. It was sitting on top of a book of poems I hadn't seen before. I recognized the handwriting on the note as Luca's.

So Nic really had told him about my assignment, and Luca had decided to help me. I tried not to wonder why, tried not to imagine him poring over this poetry book, thinking about me. It would only drive me insane.

I unfolded the piece of paper, unbearably curious to find out what poem Luca would think relevant to me, and whether I would consider it an insult or a compliment.

'Invictus' by William Ernest Henley. The poem wasn't familiar to me, but then again, few were. Luca had handwritten the words in small black script. It felt . . . personal. I shook the thought away and read the first line aloud.

> Out of the night that covers me,
>   Black as the pit from pole to pole,
> I thank whatever gods may be
>   For my unconquerable soul.

By the time I reached the final verse, my arms were covered in goosebumps.

> It matters not how strait the gate,
>   How charged with punishments the scroll,
> I am the master of my fate,
>   I am the captain of my soul.

I read the poem three times, Evelina Falcone's oil painting hanging over me, her gaze on the back of my neck. Another one of my father's victims, another blot on his soul.

In my hands, the words seemed to grow bigger and bigger.

I understood.

I understood then why Luca had chosen this poem the day after Valentino had handed me my first official target.

*Subtle, Luca. Real subtle.*

That night, as I drifted off, those words swam around in my head, beside visions of dark eyes and gold teeth.

*I am the master of my fate,*

*I am the captain of my soul.*

Five days.

Five days and everything would change.

# CHAPTER THIRTEEN

## WHEREABOUTS

I was attempting to instil my artistic flourish on a sketch of
the humble mitochondrion when the familiar *beep* of the
school intercom sounded. The flurried scratching ceased
as twenty pencils disengaged from their diagrams.

'Can Sophie Gracewell please report to the principal's
office immediately.'

I could feel the colour draining from my face, the stares of
my classmates. A small chorus of *ooooh*s came from the
back of the room.

Ms Henderson, my biology teacher, glared at me over her
glasses. 'You'd better go, Sophie.'

I rolled my shoulders back and pushed my chair from the
desk, trying not to appear worried. I walked, a lot slower than
I could have, out the door and down the corridor to the

principal's office, praying that whatever was bringing me there was something minor.

The secretary was already on her feet, ushering me into the office, her cheeks flushed bright pink as she muttered her own chorus of 'Come on, come on, hurry up now,' her hands flapping around me as if the slight breeze would move me faster.

'Ms Gracewell, we meet again.'

*Oh, God, kill me now.*

'Detective Medina. Detective Comisky.' I nodded curtly to each of them, keeping my smile tight, all the panic inside me corseting me in. 'This is a surprise.'

'Is it?' said Comisky, his eyes slitting. He was leaning back against the desk. His suit was the colour of vomit. He gestured for me to sit. I sidled around Medina, who was hunched by a disused bookcase, and did as I was told, all too aware that by having the detectives standing above me, I was giving up vital higher ground.

I was also keenly aware that Principal Campbell was outside the door with her ear pressed up against the glass. She obviously had yet to be told that frosted glass is, in fact, still somewhat transparent.

'Yes,' I said, eyeing them both up. 'Of course it's a surprise.' I lifted my chin and met their penetrative stares with my own. I had nothing to hide.

More or less.

'We were sorry to hear about your mother,' Medina said, flicking an affected glance at his partner. His eyes were softer, his stance a little more relaxed.

'Is that why you're here?' I asked. 'Because I told the

detectives working the diner case that I don't know any more than they do, and before you ask, no, I haven't seen or heard from my uncle since it happened.'

*Oh, and the next time I see him, I'll be killing him. Kk?*

Comisky shook his head, the movement bringing the faintest jiggle to his cheeks. 'No, Ms Gracewell, that's not why we're here.'

I channelled Valentino and kept my features smooth.

'Where are you staying, Sophie?' Comisky asked, dispensing with the formalities. His big grey moustache was twitching in anticipation. Honestly, why do people grow moustaches in the first place? Do they set out to look like human terriers or does the look just sneak up on them?

'With my friend,' I said. 'Until the guardianship paperwork gets sorted out. What with my uncle still being away . . .' I shrugged, and then decided to try out the old puppy-dog-eyes routine to diminish my underlying aura of sarcasm.

Medina hunkered down until we were at eye level. I had the sudden urge to jump out the window and bolt all the way back to *Evelina*.

'Ms Gracewell,' he said carefully, 'I am going to ask you a question now, and I want to make you very aware that if you don't answer it one hundred per cent honestly, then you will be obstructing the course of justice and there will be consequences.'

My palms were starting to sweat. I pressed them together and tried to keep my movements very still. My brain was exploding with theories. I tried not to let it show. Did they know about Libero? Did they know what I was going to do on Saturday? Had the Falcones been arrested?

'Are you listening, Sophie?' Comisky asked, over Medina's shoulder. He shoved himself away from the desk and plodded over to me. 'Will you pay careful attention to what we're saying?' He looked like a very angry, very stout grandfather. But not the sweet kind. The I-drink-way-too-much-at-family-gatherings-and-shake-my-cane-at-children kind.

'I'm listening.' I tilted my head and fluttered my lashes, preparing my lie before I even knew what I would have to say. 'Ask away.'

Medina shifted forward, his elbows finding purchase on his knees. 'Sophie, do you know where your father is?'

'Huh?' I scrunched my nose. 'What are you talking about?'

'Answer the question,' he said.

'That is my answer.'

Medina fell back on to his hunkers. He looked up at Comisky and another uneasy glance passed between them.

'What's going on? Where is my father?'

Medina stood up. 'Sophie, your father was granted furlough from Stateville Correctional Center on Sunday morning for your mother's remembrance ceremony.'

'Yes.' I could feel myself nodding, but all my immediate thoughts were wrapped up in what they were now attempting to tell me, and what I was praying wasn't actually true. But I could feel it, sucking the ground out from underneath me, building and building, until it rolled back towards me like a tsunami.

'And you were seen with him at the memorial service for your late mother,' Comisky supplied.

Again, I said, 'Yes.'

'We know you two were in contact.'

'The whole town knows. It's not a secret.'

'Do you know where he went after that ceremony?' asked Medina.

'Back to prison?' I said. 'Where he was supposed to go?'

*Please say he went back to prison.*

*Please tell me this isn't happening.*

Medina's lips disappeared, his mouth settling into a hard line. 'No, Sophie. Your father didn't go back to prison.'

'He had an escort with him,' I said, shaking my head. 'I saw him. He was there the whole time. My father was being monitored. He had a guard,' I repeated, as if I could convince them.

'*Had* being the operative word,' said Medina. 'That guard is now in hospital recovering from a severe concussion . . .' He trailed off, expelling all the air in one long sigh, before adding, 'Your father's tracking bracelet has been deactivated, and your father is nowhere to be found.'

I gaped at them.

This was a joke. This had to be a joke.

'We've been searching for him for several days,' Comisky added.

'And you're only telling me this *now*?' I said, more shrilly than I meant to.

Another shared glance. 'The situation is delicate,' said Medina. 'We didn't want to alert you until . . .' He trailed off.

I narrowed my eyes at him. 'Until you definitely couldn't find him and you started to suspect my involvement, right?'

He nodded. 'Something like that.'

'Sophie,' interrupted Comisky, picking up the thread and being a lot more gruff about it than Medina was, 'let's speak plainly. We want to know if you're hiding him.'

Where were the words? Why weren't they coming out? They were all jammed in a revolving door, struggling, pushing and prodding. I opened my mouth, all the dread piling on my tongue, gathering and pooling, until eventually, a sound sprang from me.

And that sound was laughter.

Manic, terrified laughter.

'Detectives,' I half-choked out. I patted my jean pockets for good measure, pretending to check if he was inside them. 'Where the *hell* would I be hiding him?'

'You tell us,' said Comisky. 'That's why we're here.'

I flopped into the chair, my head lolling backwards until all I could see were the flecks of grey on the ceiling. 'Oh my God,' I muttered. '*Oh my God.*'

So the blood war raged on, and now my father was part of it too, standing across a trench of bloody history and relentless vendettas, right opposite me.

# CHAPTER FOURTEEN

## BLACK FRIDAY

The news of my father's escape greeted me again when I got home that afternoon. It had filtered out of the cracks of Chicago PD and crept all the way up to *Evelina*. Now it was wafting through the Falcone mansion like a bad smell.

Vince Marino walked free.

And what exactly did Sophie Marino know about it?

'Nothing,' I protested, over and over again. 'I don't know anything about it.'

It tipped the scales of my living conditions further from 'free will' towards 'captivity'. With my loyalty balanced so precariously between two Mafia families, and my father running around between them, Saturday was now going to be more important than ever. Either Libero Marino was dead, or I was.

I kept my head down. I avoided Luca, and spent my evenings in the barn with Nic, shooting at everything I could pin a target to.

I was good. I was ready.

Inside, I was terrified.

By the time Friday rolled around, it felt like a family of pirates had taken up residence in my stomach and were stabbing me from the inside out.

'Why are you so anxious today? It's the weekend.' Millie was appraising me. It was never a good thing when Millie appraised me. It made it infinitely more difficult to hide things from her.

'I don't know,' I said, rubbing the dull ache in my stomach. 'I don't feel well.'

She hmm'ed under her breath. 'No, that's definitely not it. You're up to something. I can sense it.'

I slammed my locker shut. My bag felt heavier than usual, like it was trying to drag me into the ground. All this homework to do, and a man to kill, in one weekend.

'What was that?' Millie pressed. 'What was that thought that just invaded your face?'

'I'm just thinking about my dad, that's all.' Not totally untrue, but it was certainly more lie than honesty.

'Have they found him?' she asked.

I shook my head. 'I'm trying not to think about where he could be.'

'What about that address he gave you at the funeral?' Millie said. Ever since I had told her about the address, she had become fixated on it. She couldn't believe I had thrown it away – that I had destroyed a potential lifeline. Even now, after everything, she was still so trusting of a man neither of us really knew.

'No,' I said firmly. 'My dad wouldn't escape from prison just to run away to some other state. He's with the Marinos. I can feel it.'

'Ugh,' Millie groaned. '*Why?*'

*Because of the blood war,* I screamed inside my head. *Because he wants to fight alongside his family.* 'Who knows?' I said.

She shook her head, a sigh filtering through her words. 'What a mess.'

'I'm just trying not to think about it. Otherwise it's going to drive me mad.'

'Just stick with me.' She touched her head to mine. 'I'll cheer you up this weekend. Do you want to see a movie tomorrow night? I can ditch Cris. I'm definitely the alpha in the relationship, so he'll deal with it.'

'How charming.' Outside, the air was crisp and cold. I pulled my coat tighter around me, and tried to ignore the shiver crawling up my spine. 'But I can't tomorrow night. I have plans.'

'What plans?'

'Um.' If I waited even half a beat longer, I'd be rumbled, so I said the first and only thing that sprang into my mind. 'We're having a movie night.'

'A movie night.' Millie stopped walking. 'Who exactly is having a movie night?'

'All of the Falcones.' I was really trying to sound nonchalant but the idea was *ridiculous.*

'Right . . .' she said, conveying her disbelief in a sideways frown. 'And what movie is it?'

*Think of a movie. Think of any movie. Pull this lie back from the brink of ludicrousness.* 'Goodfellas,' I said. 'We're watching *Goodfellas.*'

*Oh, take a bow.*

I tried not to flinch.

Millie arched an eyebrow. 'You mean to say a family of hot-tempered Mafia people are all cosying up with each other on a Saturday night to sit down and watch a movie about a family of hot-tempered Mafia people . . . ? Is that really what you're telling me?'

Well, there was nothing else for it now.

I turned my whole face towards her, maintained full eye contact and said, 'Yes, Millie. That is exactly what I'm telling you.'

*Hold the stare. Don't look away. Sell it. Sell it . . . Three, two, one . . .*

'Huh.' Millie scrunched her nose at me. 'Well. That is just . . . honestly? That is just weird.'

I conjured the whisper of a smile. 'Tell me about it.'

'Sunday, then?'

'Sure. Sunday.'

I tried not to imagine how I would feel on Sunday. I tried not to think very much at all, in case my stomach wound up eating itself from nerves.

Millie skipped down the steps and flounced into the after-noon, leaving me staring at her long dark ponytail as it bobbed back and forth.

I made my way towards the black SUV, threw my bag in the trunk and slid into the back seat, startling at the backs of two

Falcone heads instead of one.

'Hey?' I said, more question than greeting. 'Why are there two of you here?'

Nic and Dom turned around at the same time, their lips curving in matching smiles. 'Hey,' they chorused, the sound raising the hairs on my arms.

'There's been a slight change of itinerary,' Nic said.

Dom started the engine. 'I hope you didn't make plans for tonight,' he threw over his shoulder. 'Because we're going on a little killing spree.'

I reeled backwards, my head hitting the seat with a soft thump. 'It's tonight? I thought it was tomorrow?'

Nic shook his head, the glee still firmly plastered across his face. 'Paulie's been scouting the location. Libero is coming in tonight instead.'

'So we're going *now*?'

'Are you ready?' He flashed his teeth at me again, the smile turning wolfish.

*No. No! No!*

'Where's Luca?' I asked, suddenly feeling diminished in this big half-empty car. 'I thought he was supposed to come too?'

'He's working on the other side of the city tonight.' He waved his hand at an imaginary Luca in the faraway distance. 'And besides, it won't take that many of us. Libero is barely a match for Gino.'

I blinked at him dumbly, trying to assimilate the news.

We whirred past Cedar Hill High, my classmates streaking into scarfed blurs behind me. They were going home to get ready for weekend parties, or coffee dates or dinner with their parents, soccer practice or movies or aimless walks along Main Street . . . and I was going somewhere very far away. I scooted forward, conscious of how alone I was in the back seat.

'Soph.' Nic's voice cut in. Before I even realized it, he had twisted around in his seat and was holding my hand on top of the armrest, his thumb tracing circles on my skin. 'You look pale. Are you feeling OK?'

I tried to disengage my thoughts, to use my mouth to talk, to box up my feelings and squish them down, down, down. 'I'm fine,' I said, licking my dry lips. 'Let's do this.'

He squeezed my hand, and I squeezed back, before slipping it back into my lap, away from the intentions written so clearly on his face.

'Yeah!' whooped Dom. 'Let's do this!'

He cranked the radio up until the car was vibrating, and then he crushed his foot on the gas and we sped out of Cedar Hill, both boys singing and laughing at the tops of their lungs, while I cowered in the back seat trying to fight the urge to be sick out the window.

# CHAPTER FIFTEEN

## SICILIAN KISS

It was past sundown by the time we arrived in the city. We pulled into a run-down parking lot three buildings away from The Sicilian Kiss, a dive bar often frequented by members of the Marino family. It looked deserted as we drove past it – boarded-up windows, flaking black paint on the door, and a sign that read: *Entrance By Private Admission Only*.

When we reached the car lot, Dom cut the engine, rolled his seat back and propped his feet on the dashboard. I sat forward and stuck my head between the brothers. 'Now what?'

Nic turned around so suddenly, I didn't have time to back up. Our noses were inches from each other as he said, 'We wait for Paulie's signal. He's got someone on the inside. When

Libero comes to make the deal, we'll move in.'

'We'll disarm him and shoot his legs out,' added Dom airily. 'Then you can finish him off.'

I massaged my temples, trying not to imagine the scene before it happened. It all seemed way too straightforward. Violent, but simple. Too simple. 'And we're really going to get away with this?'

'Easily,' said Nic, confidence trilling in his voice.

Dom glanced at me over his shoulder. 'Relax,' he said. 'You look like you've seen a ghost.'

Nic smirked at Dom. 'She'll be *making* a ghost tonight.'

I just stared between them, screwing my face up. 'I don't know how you guys can be so . . . jokey about all of this!'

'Lighten up, Sophie,' said Dom. 'You're supposed to kill Libero, not the mood.'

Nic snorted, then caught sight of my scowl and glanced at me apologetically. 'It's just first-time jitters,' he said, gently. 'Don't try and talk yourself out of it. Don't psyche yourself out. Libero Marino is a slimeball. I told you that, remember? He oversees the sex trade in the east of the city, he beats his girl-friends – he put one of them in a coma two years ago. He split Luca's lip open and tried to kill him when they were still teenagers. He's not a good guy, OK? He deserves this.'

I swirled the facts around in my head. It's not like I thought he was a good guy already, but I hadn't expected him to be so hateable. It was almost too easy, that he would be the perfect villain. It was easy to hate him. I tried to harness that feeling. I would need it. I would need nothing but that burning, festering hatred. A shred of empathy and it would all go to hell.

'This is for your mother, remember?' Nic added, his gaze boring into mine. 'This is for what they took from you.'

Yes. He was right. That was why I was here. I remembered the diner, the fire, the heat . . . the smoke. This was for her.

Nic turned on some music on his phone, and closed his eyes, humming under his breath. I looked through the windscreen, at messy graffiti and overflowing dumpsters. Somewhere close by, The Sicilian Kiss was awaiting our arrival, and Libero Marino was walking to his demise. I tried to concentrate on the music, letting the melody sweep me into a different place.

Time crawled.

And then . . .

Dom swiped his finger across his phone screen, read a text, smirked at Nic, and, as simply as if he was putting on his favourite movie, said, 'Show time.'

Seven minutes later, I had scaled a three-storey fire escape and was standing on the roof of The Sicilian Kiss, my gun clenched inside my coat pocket, and my teeth chattering so hard I could barely hear myself think. According to Paulie, there were only five people inside the bar: Libero Marino, Eric Cain, the owner (a Falcone snitch who was holing himself away on the ground floor), and two of Libero's buyers, who had just shown up for the drug deal.

We went in via the fire escape on the roof, while Paulie made his way through the front entrance at the same time. Nic and Dom formed a barrier in front of me, shoulder to shoulder and dressed entirely in black, their coats zipped up past their chins. We descended the stairs quietly and quickly, leaving the cold behind us. My face was hot and my breathing was coming quick and sharp. It felt like every part of my skin was tingling. I could feel the adrenalin, like a shot of hot metal coursing through my bloodstream.

We stalled in a narrow corridor at the bottom of the fire escape. The place was dank and musty. There was a door right in front of us, with a circle of glass set in the centre. Voices wafted from a lowly-lit room with black walls and rickety old tables. Someone laughed behind the door – it was loud and sharp, and I cringed at the familiarity. That was Eric Cain, Jack's best friend. Could Jack be nearby, too? What about my father?

No. Paulie would have warned us. This was his job, and Nic said they didn't call him 'The Ghost' for nothing. He was always nearby, always watching. He moved unseen inside the shadows. Even if the time had changed at the last minute, his sources wouldn't have. I told myself that over and over, Nic's warning flashing inside my head. *Don't psyche yourself out.*

Nic crept up to the window and peered in. He held up four fingers. Dom pulled the slider on his gun back. I copied him, my fingers warm with adrenalin as they slid against the cool metal.

Nic glanced over his shoulder, one hand already pressed against the door. Dom was looking at his phone, counting under his breath. Paulie was obviously coming up the opposite stairs.

Nic gestured to a puddle of darkness behind the stairs. 'Hide until we call you.'

Something flared inside me – need, anger, excitement?

'Let me come in,' I whispered. 'Don't leave me out here.'

Nic shook his head, his attention already disengaging from

me. 'You're not ready for this part yet.'

Before I could protest, or even figure out whether I truly *wanted* to protest, the boys raised their guns, swung the door open and started shooting. And then my feet were moving too, carrying me through the gap in the door as it shut after them, and propelling me towards the gunfire, my own weapon raised.

Nic fired first, and Eric Cain went down, his body collapsing on to the table and sending glasses smashing to the ground. Everyone started roaring, and the long, narrow room exploded into chaos. I zeroed in on Libero as he rolled backwards, away from Dom's aim, and flipped a table between them. Paulie appeared from nowhere and dispatched the first buyer with two quick shots in the back. The second buyer shot at Nic, but missed – narrowly. I stumbled backwards, crouching behind the bar and trying to aim at someone – at Eric's floundering form, at the table Libero was now using for a shield. But everyone just kept *moving*.

I wasn't used to moving targets.

The second buyer went down, his body convulsing as a fresh wound gushed blood down his neck. His leg twitched and then stopped. The first buyer was out, too. Nic finished Eric Cain, his back between us as the final shot rang out, and then . . . then there was only Libero Marino, crouching like a scared rat on the other side of an upturned table.

It had all happened so quickly. A flash. And now three people were dead. My pulse was roaring in my eardrums. I stood up from behind the bar, where shards of glass and spilt whisky lay in pools. I ignored the bodies, fought the urge to turn and study them. To stare death in the face and feel it spread inside me like ice. My adrenalin put one foot in front of the other, carrying me towards Nic and Dom. Libero's gun was empty. He flung it at us as we converged on him – three angels of death. It landed with a hollow click at my feet. I kicked it away.

Paulie disappeared downstairs again, already getting to work on making the mess disappear.

The table was blocking Libero up to the neck, but there was no way out for him, and he knew it. He didn't even look afraid. He did, however, look like Sara. Those wide eyes. Dimples, too, I noticed at close range, but only because he was frowning so severely and his facial hair was patchier than it had been in the photo.

'Stand up, Libero,' Nic commanded. His gun was pointed directly at Libero's forehead. A threat, only. The killing shot was mine.

'Fuck yourself, Falcone!' Libero cut his eyes to me, hatred twisting his mouth. 'You traitorous bitch. Killing your own family in cold blood.'

'Watch your mouth, Marino.' Dom fired off a warning shot and it lodged in the wooden table between them. Libero didn't even flinch. He didn't look away from me.

'Are you proud of yourself?' he said, his voice falling deadly quiet. 'Vince Marino's daughter, a coward and a turncoat. You'll suffer when my family gets their hands on you. When my mother shows up she'll gut you and then Zola will cut you into little pieces and listen to you scream yourself unconscious.'

*When my mother shows up.* What the hell did that mean? I shook the paranoia away. He was just trying to psyche me out, to get in my head. Nic and Dom weren't reacting to it, so I took my cue from them. I stared at Libero, trying to work myself up to what I had to do. His hatred was definitely helping.

Dom ripped the table away and flung it against the bar. Libero fell forwards on to his hands, spluttering. Blood was running down his left side and staining his T-shirt. He had already been shot. The colour was draining from his face, his black goatee appearing stark against his white pallor.

Dom and Nic stepped back to either side of me, and I was conscious suddenly of what I had to do, of what they were waiting for. This was it. The time had come.

I raised my gun.

Libero laughed, and with it came another trickle of blood, painting his lips crimson. He spat it at my feet. 'They gave their plaything a gun.' He spat again, and this time it reached my shoe. I kept my gaze forward, focused on his leering grin, using all that hatred to fuel my own.

'Yes,' I said, barely recognizing my own voice as I curled my lip at him. 'They gave me a gun.'

Libero returned my twisted smile. 'Which one are you sleeping with, turncoat? Which one have you whored yourself out to? All the honour and dignity in your blood and you debase yourself like this. You disgust me.'

My composure faltered, his words breaking through my defences. 'Shut up!' I snapped. 'You don't know what you're talking about!'

'Sophie,' Nic urged from somewhere over my shoulder. 'Just do it. End him.'

'End me!' Libero shouted. 'End me the way you ended your

own mother! No wonder she didn't want to live in this world any more. No wonder she ran into those flames. Away from you!'

My finger was on the trigger. The world had fallen still. It was just me, Libero Marino and all that malevolent hatred spewing from his lips, wrapping around me, taunting me. 'Shut your mouth,' I said.

'Your hand is shaking.' Libero's lips peeled back to reveal bloodstained teeth. 'I can see it.'

'Sophie,' Nic warned. 'He's going to bleed out.'

My hand *was* shaking. But my aim was still squarely on Libero's sweating forehead. I bared my teeth at him, feeling the ferocity in my face. 'I'm going to shoot you now,' I told him. 'And you deserve it.'

His grin faltered. His eyes were big, so big. Just like Sara's. I watched his Adam's apple flare as he swallowed, and I could almost taste it – that feeling of fear. Bone-chilling fear. He knew I was really going to do it. And it made me feel . . . powerful. It made me feel completely unlike myself. And somewhere deep down inside, that terrified me.

'Kill me, just how you killed my sister.' His words tripped and slurred, the energy petering out of him rapidly now. 'What's one more betrayal?'

My heart clenched. My finger faltered on the trigger. *Come on, Sophie. Come on.*

'Now, Sophie.' I could sense Nic bristling. 'Stop letting him talk.'

Libero's head flopped forwards, his weakness dragging his body towards the ground. There was so much of his blood around him already. I could smell it. He forced his head up, his eyes glassy and red. 'Shoot me,' he said. 'You fucking coward.'

'Shoot him!' said Dom. 'What the hell are you waiting for?'

'Do it,' urged Nic.

*So shoot! Shoot him!*

I was freezing up. I was staring so hard at his face my eyes were starting to water. This face that was so like Sara Marino's. My father's dimples. My own fear reflected back in his eyes, hastily painted over with false bravado. Time slowed to an agonizing pace. A bead of sweat dripped into my eye.

*Shoot him. You have to shoot him.*

My hand was shaking.

*Your mother would be so proud of you.*

I took another step towards him, trying to propel myself into the deed.

*Do it, you coward. Show him that he's wrong.*

*He's dead either way.*

I tried to press my finger against the trigger.

*I can't. I can't do it.*

The door behind me swung open and the silence exploded. Sharp, angry shouting swept into the room behind me. My attention splintered in two. My arm lagged. My breaths were coming in quick short gasps. The adrenalin was seeping out of me and panic was rising in its place. Libero was bleeding out in front of me, and all my bullets were still in my gun.

Then there was a hand on top of mine, trying to prise the weapon from my grasp, and Luca's voice, calm and insistent in my ear.

'Give me the gun, Sophie.' His other hand pressing gently

against my back. I was still staring at Libero, his body folded over into a crumpled heap. 'Give it to me.'

A prick of relief in the back of my eyes. My grip faltered, the cool sleek metal leaving my skin.

Nic was yelling at me. 'Kill him! Kill him now, Sophie! You have to do it. She has to do it, Luca!'

Luca yanked me backwards. A gunshot rang out right beside my head just as Dom and Nic roared together.

'Donata!'

I felt the vibrations of Luca's recoil as the bullet sailed through the air towards Libero. And then, through the haze and the panic and the thwack of Libero's body hitting the floor, came the sound of Donata Marino's screams as her bullet sailed past my left ear.

I jumped away from Luca, stumbled backwards, as Donata marched through the doorway, her gun raised. Her trench coat was buttoned all the way to her pointed chin, her hair coiled tightly in a bun. Her foundation was thick and her eyes were over-rimmed in kohl. She looked like her sister's shadow – her sharp features and cruel mouth as terrifying as the gun she wielded. Her lips were a slash of crimson in the dimness. Luca lunged to the side as her next bullet exploded in the space between us. Nic grabbed the back of my coat and yanked me towards the back door, pushing Dom with him while Luca opened fire on Donata, narrowly missing her next bullet. He backed up after us, using the moment Donata noticed Libero's corpse face down beside the bar as a distraction. We sprinted back through the fire escape as her howls filled up the bar behind us like an aria.

'Il mio bambino! Mio figlio!'

'*Move, move!*' Nic snapped, as we fell into formation and ran from The Sicilian Kiss like our lives depended on it.

We dropped into the parking lot, Luca out in front and Dom close behind him. Nic came around the back of me for extra cover as we sprinted towards the SUVs, our guns raised in every direction.

'She'll have backup!' Luca called over his shoulder. 'Keep your eyes open!'

A flurry of shots exploded around us, and I didn't have to look back to know that Donata was out on the roof of The Sicilian Kiss, spending all of her bullets on us. We could all hear her wailing into the night sky. '*Ti scuoierò!*' Shot. '*E ti ucciderò!*' Shot. '*Molto Lentamente!*' Shot.

'Zigzag!' Luca roared. We covered our heads, panting as we skidded between a wave of bullets. We reached the SUV, flung the doors open as shields and threw ourselves inside, gasping and shaking. A bullet ricocheted off the windscreen – bulletproof glass – as Luca slammed his foot against the accelerator and sped out of the parking lot.

Donata's screams might have been thundering through the world outside, but all I could hear was Libero sneering inside my head, *You failed! You failed! You failed! You're a coward!*

I knew he was dead. But he would always be alive in my head, taunting me, freezing me in that moment where I had faltered.

I failed.

I was a coward.

And now I had to face my punishment.

# PART II

'We . . . are all in the same boat, upon a stormy sea.
We owe to each other a terrible and tragic loyalty.'

G. K. Chesterton, *All Things Considered*

# CHAPTER SIXTEEN
## A DIFFERENCE OF OPINION

Nic and Luca sat in stony silence up front, the car moving so fast it felt like we might break the sound barrier. Dom was beside me in the back seat, on the phone to Paulie, who had escaped to a nearby restaurant to wait out the Marino ambush. They were still trying to figure out what went wrong with their intelligence, how they didn't know the Marino boss was planning to show up when she did.

Dom just kept asking Paulie the same thing, his voice tinged with a strange mixture of confusion and awe. 'What the *hell* was she even doing there?' By the sounds of it, Paulie wasn't coming up with any good answers, because Dom kept saying over and over again, 'She must have known we were coming. She *must* have.'

Finally, they seemed to settle on the same conclusion: 'We

have a rat.'

A rat that was going to die slowly and painfully when they tracked him down.

I tried to take solace in the fact that Jack hadn't been with Donata. That would have definitely cut our chances of escape in half. I was deliberately avoiding thinking about my father's whereabouts, how easily he could have sauntered into that room with Donata too.

When we were almost back at *Evelina*, Luca turned to Nic, his voice deadly quiet. 'I told you not to do it without me.'

I watched the sides of their faces as they stared at each other. Nic could sense the rage festering beneath Luca's careful demeanour. We all could. Nic leant away from it, pressing his head against the window. When he spoke again, he sounded like a little boy. 'But Valentino said—'

'I told you to *wait*,' Luca said.

Nic blinked at his brother, once, twice, and then said, 'Why, though?'

'Why?' Luca repeated. '*Why?*'

'Donata was a surprise. It's not like I could foresee that.'

'Oh, you *think*? I told you not to do it without me.'

'I had it under control,' Nic shot back. 'She doesn't need a babysitter.'

'What the hell is that supposed to mean?'

'It means we didn't need you, Luca.' There was a sharpness to Nic's words. They hit Luca between the eyes, pulled his brows together. And it wasn't true, I knew. Because I *had* needed him. We all had. I needed him even now. If he hadn't been there, who knew what damage Donata could have done? Who knew if we would have escaped or not?

'It was always supposed to be *our* mission,' Nic added petulantly.

'Right.' Luca's voice was dangerously even. 'So, who failed then, Nicoli?'

'What?'

'If you were supposed to do it together, then I suppose you both failed,' Luca said. 'Do you want me to tell that to Valentino?'

Nic's face fell. 'N-no. Of course not.'

'So, what will I say, Nicoli?' Luca pressed. 'What will I tell Valentino?'

Nic glanced once at me, his expression torn. 'Sh-she was supposed to do it, but she couldn't. I did everything I was supposed to.' He flicked his gaze to me, apology written in the quirk of his mouth as he happily sailed me down the river of punishment. 'Valentino will understand. He'll give her another chance. With the Donata complication and every-thing . . .' Nic trailed off.

'You would have failed even without Donata's inter-ruption.'

Nic huffed a sigh. He didn't disagree, but the truth was, Luca was right. I would have failed either way. I wasn't able to do it. 'Valentino will understand.'

'Will he?' Luca said.

Nic opened his mouth to respond, and then shut it just as quickly. He didn't know. None of us did.

Luca let the silence linger, let the panic surge inside the car, which seemed to grow smaller and smaller. Then, at last, he said in barely more than a whisper, 'She wasn't ready. She's not ready.'

'Her shot is incredible,' Nic protested. 'Her aim is practically perfect.'

Luca glared at his brother, a frown twisting his lips. 'Do you really think I'm talking about Sophie's aim, Nicoli?'

For the first time, Nic looked at me like I might have the answer, but I was still dumbstruck, listening to a chorus of *coward, coward, coward* playing on repeat inside my head, feeling my own mortality hammering inside my chest. He looked back at his brother. Then he shrugged, once, heavily.

Luca shook his head, turned his attention back to the road. 'You are so unfathomably stupid sometimes.'

# CHAPTER SEVENTEEN
## WAITING

**W**e were barely in the door when Luca, Nic and Dom were summoned to Valentino's office.

A debriefing.

A progress report.

About Donata.

About me.

I was told to wait outside, so I hovered on the stairs, chewing my nails right down to the cuticles. I couldn't decide which would have been worse, having to sit inside the office with them while they walked Valentino through everything that had happened at The Sicilian Kiss, or having to wait outside on my own until he decided on my punishment for having failed.

I tried not to imagine the fury in the boss's eyes when he

heard what had happened.

*I failed. I am a coward. I am useless.*

*I am weak. I am nobody.*

Why did I ever think I could do this?

*I can do this.*

After what seemed like an eternity, my phone rang, and Valentino's number blinked on screen. I pressed a hand to my heart and lifted the phone to my ear.

'Come see me in my office.'

Was this it? Was this how it ended? Where would I go now? What was the punishment for failing the initiation? No one had ever told me. I tucked my phone in my pocket and stood up, rolling my neck around to try and ease some of the tension.

I walked slowly, listening to my quiet footfall on the marble floors, and imagining myself as a criminal making my way to the hangman's noose.

# CHAPTER EIGHTEEN
## THE FIRST LIE

Valentino was at his desk, his head tilted to one side as he surveyed me with those cobalt eyes. He looked oddly refreshed for the time of night, but then again, *he* hadn't lifted a finger against any Marinos, so why should he be exhausted?

Luca stood motionless on his twin's right, his black shirt-sleeves rolled up to his elbows, his hair swept away from his face. Felice was on his left, arms folded across his chest. He was still dressed impeccably, and I had half expected he would be in some creepy silk robe, à la Hugh Hefner. Nic and Dom were side by side against the window, perched on the edge. Neither one looked at me as I came in.

I shuffled towards the half-circle of assassins. No guns on show. No guarded stances. The atmosphere seemed . . .

relaxed. I was careful not to let it lull me. The Falcone masks were well-worn.

Valentino pointed to the only free chair in the room. I had been here exactly four days ago, staring at a photograph of Libero Marino.

I sat down. I looked at Luca – his mouth was set in a hard line, his jaw tightly locked. He lifted his hand, and brushed his fingers across his mouth. Then he pressed his lips tighter together, the colour disappearing from them entirely.

*Don't say anything.*

I clamped my mouth shut. Valentino gestured to Felice, and Felice turned around and opened a cabinet. My hands seized up. I unclenched them. Why was nobody saying anything?

Felice placed two half-empty bottles on the table. One bottle of Southern Comfort and one bottle of amaretto. He bent down, opening a cabinet in the bottom of the desk, and when he straightened again, he was holding six shot glasses, all arranged in a neat tower. He separated the glasses in silence, and we all watched him as he filled them up – first with the Southern Comfort, then the amaretto.

Valentino reached for his glass first. The others followed suit, and when there was only one left on the table and all eyes on me, I pulled it towards me, thanking the universe for my steady hand.

Were we about to drink to my eviction?

Valentino raised his glass, and then did something totally unprecedented. He smiled at me. It felt, for the first time, like it was real. And it was undeniably dazzling.

'I thought it might be fitting to celebrate this with a Sicilian

Kiss shot,' he said, nodding at the glass in his hand. 'Considering what happened tonight.'

We were celebrating?

I looked at my shot glass, detecting the faint smell of almonds swirling inside it. 'I've never had one,' I said. Like it mattered.

Valentino smiled again. 'You did a brave thing tonight, Sophie. You dispatched Libero Marino, and cemented your loyalty to the Falcone family.'

*Wait, what?*

Luca glared at me.

I let Valentino continue.

'Now Donata will return to the city with your uncle at her side. The blood war has begun in earnest, and we are going to win it.' I tried not to let my shock show. I just sat there, stony-faced, as Valentino lauded me. 'Tonight, you became a true Falcone *soldato,* Sophie. So with the others here to witness, I want to raise a toast to you, and say, officially, *Benvenuta nella famiglia, Sophie.* Welcome to the family.'

He lifted his glass once more, and the others chorused him, raising their shot glasses to the ceiling, to me, to the lie. The lie that Luca, Nic and Dom had told their boss. '*Benvenuta nella famiglia, Sophie.*'

We drank as one. I tipped the shot of alcohol into my mouth and let it slide, warm and fragrant, down my throat. The fire burnt in my stomach, the faint flavour of almond still dancing on my tongue, and my gaze never left Luca's, just as his never left mine.

# CHAPTER NINETEEN

## FALLING STARS

It was just after two a.m., and the house was silent as I crept along the darkened hallway on the third floor. Before I could psyche myself out, I knocked on Luca's door.

No answer.

'Luca?' I said softly.

Still nothing.

After a minute of waiting, I decided to indulge my rudeness. I was too antsy to go back to my room. I was too nervous to sleep another night without talking to him, without trying to bridge this strange distance between us – especially after tonight.

I opened the door, still knocking to alert him to my presence. The room was dark, the only light streaming in from the moon outside. I couldn't help thinking of the last time I had been here, of how tightly Luca had held me to him, of how passionately he had kissed me. That seemed like a world away now.

The room was much bigger than I remembered it. I had never really studied it before. It was about three times the size of mine, with a line of bookshelves, a desk, two wardrobes and a king-size bed. It was cream, with artwork hanging around the walls – contemporary prints I didn't recognize. There was one with a melting clock, another one of a ship made of strange butterflies. The room was unexpectedly neat, and even the bed was still made.

His phone was on his bedside table, the time showing on his home screen. It was 2.13 a.m., and Luca Falcone was nowhere to be found. The window was wide open. I peered out to where the roof plateaued before tapering off to a three-storey drop below. And there he was, right on the edge of the roof, his legs stretched out in front of him, his weight resting on his elbows as he looked at the sky.

Luca was watching the stars.

Seriously. This guy.

I clambered out of the window, my knees wobbling until my feet found purchase on the roof. I slipped and caught myself on the ledge, cursing under my breath.

Luca's head snapped towards me. 'Sophie?' he said, bewildered. 'What are you doing out here?'

I offered him an awkward half-wave as I crouched in front of the window to get my balance. 'Um, star gazing?' I said. 'Mind if I join you?'

I couldn't see his eyes in the darkness, but he tilted his head to one side. 'Suit yourself.'

I scooted towards him, crab-walking with my hands and feet.

'It's really not hard,' he pointed out. 'You can walk, you know.'

'What if I fall?' I said, horrified.

'I won't let you fall.'

I finally reached him. He pulled his legs up, resting his forearms on his knees as he regarded me in the darkness.

I mirrored his pose. 'Hi,' I said, feeling a little breathless.

'Hello.' Luca tilted his head back, and I looked up, too. The sky was clear, and blanketed with thousands of stars. It was beautiful out here in the countryside where there were no street lamps to steal the natural light, no distractions to block it out. It was bright, and magical, and I had never noticed before. Because I never looked up.

'There's a meteor shower tonight,' he said. 'Have you ever seen one?'

'I've never even seen a shooting star,' I said, still watching the sky, hoping to catch a glimpse of something. When I looked at him again, I found he was looking at me too. We were right next to each other, his fingers so close to mine that if I moved an inch, we'd be touching. It was the closest we had been in weeks.

'Are you mad at me?' I asked.

'Yes,' he said without hesitation. 'I am mad at you.'

A part of me wanted to ask why, but I already knew. I was a different person now. I wanted things he didn't want me to have. I wanted revenge and he couldn't stomach it. He couldn't stomach who I was becoming.

'I'm sorry,' I said quietly. I didn't dare look up at him. I could feel the heat of his gaze on my cheeks.

'Are you sorry that you were prepared to go through with it tonight, or that in the end, you couldn't?'

I looked at our fingers, almost entwined. 'I'm sorry that I'm not good enough for this family. I'm sorry you had to fight so hard for me, and this is what you got.' I hesitated, waiting for my voice to stop wavering. 'I'm sorry I'm such a coward.'

Luca dipped his chin, the movement dragging my gaze back up.

He was frowning at me. 'You think shooting someone makes you brave?'

'I don't know,' I said. 'All I know is I couldn't do it when the time came. All I know is I failed my test.'

'I'm glad you failed,' he said.

'You had to lie for me. You made them all lie for me. You made them lie to their boss.'

'I don't care.'

'But you never lie to Valentino.'

'This is different.'

'How?'

He looked at me, nonplussed. 'It just is.'

'I don't understand why,' I said, my voice just a whisper. 'I don't understand why you would do that for me.'

Luca's lips flickered into a half-smile. 'No,' he said. 'You don't, do you?'

'I wish I had just done it.'

'I'm glad you couldn't pull the trigger.'

'You're happy I'm a coward?' I said.

'You're not a coward.'

'I'm not a Falcone,' I pointed out. 'Not really.'

'*Good*,' he said, his expression turning fierce.

'If I'm not a Marino and I'm not a Gracewell and I'm not a Falcone, then what am I?'

Luca leant closer to me, intensity burning in his eyes. 'You're free.'

I pulled away from him, from his heady scent and the hardness in his voice, and rested my elbows on my knees. 'Then why am I so unhappy?'

Luca stayed where he was, his gaze prickling along the back of my neck. 'You just lost your mother, Sophie. You need to give yourself time.'

'I don't *have* time.' A familiar wave of frustration was rising inside me. 'I want to make them pay, Luca. I know that's the right thing, but tonight when I held that gun to Libero Marino's head, and I listened to him cursing at me and taunting me, and calling me a traitor, I just *froze*.'

He stayed silent, and I don't know why, but all the things I had been feeling started to tumble out. 'I hate that I froze. I hate that I failed. I'm so embarrassed that I couldn't do it, and then when I really think about it, I find myself feeling terrified that a part of me thought I could. That a part of me was ready to end a man's life. That a part of me felt so powerful standing there with him shaking in front of me. I don't know what I want. I don't know what I'm capable of, but I know tonight was a failure for me.'

Luca turned to face me so I couldn't look away even if I tried. 'Let me uncomplicate this for you, Sophie. You don't want this. I promise you, this is not the path for you.'

Felice's words from the study came flooding back to me. Was this really what Luca thought or was it a projection of his own desires? 'How do you know what's right for me? I'm not you, Luca. I'm my own person. I want to let my mother know she didn't die in vain. I want to embrace this life, the blood in my veins. I don't want to be on my own.'

Luca pressed his palms against his eyes, his fingertips scraping through his hair. 'You're wrong, Sophie. You are so deeply, unbearably wrong, and I don't know how to show you that. And it makes me so angry, I could scream.'

'That's why you keep avoiding me,' I said. 'I get it. You don't believe I'm cut out for this life. You don't think I can do it.'

He uncovered his face. '*What?*'

'It's true,' I said, frustration turning to anger now. 'You think I'm going to shoot myself by accident or stab myself, or that I'm not strong enough or smart enough to do the things your brothers do. I know you don't think I'm cut out for this, and you hate that I'm even trying to be, but I have to. I don't care if it makes you angry with me,' I lied. 'I don't care if you don't believe in me.'

He rubbed his temples very slowly, and I watched him work his anger into submission. Then he said, as if it was the most obvious thing in the whole world, 'Of course I believe in you.'

'What?'

'I believe that you're smart and funny and brave and determined. I believe that you're loyal and kind. I believe that you're a good person, in your heart. In your soul. You're right about one thing, though. I don't believe that you're an assassin. I don't think you can kill someone and be OK with it. And that is not an insult, Sophie. That I believe you're too good and too kind to hurt someone, no matter how much they've

**151**

hurt you. That your heart is too big. That your empathy runs too deep. That's *why* I believe in you. I believe in you more than I could ever explain, and you expect me to stand by and watch while you destroy yourself right in front of my eyes. You expect me to let you point the gun at Libero Marino and shout at you to shoot him?'

He was really asking me, waiting for me to answer. 'I want you to want what I want,' I said slowly. 'I want you to support me . . .'

'No,' he said. 'I will not raise you up and give you a gun. I will not take you shooting and fawn over how great your aim is. I won't tell you how brilliant you can be or how many Marinos you can murder if you really put your mind to it. I won't walk you into danger and clap as you shoot to kill. I will take the gun from you and tell you you're a thousand times better without it. I will always take the gun from you, Sophie. I will always tell you that you don't need it. I will always support you, but I will never support that. *Never.*' He scrubbed his hands across his forehead, dragging his hair away from his face. 'You always manage to work me up,' he said ruefully.

All this time, I thought he put himself on a pedestal, but it was me he had raised up. He thought I was better than him – than his life, than his family – but I wasn't.

'We're the same,' I said. 'We come from the same kind of blood. How could you say all these things to me, and not say them to yourself? How do you expect me to take any of it to heart, when it's said with such hypocrisy? If you really believed your family was truly bad then you'd walk away from it. I know you're strong enough.'

Luca shook his head. 'It's not the same.'

'Why not?'

'It's too late for me. I've done too many heinous things already. There is no getting out.'

I lay back on the roof, a wave of exhaustion washing over me. Couldn't he see it was the same for me? Couldn't he understand I felt the same way? It was pointless having this argument with him. We would never agree, and the truth was, he had lied to Valentino to keep me here – and that meant I was staying.

'I'm tired, Luca. I'm tired of this conversation.'

Luca lay down next to me. 'I know,' he said. 'I'm tired too.'

We welcomed the silence, and the respite it brought. He wasn't the enemy and neither was I. Our world was the problem, and we were both stuck in it. We lay side by side, at an impasse, but not wanting to separate. My chin brushed against his shoulder. Our arms stretched out next to each other, my pinky finger brushing his. I ached for the fleeting closeness we had once had, couldn't help but wonder whether we would ever have it again.

'Tell me about the life you would have had,' I said, into the big expanse above us. 'Tell me about the person you would be if you weren't a Falcone.'

I had never delved this deeply before, and I didn't know if Luca would let me. But the moment was quiet again, and I just wanted to talk, to be with him, even if the conversation was hypothetical, even if it didn't really matter.

'I would have gone to college.' His breath fogged the air above us. 'Studied astrophysics. I would have been the biggest *nerd*.' He imitated my voice on the last word. 'When I was a kid, I wanted to be an astronaut more than anything.'

'Did you have those sticky glow-in-the-dark stars on your ceiling?'

'Of course,' he said. 'What aspiring astronaut doesn't?'

'So what happened? Didn't you think you were smart enough?' I said, teasingly.

'Oh, I'm definitely smart enough, Sophie.' His laughter echoed mine. 'I just didn't like the idea of having to eat cardboard food for months at a time. When I was seven, my dad bought me a star for my birthday. It came with all these specific coordinates and a certificate with my name on it, and we waited for it to get dark and then found it through the telescope.'

'Of course you had a telescope,' I interjected.

I caught his smirk. 'So we found the star – The Gianluca Falcone Star – and my dad helped me get the coordinates until it lit up right in front of me. When I pulled back from the eyepiece, he clapped me on the back, and asked me what I thought about it.'

Without meaning to, I had rolled on to my side and hitched my head up with my hand, so I could see him better. I liked looking at him when he was telling a story. One, because he was abnormally handsome, and two, because his face lit up when he spoke. 'And?' I prompted.

He glanced sideways at me, a smile flickering at the edges of his lips. 'I turned around to my father, who had just spent all this money on a really thoughtful, unique gift, and I said . . .' He cleared his throat, and did his best impression of himself as a child. '"Dad, are you aware that the light from this star takes so many years to reach earth, that in reality it's probably already deteriorated into a ball of dust and ash, and so

154

the gift, technically speaking, is dead, and therefore useless?"'

'Oh, man,' I said, lying on my back again, my laughter warm inside me. 'Remind me to never *ever* buy you a gift.'

'Just make sure it's a *real* star, not the memory of one,' he said. 'In my defence, I was only seven. I didn't know about conventional rules of present-acceptance. I thought I knew everything.'

'Some things never change.'

'Well, the only difference is, now I actually *do* know everything.'

'What else? What else would you do?'

His attention was trained on the stars again. 'I'd visit Machu Picchu and do the Inca Trail, I'd travel Route 66 on a shoestring budget in an old Camaro. I'd study the Renaissance in Florence, I'd sleep under the Northern Lights in Iceland . . .' He trailed off, and I could feel it, just as I knew he could – the sense of sadness creeping over us. He had *really* thought about it. All the things he would be, all the things he would do. Whispers of a life unlived, of dreams unmade. It hurt, right down in my core, to know that he would never have those things – the things that made his eyes light up and his smile stretch like a little boy's again.

We lay together under the stars and the melancholy, and I tried my hardest to think of something that might make him feel better, to wade into that dark, empty space inside me and pull out a spark of light for him, but there was nothing, just hollowness and fear and anger.

He rolled on to his side, his whole body brushing mine as he looked down on me. 'What about you, Sophie? What would you do?'

I had a million things I wanted to do – they used to play on a loop in my head, before all the nightmares took their place. 'When I was a kid, my uncle used to take me to the Oriental Theatre in the city whenever there was a new musical playing.' I rushed on, thinking of my old uncle Jack as a separate entity to who he really was – Antony Marino. 'I saw *Wicked* four times in one year. And *Billy Elliot* and *Aladdin,* all these wonderful stories brought to life, and I remember thinking when I was only eleven years old that if I was going to do something for the rest of my life, it would be that. Stories. I'd work in movies or musicals, behind the scenes, bringing it all together. I'd be the producer or the director, or I'd stand there all day and happily hold a boom mic. I didn't care, I'd just be part of it. Something bigger than me.' My breathing had doubled, and the excitement of my rant was catching in my cheeks. I didn't realize I was smiling, and Luca was so close to me, I could see the scar above his lip stretch as he smiled back.

'What else?' he asked, leaning closer. 'What else would you do?'

'I'd go to England and see where Millie grew up. I'd go to Buckingham Palace, and the West End. Millie says they do *Wicked* in British accents over there. How weird is that?' I didn't wait for him to answer. 'Or maybe I'd see *The Phantom of the Opera*. I never got to see that one, and it was my mother's favourite show. We were going to go but we . . .' I trailed off.

'Anything else?' he said, softer now.

'You know they think there are more tombs left to be discovered in the Valley of the Kings in Egypt? Imagine if I found one? I'd be so famous.'

Luca's laughter burst out of him, flashing warmth into the air between us. 'This is getting pretty elaborate . . . even by your standards.'

'Don't act like you wouldn't want to see the pyramids.'

'Of course I would,' he said leaning in until he was distractingly close. 'Maybe in this version, I could come with you . . .'

I tried to ignore the scent of his aftershave, the warmth of his body heat as he pressed against me. 'You'd probably get motion sickness on the way there.'

'*You'd* probably get sunburnt.'

'And *you'd* spend all the time reading lame poetry. Or *The Iliad* for the fiftieth time.'

'Look at you, knowing the name of an actual book. I'm impressed.'

I punched him in the arm. 'You're evicted from my dream.'

He laughed again but there was something else in it this time, a sense of empathy, of understanding. 'Oh well,' he said, leaning back down, away from me. 'It probably wouldn't have worked out anyway.'

I laid my head beside his. The excitement had drained away again, and the blanket of reality floated down to cover us. Our sighs weaved together, into the air above us.

'I killed a man tonight, Sophie,' Luca said into the silence.

The meaning was implicit. There was no other life, there was only this one. And his die had already been cast.

'I feel heavy,' he said quietly. 'I feel heavy inside.'

'I know,' I said softly. 'I'm sorry.' I *was* sorry. I was sorry that I had failed to do it; that he had had to take that burden from me, and that he was sad, right down in his bones, because of it.

I felt for his hand. He spread his fingers and laced them through mine.

Overhead, a star streaked a line of bright white across the sky. 'Look,' I said. 'A shooting star.'

'Mmm,' said Luca, the sound rumbling in his chest. Another flash, this time over to the left. 'There's another,' he said, clasping my hand a little tighter in his own and pointing with his other hand.

'Do you wish on them?' I asked.

'Not in a long time,' he said. 'When I was young, Evelina and I would lie out here all the time and look at the stars. She taught me the constellations. Told me the stories behind them. We used to wish on them.'

'She sounds amazing.'

'She was.' His voice changed, a sense of reverence in his words. 'She used to talk about it all the time – this sense of possibility. You couldn't see it, or touch it, but you had to chase it. She told me to chase it, no matter what . . .' He trailed off, and I felt the sadness rise up around us like a lake. I was determined to keep us afloat.

'Let's wish tonight, then,' I said softly. 'In her memory.'

'OK,' he said, after a beat. 'Let's wish.'

'OK,' I said, smiling too, as more stars began to burst overhead.

We stayed like that for a long time, watching the sky as it lit up in silver streaks.

I wished on every shooting star, and all my wishes were for him.

# CHAPTER TWENTY

## THE CLICK

**B**y Sunday morning, Libero Marino's 'gangland' murder was all over the newspapers. His brother, Marco, had released a chilling statement on behalf of the family. They were coming out for their revenge, and they wanted the world to know it. They wanted *us* to know it. Millie rang to tell me it was trending on Twitter. I feigned surprise and withheld the truth until she hung up.

The news was out there but *Evelina* remained, happily, police-free. I knew we had covered our tracks, but I still couldn't figure out how the boys were escaping interrogations. Everyone knew the bloody history between the Falcones and the Marinos. At first, I thought that perhaps the police were just monumentally bad at their jobs, but it became clear that when two Mafia clans are at war, it makes more sense to turn a blind eye and let the criminals take care of each other. That was what Paulie told me. As long as innocents weren't being killed, we were doing the city's job for them.

I had been staring at Libero's face in my mind all night, and I decided that eating some cereal at seven a.m. on Sunday morning would be preferable to trying to ignore the mental chant of *Traitor! Traitor! Traitor! Failure! Failure! Failure!*

And that god awful question that pulsed uneasily in my mind: *How are you going to shoot Jack? How are you going to avenge your mother?*

I told myself it was different. I didn't know Libero. He had never wronged me directly. His only crime was looking like Sara, and his face reminded me of how I had failed her. I couldn't shoot him because it would be another betrayal. I owed Sara – I convinced myself that that was why I hesitated.

On the other, bloodier hand, I definitely wanted to shoot Jack. I had slashed a blade across his eye without the slightest hint of freezing, so when he did resurface, it wasn't going to be a problem. I told myself that over and over again, hoping that if I said it enough times then it would become true.

I finished two bowls of Lucky Charms and washed up, enjoying the morning silence. I was even considering reading a book in the library to take my mind off everything. I wanted to lie low – at least from Valentino – while the lie worked itself into my bones, and I started to believe that I deserved to be here. I made my way down the hallway, appreciating the quiet while it lasted. In about two hours, Dom and Gino would be making enough racket for a small concert hall and Nic would probably come search me out for more target practice.

I padded down the hallway, following the faint sound of voices wafting through the house. I paused with my hand on the door to the sitting room, already ajar, and pushed just a little. It yielded easily, and I peered around it.

Felice was bent over himself, his words muffled by his fingers.

Paulie was beside him, perched on the armrest of the couch, one hand clapped on his brother's back. '. . . time and time again. You have to let him lead the way he sees fit.'

Felice rolled his head around, venom oozing from his voice. 'He is a child, Paulie. He will derail this family.'

Paulie sighed. 'Killing Libero was the right choice strategically. And to have a Marino do it . . . well.'

'Nonsense,' Felice spat. 'The whole thing is off. He has his *soldati* wrapped up in cotton wool – all of us barricaded in the same place.'

'I think,' said Paulie, edging lower, on his hunkers now, so he could look at Felice straight on, 'perhaps you are indulging a little too hard right now.'

'*Stai zitto*,' Felice hissed like a rattlesnake. 'You know why I'm drinking.' He dropped his head back and closed his eyes at the ceiling. 'I. Hate. This. Time. Of. Year.'

'I know it's hard for you, but self-medicating is not helping,' Paulie said. 'You're not angry with Valentino.'

Felice waved Paulie's words away, almost swatting his brother on the cheek.

'You're mad because she left you,' Paulie added, his voice turning soft.

'Say it,' said Felice, looking at the mantelpiece, at a photo of him and Evelina laughing and toasting each other with champagne on their wedding day. I edged backwards, pressing myself against the wall so I was hidden behind the door. 'Say the rest.'

'Brother . . .'

'She's not coming back.' He cursed. 'She's never coming back.'

'It's been a long time.'

How long ago had she been taken from him? How long did a broken heart last? I thought of my own grief, the constant ebb of it at the edges of my awareness. It hadn't lessened; I had just accommodated it. It was part of me now – this blur of sadness. Maybe in five years' time, I would be like Felice. Still angry, still questioning . . . still baying for revenge. His mask was almost perfect. Maybe mine would be too.

'I want to see my child,' Felice said.

'Look forward.'

'I built her a palace,' said Felice. His voice was vibrating with emotion – it was strange to see him so vulnerable, to see beneath that carefully polished veneer of his. 'I gave her the world and she walked away from it without so much as a *goodbye*.'

'Look to the future.' Paulie gripped his brother's arm, but Felice wasn't even looking at him now, he was looking at his expensive shoes.

'It was Angelo's fault,' he said quietly.

I caught my gasp on the palm of my hand. Did he know Evelina was dead? Did he really think his own brother killed her? If only he knew the truth. If he knew about my dad, or the safe, or the ring . . .

I told myself to leave, to get the hell out of that room

before he caught me spying, but I had never seen Felice so . . . vulnerable, and I was compelled by it.

'I know he helped her to leave. I know he convinced her.'

'No.' Paulie was shaking his head. 'He would never do that to you.'

'We'll never know,' said Felice bitterly. 'We'll never know what he did with her.'

'You are talking nonsense.'

'I know what I know,' said Felice. 'Angelo was a snake.'

Something cold rippled up the back of my neck. Felice wasn't talking about Angelo as a brother . . . but as an enemy. I was starting to wonder just how deep his resentment ran, and whether he had felt like this the night he watched him get shot. Was that why he hadn't intervened?

'He was your brother. He was loyal to you.'

'If he was loyal then I would have been his underboss, not his useless—' Felice stopped himself, swallowing the slur. 'Angelo destroyed this family's prospects long before he got himself killed.'

'Careful,' Paulie warned. 'Clean yourself up. Try and sleep. Don't let the others hear you speak like this.'

'Why?' Felice looked like he was about to pass out. 'Because his little bastards run this family? They take in strays and undermine our safety, and I should worry about voicing the obvious opinion of—'

'Enough!' snapped Paulie, losing the last dregs of his composure. He gripped his brother by the shoulders and shook him. I couldn't imagine ever doing that to Felice; I'd get my head sawn off. '*Get a grip.*'

Felice shrugged his brother off. His suit was crumpled, his

slacks turned up at the bottom.

Paulie crossed the room, pausing in the doorway that led directly into the study. 'I'm going to take a nap, and then I have the girls for the afternoon. Pull yourself together before the others wake up. I can't keep babysitting you like this.' He disappeared, shutting the door behind him with a quiet thud.

Felice raised his head so suddenly I didn't have time to jump backwards. We locked eyes, and he shot to his feet so fast he became one big streak of silver hair and spidery limbs uncramping themselves. I stumbled backwards out into the hallway, heading for the first room I could find.

I was halfway into the library when I was yanked backwards, my feet dragging against the floor as I struggled upright. Felice spun me around and shoved me into the alcove in the hallway, his left hand crushing my windpipe.

I grappled at his fingers. 'Get off me!'

'Eavesdropping were we, Marino?' He tightened his grip and pushed me further into the alcove, until the shadows fell across us both.

'I don't know what you're talking about!' I choked out. 'I'm just trying to do my homework!'

There was a strong whiff of whisky on his breath. He peeled his lips back, his teeth glistening at me like fangs. 'I don't trust you as far as I could throw you, Persephone.'

I blinked dumbly at him, trying to convey innocence.

'You walk around here like you belong, like these floors are yours to traverse, but they don't belong to you, nor does this family. You will always be an *outsider* to us.'

If I wasn't concentrating so hard on dragging tiny morsels of air into my bruising trachea I might have said something

**164**

about his own botched loyalty, but I couldn't force the words out.

'I don't know what went on in Valentino's office on Friday night, but if you think I believe the diatribe Luca spun about Libero Marino, then you're sorely mistaken.' He relaxed his hold an inch, and I gulped down a breath of fresh air. I thought he was going to relinquish me, but instead he whipped his gun out of his jacket, cocked it, and pressed the barrel into the underside of my jaw. My tongue stuck to the roof of my mouth.

'As far as I'm concerned, Persephone Marino, you are still an active threat to me.' The gun was cutting off my oxygen supply. Felice's eyes were wild, his lips quivering violently. Even his hands were shaking. 'If you even *consider* breathing a word about *anything* you *think* you just heard to *anyone*, you will be facing your death at my hands. Mark my words, I will show you the depth of my wrath if you so much as tiptoe out of line.'

I had frozen in place, my pulse vibrating against the cold metal, trying not to move a muscle. Any wrong move, wrong word, could set him off. The truth was, he was crazy – drugged up and strung out. If he wanted to, he would kill me right there and then, and I would only get half a strangled scream out before he did.

'I'm never going to stop watching you, Persephone.' Spittle foamed at the sides of his mouth, the words coming in heaving gasps. 'If you presume to undermine me in any way, or do anything that places this family at risk, I will put a bullet in your head.' He dug the barrel of the gun in further, and I gagged, trying to suck in air. I was about to pass out.

'Just. Like. This,' Felice whispered.

The click was as loud as a bomb. It echoed inside the alcove, and grew louder and louder inside my head.

Nothing happened. There were no bullets in his gun. A warning.

He bared all his teeth at me – that shark grin, full of malevolent amusement – and as unsightly as it was, I almost fainted in relief.

Then another sound echoed around us. Felice froze, the empty gun still pressed against my neck as the sound of a hammer being pulled back filled the small space. A black gun appeared beside Felice's head, the pressure of the barrel puckering the skin around his temple.

His face drained to a ghostly white.

Luca stepped into the alcove and brought his lips right up to his uncle's ear. 'That gun might be empty, *scarafaggio*, but this one is loaded,' he growled. 'If you ever threaten her again, I'll blow your brains out.'

The shark grin died, and real, chilling fear consumed Felice's face. His eyes grew lidless and wide. Luca kept the gun pressed against his uncle's head, and slowly, Felice lowered his own from my neck. My jaw clicked back into place and cool air rushed down my throat. I gulped it down. Without turning around, Felice addressed Luca, his grey eyes still trained on me.

'So,' he said, his lip curling. 'There are some things you deem worthy enough to kill for, Gianluca.'

Luca's reply came in one steady breath. 'Only one.'

# CHAPTER TWENTY-ONE
## HOMEWORK AND HEADSHOTS

The next few weeks passed by in a blur of classes, endless assignments, nightly phone calls about the upcoming Masquerade Ball, and meetings back at *Evelina*, where I learnt the names of every Marino in existence and watched as the Falcone boys disappeared at random times of the day and came back in the dead of night. They were in the city, scoping out Donata's usual haunts, collecting information, turning Marino allies into snitches, dispatching those that couldn't be persuaded. The house was busier than an airport at Christmastime. Donata and her remaining children, Marco and Zola (Franco, I learnt, was still in prison) had come back for Libero's funeral – the most heavily guarded procession in Chicago's history.

My father was still on the run, but I hadn't heard so much

as a peep from him. The police were patrolling Cedar Hill, on the lookout, following fruitless tips and making nuisances of themselves. I almost felt bad for them. It wasn't hard to guess where my father was – at least if you knew what I knew. It wasn't hard to guess what he was planning, but I couldn't figure out what the hell I was going to do when I came face-to-face with him again. I wasn't sure he truly wanted to protect me by sending me away to Colorado, but I knew he wouldn't harm me, not deliberately. But if he was with Jack when we tracked him down, then we were going to have a problem.

The anniversary of Evelina's disappearance passed and Felice sank back into his usual cartoon-villain self. I found it harder to be around him, knowing what he was capable of, and seeing how close he had come to actually doing it. He had left a ring of bruises around my neck, and I knew if I ever found myself alone with him away from *Evelina*, it might be the last thing I ever did. He could never know what my father had done to his wife, or I'd be dead for certain.

Luca spent all his time with Valentino, painstakingly planning and dispatching Falcones to far-off places in the state. For now, I had one duty and one duty only: go to school, stay in school. In the afternoons, I sat beneath the oil painting of Evelina Falcone in the library and forced myself to complete assignments I didn't care about. As time wore on, Evelina's eyes seemed to grow deeper, the sadness behind them rising to meet me like a terrible wave. Her face haunted my dreams, her lips twisting as she whispered to me in the night, *I see you, Sophie Marino. I see your fate.*

I knew Luca was against my role in the family's violence, but he knew, too, that when the time came to face the Marino family in earnest, he wouldn't be able to keep me away. I still had to prove myself. It was the only thing I cared about, the only thing I spent my nights thinking about. I was not going to be afraid. I was not going to hesitate. I was not going to fail again.

I spent the weeks getting myself ready mentally, honing my shot, preparing to face my uncle and Donata again, and hoping against hope that my father would be caught and hauled back to prison before then. At school I was a different Sophie – upbeat, engaged, innocent. The mask slipped on so easily, sometimes it was hard to take it off again.

A couple of days before Halloween, I was loitering in the Falcone foyer reluctantly waiting to be chaperoned to school, when Nic barged through the front door, a half-eaten break-fast burrito in one hand.

'Hey,' he said, lighting up. 'How are you?'

'Fine,' I said, shaking my head as he held out the burrito in offering.

'You sure?' he pressed. 'It's delicious.'

'I'm sure you need the energy more than me.' *You're killing people; I'm studying poems and doing calculus.*

'I don't mind sharing with my girl.'

He had taken to doing that a lot – referring to me as 'his', despite my repeated protestations to the contrary. Some-times I wondered if he was just doing it to wind me up. 'I'm not your girl,' I reminded him. 'As we've been over several thousand times.'

Nic rolled his eyes. 'Right, right. I'm still in the friend-zone, but that doesn't mean I can't hop the fence.'

'Actually, that's exactly what it means.'

'For the record, I disagree,' he said, taking another bite of his burrito and laughing at my grimace.

'What's got you so giddy so early anyway, *platonic male friend*? Where were you last night?'

I was really asking *who did you kill?* But I had quickly learnt that at the Falcone mansion, it is terribly uncouth to come right out and address the elephant in the room. They didn't speak so openly of their murders. They were implicit things that happened beneath the fabric of their family.

'You're damn right I'm giddy,' he said, shoving the rest of the burrito in his mouth and swallowing it in one giant gulp. 'You're not going to believe what I've got in the car with me.' He bounded back outside. 'Wait there!'

Dom came thudding down the stairs, and I scooted to the side before he shoved me out of the way. 'Are they back?' he asked. 'Do they have the stuff?'

'The stuff?'

He wrenched the double doors open so Gino and Nic could drag three black duffel bags into the foyer and deposit them on the marble crest. Gino was just as excitable as Nic, and Dom was rubbing his hands together as he stared at the duffel bags.

'Who wants to do the honours?' Nic asked, his gaze resting on me. 'Wait until you see these, Soph. You'll love them.'

'Should we wait for Valentino?' Gino asked.

'He's coming,' said Dom, bending down and unzipping the bags. 'I texted him. Come on, dig in. I want to pick my one first.'

Like little boys on Christmas morning, the three of them got on their knees and started rifling through the bags, pulling out guns bigger than my arms and legs. The kind of guns you see in war movies. The kinds of guns that spell instant, irrefutable death.

'Whoa,' I said, drifting towards the treasure trove of weapons. I knelt down next to Nic. 'These are *huge*.'

'Yeah,' he said, smirking at me. 'Eighteen automatics plus ammunition. Let's see your uncle survive an assault from one of these.'

Before, a comment like that would have shocked me – scared me, even – but it barely registered now. The idea was as commonplace as the guns themselves.

He picked up a gun and hefted it into the crook of his arm, moving his shoulders around to get comfortable. Beside him, Dom and Gino were doing the same. 'It'll be heavier when loaded,' said Dom, aiming his gun at me. 'You think you can handle that, Sophie?'

Nic grabbed another gun from the bag and handed it to me, nodding at me to take it. I picked it up – it was heavy, even without the ammunition.

'Relax your shoulders and grip it,' said Nic, still watching me intently. 'Here, like this. Look.'

He held the gun lower, at his chest, one hand on the front handle that jutted out almost parallel to the back handle, which he tucked into his ribcage, his elbow pulled back to make it fit. He directed it at Gino.

'Say hello to my little friend!' he said, before making a *thud-thud-thud* sound at him. Gino pretended to clutch at his heart and fall over. I had seen Gino like that before – only with real blood gushing down his shirt, his face as white as snow. Now, he was giggling in that high-pitched voice of his and writhing around on the floor, and I couldn't help but find it strange how much he had distanced himself from the time he almost died. And yet, I was here, too, holding a machine gun to my chest and practising my aim in a puddle of assassins on a hundred-year-old marble crest that stood for blood and honour. And I don't really know why, but I was laughing too.

Nic stopped faux-shooting and turned back to me, his smile as wide as I had ever seen it. There was something infectious about his excitement. I wanted to feel like that. I wanted to smile like that.

'See?' he said, still laughing a little. 'Easy as that.'

I adjusted the gun as Nic had done, trying to push away the faint unease inside me. 'Like this?' I asked, swivelling to see if the gun was snug enough with movement. It was a little cumbersome.

'Exactly,' said Nic, winking at me. 'You're a natural with it. I knew you would be.' Though I knew it shouldn't, his approval made me smile.

Dom leant towards me, his pungent aftershave mixing with the faint whiff of hair gel that always emanated from him. 'Maybe with this gun, the next time you shoot to kill, you'll actually pull the trigger.'

Gino sat up. 'What?' he said, blinking at me and then at Dom. 'What's that supposed to mean?'

Nic thumped Dom in the side of his head. '*Io non ci scherzerei tanto, fratello!*'

'*Calmati,*' said Dom, returning a jab to Nic's right arm. 'It's a joke.'

'I don't get it,' said Gino, still glancing between us.

172

I glowered at Dom. 'A bad joke.'

'A dangerous joke,' cautioned Nic.

Dom shrugged. 'She should have thought of that before she—'

'Dom!' I shouted, casting a wary glance at Gino. He didn't know about my cowardice at The Sicilian Kiss, but the way Dom was dangling it in front of him, he was about to. And that would be one more chink in the secret, and one more step towards my eviction. Or worse. 'Seriously, shut up!'

Dom raised his palms to me. 'Calm down, tetchy. I'm just kidding around.'

'What's going on down here?' Felice descended the stairs, his loafers padding softly on the stone floors, his grin fixed perfectly in place. Even now he was back to his old impeccably-turned-out self, I would never forget the version of Felice that had cornered me in that alcove, the manic look in his eyes, the thirst in his voice when he spoke to Paulie about Angelo. I would never forget how deeply he despised his role in the family, or how little respect he had for Valentino. He was more dangerous to me now than ever, and no amount of forced pleasantries or blithe indifference on his part was going to change that. 'A special delivery, and no one thought to call me?'

'We were picking our favourites,' said Gino, twirling his own choice in front of him. 'Didn't want to get stuck with any duds.'

Felice arched a brow. 'A delivery this precious from New York is unlikely to have any duds, *Giorgino*, and if the Di Salvos heard you say as much, they'd have your tongue cut out before lunchtime.'

'Calm down, Felice.' Nic was examining a longer, thinner gun now, which had a little tripod stand.

Felice hunkered down and took a gun for himself. I didn't fail to notice the look of disdain he offered to the one sitting in my lap. It was probably the one he wanted. I clutched it harder, indicating just how sure my choice now was.

Elena swept through the hall a moment later, her pixie-like nose upturned at our huddle. 'What a mess you all make sitting there like vagabonds,' she said, eyeing the weapons over Dom's shoulders. 'Can't we act like adults and place these elsewhere?' She frowned at me. 'And shouldn't you be in school, girl?'

'Valentino wants her chaperoned to and from school,' said Dom, without looking up at his mother. 'I'll get around to it once I've chosen my favourite.'

'Boys and their silly toys.' Elena rolled her eyes and sashayed off into the kitchen, her heels clacking on the ground as she went, her voice fading. 'And the Lord gave me five of them. *La vita sa essere terribilmente ingiusta . . .*'

'So she doesn't want a gun, then,' I surmised.

'Mama doesn't get her hands dirty if she can help it,' Nic supplied. He was still examining his gun. His lips were puckered in concentration, his brows pulled together.

'A lot of the girls don't get their hands dirty,' said Gino. 'That's what makes you so cool, Soph.'

Something fluttered inside me. Oh, God. Was I really this starved of praise and acceptance that this was making me smile? The answer: yes. 'Thanks, Gino.'

'Yeah, that's what makes you *different*,' leered Dom. 'Your extreme readiness to shoot people.'

174

I balled my fists. He just couldn't help himself.

Felice was staring at me. Before he could interrogate Dom over that stupid comment, Valentino arrived. The wheels of his chair were almost soundless on the smooth floor, but Luca was with him, and their conversation, low and in Italian, preceded them.

'Good,' said Valentino, eyeing the delivery. 'So the exchange went well?' he asked Nic.

Nic disengaged from the guns and puffed his chest up. 'And we have the Di Salvos' support in New York too.'

'Well done.'

Nic nodded, pride straightening his spine. 'No problem.'

I stole a glance at Luca. He was staring at the automatic machine gun in my lap. To say he was frowning would be a colossal understatement.

'Shouldn't you be at school?' he asked me.

'I'm just waiting for Dom,' I said.

Dom was rotating two guns in either hand and humming under his breath. They looked exactly the same to me. 'I'm nearly ready,' he said, without looking up. 'Just have to make one last decision . . . or can I just have both?' He looked at Valentino hopefully.

'Obviously not,' said Valentino.

Luca muttered something to Valentino and then pulled his car keys from his pocket. 'I'll take you, Sophie,' he said. 'Come on.'

'Don't you want to pick your gun, Luca?' said Nic. 'Before all the good ones go.'

Luca was halfway to the door. He didn't bother turning around to answer. 'A gun is a gun, Nicoli, not a trophy. Just get them out of the way before the others come downstairs. I don't want Sal and Aldo seeing them.'

Dom started laughing. 'Geez, I can't wait for Christmas so you can suck the joy out of that too.'

Luca raised two fingers over his head, and then disappeared into the driveway. I put my gun down and shrugged my bag on to follow him outside.

'Good luck going to school under that black cloud,' said Dom sarcastically. 'At least we'll all get a break from him.'

'Grow up.' Valentino slapped the back of Dom's head. 'Just because he doesn't want to play with guns like they're toys.'

'Blatant favouritism,' Dom muttered.

Nic caught me by my hand, tugging my attention back to him. 'I'll save this one for you. Jack won't know what hit him, Soph.' He smiled up at me.

I smiled back. 'Thanks.'

His fingers were pressing into my palm, jolting warmth up my arm. 'How high is that friend-zone fence now?'

Frustration careened over my gratitude. 'One hundred feet high, and covered in barbed wire, Nic.'

Dom, who had clearly been listening in, snorted. 'Keep climbing, bro, and die trying to get over it.'

Nic slammed the butt of his gun into Dom's arm, and I left them behind me, bickering.

In the driveway, I slid into the front seat of the car and dropped my bag in front of me so I could put my seatbelt on. 'Thanks for babysitting me,' I said. 'I think Dom is finally getting fed up of being my driver.'

Luca started the engine and reversed around the driveway in a wide arc, his hand slid across the back of my chair, his gaze over his shoulder. 'I'm just sorry I interrupted such a precious bonding moment.'

'With me and Nic, or me and my new gun?' I asked the side of his face.

His laugh was short and mirthless. 'Aren't they one and the same now?'

I rolled my eyes. 'Let's not do this, Luca. We're never going to agree about this, so why keep going round in circles?'

He wasn't looking at me, and I wasn't looking at him. 'Sometimes I wonder if you make decisions just to piss me off.'

I glared at the road. 'Sometimes I wonder if you give yourself too much credit in my decision-making.'

'Do you have a death wish?'

'I have a revenge wish.'

'I have a problem with that.'

'Then evict me.'

'No.'

'Then deal with it.'

He ground his fingers around the steering wheel. 'And you wouldn't consider taking a step back from the guns,' he said, 'and letting me handle it for you?'

'What do you mean, *handle it*?'

'Let me take care of your uncle and Donata.'

'And what, I just stay at home, looking wistfully out the window as you go forth and massacre my family?'

'I'd prefer it to the alternative.'

'Well, that's not your decision to make,' I said, carefully. 'We're all in this together now, and I don't plan on failing again when my time comes.'

He set his jaw, a muscle feathering below his cheekbone. He chewed on the silence, and I fell into it, preferring it over the constant need to convince him, to avoid being convinced by him.

We were pulling up outside Cedar Hill High before he spoke to me again. He shut the engine off and turned to face me. My heartbeat immediately kicked into high gear, but I knew he wasn't going to kiss me. That side of us was long gone. We were more like adversaries now, with a vague sprinkling of friendship every now and then, when we weren't arguing.

I raised my eyebrows. 'Yes?'

'Sophie.' His eyes were the purest blue in the morning sunlight, his lips lightly parted so that his breath warmed his words. 'Can't this just be enough for you?'

'W-what?' I stammered.

'School,' he said. 'Your friends. Normality. Isn't it enough?'

My face fell. 'Oh,' I said, trying to harness myself again. 'School. Normality.' I grabbed my school bag, and popped the door open before my embarrassment could swallow me whole. I hopped out and ducked my head inside, towards him, trying very hard not to look at his lips.

'Look,' I said. 'If it makes you feel any better, I haven't totally disengaged from my old life. I'm doing the most normal high school thing ever tomorrow night. I'm going to the masquerade dance.'

'The what?'

'The dance,' I repeated. 'You know, Millie's dance?' And then I realized I had never once mentioned Millie's dance to him, because, why would I? We didn't talk about the lighthearted stuff, the falsities of my second life. 'Tomorrow,' I clarified. 'I'm going. More or less against my will, but Millie was very adamant from the start and I kind of owe her, y'know?'

He was staring at me. It was not in a sexy way.

'It's going to be horrible,' I added, feeling like I needed to play it down, like the idea of me having fun while he was at home helping Valentino with assassination logistics was an unfair one. 'But I'm going. So there. That's something normal. Will that tide you over?'

'This is obviously a joke,' he said. 'This *is* a joke, yes?'

'What? No.'

His lips parted in surprise. *Don't look at his lips.* 'I don't believe you.'

'Why?' I asked, a familiar flash of irritation taking hold of me. 'Is the idea of me in a dress at a dance really so shocking to you?'

He tilted his head to one side. 'You're actually serious.'

'No, duh,' I snapped.

'No,' he said firmly. 'No way.'

'I wasn't asking you,' I pointed out.

'Well, you're going to listen to me.'

I grabbed the doorframe. 'Exsqueeze me?'

He came closer, undaunted. 'I said there's no way you're going out at night unattended to a dance while we're in the middle of an active blood war.'

My fingers tightened on the doorframe. 'Do you want me to do normal things or do you want me to shoot guns? Make up your damn mind, you yo-yo.'

He glared at me. 'You're not going to that dance while

**179**

Donata has her *soldati* out looking for you. She's put a bounty on all of our heads, and I guarantee you, as a former Marino, yours is the highest.'

If he was trying to scare me into submission, it was working, but I was definitely not going to let him see that. 'I go to school, don't I? You've always been so insistent about that.'

'That's different. It's the middle of the day, full of witnesses, and we bring you here and pick you up.'

'There'll be witnesses at the dance,' I pointed out. I never imagined I'd be fighting this hard to actually attend the stupid dance, but now I really wanted to go, just to prove to him he couldn't control me. 'And I'm going with Millie and Crispin, so it's not like I'll be on my own anyway.'

'And what exactly is a Crispin?' Luca sounded like he could taste the word in his mouth and didn't like it one bit.

I rolled my eyes. 'A Crispin is a *person*, Luca. He's Millie's boyfriend. And the dance is being supervised in the gym. It's perfectly safe. It's the same as going to school.'

'No, it's not.'

'Yeah, well.' I shrugged my bag on to my shoulder. 'Whatever.'

'You're not going, Sophie. I'm serious.'

'We'll see.' I shut the door and flounced up the steps, feeling his glare on the back of my neck.

My phone buzzed.

It's not happening.

I rolled my eyes. It was so happening. Otherwise Donata Marino would have to get in line behind Millie for my head on

180

a plate. There was no logic in Luca keeping me from the school dance if he was prepared to make me go to school every day. The two were basically the same thing, and it's not like Donata had the timetable for Cedar Hill High's social events. Still. Best not cause an all-out civil war with Luca over it. A well-placed emoji should smooth things over. A giggling monkey? No. Too frivolous. Dancing Señorita lady? A definite contender, but perhaps a bit too taunt-y. Something that says 'I'm not going to listen to you in this instance, but let's just move on and not be mad about it, OK?'

*I don't respect your authority, remember?* ☺

I made my way along the deserted corridors. I was definitely late. Another ping back.

You are such a brat.

Talk about the pot calling the kettle black. I stalled outside my biology class and sent back one more text.

Try and stop me.

I shuffled inside, made my hasty apologies and slid into my seat, glancing surreptitiously at my phone one last time.

Watch me.

At lunchtime, Millie and I convened with sandwich wraps and smoothies outside on the bleachers. I had pushed the argument with Luca right to the back of my mind – into the filing cabinet with all the other ones.

'Why do we have to do this here?' I asked Millie, rubbing my arms through my coat. 'I'm going to freeze.'

'Well, at least don't freeze with that frown on your face, cranky-pants. I don't want anyone else to see these dresses. It would be a huge spoiler.' She took a swig of her smoothie and nearly spat it out. 'I hate kale so much. Why do I do this to myself?'

Mine was berry. And it was de-lic-ious. I gulped it down. 'Because you're trying to be healthy?'

'It's not worth drinking grass over. And my wrap is just feta and *lettuce*,' she lamented.

'At least it won't get stuck in your braces,' I pointed out. Millie had just gotten her braces off and we were taking every opportunity to point out how bling-tastic her teeth were now that they weren't hidden. Millie was beautiful already, but her new smile was an explosion of loveliness. It suited her. Pearly white, straight teeth to go with her long dark hair, a smattering of freckles over porcelain skin, and those shiny blue eyes.

She gnashed her teeth at me, scrunching her nose at the same time. 'At least I can now eat things in an orderly and timely fashion.'

'And look amazing all the while,' I said, 'not that you weren't a vision before.'

She slapped my arm playfully. 'You flatterer, you.'

We sat down and she pulled out two floor-length dresses from her bag and laid them in front of us, side by side.

My eyes grew, and something hitched up in my chest.

Something small and slumbering awoke inside me. A new

sensation – or at least one so long forgotten that it felt new. It was a feeling of anticipation . . . of wanting. I was used to frequent pinches, feelings of anxiety, of fear . . . but this, this was unexpected. I thought that excitable, girly, teenager part of me was dead and buried, but here was a sliver of it, getting geared up for the Masquerade Ball. Suddenly, I really *really* wanted to go to the dance.

'Royal blue or emerald green?' Millie asked. She was still fluffing them out, showing their shape.

'They're amazing.' I fingered the delicate green material, lifting it up and letting it flow between my fingers. 'Are you sure? Won't your mom mind?'

'No way,' she said, grinning. 'She'd give you the moon right now if she could. Pick whichever one you want. I'm wearing a black fishtail one so you can have either of these. They're pretty tight, but you're outrageously hot, so it's fine.'

I slapped her arm playfully. 'Now who's the flatterer?' A smile caught in my cheeks. I stroked the material, loving the softness beneath my fingertips. And to think, just this morning I was as enthusiastic about the gun in my lap. What was wrong with me?

Which Sophie was I?

'Hmmm.' I lifted up both so I could see how they fell.

'I think the blue one would bring out your eyes,' Millie pointed out. I swished it around, admiring how the material tumbled like a waterfall. It was Grecian in style, with delicate straps that criss-crossed near the bodice. It was tight around the waist and flowed to the ground in tumbling waves.

'The material slits halfway up the side so it swishes when you walk.' Millie made a swish-swish sound and moved her hands in front of me in squiggling lines to demonstrate.

'I do like to swish,' I said.

'Don't we all?' said Millie, wistfully. 'Those Falcone boys are going to drool when they see you.'

All the little butterflies inside me seized up. 'That reminds me,' I said, leaving the dress down again, smoothing out the bodice with my fingers, like I was lovingly petting a dog. 'Luca says I can't go to the dance.'

'Huh,' said Millie, screwing up her nose. 'I didn't realize Luca Falcone was your evil stepmother.'

'What?' I feigned surprise. 'Are you *sure?*'

'Pretty sure,' she said, stroking her chin. 'So, what gives? Do I need to get you a pumpkin? Some helpful kitchen mice? A fairy godmother, perhaps?'

I was wondering how I could conjure a lie that would aptly cover up the fact that I was in the middle of a giant blood war with another Mafia family, reignited by the fact that they all thought I had just murdered a Marino *soldato* who I was also, conveniently, related to. 'Luca's just being protective.'

'Buy him a kitten and let him protect that. He's not your guardian.'

'Yeah, I know,' I said slowly. 'I just don't think he's going to be pleased about me going. I'm not saying I'm not going to go, I'm just saying he'll probably try and stop me, that's all.'

'Sophie.' Millie levelled me with a dark look. 'Luca Falcone does not want to get in the way of me and my dance. He'll regret it.'

A laugh bubbled out of me. 'Oh, yeah?'

She nodded, eyes wide. 'Nobody messes with my plans. I don't care how murdery they are. He'd better step back. Now.'

'He's a formidable foe,' I said. 'Trust me.'

'Wait,' she said, her eyes lighting up. 'Why don't you just *invite* him?'

I threw my head back and laughed. The idea was so ludicrous, so improbable . . . so pathetic. Pathetic that the only boy I was interested in would rather gouge his eyes out than accompany me on an actual date to a high school dance. I stopped laughing. It really wasn't that funny.

'No,' I said, composing myself. 'That's not the solution, trust me. We haven't really been getting on lately.'

'Why? Are you flirting with Nic?'

'I do not flirt with Nic! Why does a girl being nice to a boy always have to be construed as flirting? I am capable of having more than one agenda in my head at any given time.'

'OK, OK, relax, I was just asking . . .'

'And Luca doesn't see me like that any more, anyway,' I added.

'OK, fine, no Luca. I get it,' Millie conceded. 'That's probably a good thing. I really don't want to scare Cris away.' She smiled involuntarily at the mention of Cris, who had made the transition from casual hook-up to bona fide boyfriend in a matter of weeks. He was nice: normal, kind, and most importantly, safe. I liked Crispin. Even despite the hideous name. He couldn't help that.

'Don't worry, for the sake of your burgeoning relationship I'll keep my assassins as far away from your boyfriend as I can. But I can't imagine anything would put Crispin off you,' I added. 'You are, after all, utter perfection.'

'You can just call him Cris, you know.'

I smiled sweetly at her. 'I actually really enjoy saying the

185

full version, so you'll just have to indulge me.'

I was rooting for Cripsin. I was rooting for anyone that didn't live in my world. I think deep down, I knew that I would have to leave Millie some day, in one way or another, and when I did, I didn't want to leave her on her own.

'How's it going with good old Crispin anyway?' I had been spending so much time worrying about myself that I hadn't given her half enough opportunity to talk about herself – or let her gush about her love life.

Millie beamed at me. 'I'm pretty sure he's in love with me.'

'No way,' I said, stifling a squeal, the inner romantic in me alive and well. 'How do you know? What did he say? When did he say it? Start from the beginning. Leave nothing out.'

She glanced away, as if checking for possible eaves-droppers. There was a thirty-yard radius around us, care of my infamy. 'OK, so basically, the other night, we were watching *Ghost* at my house, you know that movie with Patrick Swayze and Demi Moore when they were both at peak hotness?'

'Of course.'

'So, we were on the couch and Cris had his arm around me and I was lying back against his chest, and we were watching that scene where they get all sultry with the clay while 'Unchained Melody' plays in the background, and I was saying how *Ghost* did for pottery what Benedict Cumberbatch did for Sherlock Holmes. Made it sexy, you know? Anyways, next thing I know, he's stroking my hair, right . . . and then . . . he kissed me on the head! Like he just leant down and kissed the top of my head.'

She was practically jumping up and down in her seat.

'Um . . . what?' I said.

She pointed to the crown of her head, where her parting split her long hair evenly. 'He kissed me here. On the head.'

'He kissed you the way a parent kisses a newborn baby? He kissed you . . . like, paternally?'

'Oh, Jesus, Sophie.'

'What? I don't understand! Your rants are always so vague. I feel like I need CliffsNotes.'

She placed her palms on her knees and drew in a deep breath. 'Have I never told you this theory of mine?'

'Oh, I love your theories,' I said, leaning back in my seat and getting comfortable. 'Please. Proceed.'

She smirked at me. 'I have long been convinced that when a boy kisses you on the head – not in a sexual way or a hint-hint-I-want-to-have-sex-now way – just tenderly, like in a way that comes naturally to him, almost like a reflex, it means he has crossed over the threshold of "like" or "lust" and has fallen in love with you. Sometimes they don't even *realize* it. It's like their body and their reactions understand it first and then their brain gets it a while later. But mark my words, it is *a sign*.'

I was trying my hardest not to smirk.

'A kiss for the sake of a kiss, and nothing else,' she said. 'I'm telling you, it's a sign.'

'Where did this theory come from?'

'My mum,' said Millie. 'About two months after she started seeing my dad, they were standing outside the cinema and it was freezing cold. He had his arms around her and she was hugging him back, trying to steal his body heat, and they were laughing about something in the movie they'd seen, and he just leant down and kissed her on the head, and she said that's when she knew.'

'Knew that she was in love with him?'

'No!' Millie scoffed. 'That *he* was in love with *her*. Have you *seen* my mum? She's way hotter than my dad. He had to play the personality game to get her. It was a longer process.'

'Uh-huh . . .' I said, coming around to the idea. I had never really experienced it, so I supposed I couldn't say for certain whether it was bull or not. Even though it did sound pretty suspect. I could, however, believe that a boy was madly in love with her. That part on its own was easy. 'So, Crispin loves you, then?'

She nodded, her hair curtaining either side of her face. 'I could just feel it.'

'Well, that's cool,' I said, grinning at her. 'And I'm not surprised, either.'

'He'll probably say it at the dance. I don't know what I'm going to say back yet.'

'Do you love him back?' I asked.

Millie shook her head. 'Nah, not yet.'

'You could pull a Han Solo, and say "I know" when he tells you.'

'Your nerdy sci-fi knowledge notwithstanding, Soph, that is actually not such a terrible idea.'

'Yes, it is!' I said, alarmed. 'Don't say "I know". That's so mean! I was kidding!'

'I'll think of something,' she assured me. '*Anyway*, returning to my earlier point. You don't need to worry about some poxy Falcone curfew barricading you in your princess tower. Cris and I will just come and get you tomorrow evening, and we'll all go together. You can have your Cinderella moment. I will make sure of it.'

'Thanks,' I said, in earnest. 'I think I'll make a rather dashing third wheel.'

'You'll be the sexiest third wheel in the history of Cedar Hill High. And if you're feeling uncomfortable, just say the word and we can ditch Cris, because as I've always said, Soph, you're my real true love.' She grabbed my hand and squeezed it. 'There's no love as real as that of a girl and her best friend.'

'Damn straight,' I agreed. 'I love you, Mil.'

She winked at me. 'I know.'

# CHAPTER TWENTY-TWO

## NORMALITY

When I stood in front of my mirror and saw myself in the royal-blue gown – my blonde hair framing my face in waves, my cheeks lightly rouged, my eyes made bigger and bluer with shadow and mascara – I started to cry. This girl I barely recognized. This girl my mother would have fawned over. This girl who looked elegant and happy.

This girl who wore a mask so convincing she almost fooled herself.

My reflection seemed so far away from who I had become. It wasn't me, this new image. Inside I was dark and broken. White-hot with rage. Weakened by grief. Inside, I was a black hole, waiting to devour any semblance of happiness.

This wasn't me, but for tonight, I desperately wanted it to be. And the realization, when it came, was like a punch in the gut. So I cried, just a little, and then I cried a lot. I sank to the floor, pulled my knees into my chest, buried my face in my mother's sweater, and wept.

God, how I missed her. I missed who she was, and who she made me believe I could be. I missed the way she made me feel. I missed the world I used to know, and all the wonderful people in it. I missed the possibility of a different life.

*Be strong. Be brave.*

When I stood back up, reapplied my make-up and fixed my dress, I realized that for the first time in a long time, I looked like her. I didn't look like my father. I didn't look like a Marino. I looked like Celine Durant, my mother. Not a Marino. Not a Falcone.

Tonight, at the Masquerade Ball, I would wear two masks. The gold-embroidered one from Millie, and this painted smile that spoke of another life.

Millie texted me just after sundown to let me know her and Cris were almost at *Evelina*. I didn't know who was downstairs so I decided it would be safest to meet them at the end of Felice's driveway, far away from any prying eyes.

I gave myself a final once-over in the mirror. The dress fitted like a glove, hugging me in at the waist and parting in gentle ruffles towards the floor. I had redone my make-up – this time with waterproof mascara – but the urge to cry had passed, and in that moment, I felt strong. Excited. I unearthed my mother's favourite sapphire necklace and earrings and put them on.

I grabbed my bag and my mask, and sneaked downstairs, treading as softly as I could so my heels on the marble floors wouldn't give me away. I kept my breath bound up in my chest as shivers of anxiety coursed through me.

In the foyer, I ran into Gino. He was crawling along the floor on his hands and knees and squinting at the tiles. I probably could have stepped right over him, but I figured I wouldn't take the chance.

I bent over him. 'What are you doing?'

He snapped his head up, and his face broke into a grin. 'Sophie!' he said. 'Wow. Nice dress. You look like a young Brigitte Bardot.'

'I—what?'

He sat up on his hunkers, disregarding his search. 'She's a French actress from back in the day. I like her movies.'

'Um, OK. Cool. Thanks?'

'You're welcome,' he said, still beaming.

*Ah, Gino.*

I gestured at the floor. 'Everything OK?'

'I lost my earring,' he said, tugging at his ear and frowning.

'Oh.' I didn't add that that was probably an improvement. 'Do you want me to help you look for it?'

'That's OK.' He paused, and looked up at me again. 'Do you want me to help you sneak out?'

I smiled sheepishly. 'That's OK. I think I can take it from here.'

'Where are you going, anyhow?'

'To a dance.' I waved the mask in my hand. 'A masquerade dance.'

Gino sighed, and his eyes glazed just a little. 'I love dancing,' he said. 'But no one ever seems to make time for it. Not since Evelina left.'

I almost would have taken him with me, if it wasn't for his

position as a complete and totally unsubtle loose cannon. 'I better go,' I hedged.

He had already resumed his search.

I unlatched the front door and slipped outside. The sky was a myriad of pink and orange brushstrokes, growing dark at the edges. It would be a clear night, and a smooth getaway. The sense of possibility, of *before*, carried on the soft wind, and I embraced it.

The lanterns around the driveway were already lit up. I walked slowly, concentrating on the determined crunch of gravel beneath my feet. I passed the one and only SUV in the driveway and reached the edge of the circular parking area, and then, I don't know quite why, but I stopped walking. I stalled, and I knew, without knowing how, that there was someone behind me, watching me. I could *feel* it in the hairs on the back of my neck.

I didn't dare turn around. I kept going, determined to have one last night of normality before it all went to hell. One last night of the old Sophie, before the underworld swallowed me up for good.

It would be enough.

# CHAPTER TWENTY-THREE

## MASQUERADE

For a place that usually smelt of old sneakers and looked like something the 1940s threw up, the school gym was really working it tonight. All the walls had been covered in thick black drapes inlaid with crystalline stars. They even lit up and twinkled. Crêpe paper snowflakes hung from the ceiling around a giant disco ball that cast swirling silver streaks all around the room. The ground was covered in faux snow sprinkled over a white roll-out dance floor, and the tables were adorned with shining silver tablecloths.

Most of the girls were wearing floor-length gowns of black and silver and gold. Their masks were intricate and elaborate – some on ornamental handles, others fastened around their heads with a band. The guys were well turned out in tuxes, although some had opted for Converse instead of dress shoes. One girl was wearing a fitted tuxedo with tails at the end. Her shoes were black and white, and shiny, and she was carrying an actual cane with her, as if she was about to break into an elaborate tap-dancing routine at any moment. She had a dark pixie cut that stuck up around the edges of her white mask. I couldn't see beyond the upturned nose and dark purple lips to fully recognize her, but I was definitely impressed by the eccentricity.

It was pleasant to not have to look anyone in the eye and see their judgement or fear staring back at me. The anonymity was freeing, and with my mask tied snugly around my head with a ribbon, and the upper half of my face covered, I sank into the music and the mingling, and felt a sense of freedom I hadn't experienced in a while.

'It's perfect!' I told Millie, who was swigging from Crispin's concealed hip flask by the punch table. He was standing behind her, a protective hand on her waist, and she was leaning into him, swaying in time with the music. Being a third wheel wasn't really that excruciating as it turned out. I was just happy to be out of *Evelina*. I was happy to be any kind of wheel at all.

'I know, right!' She beamed at me. 'Everyone is in such a good mood.'

'Of course it's perfect,' Crispin chimed in. He was talking to me but staring at Millie. He did that a lot. It was cute, if a little vomitous, but hey, who was I to judge? 'It's perfect because Millie is perfect.'

Millie giggled. 'Thanks, babe!' She gave me a look that seemed to say *I-told-you-he-was-in-love-with-me*. I took a swig from the hip flask and winked at her.

Watching the two of them together, I now understood exactly what she had meant on the bleachers yesterday. Cris was *so* in love with her. There was no doubt about it. And she was in love with love, and I felt a huge burst of happiness for her, because of all the people in my life now, she deserved that joy the most. I couldn't give that to her any more – not for more than one night – but Cris could. He was all-in. And Millie deserved someone who could go all-in for her.

'I'm going to run to the bathroom,' I told them. 'I'll be back in a minute.'

'Do you want me to come with you?' Millie had already started to disentangle herself from Cris.

'No, no, I'll be fine. There are loads of people in there already.' I waved her back into her suitor's arms and slipped across the dance floor until the throngs of people started to thin out and I could relax a little. I didn't really need to go to the bathroom, but I wanted to give Millie the space to make out with her boyfriend for a while. I didn't need to witness that, and I could tell she was dying to kiss him. He *was* pretty hot, in that blond, all-American track-and-field-star kind of way. Abercrombie attractive. I guessed I only had eyes for nebulous assassins these days.

The song changed, and I almost squealed with delight. It was 'Africa' by Toto, old but epic. I thought about dancing on my own, then I thought about my dignity and if the rest of it was worth salvaging. I was half considering actually asking someone to dance – I had been getting a lot of appreciative looks, and since the mask hid my identity – more or less – what was the harm in a simple moment of escapism? Wasn't that the point of tonight?

I hesitated, scanning the crowds. Who was I going to ask? My nerves kicked into gear. I couldn't. Could I? But I loved this song. And the girl with the cane was dancing quite close . . . Maybe I could dance with her, though I imagined it would severely lower the air of coolness around her. Or at least sidle over and ask her where she had gotten her lipstick, because now I was near enough to see the glitter on top of the dark purple sheen.

Someone tapped me on my shoulder, and I turned around so fast, my dress swished like a move from an overly-expensive, random-actress-led Dior perfume ad.

My gasp was so intense it turned into a coughing fit, and all the grace that had emanated from my original twirl evaporated.

'*Luca?*' It took everything in my power not to press my hand into his face to check if he was real.

Luca Falcone was standing in front of me in the most pristine black suit I had ever seen. He was wearing a black silk shirt and tie, buttoned up to his neck. His hair was swept backwards and lightly gelled, and the mask he wore was thin – just a swathe of black to cover his eyes, but nothing could disguise that mesmerizing sapphire blue.

He was smirking at me. 'Hi.'

I really wanted to go for a demure, perhaps even sultry, *Hello*, but what came out was a heaving, 'What-the-hell-are-you-doing-here?'

His smirk didn't falter. 'Your own independence and self-sufficiency notwithstanding, I thought that maybe you might be open to having a chaperone tonight . . .'

'Do you mean romantically or for security?' I asked.

'Which would you prefer?'

'Which are you offering?'

The smile sloped to one side. 'Whichever one makes you happier.'

'Am I hallucinating?'

'I'm the one at a high school dance,' he pointed out. 'Maybe I'm hallucinating.'

A memory trickled into my awareness. 'It was you earlier in the driveway, wasn't it? You saw me and you let me go.'

He nodded.

'I thought you'd stop me.'

'So did I,' he admitted. 'But then I saw you sneaking out, in that dress.' His eyes travelled the length of me, slow and incredibly unsubtle. 'And I couldn't do it.'

'Thank you,' I said, my voice barely more than a whisper. I didn't have to say the rest: *I needed this. I needed this for my sanity.* He already knew.

'You look beautiful,' he said.

'I—what?'

His smile grew. It was unfairly ravishing, considering I was the one in the gown. 'Did I stutter?'

'It is a beautiful dress,' I said decidedly. 'I kind of had a moment with myself earlier when I was looking in the mirror.'

Luca stopped smiling. 'It's not the dress.' He dropped his voice, and came a couple of inches closer. 'I think you're beautiful when you wear oversized hoodies and fleece pyjamas with teddy bears on them. Or when you wear thick socks and use them to slide around on the marble floors when you think no one's looking at you.'

'I – Oh. You know about that.'

198

'And I think you are especially beautiful when you are giving out to me.'

'In that case, you must find me constantly compelling.'

His laugh was breathy. 'Come on, Cinderella.' He took my hand in his and led me on to the dance floor, and before I could process the strangeness of everything, he was twirling me into him and we were dancing together. And he was good. Damn. He was *really* good. He knew all the words, too, and he was singing along, his voice lilting and strong, and then I was singing too, way out of tune and much too excitedly. We pealed into a fit of laughter, his amusement ringing in my ears, my smile so big it could have broken my face, because we were both cheating just for one night – we were both wearing masks belonging to other people, and it was exhilarating.

The song changed to a slow number, and instead of shying away, he pulled me closer and put his arms around my waist. I wound mine around his neck and laid my head on his chest until I could feel his heartbeat against my cheek.

He dipped his head, his mouth next to my ear. 'Let's just escape. For tonight.'

I nodded against him. My eyes were closed. I was inhaling his scent and feeling it wrap around my heart. God, I had it bad for this guy. But I wasn't going to think about tomorrow, or what would happen when the game of make-believe ended. 'Just for tonight,' I murmured, resting my head against his chest, relaxing into the feeling of his hands around me.

# CHAPTER TWENTY-FOUR
## TWIST

'Well, if this isn't the most welcome plot twist . . .'

Luca and I turned around to find Millie and Cris beaming at us with matching smiles. Luca left his hand on my back, his fingers lightly trailing my waist.

'Hello, Millie,' said Luca, courteously. He didn't care one iota that she had caught us dancing together, or even that she had caught him at a high school dance.

'Hiii,' I greeted her. 'Sorry, I meant to come back to find you, but I got waylaid . . .'

Millie nodded, her eyebrows still halfway towards her hairline. 'Yeah. I can see that. Luca, to what do we owe the grand gesture?'

He laughed, and I was struck by how different we both were in this environment, how light I felt inside. 'I suppose I—'

'I'm just kidding,' said Millie, her own laughter soaring to match his. 'I know it's because you're secretly in love with my best friend but you're too proud to admit it so you prefer to nag her instead because it's the only way you can show her you care without freaking her out or encroaching on your brother who would flip out if he knew and probably try and stab you because for some ludicrous reason he still thinks they might get back together, and don't worry I won't make you admit that I'm right either so we'll just breeze on past this . . . anyhoo, this is Cris . . .' She shoved Cris in front of her. 'Cris, this is Luca. Be *really* nice to him.'

I tried not to feel the fresh heat of mortification eating me alive as I endeavoured to communicate my sudden, murderous thoughts to her. *I'm going to kill you the next time we're alone.*

Luca didn't even bat an eyelid. He took Cris's hand and shook it, reintroducing himself, as pleasant as I had ever seen him. Cris returned it, wincing just a little, and I noticed with a grim flair of amusement that Luca had crushed his fingers together, just a little, in that handshake. As polite a warning as any, I supposed, but I knew he could tell Cris was harmless.

'So, this is nice,' Millie said, taking the reins again. 'Weird . . .' she said, eyeing me, '. . . but nice.'

Luca's grip on my waist got a little tighter. He shifted, pulling me with him.

'What?' I said, turning to look up at him.

'Don't move,' he said, low and through the side of his mouth.

'Why are you backing away from us all of a sudden?' Millie

asked. 'What's going on?' She sniffed the air around Cris, her face scrunching with confusion. 'I don't get it.'

Luca, who had gone completely rigid beside me, was on high alert. I tried to follow the direction of his eyeline but I couldn't see around Cris's broad shoulders.

'Nothing,' I said, answering Millie way too late.

'What are you doing?' I hissed at Luca.

'They're here,' he said, drawing himself to his full height. His other hand flew to his waistband, checking for his gun.

Millie was still talking to us, but I was tuning her out, my whole body trained on where Luca was looking. At a throng of people who all looked the same, who all wore the same stupid masks and the same stupid Converse shoes.

*Stupid masks.*

'Soph?' Millie was clicking her fingers in front of my face. 'What the hell are you staring at? You're starting to freak me out.'

'I think it's Zola,' Luca said under his breath. 'And if it is, she won't be on her own.'

Zola. *Zola.*

*Oh, crap.*

Zola was the sister of Sara and Libero Marino, recently released from prison, and if Zola Marino was somewhere inside this gym, someone was about to die.

And that someone was probably me.

'There's no way,' I said, not bothering to keep my voice low, and fully aware that Millie was reading every single word out of my mouth to try and figure out why Luca and I had gone so cold all of a sudden. 'Zola's not here. She couldn't be here. Not in a *high school*.'

Luca untangled himself from me and I grabbed him by the back of his jacket before he could disappear into the crowd. 'Are you crazy?' I snapped. 'Where the hell are you going?'

He reeled around. 'Don't move from here, OK?' He turned to Millie and Cris. 'No one move from here until I come back.'

'Huh?' Cris said. 'What are you talking about, man?'

Luca turned to Millie. 'Stay on the dance floor,' he told her. 'I'm serious, Millie. Keep her close to you.'

'What's going on? Is . . . is it Donata? Are we in danger?' Millie was starting to panic – she was starting to get it.

Cris was still totally confused.

Luca slid between Cris and Millie. I lunged after him, but Millie pushed me backwards.

'Stop,' I said, trying to see where he was going. Straight for the girl with the cane and the cropped pixie cut! Straight for the girl who had been loitering around the dance floor all night – looking for me. Zola Marino – tall and wiry with bright purple lips and wide, dark eyes. And Luca was marching right towards her.

Millie grabbed me by the arm. 'He said wait here.'

I shook her off. 'Mil, you don't understand.'

'Yes, I do,' she said, her grip growing harder. 'I understand perfectly.'

The sound of a gunshot stole my response.

'Holy shit.' Cris grabbed Millie and yanked her across the dance floor, away from the sound. I tugged free of her grip and slunk into the pandemonium. Everyone was screaming and fleeing towards the exits. Millie shoved against Cris, reaching out for me. I pushed her back towards him, pulling further away from the waves of people clamouring around me.

'Sophie!' she screamed. 'Sophie, get back here! Come on!'

I tried to trace the noise of the gunshot, the sound still reverberating in my eardrums. Everyone was surging towards the exits, and there were no casualties in the gym – no one wounded or screaming, no one on the floor, no blood . . . and then . . . another shot!

Millie's screams followed me across the dance floor, but Cris was hauling her away. I was running entirely on adrenalin as every thought in my head pounded out Luca's name. Even though I knew he would never discharge his weapon in such a public place, I refused to entertain the possibility that those gunshots had harmed him.

I was almost across the dance floor when Donata Marino stalked into my path and slammed her fist into my face. A girl beside me screamed, pushing by us towards the exit, as Donata wound her fingers into my dress and pulled me to her. Her perfume rolled over me as I blinked the stars away, tried to keep my head upright. Donata brought her masked face just an inch from my own, her kohl-rimmed eyes flashing as she loomed over me and dug the barrel of her gun into my ribs. She walked me backwards, into the crowds, her long black dress trailing behind her, her blood-red lips twisting in disgust.

'You think you can kill my son and get away with it?' she hissed, her yellowed teeth on show. 'You think I won't gut you slowly and painfully for what you took from me?'

I heaved a breath, tried to pull my stomach in, away from her gun, but she pushed harder, scraped her fingers across my neck, her long, pointed nails, drawing blood.

'I'm going to show you what the Marino family does to

turncoats,' she snarled. 'I'm going to tear you limb from limb, make you scream all night.'

I gasped a breath, turned to stone by the feeling of her gun pressing into me, the very real possibility that she would kill me if I moved against her, even an inch.

Jack appeared, then, shoving his way through the chaos, pushing a girl so hard she fell over.

He was wearing a suit too, a full mask of glittering gold, but I'd recognize those eyes anywhere, one of them irreparably scarred, that lumbering lope. When he reached us, he pulled me away from Donata.

'Not here,' he snapped at her over my head. 'There's too many witnesses.'

He wouldn't even look at me.

'Jack,' I wheezed.

'Shut your mouth.' He grabbed me by the throat, yanked me out of Donata's grip and into his own.

'Take her out, then!' Donata moved in front of us to clear a path, her arms outstretched on either side of her. 'Let's go!'

Jack spun me around and twisted my arms behind my back. He marched me towards the exit, just as another gunshot rang out behind us and my heart ratcheted up my throat.

Donata glanced over her shoulder, her thick black brows pulling together. 'Zola.'

'She'll have to follow us,' Jack shot back. 'There's no time.'

I tried to wriggle free, tried to scream, but everyone around me was screaming and running. Hundreds of students losing their shit at the exact same time. It was the perfect distraction. Jack twisted my arm harder, and a flash of agony made my knees go weak. I cursed at him, and Donata

205

turned around and punched me in the side of my cheek. I spat in her face.

She recoiled, let her temper fly again, but this time I ducked, and her fist caught Jack on the chin. He loosened his grip for a split second, and I slammed the heel of my shoe into his foot and then dropped to the ground. The crowds surged around us, and he tripped, his foot catching on my ankle as I slid away from him. Everyone was still clamouring for the exit, and we were in a funnel of people now. I crawled through them, putting as many bodies between us as possible as shouts of 'Police! Police!' rang out.

I looked back only once, and caught the panic in Donata's expression, the wisps of dark hair coming loose around her face, as Jack grabbed her and pulled her towards the door. She was almost outside, disappearing into the pandemonium, when she pulled her gun and fired a shot in my direction. I slammed my body flat against the ground and watched the bullet lodge less than a yard from my face, nearly catching a girl in the ankle. She shrieked as I clambered past her.

Another distant gunshot blasted through my train of thought. I rolled to my feet and followed it, leaving Jack and Donata behind me, caught in swirls of panicked teenagers herding them towards the police. I knew they couldn't risk getting caught. Well, Jack wouldn't. Donata was so crazed with grief, she probably would have come back and shot me right in the middle of the gym if he hadn't dragged her away.

Another gunshot, and one thought pounded out all the others as I slipped through the double doors at the far end of the dance floor, and into the bowels of the school: *Luca.*

Here, there was only darkness. Darkness, and shouting, and hurried footsteps echoing down endless corridors filled with lockers.

'Give it up, Falcone!' Zola Marino's voice was higher than I expected, her words marked with a strange cadence that reminded me of her sister, Sara. 'Surrender and I'll let you die quickly!'

I slipped my shoes off and kept to the side of the corridor, inching along the lockers and following Zola's taunts. If she was scared, I couldn't detect it.

'Why don't you save me the trouble and just shoot yourself, Zola?' Luca's response was deadly calm. He wasn't injured, despite all the shooting. Relief rippled through me, but it was short-lived.

Another gunshot rang out.

'Come out, come out, wherever you are!' Zola cooed. The shot had shattered the CCTV camera just around the corner from me. It fell in shards just yards from my feet. I was close. 'You look so shiny in your tux, Gianluca. My mother would love to brand her black hand on it. Right after she's done with your little plaything, of course. She's probably cutting her fingers off right now.'

'You're a bad liar, Zola! Always were!' Luca's laughter echoed down the corridor, but it was strained and forced.

Zola was getting angrier, her composure slipping. 'You won't be laughing when I put a bullet in your head! I know you're cornered down there.'

Zola was right. I could tell she was closer to me. Luca was at the other end of the hallway – a dead end, and there was only so many rows of lockers that could protect him. He couldn't come out. Not before the police or Zola closed in on him. The only options were to crouch and hide, or to try and shoot his way through.

'Nothing else to say?' Zola goaded. 'Are you worried about your jewel? My mother won't be quick with her. She wants to bring her home, take her time.' Another gunshot. Zola cursed. 'My *fucking* foot.'

I edged closer, heels in hand as I peeked around the corner. Zola was limping down the corridor, half of her dipping towards the floor, her suit jacket hanging off one shoulder. She was moving away from me, leaving a track of blood behind her. She was shooting indiscriminately at where Luca was hiding.

Luca rolled out of the space between the last locker and the wall, and they shot at each other at the same time. Luca cursed, tried to shoot again, but the click echoed down the hallway. There were no more bullets in his gun. Zola fell to the side, reloading in a blur, and when she raised her gun at Luca, I knew it would be the last thing Luca ever saw. I started running, my arm pulled back, and fired my stiletto through the air, straight into the side of Zola Marino's skull. She warped sideways, flinching, and the shot meant for Luca careened into the wall.

I slammed the other heel into the side of Zola's head, kicking out the backs of her knees at the same time. She whirled on me, blocking my view of Luca. We tumbled to the ground together, Zola's gun pulsing jet black in my periphery, her fingers grappling for my throat.

Just as the distant sound of sirens cut across the deserted hallway, she grabbed me by the neck and rolled on top of me.

She bared her teeth, her tongue peeking out between them. I pushed my fingers into her eyes, grabbing my shoe with the other hand. The glitter on her lips helped me focus on my target.

'Here's your jewel,' I yelled, slamming my shoe into her face and hearing the bones in her nose crushing underneath it.

She lurched to the side, her gun held high, and then the sharp sound of a gunshot slammed into my eardrums, and for a split second I felt searing hot all over.

I keeled over, clutching at the pain lancing through my body, trying to find the source, trying to focus my thoughts.

My shoulder was on fire.

Luca yanked Zola backwards and pistol-whipped her in the side of the head. Her next shot lodged in the ceiling. Luca wrestled the gun from her and threw it sidelong towards the other end of the hallway. It clanged off a locker and skittered from my view.

Zola groaned, and Luca hit her again, the crushing sound of metal on bone reverberating around us. She slumped over, unconscious.

The blood was pooling from my left shoulder, leaving a river of warmth all the way down my arm. 'Luca,' I said, hearing the fear colour my voice. 'She shot me. I've been shot.'

'*Cazzo!*' He hunkered down and traced his finger around the wound, pulling my arm towards him. I cried out and he flinched. 'Sorry,' he murmured, examining it in the darkness. He shuttered his expression. I could almost pinpoint the moment he slipped back into commander mode, and for once I was glad of it. If we were going to get out of here unscathed, one of us had to have our wits about us.

'There's no bullet inside the skin.'

'It hurts.' I gasped a shallow breath. 'Why does it hurt so much?'

'A graze,' he said, his eyes tracking the streams of blood on my arm. 'A bad one. I'm taking you to the hospital.'

'No!' I hissed, struggling to right myself. 'I'm not going anywhere near a hospital.'

He pulled me up on to my feet using my good arm, holding me steady at the waist. 'Can you walk?' he asked, urgency flashing across his face. The sirens were piercingly loud now. 'Do you think you can walk out?'

The pain was bad, and it was only made worse by the realization that I had been *shot*. 'Yes,' I heaved. 'I can walk.'

*Ignore the pain. Use it as fuel.*

He stowed the guns on top of the lockers, grabbed my shoes, and left Zola Marino in a bloody, unconscious heap behind us.

We hurried through the corridors, weaving our way back towards the gym. I was lagging behind, but he pulled me with him.

'The blood,' I said, watching the red track across the side of my dress. The cuts Donata had left on my neck were adding to the crimson rivers on my skin. 'They'll see. They'll know.'

Luca was already shrugging off his suit jacket. He draped it around me, and then pulled me against him.

'I'm going to staunch the wound.' As he said it, the hand that had been draped around me squeezed against the bullet wound in my shoulder, pressing so hard I slumped against him.

'Urrgh,' I warbled.

'Sorry,' he said, straining. 'Just try and grit through it, Soph.'

I examined myself for any more tell-tale signs of blood, trying not to focus on the mild torture coursing through my body. Luca's suit jacket was so big it dwarfed me. It dwarfed all evidence of our scuffle.

We made our way across the now-empty dance floor. He dropped my shoes among the other stilettos that had been discarded during the chaos. There was no way I could teeter convincingly in them now.

I groaned.

'I'll get you a new pair,' he said.

'Not that,' I hissed. 'The pain. Your grip. It's so tight.'

'It'll stop the bleeding,' he said. 'We're about to walk into a huge amount of cops. Just follow my lead, OK?'

'Jack – Donata,' I tried to explain. 'They're here.'

'They'll be long gone,' he said, but there was no confidence in his voice, no confidence in the way he was scanning the gym.

I wound my good arm around his back, pressed my head against his shoulder and tried not to flinch from the pressure coming from his other hand. We stumbled through the front doors, joining the last dregs of students crying and shouting, and then I channelled every element of hysteria inside me and started screaming too.

# CHAPTER TWENTY-FIVE
## RED AND BLUE

Everything was red and blue. A line of heavily armed policeman surrounded the exit. We stumbled forward, and I slipped into the role of terrified-innocent-teenager more easily than I had hoped possible. I was crying so loudly my voice was resonating with the sirens' pitch. Luca held my head against him and whispered fake nothings into my hair. His fingers pressing tighter and tighter against the wound, the nausea curling in my stomach.

Over my head, I heard him speaking to the policemen. 'She's in shock. She was in the bathroom when it started. I had to drag her out of the stall.'

I pressed my face into his jacket, and wailed some more.

The cops were asking Luca questions about the shooter. He was batting them away expertly. 'I don't know. I was with my girlfriend the whole time. She had a panic attack. Can I take her home?'

I sniffed again. My face had grown deathly pale.

Seeming satisfied and somewhat distracted by our display, the cops ushered us behind them, out of the way, and we joined a huddle of students being herded back from the entrance.

I turned my face to Luca, blinking him into focus.

He was already looking at me, a frown rippling across that smooth composure. 'How is it now?' he asked. 'I'll ease up the pressure.'

'I need to lie down.'

He pulled me tighter against him, so I was half leaning, half standing. 'I'm taking you to the hospital. Vita will have a look at you there.'

'No,' I groaned, my head lolling against him. 'Please, no hospitals.'

'I'm not taking any chances, Soph.'

'No outsiders.'

'Vita is Paulie's wife. She's a doctor.'

'No hospitals,' I laboured. 'Can't you bring Vita to us? If the Marinos came to a school, I doubt they'll have any moral hesitancies about barging into a hospital. You didn't see Donata. She's baying for blood. She's a loose cannon now.' I nearly flopped over from the effort of those few sentences.

Luca seemed to be considering it, because instead of arguing back, he went silent. He knew I was right. It was too dangerous, and my condition wasn't serious enough to warrant the risk.

'I'll figure something out,' he said at last, the words filtered through a sigh.

We hobbled further away from the crowds, but not far enough to stop Millie spotting us and making a beeline for us. Cris struggled to stay arm in arm with her; only Millie could sprint like that in heels.

'Sophie!' She tried to grab me by my arm.

'Don't!' Luca pulled me backwards. 'Don't touch her.'

Millie dropped her hand as if I had burnt her. She narrowed her eyes at Luca, then at me. They widened, just a fraction, taking in my appearance. 'What. The. Actual. Bloody. Hell. Is. Going. On?'

'I don't know,' I said quickly. My eyes were telling a different story. *Don't talk about this in front of Cris.* 'It all happened so fast. I think the shooter's still in there.'

Millie was having a hard time piecing everything together. I was deathly pale and hanging by a thread. Every passing second, I was leaning more on Luca and less on my own two feet. I had to get the wound seen to. I had to lie down. I turned to look up at him, and as quietly as I could, I told him, 'I think I'm going to pass out.'

'We have to go,' he told Millie shortly. 'Immediately.'

Millie clocked what was happening – well, maybe not the whole thing, but she could see the strength draining out of me and the urgency creeping into Luca's voice.

'To *Evelina*?' she asked him.

'What's *Evelina*?' said Cris.

'Yes,' Luca said to Millie.

'Are you OK, Sophie?' Cris said, watching me now too. 'You don't look so good.'

'I got a fright,' I said, trying to force my head up straight. 'I had a panic attack in the bathroom.'

Cris wasn't buying it exactly, but he was a million miles off the truth and I could tell he was more concerned about Millie than me. Luca started to wheel us off in the direction of his car. 'We'll catch up with you later, Millie,' he said, a note of warning in his voice. 'You and Cris should head home.'

Millie was watching us closely, whatever she wanted to say clamped down on her tongue. It wasn't the right time. 'I'll come with you guys. Cris, babe—' She turned around to her boyfriend, fluttered her lashes and made her voice go all gooey. 'I'm going to go back with Sophie and make sure she's OK. I'll call you in a little while.'

'Millie, I don't think—' Luca began.

'Let her come,' I hissed. 'She knows.'

'She's a liability,' Luca muttered.

I pinched him in the arm. 'She's my best friend, and trust me, she's not going to let this go.'

Cris slid his arm around Millie. 'I'll just go with you,' he said, still half perplexed.

'I'll call you soon,' Millie said more firmly. She wriggled out from under his arm. 'Soph's having a hard time and I need to be there for her.'

I elongated my face and did the most unattractive grimace I could muster up. 'I'm so scared, Cris,' I said. 'I feel like I might break down any second.'

'What about him?' Cris pointed at Luca, but was still looking at Millie. 'He's with her.'

'I don't care,' said Millie brusquely. 'In times like this, a girl needs her best friend. I'll call you later. I promise.' She gave him a quick kiss on the lips and then turned on her heel. She took my other arm, and Luca steered us, arm in arm, to his SUV.

Millie dropped her voice. 'Has she been shot?'

'Yes,' Luca said. 'Just a little.'

'Just *a little*?!' Millie released an impressive string of curses. 'You have a lot of explaining to do, Falcone.'

'I told her not to follow me.'

'Shut up!' I snapped. 'Of course I was going to follow you.'

Luca shook his head. 'You are so frustrating.'

'Are we going to the hospital?' Millie interrupted.

'No,' I said. 'It didn't go into my shoulder.'

'I'm getting her help,' Luca said.

'You'd better be,' Millie snapped.

We climbed into the SUV. Luca hopped in the front and started the engine.

'How are you feeling?' Millie asked me.

'A little bit like death,' I said weakly.

'Don't even joke about that, Soph. And please tell me I did not see Donata and your uncle speeding away from the school a few minutes ago?'

'About that . . .'

'Oh, Jesus.'

'Sorry,' I murmured. The pain was starting to subside, but the heat was still raging through my arm.

Millie frowned at me. 'When we get to *Evelina*, you're telling me everything.'

'Mil, I—'

'No,' she snapped, cutting me off. 'I don't know what went down tonight but I know you are in a whole lot more danger than you've been letting on, so if you want me to be your

216

friend, then you're going to have to let me in. No ifs, no buts.'

Luca was watching us in the rear-view mirror. 'Sophie's taken a vow,' Luca reminded her. 'She can't tell you anything.'

'Excuse you?' Millie scooted forward, her head jutting between the front seats. 'Luca Falcone, you can shove that vow right up your—'

'Millie!' I interrupted, yanking her back. 'It's all right. I'll tell you.'

Millie folded her arms, her narrowed gaze on the back of Luca's head. 'You come to *my* dance and endanger *my* best friend by going off shooting your gun at random people and then you expect me to wave you off without so much as a single question as to what the hell went on. Meanwhile, my best friend is suffering from a *gunshot wound* – and let me tell you something, pretty boy, if I find out it was you who shot her, I will yank every perfect hair out of your head one by one and then slam my fist into your face. I swear to God, you'd better hope the explanation for this shitstorm is water-tight, because it will be your funeral if—'

'*I* didn't shoot her,' Luca cut in. 'Don't insult me.'

'Do you want a medal?' she retorted. 'Because the way I see it, you were the last person with her, and now she's all shot up.'

'I told you to stay put.'

'I'm in charge of my own actions,' I interjected. 'So how about you stop blaming each other?'

'OK,' said Luca. 'Shall I blame you, then?'

'For not staying behind while you went charging to your death?' I supplied.

'Stop hate-flirting, you two,' Millie interrupted. 'Who was it?

Who the hell shot her? Was it Donata? Was it *Jack*? Who do I have to maim now?'

I almost laughed. No fight skills or guns or training, and Millie was perpetually undaunted in the midst of all these assassins.

'Zola Marino,' Luca replied. 'Donata's daughter. I shouldn't have gone after her. She's a loose cannon. I was afraid of what she'd do to get your attention, Sophie, to pull you away from the crowds. I was afraid who else she might hurt in her attempt to flush you out. I was trying to neutralize her.' He stopped to bite off a curse. 'I should have looked for Donata first. For your uncle. I made the wrong call.'

'Wait, you went after Sara's sister?' Millie asked. 'What the hell was *she* doing at our dance? Does she go to Cedar Hill High?' She paused, then sucked in a gasp. 'Wait, is she dead now? Did you kill her?'

Luca and I exchanged a look in the mirror. God. Where to begin? Millie didn't even know about our involvement with Libero. She didn't know about the blood war. She didn't know about what I was planning. She didn't know about anything.

Luca was having the same thought. He scrubbed his hand across his forehead, a heavy sigh filling up the lingering silence.

Millie sat back, her face turned towards the roof of the car. 'OK,' she said calmly. 'The way I see it, you both have two choices. You can sit here covered in your lies and your silence and keep exchanging furtive glances right in front of me and thinking that I don't notice, or one of you can open your mouth and start talking.'

'I'm inclined to go for number one,' Luca said.

Millie blew a laugh at him. 'That was a fake option, Luca. If I have to track down every Marino in Chicago to find out what the hell went down tonight, then I will. You think Sophie is stubborn? Well, let me introduce you to Sophie 2.0.'

A laugh trickled out of me. 'It's a very long story, Mil.'

'Well, then,' she said confidently, 'lucky for you we have a *long* drive.'

# PART III

'Whatever is done for love always
occurs beyond good and evil.'

Friedrich Nietzsche

# CHAPTER TWENTY-SIX

## GENOVESE

**B**ack at *Evelina*, it wasn't Vita who tended to me, but Elena. She breezed into my bedroom dressed in a floor-length dressing gown, her dark hair hanging loose around her shoulders. She looked younger without her usual make-up.

'You're back,' she said, way more casually than I was expecting. She had a small case with her; she laid it on the bed between us and gestured at Luca's suit jacket, indicating with a flick of the wrist that I should take it off. 'Can I see the wound, please?' There was a note of tenderness in her voice, in place of her usual mistrust.

I shrugged the jacket off, watching as her eyes went wide. She sucked in a gasp. 'It's a little worse than I was expecting.' She took my hand in hers, pulled gently, so she could get a better look at my shoulder. There were pools of dried blood around the wound, the skin gaping open where the bullet had grazed the skin. I had to look away before I got sick.

'OK,' she said, calmly, opening the case. 'I'm going to have to stitch it closed.'

'What?' I gaped at her. 'Shouldn't we get a doctor or something to do that?'

I don't know why I was expecting her to pull out some run-of-the-mill fabric thread and a rusty old needle, but I was. She removed surgical thread and a sterilized needle instead, a frown pursing her lips as she looked at me. 'I am a mother of five active assassins, the wife of one deceased Mafia boss and the daughter of another. I am also a trained nurse. You don't have to look so horrified, Sophie.'

*Sophie.* My name. The preferred version too. Something fluttered inside me. It felt a little bit like relief.

I closed my jaw back up. 'Sorry,' I said. 'I just thought—'

'That I was going to hurt you?' she said. 'Of course not.' She applied some ointment to the area around the wound. I tried not to flinch, and failed. 'I don't usually numb first, but since this is your first gunshot wound . . .'

'Jesus,' I muttered.

Elena surprised me by laughing. 'The first prick will be the hardest, and then it will be quick. I promise.' She tapped a finger against my skin to see if the numbing cream had set in yet. 'Feel that?'

I nodded, and she pulled back, waiting.

'I didn't know you used to be a nurse,' I said.

'Yes. I trained a long time ago – before I had all these boys running around after me, dragging at my skirts, demanding five meals a day. Once they came along, I found being a mother to them was a full-time job.'

'I can imagine.'

'I enjoy it, you know,' she said, flicking a glance at me, waiting for a reaction. 'Tending to people. That might surprise you.'

Maybe it would have once, but not any more. Not after I'd seen her around her sons, the love she showed them, even when she was snapping at Dom about leaving dirty plates in the sink or giving out to Gino about his messy hair. You could feel it.

'It doesn't surprise me, actually.' That brought a fleeting smile to Elena's face. 'What made you want to be a nurse?' I don't know why I asked, but my shoulder was starting to go numb and I knew the needle would be coming next and I wanted to take my mind off it. Besides, I wanted to know more about her.

'My mother was a nurse.' She pointed towards the wall, and I looked away, trying to ignore the needle as she threaded it in my periphery. 'She died when I was very young, but the care she showed my sister and me in our early childhood never left me. She was from Texas. As far from a mafiosa as you can imagine. She taught us to ride horses and make pecan pie when we were barely able to walk. She made the most magnificent turkey dinners at Christmastime, and the sweetest eggnog. And then one day, it all went away. She died in a botched hit on my father, and all of her goodness died with her.' Her smile was sad, her voice hollow when she said, 'When you grow up around torture and violence, it does something to you, Sophie. I wanted to end suffering, not

225

cause it. I wanted to be a solution, in whatever way I could. My mother was kind. I suppose I wanted to be like her.'

I barely felt the first prick. The cream had kicked in and Elena's movements were quick and steady now. Still, I shut my eyes. 'Did your dad approve?'

She let out a snort. 'My father rarely approved of anything I did. Where my mother was kind, he was cruel. He ruled the Genovese crime family with an iron fist, and that extended to Donata and me as well. I used to think he was the most impressive man I ever met. As I grew up, that changed. I came to fear how easily he could separate his emotions from his duty. Sometimes I wondered if he had emotions at all.'

The silence rose up between us, and I was conscious of how much she was offering me, how vulnerable she might have felt in that moment, so I said, 'I can understand that. Thinking you know someone, and learning that they're nothing like what you thought. It sucks. Especially when it's your dad.'

Elena nodded. 'We look at our parents through rose-coloured glasses. Part of growing up is taking them off. We come to understand them on a human level. It's not always a pleasant experience.'

'No,' I agreed. 'It's not.'

'My father didn't believe in silly things like affection or love. He liked order and deference. He wanted me to marry my second cousin to keep the Genovese bloodline strong.'

'Ew,' I said, before I could stop myself.

Elena's laugh was a passing tinkle. 'Yes. Exactly. You can imagine how angry the great Don Genovese was when I ran away with Angelo Falcone instead.'

226

I remembered what Donata had told me about the situation. *Do you know what he gifted to my sister on the night of their wedding? My father's death.*

'Angelo killed your father.' The words were out of my mouth before I could swallow them back. I winced, feeling the prick of the needle more keenly now.

'Yes, Angelo killed my father, but not before he made an attempt on *our* lives.' She sighed, and I could almost feel it in my bones. The sadness, the weariness. 'He didn't have a choice. For us, it was kill or be killed.'

I sucked in a breath. 'Your father really tried to murder you? Because you fell in love?'

'Because I fell in love with the wrong man and tied myself to the wrong family,' Elena explained. 'He would have preferred a dead daughter over a Falcone one. I think that's why he tried to do it on my wedding night. As a lesson to others in the Genovese family. As a warning. He wanted me to die in my wedding dress.'

I wondered if my father felt the same way about me. I hoped not – though with Jack, the sentiment was clear. He had been ready to haul me away with Donata tonight – to let her torture me for turning my back on the Marino family.

'When my father sent his *soldato* for me, I was in the shower, about to get ready for bed with my new husband.' I felt her shudder at the memory, but she continued, her voice strong. 'It was my cousin Johnny. I screamed when I saw him burst in, and if his gun hadn't misfired, I would have died right there in the water. But Angelo was in the dressing room, and he got to him first. I guess Johnny thought I was alone.'

'That sounds terrifying,' I said, imagining that particular

227

brand of fear.

'It was,' she said quietly. 'Right after that, Angelo called Paulie and they paid my father a final visit together.' She swallowed hard, cleared her throat, and said, 'The end was quick.'

'God,' I said. What a mess these Mafia families made for each other. 'And your sister never forgave you.' It was a statement, not a question.

'Donata was in the house the night Angelo killed my father. He could have killed her, too, but I asked him to spare her. Despite the fact we never saw eye to eye, despite her hatred of me and what I had done, I didn't want him to harm her.' She tapped my arm to indicate she was done with the stitches. I opened my eyes to find her icy blue gaze swimming with unshed tears. 'I spend every day of my life regretting that decision. I spend every waking moment wondering whether she will take one of my sons from me, like she almost took Gino during that fire.' She blinked, and the tears vanished. 'I think it is the worst decision I ever made.'

Elena ran her fingers over the scrape wounds in my neck. 'A gift from my sister?' she asked.

I nodded.

She pulled her hair from her neck, craning it away from me so that under the light I could see three faint white lines stretching from her collarbone around to the back of her ear. 'Snap,' she said, a macabre smirk twisting on her face. 'She did this to me when the boy she had a crush on asked me to the prom instead. Of course I didn't go with him, but the offence was enough to warrant the scars.'

'She's crazy,' I breathed.

'Yes,' Elena said simply. 'I'm glad you are away from her.'

The sentiment pricked my heart, and I thought for a horrifying moment that I might cry. It had been a long night. 'Thank you,' I said quietly. 'For helping me tonight . . . and for being nice to me.'

Elena nodded. 'It is not unheard of to leave one Mafia family for another, if you feel there is something or someone calling out to you.' I avoided her gaze, tried to ignore any implicit meanings that may or may not have existed in that statement. 'If you are prepared to endanger yourself for the safety of my boys, I am prepared to do the same for you. We look after each other, now. All of us. If my sons can trust you, then so can I.'

She went back to work, fixing a square bandage over the stitches in my shoulder. She pulled back, took two pills from the case and then closed it up, folding the pills into my hands. 'You'll need these painkillers. I'll get you a prescription for more and I'll send one of the boys to pick them up. Try not to move around too much over the next few days, and get a good night's sleep.' She squeezed my good arm once, then got to her feet. 'You did well tonight, Sophie. You were brave. You were a Falcone.' She turned from me then, her silk robe trailing behind her as she left.

I swallowed the pills without bothering with water. A few minutes later, Nic appeared in the doorway to my bedroom. 'Well?'

'Twelve stitches, no bullet,' I said. 'Lucky me.'

'Congratulations!' His smile was all teeth. 'Your first official Mafia wound. And twelve stitches. That's impressive.'

'Is it?' I pulled the blanket tighter around my arms, covering up all the skin that had been marred with blood.

'Don't,' he said, coming into the room. 'Let me see.'

Reluctantly, I dropped the blanket, revealing my heavily bloodstained arm. There was a thick gauze plaster covering the wound on my shoulder.

He whistled. 'Whoa. That's intense.'

I smiled weakly. ''Tis but a scratch.'

'You're hardcore, Soph.'

My head was starting to swim. I didn't know what Elena had given me, but I was going all bendy and light-headed. 'I feel very soft and squishy right now,' I said. 'And also, bloody. Very bloody.'

'Hang on.' Nic left the room, returning a moment later with a hand towel. He sat down beside me and took my hand in his, laying it across his knee. I just sat there, all floppy, as the painkillers slipped into my system and my lids grew heavy, and watched as he pressed the wet towel against my arm.

'Thanks, Nic,' I said, watching him clean the blood away, bit by bit. His head was bent at an angle, his dark brows pulled together. His touch was so gentle I barely felt it.

'It's kind of sexy,' he said, taking my fingers in his, and carefully scrubbing the towel across them, removing the dried blood in my fingernails. 'All this blood.'

I smiled blissfully at the crown of his head. 'That is such a stupid thing to say.'

His laugh was a low rumble in his chest.

'Did Luca speak to Valentino yet?'

'He's briefed him,' Nic answered without looking up.

'Was Valentino angry?' I asked.

Nic shrugged. 'Valentino's always angry. Luca wants him to push for a truce. Valentino is considering it.'

'Really?'

'Yeah.' Nic snapped his head up. 'Stupid, right?'

'What did Luca say?'

'I guess he just can't believe they all showed up at a high school. I mean, that's so messed up.'

'Yeah,' I echoed.

'Luca says there are no rules any more, no shred of honour left between our families, and if we don't agree to a truce now, then we're all going to suffer for it.'

It was too much to process. I could only hang on to one thought at once. 'What happened to Zola Marino?' I asked. 'We left her unconscious in a hallway.'

'She's been taken into police custody,' he said. 'They're calling her a lone shooter on the news.'

'Will she talk?'

A mirthless smile. 'Not a chance.'

'Will she get bail?'

'If Donata has anything to do with it. She's got half of Chicago PD in her pocket.' He pulled the towel away and lifted my hand to inspect it. 'Tonight was a disaster.'

'It won't be like that next time.'

'There might not be a next time, if they get their truce.'

'No,' I said. 'We can't cower, not now.'

'Tell that to Valentino and Luca,' Nic said, his tone clipped. 'There's no speaking to them when they get like this.'

'I don't want a truce, Nic.'

'And you think I do?' he said, incredulous. 'We deserve revenge. *You* deserve revenge. Tonight was difficult, but you

231

escaped. Donata ended up losing, not us.' He rolled his eyes, frustration gathering in the corners of his puckered mouth. 'I don't know why Luca can't see it like that.'

'I'll have a gun next time. We'll be better prepared.' I don't know why I was fighting so hard. I suppose beneath the fear and the pain and the sudden realization of my own precarious mortality, there was a feeling of strength, of my own determination. I was strong. I had survived tonight. I had helped Luca. And I would survive again. We all would. 'I'm not afraid, Nic. I'm not afraid of what they'll do, and I'm not afraid of what *I* can do.'

He smiled at me, a slow curl of his lips. 'See,' he said. 'You *are* hardcore.'

He moved the cloth up my arm, brushing the inside of my elbow, his fingers inching around my wrist.

He slid his arm back down. Without meaning to, he was holding my hand, and my fingers were curled inside his. We were much closer than I realized. He was tracing small circles around the wound in my shoulder with his free hand, tenderly cleaning off the dregs of disinfectant and blood.

'What are you doing?' I was suddenly so unbearably tired.

He took his hand away, folding the cloth in his lap. 'I'm proud of you, Soph,' he said earnestly. 'You were amazing tonight. A true Falcone.'

I smiled at him. 'Thank you.' The words slipped off my tongue, husky and far more intimate than I intended. 'You smell like a forest.'

The corner of his lip flickered. 'Looks like the pain meds are kicking in.'

# CHAPTER TWENTY-SEVEN
## ONE HUNDRED GRAVES

'What unique brand of violent romanticism is this?' I snapped my head up to find Millie standing in the doorway to my room. 'Because I do not love it.'

'It's called friendship,' I said, pulling back from Nic, realizing in a moment of fleeting clarity that perhaps it did look like something different, something I didn't intend.

She strode into the room, her heels and dress still miraculously intact, the black fishtail trailing behind her. 'I have now been fully debriefed and suitably threatened by Valentino as per your request, Mr Falcone, sir.'

'I didn't tell him to threaten you,' Nic said. 'I told him to calm you down. You were getting hysterical.'

'Huh,' Millie mused. 'Well, I guess he threw that part in for free. Anyways, consider my lips sealed. I do want to see my parents live into old age, you know.'

Nic ground out an unintelligible curse. 'Did he really threaten your family?'

Millie smiled sardonically at him. 'Only a smidge. May I have a word with my best friend now, please?'

Nic got up, muttering something to Millie before taking his leave and shutting the door behind him.

Millie wheeled around and flipped her hair away from her face. 'A blood war,' she said.

It felt like my head was floating several inches above my neck. My fingertips were a little numb. I nodded.

'Are you freaking *kidding* me, Soph? Is this some sort of cruel Halloween prank where you dress up as someone I don't *know*?'

I flinched at the implication. If only she knew what the real disguise was – the person who had been hanging out with her these past few months, forcing smiles and feigning interest in a future that was no longer within reach.

'You're in a *blood war*!' she repeated. 'When the hell were you going to tell me? Or was I supposed to just join the dots at your *funeral*?'

I raised my hands in the air, trying to placate her. 'I'll explain, Mil.'

'You can definitely try, but I doubt you'll talk your way out of this.'

'I didn't want to worry you,' I said. 'That's kind of how it works in the underworld. The less you know, the safer you are. I never in a million years thought something like tonight would happen. I never would have knowingly put you in danger like that. I'm sorry.'

She pinched the bridge of her nose. 'I would actually throttle you if you weren't already injured, Soph. I swear to God, for a smart girl, you are acting like the dumbest person on the planet right now. You think my main point of contention is that you didn't tell me about the blood war? No, my main issue is that you *are in the middle* of a blood war. How the hell did that happen?'

I blinked at her, feeling an overwhelming urge to slump over and sleep for a hundred years. 'You know I'm a Marino. You know what they did to Mom.'

'What exactly are you trying to achieve by living here in the middle of all this violence? Do you *realize* you almost got killed tonight?'

'I realize that.'

'Hanging out with this family is probably the worst thing you could be doing right now,' she pressed. 'They've painted a big fat target on your forehead.'

'The target was already there, Mil. The Marinos are after me too. We're safer if we stick together. Without them, I'm like a sitting duck.'

'And?' Millie prompted. 'Is that it?'

'What?' I said.

'Is that the only reason why you're here?'

'What are you talking about?' Her meaning was not connecting inside my fuzzy head, but I could tell she was angling at something.

'I spoke to Gino downstairs,' she continued. 'I guess he thought you had told me everything on the car ride here . . .'

'I did,' I lied.

'Did you?' she challenged.

I shrugged.

'You didn't tell me you have a gun now.'

'I—'

'Oh, I'm sorry. *Two* guns,' she clarified.

I flinched again. 'Gino should not have told you that.'

She dropped her jaw. 'So I'm an outsider now?'

'Not like that,' I said, instantly regretting my tactlessness. 'I just meant, he should be more discreet. It's not like he—'

She raised her hand to cut me off. 'You also didn't tell me how good a shooter you've become.'

I looked at my hands, the shame painting circles of warmth across my cheeks. 'I didn't see the point in telling you. It's nothing.'

'It's nothing,' she repeated. 'So, it's a hobby?'

I didn't dare meet her eyes. 'Something like that.'

'You expect me to believe that? You think I haven't seen how angry you've become? How different you are? You think I can't look at my best friend and see that jagged, broken heart – the darkness in your eyes when you speak about Jack, the way you bristle when I mention your dad? You think I don't know how cut up you are over your mother? You think,' she sucked in a breath, her voice wobbling, 'I don't know that the reason you spend so much time shooting that gun is because you want to point it at your uncle's head the next time you see him and pull the trigger?'

My face fell. I was too tired to rearrange it in time. Of course she could see through me – I don't know why I ever believed she couldn't. She knew me better than anyone.

'I see it,' she said. 'Even now, you can't hide it from me, so don't bother trying. You're here for safety, sure, but you're also here for revenge. Admit it. If you value the trust we have, then you'll stop lying to me.'

I forced myself to look at her – my best friend, beautiful and funny and smart and brave and still glowing in her gown. And here I was, bullet-wounded below her, crumpled in her mother's blue dress, and still afraid to show her who I really was inside even though she already knew.

Millie was the only one left. *Take off the mask.* If tonight had proved anything, it's that you can't run from who you are.

'OK,' I relented.

'OK?' She stood in front of me, her arms folded.

'I've allied myself with the Falcones because I want Jack to suffer the way he made my mother suffer, the way he's made me suffer,' I told her. 'I want to kill him. It's not a whim or a stroke of grief. It's the right thing, and I want to be the one to do it. The Falcones will help me, and after I'm done, I want to kill Donata Marino, too. I won't rest until I have my retribution. I won't rest until Jack has been brought to justice. I've always been part of this underworld, Millie. I have it in my blood and my heart. I'm not running from it any more. I'm not running from who I am.' I leant back on my elbows, so she could see the truth in my expression.

A strangled laugh caught in her throat.

'That's the truth,' I said. 'The old Sophie is dead. She never really existed, and this person is who I'm supposed to be.'

She gaped at me. All of her teeth visible at once, her jaw slack with surprise. 'Oh, Soph. You can't be serious.'

'I am as serious as this gunshot wound in my shoulder.' I was on a roll now. She might as well know all of it. 'In fact, I have never been more serious about anything in my life. I didn't want to show you this side of me. I didn't want to frighten you or put you in danger or have you look at me the way you're looking at me right now but the truth is I'm sick of being weak and helpless, I'm sick of being on the sidelines of my own life, and I'm sick of letting other people make decisions for me. I'm taking back my power. It's messy, and it's dark and it's scary, but I'm not afraid, Millie. This is who I am.'

She let the silence stretch out between us. Horror roiled over her face. She crossed her arms over her chest, pushing her silver-diamond pendant upwards until it flickered underneath the lights.

'I'm sorry,' I said. 'I'm sorry I'm not the friend you deserve and I'm sorry I put you in danger tonight. I'm sorry I ruined your mother's beautiful dress, I'm sorry I ruined your dance, and I'm sorry you have to stand here with me right now, with that look on your face.'

Her face crumpled. 'Soph—'

'I love you,' I continued, pushing on despite the discomfort in her expression. 'You're my rock, my best friend, my sister, the best thing in my life, but I know you can't stand by me in this. I would never ask you to. I don't expect you to understand me, and I don't expect you to forgive me for the things I'm going to do, so I want you to know that you can go. And that's OK. You don't owe me anything. You can go.'

'Go?' she repeated, like the word made no sense. 'Go where?'

I gestured half-heartedly at the room, and then at myself, letting my hand flop into my lap. 'Away from here,' I said, trying to sound strong and sure, when all I felt was shaky and sad. 'Away from me.'

A frown, a shadow of bewilderment, and then she rolled her eyes. 'Oh, for God's sake. Don't be so dramatic.'

'I'm not being dramatic,' I protested. 'I'm serious.'

'Well, I'm not about to walk out on you and leave you to this giant shitstorm. You are just one big cluster of bad decisions and misinformed ideas right now, but that's not your fault. You've lost a lot. I understand why you're adrift, but that doesn't mean I'm going to walk away. Not now. Not when you clearly need me the most. I mean, what kind of person do you think I am? Seriously?'

'I wouldn't blame you.'

She waved away my response. 'Not only am I going to stick by you, I'm going to drag you out of this mess while I'm at it. We have plans. We're going to finish school and go travelling and have adventures. You're not going to end up dead or in jail from chasing around some lame arsehole who doesn't deserve a second of your attention. Leave Jack to the police, or to Nic or even that oddball Felice, if you like, but don't waste your own future on this idiot. He's already taken enough of your past.'

'I'm not leaving here until it's done, Mil.'

She plonked herself down on the bed beside me. 'Yes, you are.'

'No,' I repeated, more sternly this time. 'I am not.'

The moment grew tight. We stared at each other, each waiting for the other to break, for someone to concede defeat. She couldn't see the situation the way I could. She was looking at it logistically, and I was looking at it personally, and that made all the difference. This was my task. My retribution. My journey to healing.

'I'm going to kill him,' I said. 'And there's nothing you can say to stop me. Nothing.'

Her hand flew to her mouth, her words muffled by her fingers. Finally, she was getting it. She knew I meant it. 'Jesus Christ, Sophie.'

I stared at her, unblinking.

'You can't be serious.'

'I am.'

'I am not hearing this.' She shut her eyes. 'This is not real. I am not hearing this.'

'It's the truth,' I told her. 'I'm going to kill my uncle.'

She was quiet for a few moments, shock and disbelief warring across her features. Then she spluttered back to life, snapped her eyes open and glared at me. She waved her hand around, as if she was painting a picture in the air. 'So dig two graves then, Sophie. One for Jack and one for you. Actually, better yet, why don't you dig a hundred?' She wheeled around, pointing towards the hallway. 'Dig one for every Falcone and every Marino and every goddamn idiot who loves you all. Dig all the graves you can before you go shooting anyone up because when this stupid-arse blood war hits we're all *fucked*! The people who love you won't walk away, and it's your stubbornness that will get them killed, just like it will get *you* killed.' She brandished her finger towards my shoulder. 'Just like it almost did tonight. Or don't you realize how close your shoulder is to your heart?'

'You don't have to be involved,' I said. 'I told you that.'

'Don't be so reductive!' she snapped. 'Of course I'm involved. You're involved, so I'm involved. And you'd better pray I go down before you, because if you get killed before me then I'll have to die twice!' Her eyes filled up, but she kept shouting, her voice climbing higher and higher. 'How could you have so little regard for your own life?'

'What life?' I asked. 'The one Jack took from me? *That* life?'

'You control your own life, Sophie!'

My head was starting to swim. I needed to lie down. I needed to sleep. 'I'm tired, Mil. I can't have this argument again.' Not with her, not with Luca. 'I know what I'm doing. I know where I'm going.'

She shook her head at me, her hands coming down to my wrists, clasping around them as though she could pull me out of my thoughts. 'Get out of here, Sophie. Before it's too late.'

'There's no way out. Can't you see that? I'm marked by the Marinos. They want me just as much as I want them.'

Millie scrunched her nose. 'No,' she said, searching for something to say. 'This can't be it.'

'It is,' I said firmly. 'This is the safest place. The only place.'

'Then go to the address your father gave you,' Millie said. 'At least for a while. Until you figure out—'

'Are you crazy? What makes you think I trust my lying, murdering father?'

'He loves you, Sophie. He wouldn't trap you.'

'Wouldn't he?'

Millie shook her head. 'He wants to help you. And now I get it. I didn't understand it at the time, but he knows how deep in you are.'

'I threw the address away,' I reminded her.

'You must remember it. At least some of it. Isn't it worth investigating?' she pressed. 'It could be like a safe house . . . they wouldn't look for you there.'

'Unless my father tells them to.'

'He's not a monster,' Millie said. 'You know he wouldn't do that.'

'That's the thing,' I said, another wave of exhaustion careening over me. I sank backwards against my pillow. 'I don't know that. Not any more.'

'You're fading.'

'It's the pain meds,' I said, struggling to keep my eyelids open.

Millie huffed a sigh. 'Let's put this on pause until you've slept it off. Let's get you into your pyjamas.'

'I'm sorry,' I murmured, unzipping the dress. My hands were moving in slow motion. The sides of my vision were fuzzy. There was no pain in my shoulder now. 'The dress is stained.'

Millie helped me shimmy out of it, doing most of the work while I just flopped around like a marshmallow.

'I don't care about the dress, Sophie.'

I wriggled into a T-shirt and sweatpants. 'I wish you did.'

'No, you don't,' she said.

'I wish you were less observant.'

'I wish you were less stubborn.'

'You're just as stubborn as me.'

'Yup,' she said, helping me under the blankets. 'That's how I know I'm going to win.'

'Win what?'

My eyelids were drooping. I felt at peace, like I was floating above myself. The argument was far below me, in another place.

She tucked the duvet around me. Dropping her voice, she

brushed the hair from my face, and her voice followed me into the darkness as I drifted off. 'I'm going to win this argument. I'm going to drag you out of here if it's the last thing I do.'

Then I was gone, and so was she.

# CHAPTER TWENTY-EIGHT

## BREAKFAST

'**M**y cereal tastes funny.'

'That's because you're still high,' Nic pointed out. 'How many painkillers did you take this morning?'

I held up two fingers to him while I crunched. 'Everything tastes like marshmallows.'

'That's because you're eating Lucky Charms,' he said, laughing.

I smiled at him, my mouth still full. I imagined I looked like a chipmunk.

'How's your shoulder this morning?' asked Elena, who was making an elaborate fry-up across four pans.

'It's OK,' I said, rotating my arm to see how much it hurt.

Yup. Still hurt.

Felice was at the head of the table, peering at me over

his frothy cappuccino. 'Welcome to the Gunshot Club, Persephone. Do you feel invincible?'

'No,' I said. 'Should I?'

'No,' he said, his smile curling. 'You shouldn't.'

I stored that veiled threat along with all his others and demolished another spoonful of Lucky Charms while the smell of bacon filled up the kitchen.

'How many eggs, Gino?' Elena asked over her shoulder. She was still dressed in her silk dressing gown, her long dark hair spilling in waves down her back.

'Six,' he called out, his words warping around a mouthful of toast.

'Dom?' she asked.

I had come to discover that Dom didn't speak all that much before 11 a.m. It was a delightful Falcone fact. He held up four fingers.

'Four,' said Gino for him.

'Nic?'

'Three. Double bacon, please.'

'CJ?'

'Three,' CJ said, glancing at Nic. 'And double bacon too, please.' Dom had caught CJ trying to drive his car the other night and had nearly slapped him into the next state, so CJ had temporarily directed his hero worship to Nic.

I slurped another spoonful down, barely tasting it. I had only been up a few hours, but I was exhausted already. My shoulder was throbbing dully, my eyelids were heavy from the painkillers and I could feel Felice staring at me across the table.

'Sophie?' she asked after another beat.

'No, thank you.'

'Where's Valentino?' asked Gino. 'He's usually up early on Saturdays.'

'With his brother,' said Felice.

Dom rolled his eyes. 'Valentino is probably helping Luca turn into an actual punching bag so he can beat the shit into himself in a more efficient way.'

Felice snorted, then dipped into his cup to hide his amusement.

'Leave him alone,' I chided Dom. 'You weren't there.'

'Eh, yeah, because I'm not a stupid teenager who gets off on drinking spiked punch and playing dress-up at the local high school.'

'You also weren't invited,' Nic pointed out. 'Because girls find your hair gel repulsive.'

It was my turn to laugh. Nic exchanged an appreciative glance with me. CJ bit back his smile. He wasn't ready to go full Judas on Dom yet.

'That's hilarious,' said Dom, not smiling remotely. 'Almost as hilarious as Sophie inviting *Luca* and not you, the person who's still desperately trying to screw her.'

I spat out my next spoonful.

'Dominico!' Elena shrieked, whirling around. 'You will not speak like that in this house. And certainly not in front of the younger children.'

'I'm not a child,' CJ snapped.

Nic fired his fork at Dom, catching him in the side of the face. Their chairs screeched back at the same time, both of them lunging across the table at each other. Gino grabbed Nic by the waist and spun him around, away from Dom. I was on my feet, too, swatting Dom's hands back across the table. 'Sit down, you moron.'

'He could have cut my eye out!'

'And you would have deserved it,' Elena snapped. 'Have I raised a pack of wolves?' She threw her hands up at the ceiling. '*Ti prego, Dio, dammi la forza!*'

Felice remained where he was, smirking and sipping. I half wished Nic's fork had missed Dom and embedded itself in his uncle's face instead. How could no one see how much of a snake this guy was?

'*Relax*,' said Dom, sitting back down. 'I was just saying.'

'Sophie didn't invite Luca,' said Nic. 'He went to keep an eye on her.'

'And good thing too,' said Gino. 'Otherwise she'd be toast.'

'*Luca* would be toast,' Nic clarified. 'It was Sophie who disarmed Zola.'

'But didn't choose to kill her,' Felice finally weighed in.

I didn't break his stare. 'The circumstances were too complicated, Felice.'

'Is that right?'

Elena turned around again, her voice weaving with the crackle of grease on the frying pan. 'Did you have something to say, Felice? Perhaps you should be direct about it.'

Felice offered her his shark grin. 'I was merely pointing out that regardless of who subdued Zola Marino, Luca or Persephone should have killed her while they had the chance. That woman will have been released on bail by now, and we all know she's a loose cannon. Showing up to a high school dance full of innocent teenagers and discharging her gun can certainly attest to that.' He sat back in his chair, his fingers

247

drumming a steady beat on the table. When no one said anything, he repeated himself. 'Luca should have handled it.'

Elena pointed her knife at Felice, swirling it around in the air as she circled his head. 'You think he should have shot Zola and been taken away in handcuffs for it, and locked up for the rest of his life?'

Felice shrugged. 'Who's to say what would have happened?'

'Common sense,' Nic answered. 'The police were every-where. Jack and Donata didn't even stick around, and she's their family. Luca would have been dragged to prison for it.'

'Making one less active member of this family,' said Dom tightly.

'And one less person in your way to the top,' I added.

Felice's eyes widened just a fraction.

The others fell silent.

'Careful,' he said, baring his teeth at me.

# CHAPTER TWENTY-NINE
## TRUCE

I was sitting in the library, my feet on the coffee table, when Luca swung the door open and let himself in. All the others had gone out for the afternoon, so I hadn't expected to see him any time soon.

'Hey.' I set my phone down, pausing the intense gif-only conversation I was having with Millie. I tried to sit up, but my movements were more laboured than usual and it took twice as long.

'Hi,' he said, looking me up and down, his gaze lingering on my bandaged shoulder even though it was covered by an oversized hoodie.

'Stop checking me out, Luca. I'm not looking my best.'

He leant against the arm of the chair beside me and his aftershave rolled over me. I tried not to be sucked into memories of secret moments and stolen kisses. 'How are you?' he asked.

'Oh, you know, not dead,' I said, looking up at him. 'So that's something at least.'

He didn't laugh. His usually bright eyes were wired with red, the skin under them rimmed in dark circles. His hair was messy and swept away from his face, and the grey sweater he wore was creased around the neck. And yet, despite everything, he still looked like he had just tumbled out of a GUESS commercial.

'Not funny,' he said, decidedly. 'Not funny at all.'

I straightened up, released a sigh. 'Where have you been? I haven't seen you since last night.' *You know, since we nearly died together in that corridor.*

He raked a hand through his hair. 'Talking with Valentino. Coming up with a way to end all of this for good.'

'What do you mean?' I asked.

'I've been in the city all morning, trying to get a message to the Marinos. We're scheduling a peace talk for next week.'

'A *peace talk*? What are you, two warring countries?'

'We may as well be,' Luca said seriously. 'We're going to call a truce.'

'A truce?' I repeated. 'Just like that, it's *decided*? I thought you and Valentino were just discussing that possibility.'

'We *were* discussing it,' Luca said, nonplussed. 'And now we're done discussing it. The decision has been made.'

I blinked at him, incredulity filling me up. 'Without the rest of us?'

He tilted his head. 'It was our decision to make.'

I got to my feet. 'You're kidding, right? I can't believe you did this behind my back.'

'Behind your back?' Frustration curled his lip, brought out a hint of the feral Luca I had seen many times before. 'I thought you'd be *relieved* about this.'

'You thought I'd be relieved that the day after Donata Marino *opened fire* on me at my high school dance you're extending an olive branch to her? Are you out of your *mind*?'

Luca got to his feet too. 'Are *you*?'

I shook my head. 'I can't believe you're giving up like this.'

When he spoke, his voice was deadly calm. 'You almost *died* last night, Sophie. I almost had to *watch you die*.'

I took a step towards him, propelling all my anger and frustration into the space between us. 'But I didn't die, Luca. That's the point. I'm still here, and they're a man down. Now we have the upper hand.'

'I don't care about the upper hand!' he said, his composure unfurling almost as fast as mine. 'I care about lives! I care about *your* life! At least one of us should!'

'What the hell is that supposed to mean?' I hissed, venom pooling on my tongue.

He glared at me. 'It means you have a life outside of this war, Sophie. You have *possibilities*. I want you to stop looking at all the things you want to damage and start looking at all the ways you can be happy. That life you imagine for your-self? The one we talked about? You can have that. You can still have all of it. Start thinking about that. Start thinking about possibility.'

There he was, on that damn pedestal again, and it made me so mad that he couldn't understand how badly I needed this. How badly I wanted Donata to pay.

I reeled my temper in, made myself sound calm as I said, 'And what if I want something different? Does that count for anything?'

'We're calling a truce,' he said firmly. 'This isn't a negotiation. I just wanted to let you know. Stupidly, I thought you'd be pleased.' Before I could respond, he turned from me and stalked out of the room.

I marched after him. 'Hey! Get back here!'

He turned around, his eyes flashing in the dusky hallway. 'What?' he spat.

'Is that it?' I said. 'The blood war is over, so you're just going to go back to ignoring me. Pretending I don't exist.'

He took a step towards me. 'When have I ever pretended you don't exist?'

'When you don't look at me for days at a time!' I shouted. 'When you don't talk to me. When you make decisions without consulting me! When you walk around here acting like I don't exist! When you spend days not even *thinking* about me.'

He scraped his hands through his hair, then flung them down by his sides. 'Sophie, I'm *always* thinking about you! Don't you get that?' He took another step, frustration tripping through his voice. 'I can't do anything *but* think about you. I spend all my time worrying about your safety, whether you're happy, whether you're healing, and you're standing here asking me to throw you back into the fire!'

His words slapped the retort right out of my mouth. I just hovered there, marbled in my surprise as he stood in front of me, waiting for his breathing to slow.

He came a little closer, and I stayed still, wanting him to

explain. He took his switchblade out, brandished the handle between us, his name scrawled on top. A piece of paper came with it, upheaved from his pocket.

'I gave you my *knife*,' he said, as I caught the paper fluttering to the floor. 'I gave you the most important thing I own.'

I held the paper between us like a white flag. 'What's this?'

'Oh,' he said, frowning at his pocket. He stowed the knife away, his voice falling quiet. 'That.'

I unfolded it slowly, waiting for him to stop me. He didn't.

It was a note.

It was *my* note.

From a million years ago.

*Aren't you glad I have no respect for your authority?* ☺

I held it between us and stared at it, my fingers shaking.

'I'm always thinking about you,' he said, his voice resigned. 'I'm just trying to make it right, Soph.'

I looked up at him. 'You kept my note?'

'Yeah. I did.'

I could sense he was embarrassed, so I folded the note up and handed it back to him. He slipped it into his wallet and stashed it in the back of his jeans. I didn't want to argue with him any more, about this, about anything. He was too important to me. I just wanted to see him smile and hear him laugh. I just wanted to be near him. When I was around Luca, my heart opened a crack, and I became less afraid of my true feelings. Sometimes people pretend they're listening, but really they're waiting for a gap in conversation to say something about themselves, or until you are finished talking about your sadness so they can move on to brighter topics. Luca *really* listened to me. He really cared.

'I don't want to fight with you,' I said.

'I don't want to fight with you either.'

I made the mistake of trying to hold his gaze. It shot right through me, into my heart.

'Truce?' I said, my voice ragged with a sudden flare of desire.

'Truce.'

'You know, you're very confusing, Luca,' I said softly. 'I feel like I need a cheat sheet sometimes. I never know what you're thinking or what you want.'

The whisper of a smile spread across his lips. A beat of silence, and then he came a little closer. 'Do you want to know what I want, Sophie?'

I nodded. 'Yes.'

'I want to kiss you.'

I swallowed hard. 'Then why don't you?'

He didn't move. 'Because I'm not supposed to.'

I hesitated a beat too long, distracted by the raucous thudding in my chest. He straightened up, as if remembering himself, and took a step away from me. Then another one. He regained his composure, wiped the look of indecision from his face, and cleared his throat.

I came towards him. 'You think too much, Luca.'

'Yes,' he said.

'You're used to making all the decisions.'

'Yes.'

'Well, there's two of us in this, you know.'

'Yes.'

'Then I'll decide.' A rush of desire seized me, and before I could stop myself, I was grabbing the collar of his shirt and pulling him towards me. He responded instantly, wrapping his arms around my waist, his body curving against mine as he walked me backwards with him.

'Yes.' He spun me into the alcove halfway down the hall, his hand pressing against the small of my back, the other grabbing the back of my head. He crushed his lips to mine and I opened my mouth to let him in, and when his tongue brushed against mine, I could taste his need as keenly as my own. He ran his fingers through my hair, pulling me tighter against him. I wound my hands around his neck, ignoring the flicker of pain in my shoulder and pushing up on to my tiptoes so I could taste every part of him, so I could feel how much he wanted me.

He pulled back, panting, his fingers tracing my lips as he caught his breath. Our foreheads were pressed together. I smiled beneath his touch and he kissed the corner of my mouth.

'More,' I whispered.

A groan caught in his throat. 'More,' he said, pressing his lips to mine. The entire concept of time was obliterated as we stood moulded to each other inside that alcove, kissing and gasping for breath. I forgot where I was, and with every press of his tongue on mine, the darkness inside me seemed to shatter, just a little.

After what seemed like an eternity, but not nearly long enough, I pulled my lips from his. I touched my nose against

255

him. 'See what happens when you don't overthink?' I said softly, my fingertips still lost in his hair.

He moved his palm against my neck, his thumb caressing the sensitive spot behind my ear. 'I could do this for ever,' he murmured. He pressed his lips against mine, warm and lingering, before drawing back again to look at me. 'I can barely remember my own name.'

I smiled against him. 'We should probably go before someone finds us.'

'You're right,' he said, kissing me again. 'But you taste so good.'

'And you smell amazing.' The truth was I never wanted to move from that alcove. The bubble we were in was perfect – it was full of fire and adrenalin and giddy joy.

'Just six more,' he said, smiling as he kissed me several more times in quick succession.

I could not take my hands off him. It's like we had started something that neither of us could pull away from. Self-control be damned – I couldn't remember a time when I had had any.

'Three more,' I said, pulling him against me again. He yielded willingly, laughing as he opened his mouth to mine.

When the shout shattered the silence, I thought someone had been shot, or at the very least that the person who'd shouted wasn't standing so impossibly close to us. I reeled backwards, a gasp sticking in my throat, as Luca spun around. The blow landed against his right cheek and he slammed backwards, his head smashing against the wall.

Nic grabbed Luca by the collar and yanked him out of the alcove, his shouts turning to a violent string of curses as he launched himself at his brother. I shot out after them, almost crashing into Dom and Gino who had been following behind Nic. Their coats were still fastened and they were staring bug-eyed at their brothers, bewilderment screwing up their faces. They had all come home together, and Luca and I had been so wrapped up in each other that we hadn't heard a thing.

Luca ducked out of Nic's next punch and backed into the foyer, his hands raised at his brother. 'Calm down, Nicoli.'

Nic charged at him like a bull, slamming into Luca's torso and carrying them both against the far bannister. Gino, Dom and I followed them, their shouts joining with mine. Valentino was in the foyer. He was still wearing his coat, but his face was twisted up in horror as he took in the scene.

Nic lunged at Luca again, but missed, his fist cracking into the wall. His scream was primal.

'Stop them!' I yelled at Valentino. 'Make them stop!'

'I can't,' he said, exasperated. 'Look at them.'

I turned to Dom and Gino. 'Break them up, before one of them gets seriously hurt.'

'What the hell happened?' asked Dom. 'What's going on?'

Felice came in through the front door, slamming it behind him. He was wearing a purple scarf, the collar of his black trench coat flicked upwards. He stopped mid-stride, his mouth agape, as Luca kicked Nic in the back of his knee, momentarily immobilizing him.

Nic fell to the ground, grabbing at Luca's ankle. Luca lost his footing and collapsed on to Nic, and they began brawling again.

'Dom,' I said, tugging him by the arm. 'Please. Break them up.'

'What's it about?' he said, circling the huddle. 'I need to know whose side I'm on first.'

Crap. I didn't want him to jump in against Luca too. And he would if he knew why Nic was so angry.

Valentino fired his gun in the air.

The resounding crack shocked everyone into stillness.

Luca and Nic fell apart from each other.

'My ceiling!' Felice shrieked. 'Have you lost your mind, Valentino?'

'*Calmati*,' Valentino cautioned. 'It was getting out of hand.'

Felice was examining the new hole in his ceiling. He looked like he was about to cry.

Valentino was examining Luca and Nic. The boys hadn't done any real damage to one another . . . yet. Luca's lip was bleeding. Nic's chin was turning a vicious shade of purple.

'It's over,' Valentino told them. 'Whatever it is, it's over.'

Luca raised his hands. 'Sorry,' he said, looking genuinely ashamed of himself.

'No!' Nic hissed, snapping out of his sudden stillness. He whirled around, his finger jabbing at Luca's chest. '*Ti dovrei fare a pezzi, traditore!*'

'Oh my,' said Felice, his attention refocusing on the boys. He looked like he was tasting something particularly delicious.

'Restrain yourself, Nicoli!' Valentino warned. 'You've lost your head.'

'Why the hell does Nic want to slit your throat, Luca?' asked Dom.

Luca raked his hand through his hair, trying to compose himself. 'It's between Nicoli and me.'

'And Sophie,' said Nic, casting me a look so full of venomous hatred that I felt for a moment like I was shrinking.

'Ah,' said Valentino. He rolled his shoulders back. 'I see.'

'What do you see?' asked Gino. 'I don't see anything.'

My cheeks were burning up. I should say something. What should I say? What would make it better?

'You're messed up,' Nic spat at Luca. 'You talk about love and honour, you tell us to pour all of our time and efforts into *la famiglia*, to forget any other pursuits that might split our attention . . . You tell us to remain loyal to one another at all costs, and then you do *this* right under my nose! How long, Luca? How long have you been betraying me?'

'Nic,' I said, trying to wade in. 'It's not like that.' I could feel Valentino's glare on my back.

'I haven't been betraying you,' Luca said carefully.

'Are you *fucking kidding me*?' Nic shouted. 'What the hell do you call sticking your tongue down her throat?' He pointed to the alcove. 'What did I just walk in on?'

'Ooooh,' said Dom, finally getting it. He smiled lecherously at me. 'Bad Sophie. Very bad.'

I returned my middle finger.

'*Che sorpresa!*' Felice chuckled. No one else was sharing in his amusement.

'Just calm down,' said Luca. 'We'll talk about this somewhere else in private, just us.'

'No!' Nic roared. 'You don't deserve privacy. You've obviously had it long enough. I want to know what sick game you're playing here. I want to know why you're trying to punish me!'

'I'm not playing any game,' Luca protested, the heat rising

259

in his voice too. 'I'm not trying to punish you!'

'Bullshit!' Nic snapped. 'I know you're angry at me! You're mad because I'm teaching her how to defend herself. You're mad because I won't do what you tell me to, because I won't wrap her up and force her to stay away from her destiny!'

'Stop,' warned Luca.

'Newsflash,' said Nic, coming towards his brother again, his voice rising. 'She doesn't want a fucking shield, she wants a sword, so I gave her the sword, and it cuts you up. It makes you feel small and ignored, because we're not listening to you, because for once, we're not falling under your instruction and you can't control us—'

'I mean it, Nicoli.' Luca was seething, his features turning feral. He was dangerous like this; he was unpredictable, and everyone knew it. 'Sophie doesn't belong to you. She doesn't belong to anyone.'

Nic wouldn't relent. 'You're mad because you have no control over what will happen. You feel small and pathetic, and you should! You couldn't handle not having all the power. You wanted to take it from me. You wanted to take *her* from me! You wanted to win!'

I waded in between them. 'Stop!' I shouted. 'This isn't some stupid power game, Nic. He's not using me!'

Nic turned on me, his eyes flashing. 'He's using you to get to me.'

'You and I aren't together,' I said, exasperated beyond words. 'We're over. We've been over for a while.'

'I was going to win you back,' Nic said, pushing his temper towards me like a storm cloud. 'But he took that chance away!'

260

Enough. I had had enough of Nic treating me like some kind of trophy. I had had enough of him treating my desires and opinions like transitory thoughts that could be changed and manipulated at his leisure.

'*I* kissed *him*!' I shouted. '*I* wanted it!'

He levelled me with a dark look. 'I know him better than you, Sophie. Don't be an idiot. Get out of my way,' he hissed. 'I want him to admit it.'

He shoved me aside and stalked towards Luca. Dom and Gino moved in beside Nic, a cautionary hand on each of his shoulders, holding him back.

Luca stood stock-still, unblinking, as he raised his finger at his brother. 'Touch her like that again, and I'll end you.'

'Admit it,' Nic spat, ignoring the threat. 'Admit that you kissed her to get back at me. Admit that you wanted to teach me a lesson! You selfish son of a bitch!'

Luca bared his teeth at Nic. 'Shut your mouth, Nicoli.'

'No!' Nic screamed.

'Fine!' Luca shouted, coming right up to Nic's face, his hands clenched into fists at his sides. 'You want the truth?'

'Yes!' Nic yelled, refusing to budge. 'Give me the fucking truth!'

'Here it is!' Luca said. 'I didn't kiss Sophie to get back at you, I kissed her because I'm in love with her!'

Nic reeled backwards, as though the blow had been physical.

Gino and Dom gasped in unison.

My jaw unhinged.

Valentino buried his face in his hands and groaned.

And Felice threw his head back and laughed.

# CHAPTER THIRTY

## PLEA

I kissed her because I'm in love with her.
*I kissed her because I'm in love with her.*
*I kissed her because I'm in love with her.*

I was trying very hard to keep the smile from my lips, to keep my eyes downcast. My heart felt like it had swollen to twice its size, and all I could do was stand there and try not to get lost in the commotion.

Luca loved me. Luca was in love with me.

Nic was gaping at him, like he was trying to assemble a puzzle on his brother's forehead. Dom and Gino had fallen still – even Dom had shut his mouth. They were waiting for Luca to break, for the joke to be revealed.

After a few more loaded breaths, Nic spluttered into life again. 'No,' he said. 'I don't believe you.'

'It's true,' Luca said.

'Since when?'

'I don't know.'

'*How?*' said Nic.

Luca's smile was rueful, the guilt of the revelation tinged in his words. 'You of all people should be able to answer that, brother.'

Nic screwed his face up. 'But you used to find her so annoying.'

'I still find her annoying.'

Nic narrowed his eyes. 'You don't deserve her.'

'I know.' Luca tilted his head, just a little, and it was as though I could read the rest of his response in the careful lift of his brow. *Neither do you.*

'*Bravissimo,* boys.' Felice clapped his hands together. 'The blood of betrayal runs deep here at *Evelina*. I can't say I'm surprised, given the DNA you all share. Now, a word from our female protagonist, Persephone, perhaps?' He swivelled around to me, his face a mask of glee. 'Do *you*, Persephone, in fact, love Gianluca or will you remain loyal to our beloved Nicoli, the one who has been so selflessly training you for your revenge, probably under the impression that he was winning you back? Just how deep does your deception run in this little charade?'

Felice was threading a line of guilt right into my soul. I had known my feelings for Luca would hurt Nic if they ever got out, but I hadn't thought about it so starkly – at least not like that. I hadn't really been thinking at all, just searching for that solace that I could get from Luca's kiss, from his skin against mine, his breath against my ear . . . I looked to Luca, searchingly, but he was facing away, grinding his jaw. He would not play into Felice's spectacle.

'Can you show some respect?' I hissed at Felice. 'Clearly this isn't funny, and it's got nothing to do with you either.'

I was losing my footing – caught between wanting to respond directly to Luca, and wanting to run a million miles from the roomful of Falcone spectators.

'What's that, Persephone?' said, Felice, wearing his classic expression of faux surprise. 'Or should I start calling you Marilyn?'

'What?'

'Marilyn Monroe.' He licked his lips. 'I believe she slept with both Kennedy brothers, yes? And what happened to her then . . . ?' He trailed off, tapping his chin.

'She committed suicide,' Gino said.

'Nah. That's what they want you to think. She was definitely murdered,' Dom supplied.

'Was she?' Felice leered at me.

'Enough!' snapped Valentino.

'Valentino!' said Felice, shocked. 'You cannot end a soap opera midway through. I want to watch the finale.'

'Shut up,' said Valentino, his weariness transforming into a biting cruelty. 'Stop getting in their heads. It's counter-productive.'

'I am merely expressing curiosity,' Felice pointed out.

'*Stronzate!*' Valentino levelled his uncle with a dark look, his finger raised in accusation. 'You're so full of shit, if you ever had an enema you'd evaporate into thin air.'

The laugh burst out of me before I could stop it. It joined a spate of other sounds of uneasy amusement. Suddenly everyone was clearing their throats.

Felice looked like he had been stabbed.

He curled his lip, his words now thick with rage. 'How dare you speak to me like that, you insolent, incompetent, ill-prepared—'

'*Basta!*' Luca shouted, his demeanour as feral as it had been with Nic. 'One more word and you'll lose your tongue.'

Valentino seemed unaffected by his uncle's tirade. Then again, he always wore the best mask. 'You have work to do, Felice, and I have a family to run. Nic and Luca, I suggest you take some time apart from each other before this gets any more out of hand. Dom and Gino, you're on security. CJ has been manning it alone long enough. Sophie, I want to see you in my office right now.'

I wasn't sure whether I should have been grateful or terrified, but Valentino was plucking me out of this impending shitstorm, and I didn't have any choice but to follow him. He was the boss after all, and the last person I wanted to piss off. I traced a wide arc around the others, trying to catch Luca's eye, to say something, anything, to make him feel like he wasn't in this alone.

He glanced at me, his face awash with confusion – with regret. I did the only thing I could think to do without stirring up more dissension. I smiled at him; it was shy, tentative almost, but I watched him exhale heavily, a kernel of relief caught in his expression.

I shut the door to Valentino's office behind us. Instead of rounding the desk and leaning across it, Valentino placed himself just opposite the leather armchair, and gestured for me to sit. It was almost like we were two old friends, about to

265

have a catch-up. You know, if you disregarded the massive implosion and my starring role in it.

I sat down opposite him, looking as contrite as I could. I did feel guilty for hurting Nic, but nothing in the world would convince me to erase that kiss from my memory, the lingering sensation of Luca's lips on mine . . . I shut down my thoughts. I definitely did not want to get all hot and bothered in front of Valentino. It was already awkward enough given how similar they were in appearance.

'Well, that was unexpected,' he said evenly.

'Yes . . .' I tried to gauge his mood. He seemed totally impassive, lips set in a hard line, lids drawn low over his eyes. He was lethal, this kind-faced boy, who could snap in the blink of an eye – acid-tongued and cruel when he wanted to be, placid when he felt safe. 'It kind of got out of hand.'

'Which part?' he asked wryly.

Was he kidding? I was on my guard, sitting in what had now become my usual chair, my arms crossed, my legs crossed, my voice as neutral as I could make it.

'I-I don't know,' I hedged. 'All of it?'

Valentino smiled – it was quick and sudden, like a light being switched on. 'I don't want to make this even more excruciating for you, Sophie.'

'You don't?'

'No,' he said, bemused. 'Why would I?'

'I thought you'd be mad.'

Valentino shrugged. 'I'm not in the habit of getting in the way of someone's romantic inclinations.'

'Oh.'

'Your happiness is your own to navigate . . .' He paused,

swallowed, and then added, 'Luca's happiness is his own.'

'So we're not in trouble?' I asked, feeling a little bit like I was being set up.

Valentino smiled at me again, a hint of his yellowing teeth winking through. 'For falling in love?' Heat crawled into my cheeks. 'No,' he said quietly, answering his own question. 'You're not in trouble.'

I lifted my brows. 'So, then . . .'

'You're wondering why you're here?' He gestured to the hallway behind me. 'I thought you might want a few moments of composure, away from the fighting and the arguing, not to mention my uncle's endless propensity for other people's drama.'

'Thank you,' I said, letting my guard down just a little. 'I appreciate the reprieve.'

'Did you think I wouldn't be sympathetic? That I wouldn't understand?' he asked me.

His voice had gone a little funny. We were in uncharted waters, and all I knew for certain was that Valentino was sad about something. I couldn't guess at what it was; there was a wall between us, and he was keeping it there, deliberately.

'I don't know,' I told him quietly. 'You always seem so . . .'

'Cold,' he finished for me.

'Yes,' I admitted.

He nodded contemplatively. 'I'm not cruel, Sophie. I'm intelligent. I use my intelligence in a way that is unencumbered by emotion or affect, and so to others it seems cold. *I* seem cold. But that doesn't mean that I don't know the value of love, or how precious it is, or how unlikely it is that Luca has found it at all. I am not cold,' he repeated. 'Despite the

267

mask I wear.'

'You wear it a little too well, I think.' I was still searching for the person underneath it. I had never seen him act so human, so relatable. I never thought he would be that way with me.

'Yes,' he agreed. 'I've been wearing it far longer than the others.'

I traced a pattern on my jeans, too shy to look at him, as I said, 'I didn't mean to make such a mess . . . with Nic and Luca. I just . . . I couldn't help it.'

Was I really talking about making out with Luca directly to his twin brother who was also the boss of our entire Mafia family?

Yep.

Valentino steepled his fingers in front of his mouth. 'For someone who has waded through so much violence and hate, and had her world tipped upside down and all those she loves fall out of it, I think your decision to open your heart to love is a commendable one. You know, it is braver to love when hate is the easier option. Impassivity is an easy mask to wear, but it takes the most out of you.'

'Don't you think it makes you vulnerable?' I asked. Wasn't that why I had been hiding my desire for Luca all this time, trying to stamp it down, trying to ignore it?

'Yes,' said Valentino. 'But allowing yourself to be vulnerable does not make you weak, it makes you strong. It makes you brave. And most importantly, it gives you more to live for.' He made the shape of a gun with his thumb and forefinger, and pointed it at an imaginary target behind me. 'It is hardest to kill the man who has the most to live for.' He took a pretend shot. 'The empty, the soulless, the hate-filled enemies drop like flies. Those who love, and love hard, are the ones left standing.'

'Well, damn,' I said, smiling. 'I forgot how wise you are.'

Valentino's laugh was a lilting melody. 'I think too much, Sophie. It's not always a good thing.'

It was infinitely harder to dislike or mistrust Valentino when I was on the same side as him. Here he was – funny, charming, empathetic and interesting, everything I thought he wasn't. It was as if gaining Luca's affection had loosened Valentino up too. He was showing me a sliver of who he really was. In the end, they weren't all that different from one another.

'You surprise me,' I told him candidly. 'I never thought we would get to talk like this.'

Valentino pitched forward again, closing the distance between us. I mirrored him unconsciously. 'Here is another surprise, Sophie,' he said, his voice low. 'I know you didn't kill Libero Marino at The Sicilian Kiss.'

*Abort. Abort. Abort.* Every drop of colour drained from my skin as I sat beneath that icy gaze, struggling for a way to respond.

Valentino's grin turned wolfish. 'Don't try and lie,' he said, raising his finger as if to wag it. 'I find it personally offensive when people lie to me. It insults my intelligence.'

*Oh God. Oh God. Oh God.*

I forced myself to say something. The longer the silence, the deeper his thoughts. 'How?' I asked. 'How did you find out?'

'I know you, Sophie. I also know what my brother, Luca,

sees in you. Does that surprise you?'

He was speaking in facts. The emotion was gone.

'I don't know,' I said.

'If you had put a bullet in Libero Marino's head that night, it would have changed you. And despite a slightly increased desire for bloodshed and, evidently, romance, I find you decidedly unchanged.'

'Oh.'

He smiled, and it made his eyes look . . . kind. It made him look like Luca. Not just on the outside, but on the inside, too. 'Yes,' he said. '*Oh.*'

'I'm sorry,' I said hastily. 'I was going to. I really wanted to, but I stalled at the last second and I couldn't make myself do it. I froze.'

'It happens.' He waved away my response. 'I can only assume Luca deigned to dispose of Libero on your behalf.'

'I don't know. I can't remember.'

Valentino's laugh caught me off guard. 'That's good,' he said, still chuckling. 'I was hoping you'd lie for him. Luca deserves someone who would lie for him. Even to her boss.'

I squeezed my eyes shut. If only I could make myself disappear.

'Just as he lied to me that night,' Valentino continued. God, he had the whole thing figured out, and I had been skipping around like a regular Houdini, thinking how fortunate I was for getting away with my cowardice.

'Please don't be mad.' I looked up at him imploringly. 'It was such a crazy situation, and everyone got their wires crossed . . .'

Valentino's laugh reignited. 'Still lying!' he said, mock-

270

accusingly. 'You can stop now, OK?'

I decided to shut my mouth. I was probably just adding insult to injury at this point.

He sat back in his chair with a sigh, the smile still fixed on his face. 'You know what I felt tonight when Luca told Nic that he loved you?'

'Abject horror?'

'I felt relief,' he said. 'I'm relieved that my brother is in love with you, because it makes the lie he told me easier to stomach. I can understand it. He was protecting you. He wasn't putting distance between us, but placing himself in front of you. That, I can understand. That, I can forgive.'

'Why didn't you say anything? If you knew all along?'

'I didn't want to tip Felice off.' Valentino scrubbed a hand across his buzz cut. 'If he knew Luca had lied to me, he would see it as a weakness in the family, and he would find a way to exploit it.'

'Ah,' I said, nodding in agreement.

'It's a full-time job keeping things from him.'

'I can imagine.' Evelina's ruby ring flashed through my head. I blinked the image away, replaced it with the image of Felice's face inches from mine, his hands around my neck as he slammed me into that alcove, whisky on his breath, hatred in his eyes. All the things I had overheard, all the lies inside him. And in that moment, I knew I had to say something to Valentino. If I could throw myself in the firing line for Luca, for loyalty, I could do this too. I could be a good Falcone, even if it meant standing against another member of the family.

'I want to tell you about something that's been troubling me,' I said.

271

Valentino went very still, his eyes narrowing. 'Oh?'

'I don't like Felice, Valentino. And I definitely don't trust him. I thought it was because I was an outsider, but ever since I came to live at *Evelina*, I've realized it's not me, it's him . . .'

Valentino raised his eyebrows, as if to say, *Continue.*

I knitted my hands in my lap, took a breath, and said, 'I heard him talking to Paulie early one morning a little while ago. He didn't know I was there. I didn't intend to eavesdrop, but I couldn't walk away. Not when the things he was saying were so troubling.' I paused, studying Valentino's face for a reaction. It was perfectly impassive, which I had come to realize meant there was a whirlpool of thoughts going on inside him. 'When Felice noticed me listening, he followed me into the hallway and threatened me with his gun . . .'

'I remember,' Valentino said. 'Luca told me about this.'

'I think Felice had been drinking . . .'

'Yes,' he confirmed. 'He always loses himself around the anniversary of Evelina's disappearance.'

'Well the stuff he was saying to Paulie . . .' A flicker in Valentino's jaw betrayed his mounting interest. 'He was complaining. At the time, I didn't think to mention it because Luca was already so angry with him. I guess I thought it might stir up more trouble, but seeing the way he reacts to the others when they fight at home, or how he never seems to interfere in the name of peace, has got me thinking that maybe there's more to it than that . . .' I trailed off.

'What was he complaining about?'

'You.'

'Me,' Valentino repeated evenly.

I nodded.

Another flicker of interest, his lashes lowering. 'Why?'

Why hold back now? I didn't want to keep any secrets from the family, especially not something that might be vital. With the blood war looming, we needed to be sure of everyone's loyalty, and as far as I was concerned, Felice was walking around with a giant question mark over his shiny silver head.

*Here goes nothing.* 'Felice doesn't think you're equipped to lead the family. I think he reckons he'd do a better job . . . that it should have been him.'

'As we've always known,' Valentino said, unsurprised. 'Felice has long suffered from delusions of grandeur.'

'I think it's more than that,' I hedged.

'How do you mean?'

'He was complaining about your dad.'

Valentino's fingers tightened on the wheels of his chair. 'Elaborate.'

'Well, I think Felice resents your dad for overlooking him, but as well as that . . .' I was starting to think that maybe this constituted 'stirring' rather than 'briefing', but I couldn't back down now, not while Valentino was hanging on my every word. 'I think Felice is under the impression that your father had a hand in Evelina's "escape" all those years ago . . . He always thought your father was too sympathetic towards her.'

Valentino chewed on this new information, digesting it in silence. 'I see,' he said at last.

'Why would he think that?' I asked delicately. 'Why would there be a side for your father to choose in the first place?'

'Felice used to drink a lot,' Valentino said. 'He has since

273

directed his addictive nature to bee-keeping, more or less, but back when he was married to Evelina, there were many times when he would . . . mistreat her.'

'Mistreat her,' I repeated, hearing the sudden coldness in my voice. 'In what way?'

'He would push her around. Berate her. She was careful about hiding it from us. She didn't want us to see that side of Felice, of their relationship. But you couldn't miss it.' His voice got quieter, threads of something else woven inside his words as he went on. It sounded a little bit like regret. 'She drifted through the house like a ghost. You could see shades of black and purple around her eyes, even beneath the make-up.'

Suddenly I understood the sadness simmering behind Evelina's eyes. All that beauty tinged with melancholy. A palace ruled by a violent king. A diamond choker for a noose. 'Did you ever say anything to her?' I asked. 'Or him?'

Valentino shook his head, a frown tugging at his mouth. 'I wish one of us had done something, Sophie. Luca and I talk about it often. But we were young, and as much as I hate to admit it, we were afraid. We didn't have a voice. She always spoke up for my brothers and me, but we never spoke up for her. She was kind to us and we failed her every single day.'

I could feel the respect he had for her, and the sense of grief now tangled up inside it. 'You were young,' I said softly. 'It wasn't your battle.'

'It wasn't hers either.'

'Why did he do it?' The memory of Felice's hands on my throat, of his breath in my ear, made me shiver. 'What's wrong with him?'

'He was obsessed with her,' Valentino said, his words

woven through a heavy sigh. 'Rather, he was obsessed with the *idea* of her. The idea of someone and the reality of someone, when they merge, can make for a dangerous disparity. Felice picked her out of a church choir when she was barely twenty. She was an angel. He fell in love with her and built her a palace, and then when she started speaking up and voicing her own opinions, he didn't like it. He wanted a doll, not a wife, and Evelina was not a doll.'

'Oh.'

Valentino went on. 'Evelina hated how active Felice was in the family, and how much he enjoyed the theatrics of bloodshed. They argued constantly. Felice can't seem to love in a healthy way. He hit her in front of everyone one Christmas Day. My father ended up knocking him out. He wasn't going to stand for that in his family, under his rules. My father was a decent man. Felice was always somewhat of a . . . challenge. Believe it or not, this version of him is much more palatable than the old one.'

'And just when I thought Felice had reached the lowest ebb of my respect,' I said sourly. 'What a creep.'

Valentino didn't disagree. 'It doesn't surprise me that he would suspect my father in her disappearance. My father was always kind to her, and Felice never liked that.'

'That was his own fault.' I could feel myself getting riled up. 'He didn't deserve her. He doesn't deserve anyone if that's the way he carries on.'

'Well, he doesn't have anyone,' Valentino said, pointedly. 'Not any more.'

And there it was – the sting in the tail. Felice might have been horrible to Evelina, but my own father had been worse.

275

He had taken her life from her. Did Valentino suspect she was dead? Or did he really think her missing all these years?

'She and Luca were close, weren't they?' I remembered what he had told me about her, how she had made him believe he could be anything he wanted to be. How she had made him believe in possibility. I looked at my lap, suddenly unable to look Valentino in the eye.

I could sense him nodding. 'He idolized her. She was less like a mother and more like . . . a kindred spirit, I think. When she left, she took a piece of his heart with her.'

I couldn't untangle the emotion in his voice – was it regret, or sadness, or something else? Empathy for his brother, for the closest person to him in all the world? Guilt surrounded me, tinged my words, as I tried to keep them even. 'That's so sad,' was all I could say, because *Maybe she's better off* would have been a lie, and I wouldn't lie, not about this.

'She was a dreamer,' he said evenly. 'She wasn't meant to last in our world.'

There was something about the way he said it – the finality behind the words. He knew – or heavily suspected – she was dead, but he couldn't have known it was my father who did it. I would have felt it, and there was only sadness, heavy and dark, between us now. No suspicion, or resentment. I was careful not to look at him, careful not to push for answers I already had.

She was a dreamer.

There it was: the simple truth.

Wasn't Luca a dreamer too? Or had he stamped down that part of him just enough to claw by, to do what had to be done, to sacrifice a little part of himself every day? Or was he destined to meet the same fate as Evelina some day, at the hands of someone just as depraved as my father?

'Try not to worry about Felice,' Valentino said. 'He's capable of a lot of bad things, but he would never turn on us. He's too interested in self-preservation. Besides,' he added, 'if he truly was that angry at my father, then why did he never stand up to him?' He didn't wait for me to guess. 'Because he's a coward. And cowards might dream of higher planes but they know their place, and they don't step outside of it. Felice talks a big game, but he doesn't stand behind his words.'

I wasn't so sure. If Felice was truly loyal to Angelo despite his resentment, then where the hell was he the night my father shot him? He saw the entire thing, and yet by the time the ambulance came, he had already absconded. There was something not right about it – a niggling feeling at the base of my spine that had been growing ever since that night I over-heard him ranting to Paulie. But what good would it do to bring it up? Angelo was dead and, like Evelina, it was my own father who had been the killer.

'So, Sophie,' Valentino said, 'here we are, with the truth between us.' He moved around the other side of his desk, and started rummaging in a drawer. I watched him in silence – the frown puckering at the edges of his lips, the way one eyebrow arched higher than the other. After a moment, he pulled back, with a box. 'And now I'm going to give you some-thing.'

'A gift . . . ?' I tried to decide what could possibly be in the box.

'You don't have to look so scared,' he said. 'Haven't we already established that we're on the same side?'

'I thought that once before,' I said.

Valentino sucked a breath in through his teeth. 'A fair point.'

He rounded the desk and handed me a knife. I took it, and stared at the switchblade – now so familiar to me – as it sat innocently in the palm of my hand.

'Your switchblade?'

Valentino rolled his eyes. 'Obviously not *my* switchblade.'

I turned it over.

## Persephone, June 30th

'Oh.' I traced the perfect calligraphic letters, the flourishes, the etching of a falcon, wings half-spread.

'A Falcone switchblade,' I whispered. 'My own switchblade.' I glanced up at him, a smirk twisting my lips as a flurry of giddy energy rushed through me. 'Val, you simply must stop giving me weapons like this, you're absolutely *spoiling* me.'

He gaped at me for half a second, and I instantly regretted the levity of my response.

Then he laughed, and the sound was open and honest. 'I was trying to think of an appropriate time to give it to you. This seemed like a good diversion.'

I fingered the engraving. 'You got me this even though you know I didn't go through with killing Libero Marino. Why?'

'I need allies,' Valentino told me plainly. 'I know you're loyal. I trust everything you just told me. Luca fought hard to have you accepted here, and I trust his judgement too. I wouldn't deny him that. I wouldn't deny him anything, in fact. But I want you on my side, Sophie.'

I nodded, probably a bit too enthusiastically. 'Of course I'm on your side.'

'Good.' Valentino's smile was fleeting this time. 'Because I need you to stay here, with us.' There was an unexpected intensity to his words. I glanced up at him. 'I'm afraid I might be losing him,' he said.

'Who?'

'You know who,' he said.

'You're not losing Luca. He loves you. You're loyal to each other.'

'I am losing him,' Valentino insisted. 'To you.'

'It's not a competition, Valentino.'

His eyes creased, sadness brimming at the surface. 'Don't make him choose.'

'I won't.' I pressed my hand to my heart, without quite knowing why.

We fell into silence then, Valentino's thoughts turning to somewhere beyond that room, the switchblade heavy and sure in my hand.

# CHAPTER THIRTY-ONE

## NOTES

Paulie and Luca were on their way into the city by the time I was done in Valentino's office. Nic had tried to attack Luca again, and then a call had come through about a logistics meeting with a Marino emissary ahead of next week's peace talk. I wandered upstairs feeling incomplete, and a little anxious. Luca had said he loved me and I didn't get to say it back.

I paced back and forth in my room, and ate an entire bag of Cheetos. I didn't want to go downstairs – Nic was there, and I wasn't ready to have that talk with him, and it was more than obvious he wasn't ready to have that talk with me. Luca wasn't due home until much later.

I decided to go back to basics.

I was going to leave him a note.

A poem.

But I was going to out-gesture him and make my own.

I opened my notepad and started scribbling, and before I could talk myself out of it, I slid the note under his door and scurried back to bed.

Luca, I think it's time I told you something true,
Like how your eyes are the most amazing sapphire blue,
Or how your smile makes me giddy and silly and shy,
How I love your voice and the way that you sigh
I swear my heart jumps whenever I'm with you,
Because you are my favourite, and I love you, too.
PS I almost forgot this last message from me,
I will still never respect your authority ☺

# CHAPTER THIRTY-TWO

## DORK

When I rolled out of bed in the morning, a piece of paper had been shoved under my door. I unfolded it, glee quickly replacing exhaustion.

Sophie,
You are such a dork.
I'm keeping that in my wallet for ever.
Come get me when you wake up.
Luca x

# CHAPTER THIRTY-THREE

## ALL SOULS

**U**nfortunately for me and my intended Sunday morning cuddle session with Luca, Valentino had other plans. It was All Souls' Day, and since we were entering into peace negotiations with the Marino family, that meant we could all go out together on a family outing.

To church.

Kill me.

I was told we were to assemble at 10 a.m. in the foyer, which afforded me exactly twenty-nine minutes to spruce myself up. Dire. I caught a glimpse of Gino bounding down the hallway on my way back from the shower and noted with some degree of horror that he was wearing a suit. I hastily straightened my hair, wound it into a high ponytail and then swiped on some mascara, lip gloss and blusher.

There were more of us than usual today – a few of Luca's great-uncles and -aunts, some errant cousins, Paulie and his three girls, Cecilia, Pia and Greta. There was Sal, Aldo and CJ, and of course, among them all, Nic. He wouldn't look at me, and he made sure to stand as far away from Luca as possible. I was thankful at least for the crowd that pushed us apart from one another.

It was tradition, the others told me, to attend church in the city on All Souls' Day to remember their dead. Today was no different, only this time Valentino had cautioned Nic and Luca to use the outing and the confessional afterwards to bury their problems with each other. A family divided was weak, and we needed to be strong.

I had already gathered that the Falcones were Catholic. Like, super-Catholic. I wasn't, but the excursion fell under the heading of 'family business', and that meant I was a part of it.

I hadn't spent very much time in churches, but I was pretty sure Holy Name Cathedral in Chicago was one of the most decadent in existence. It was huge – this majestic structure with tall, bright ceilings, vaulted archways and marble pillars that probably cost more than I would ever earn in a lifetime. I remembered the outside facade from the article about Angelo Falcone's funeral Mass, but inside was even more impressive.

We arrived early and shuffled up the aisle, lulled by the faint sounds of hymnal music floating down on us. It was peaceful, and the tension that had been boiling among the family seemed to quell just a little, replaced by soft melody and candlelight.

'You're like a kid in a candy store,' Luca murmured as we

made our way up the centre aisle.

I had been staring open-mouthed at the altar. 'It's cool,' I breathed.

'Is it?' he asked, amused.

I nodded. 'Very *Hunchback of Notre Dame*.'

His laugh was low against my ear. 'Why am I not surprised by that comparison?'

I winked at him over my shoulder. 'I'm just a Disney princess stuck in a Mafia world.'

He trailed his fingers around my waist as we walked, planting a quick kiss below my ear before anyone could see. 'Yes, you are.'

The Falcone family took up two entire pews. Luca and I sat in the second of the two rows, and Nic was, by awkward coincidence, just in front of us, his shoulders tensed. Elena was on one side of him and Gino on the other. Paulie's girls were giggling down the far end of their pew, sandwiched between Sal and Aldo, who looked positively miserable.

I was enjoying the way Luca's leg was brushing against mine. That quick kiss in the aisle had sent my mind spiralling somewhere entirely un-church-like. The trade-off for this wonderful closeness meant I was also sitting beside Felice and was, as a consequence, detecting the faintest scent of honey every twenty seconds. It still reminded me of death. Valentino was on the other side of Felice, positioned at the very end of the row beyond where the pew ended.

As the church filled up, the choir began singing – their soaring voices pealing across the aisles and reverberating inside the sloping arches. Some of the Falcones around me joined in. Felice stayed silent, thankfully. Luca had his eyes closed. He must have been thinking about something serious because there were little ripples forming above his nose.

Elena was the first to notice the arrival of her sister. Her hand flew to her mouth, a gasp only half stifled at the sight of Donata Marino and two of her lackeys right across the aisle. I slammed my fist into Luca's leg, and his eyes flew open. Whispers rippled along the pews, as half of us turned to Valentino, waiting for instruction.

He raised a hand slowly, as if to say, *Calm down. We are at peace.*

Elena was deathly pale, her bright pink lips twisted into a scowl. Her head was tilted away from her sister, her fingers gripping the pew so tightly they looked like they might break off. She wore her hair long and loose in contrast to Donata's bun, which was so tight it stretched her eyebrows. Still, the Genovese sisters were similar – the same brightly painted mouth, the same piercing eyes. Their noses were upturned, their pointed chins naturally raised as though they were looking down on the rest of the world. Dom and Gino were staring so hard at Donata that they looked like statues. Paulie was subtly casing the rest of the place while Luca was working on matching Valentino's impassive expression. Only I could hear how uneven his breathing was.

With my heart in my throat, I dropped my voice, barely moving my mouth as I asked, 'Did you know Donata was going to be here?'

Luca's jaw hardened. He shook his head, an inch to the left, an inch to the right.

'Are we in danger?'

'No,' he whispered, at the same time as Felice, from the

other side of me, leant forward and said, 'Of course.'

I was conscious of Felice's eyes on the side of my face, so I kept my arm pressed against Luca's as we waited for the priest and the servers to ascend to the altar. I felt the weight of my switchblade in my pocket and was grateful for it. I would use it if I had to.

'What should we do?' I said.

'Nothing,' Luca said.

'Yet,' Felice added.

I stole a glance at Donata. She wasn't facing us. She was watching the priest take his place at the altar, a serene smile spread across her face. Maybe it was my imagination, but as I studied her, it seemed to grow, curling into a smirk that raised the hairs on the back of my neck.

Everyone was on high alert. *Peace talks, peace talks, peace talks,* I kept repeating inside my head, but the words only seemed to raise my heart rate, and all I kept thinking was: if Donata was here, across from us, where were the rest of them? If it really was a gesture of goodwill, why weren't they here, too, where we could see them?

Why wasn't my uncle sitting across from us too? Why wasn't my father here?

The Mass began in Latin. After a few minutes, Paulie shifted his position, so that he was sitting sidelong, facing the other side of the church and the back of it, his cheek turned to the priest and his sermon. This, evidently, was more important, and it was telling that neither Valentino nor Luca told him to stand down.

Time crawled, and instead of sinking into a feeling of serenity, I became more alert. Finally, everyone was getting up and shuffling to the front of the church for communion. Felice brought Valentino, Paulie walking in front of them, just in case. Luca waited for them to return before going up. For once, I was glad of the protection. The choir was singing another soaring hymn. An old lady behind me was singing out of tune, her voice like broken glass. I stayed where I was, my hands folded in my lap.

The Falcones filed back in, one by one. I had to stand up to let Luca and some of the others by me. He knelt down, his face pressed to the pew in front of him, his eyes still open. They were all kneeling, even Felice, his lips moving soundlessly. Nic was praying, too. I hoped they were praying for peace among themselves. I stayed sitting up, unsure of where to put myself. I watched the sea of faces streaking by – made pale by the encroaching winter, their necks wrapped up in scarves. It was a bit eerie – this wordless procession, the deep, rousing music that fell upon us from above. Nobody was even looking at each other. They were looking at their hands, their feet.

I watched Donata and her two lackeys receive communion, heads dipped in reverence and hands clasped as they passed us by. As they passed us by and kept walking. Towards the exit, away from the final blessing.

I sneaked a glance at Valentino. Of course, he wasn't kneeling – his chair was apart from the pews – but his head was down, as though he was sleeping.

I looked back at Luca. He was frowning, but his lips were still. Was he wondering about Donata, too? Why she wasn't staying? Elena was sitting bolt upright in her seat, watching the back of Donata's head as she made her way down the centre aisle. Everyone was watching her go. Felice cleared his throat. There was a scuffle somewhere to my right, but by the time I looked back, everything was normal again. Valentino was still praying, his head bowed slightly.

I looked again, leaning closer to Felice and ignoring all that honeyed scent to see around him properly. Head bowed, shoulders slumped. I couldn't see Valentino's face, but his body was creasing, his forehead inching towards his knees, slowly, slowly.

I grabbed Luca's arm and shook him.

He snapped his head around, forgetting to whisper. 'What?'

I jabbed Felice in the shoulder. He was already looking at me.

'Valentino,' I hissed. 'Valentino!'

I stretched around Felice, without bothering to ask permission. His head turned slowly, following me. The others were turning around now, too, following the disturbance and ignoring Donata Marino as she left the church.

Valentino was still falling forwards. Not praying. Not sleeping. Felice, seeing that I couldn't reach, grabbed Valentino by the shoulder. He didn't raise his head.

'No,' I muttered, 'no, no, no.'

'Valentino!' Luca said, his voice carrying over the dying music. Felice pulled Valentino back with a stiff yank. His head lolled backwards until he was gazing at the ceiling, his eyes wide open. A trickle of blood striped his chin.

Felice gasped, and his hand fell away from his nephew. 'No,' he breathed.

*No. No. No.*

I looked down, to where Valentino's hands were folded across his middle, his fingers still half clenched. I saw the handle of the knife, long and sleek, and the dark pool spreading across his jacket, right over his heart, at the same time as the others.

Elena screamed.

The choir stopped singing.

Nic and Dom jumped over the pew and barrelled down the middle aisle, shouting as they pulled their guns out. A lone figure crashed through the doors, just a shadow at the end of the church, her laughter rising up like a chorus. Laughter I had heard for the first time recently, trapped inside a darkened hallway in my school.

Elena's scream echoed down the aisles of the church, reverberated around us as she folded in on herself, her face pressed to the pew as she gasped and heaved. Luca stumbled past me, past Felice, and out into the aisle. He sank to his knees in front of Valentino, his arms encircling his middle, his head slumped forward, touching against Valentino's knee – his position a mirror image of his twin brother's. When the sound gurgled in his throat, it was a scraping, primal thing, carved from pure, soul-shattering grief, and I could feel it, this sharp, twisting wound, right down in my own heart.

Valentino was gone.

The boss was dead.

# PART IV

'Vengeance is in my heart, death in my hand,
Blood and revenge are hammering in my head.'

William Shakespeare, *Titus Andronicus*

# CHAPTER THIRTY-FOUR
## WINTER

The weeks passed slowly. Every day was a trickle of time, of renewed pain and loaded silence. A thick blanket of snow draped itself over *Evelina*, and with it came the ice. It made spectres of us all, roaming the halls, looking for something to say, and knowing there were no words left.

There was no laughter, no joy.

Just rage.

Intent.

My father remained elusive – no sightings, no word of him anywhere. I started to wonder if he had been there that day, too, hiding somewhere with Jack, laughing behind a church missal as Elena's screams filled up the church like an aria.

Over twenty witnesses at Holy Name Cathedral on All Souls' Day pointed to Zola Marino as Valentino's assailant.

They had seen her in the communion procession, hooded and in plain clothes, as she approached Valentino in the aisle and leant over him from behind. They had passed it off as a friendly greeting at first, a hug that lasted just a little too long. By the time they understood what had happened, Elena was screaming the walls down and Nic and Dom were already charging out of the church.

The boys never caught up to Zola.

They never even fired their guns.

The incident made every single local paper, and most of the national ones, too. News of the escalating blood war between the Falcones and the Marinos was now public knowledge. They rehashed old murders – details of my paternal grandparents, Vince Marino and Linda Harris, splashed across the pages, photographs of Angelo Falcone, of Felice, and even Luca – the 'striking blue-eyed twin' of the latest Falcone victim.

Zola had been discovered hiding in the back of a well-known Marino-friendly restaurant eighteen blocks from the church and was taken away in handcuffs by the police. On her second day in jail, she was found hanging by the neck. The newspapers called it suicide. The Falcones called it retribution. They had people everywhere. Prison wasn't good enough for Zola, so death would have to do.

The war had truly begun.

In the blink of an eye, everything had changed, and we all did too – morphed by the weight of our guilt, of how close we had been to Valentino and how drastically we had failed him. It was the hardest blow they could have dealt, and they had done it because we had underestimated them. Because we had dared to ask for peace when they were thirsting for war. Because we had dared to believe in the possibility of a truce. Nothing was off limits any more.

The rules had changed.

Luca's desires now were singular, the sharp edge of his grief directed outwards, like a weapon, at all those Marinos who still walked free. He talked a little crisper, walked a little faster, drew his gun a lot quicker. He didn't lie out on the roof any more, looking at the stars. He didn't read poetry or spar with his brothers. He didn't talk about the what-ifs. He didn't talk to me, either. Not the way he used to. The old Luca was gone, replaced by a harder, darker version. The Falcone he was always supposed to be. The Falcone who would avenge all that was taken from us.

No one else talked about the what-ifs, either. The idea of possibility was gone. Luca had finally let it go. He had finally succumbed to the family, and without him trying to block me from it, I did too. We were united at last in our purpose, but instead of bringing us closer together, it pushed us apart. We stood on opposite ends of a dark cloud, our ever-present grief licking the happiness from our skin.

On November 10th, Valentino was interred next to his father in the family mausoleum.

That evening, Luca was sworn in by the family elders as the new Falcone boss.

He made Paulie his underboss.

Security measures at *Evelina* were tightened.

Shoot-on-sight orders were distributed.

Luca swore revenge on every living, breathing Marino in the state of Illinois while Felice stood by and watched, a quiet smile painted across his face.

And I kept wondering, as the weeks dragged by, how exactly the Falcone *consigliere* had failed to notice Valentino's murder, when he was sitting shoulder to shoulder with him when it happened.

I played his reaction over and over in my head – the wide eyes, the gasp, the slow turn of his head, as though the scene had been written and it was time for Felice to play his part. The more time passed, the less I believed in his shock. His grief. The less I believed in his loyalty at all.

Felice spent his time watching Luca, and I spent my time watching him.

# CHAPTER THIRTY-FIVE

## DECEMBER 23RD

I n the Council room at *Evelina*, Luca stood at the head of the table with his back to us. His black hair brushed against the base of his neck, his head tilted to the side as he faced the photographs on the wall. The others were looking at them, but I was looking at Luca, the way his shoulders tensed, how his voice arced. I could hear the exhaustion in it. He swept a hand through his hair, then gestured towards the photo on the far right.

Uncle Jack. A recent photo of him coming out of Eden and ducking into a car. His grey hair was buzzed short, his right eye still scarred and pink around the edges. My handiwork.

It was two days before Christmas, and I had never felt so joyless. We were planning our final, full-force strike, and every active Falcone member in the state had been called in to prepare for it. D-Day was approaching and I was right smack in the middle of it, finally about to get my revenge.

I didn't want to be anywhere else.

'Jack Gracewell aka Antony Marino will be at Donata Marino's house, along with the others,' Luca said without turning around. 'Marco, her youngest son, will also be present. We suspect he has been appointed underboss following Zola's death. Her cousin, Romano Marino, recently released from prison, has also risen in the ranks. Our sources tell us he's become a key player in Zola and Libero's absence.' He shifted his attention to the photo on the far left, where a stocky skinhead boy was glaring at the camera. Beside him, a photo of a scowling Marco Marino: cropped brown hair, a hooked nose and a silver lip ring. Sara's eyes, Donata's harsh curving mouth. 'And of course, Donata will be hosting.' The photo of Donata was taken at Zola Marino's funeral. She was mostly hidden under a netted black veil, those piercing eyes glazed over. She wasn't crying. She was a woman who had spent all her tears long ago.

'And what about Michael Gracewell?' asked Dom. 'Is he expected at Donata's too?'

Luca straightened just a little. 'We have no recorded sightings of Vince Marino Junior.'

Not since my mother's goodbye ceremony.

Where the hell was he? Hidden so deeply inside the Marino framework, we had barely heard a peep from him. Was he that afraid of being hauled back to prison? Or was it us he was hiding from?

'Well, if he's there, we'll just kill him, too,' Felice remarked, his eyes on me while he said it. 'The same rule applies to all of the Marinos. Is that not correct, Don Luca?'

There was no respect in the way he addressed Luca, and everyone around the table knew it. He was still looking at me while he played his game, while he tried to make Luca sign my father's death sentence in front of me.

'I doubt Vince Marino will be there.' Luca's voice was even. 'He might be halfway to Fiji by now.'

'But if he is,' Felice pressed, grinning at me, 'we are to kill him too, yes?'

'Yes,' I said, taking the reins before Felice could do any damage. 'Of course we kill him. Why wouldn't we? He's a Marino.'

I tried not to let the pain of my response show on my face. If Luca couldn't confirm my father's impending death, then I could. It didn't matter how deeply it cut into me, how jagged the words tasted in my mouth. There was no going back now, and the father I knew was long gone.

Felice's eyebrows shot up. 'Persephone,' he said, his smile curling. 'You surprise me. You would put your own father to death . . .'

Luca whirled around so fast that Gino jumped in his chair. He had his finger half an inch from Felice's face, his twin brother's thick ring shining on his left hand. Pure, unfiltered rage flashed behind his eyes. 'I will tell you this once, Felice. You will not, under my leadership, presume to exploit the grief or pain of anyone in this family for your own amusement. You will not goad or tease or stir any more. If you do, I will demote you. If you push me, I will punish you.'

Felice swirled his response around in his mouth. We were all tellingly silent. It was a game, and it was not for us to play, but to wait on edge for it to end. Of course Felice would not cower, not in front of his audience, not even against his better judgement. He raised his eyebrows, and as innocently as he could make himself sound, he said, 'Are you speaking to me as my boss or as Persephone Marino's lover?'

Luca backhanded him.

The sound was a thick, hulking smack in the airless room. The ring smashed into Felice's mouth, nicking a cut along his lower lip. Felice blinked up at Luca, the blood dribbling down his chin. He sucked it into his mouth and hummed as he tasted it.

'Felice,' Paulie warned. 'Don't.'

Felice stared at Luca. 'You are crueller than your brother was, Gianluca.'

Luca hunkered down, his face inches from his uncle's. 'This is a different family now, Felice. Your words will have consequences, as will your actions . . . or lack thereof.'

He held his stare. The room seemed to grow colder. Luca would never forgive Felice for what happened that day in Holy Name, just as he would never forgive himself.

Felice swallowed a mouthful of his own blood. He broke eye contact, moving his gaze back to the photographs behind Luca. It was over.

Luca straightened up. '*Capisci?*'

Felice nodded. '*Capisco.*'

Uneasiness bound us into silence as we watched this new version of Luca, a boss just like the one his grandfather thought he would be. He was cold, calculated, intelligent.

Grief had made him something to cower before – he held his temper on a short leash but it still flared inside him, and we could all feel it.

Luca turned back to the photographs, clasping his hands behind his back, the Don's ring glinting at me. 'These people are the reigning command of the Marino family. When we ambush Donata's home, I want them taken out first. Prioritize. Keep your wits about you. They will be expecting our retribution. They will be armed.'

Cosimo, a Falcone elder, tapped his cane on the table. 'Who will go?' he asked.

Luca turned around again, his face placid. How eerie it was to see how much he looked like Valentino now, how steady he seemed in the role he never wanted.

'Everyone who is able and willing. Elders excluded, unless they choose otherwise.'

'We are all willing,' said Paulie. 'Naturally.'

'Naturally,' Elena echoed him, her voice hollow. She didn't speak much any more. It was like the effort of being present was too much for her now, the sadness was too great. It took all of her energy just to wade through it, day after day.

'Gee, I don't know,' said Dom. 'I'm kind of scared?'

We all turned to look at him. He burst into a fit of laughter. 'Just kidding,' he said, smiling at his own apparent hilarity. 'I can't wait to blow Antony's one-eyed head off!'

'What time, Luca?' asked Paulie. 'I'd like to see my girls in the morning when they open their presents.'

Felice side-eyed Paulie. 'This whole operation doesn't rest on the reception of your My Little Pony gift sets, brother.'

Paulie ignored him.

301

'And Calvino's younger boys,' grumbled Tommaso, another elder, from the far end of the table. 'They deserve a Christmas morning, too.'

'They will be with Vita,' said Paulie. 'Far from here.'

*Good*, I thought. Let there be joy, at least, for the children. Let there be joy until they grow into their destinies and turn into the rest of us.

'Donata will begin lunch early,' Elena said quietly. 'She keeps with the tradition of how our mother raised us. It will be an all-day affair.'

She slumped back in her chair, her eyes downcast, her sadness draped around her like a shroud. It's like someone had doused a bucket of water over the fire inside her. I wondered if she would ever be the same again. I wondered that about Luca, too.

'Pity we can't jump out of the panettone,' murmured Tommaso, much to the chagrin of his wife.

'You're not going,' she hissed. 'You've just had a knee operation.'

'I was just saying,' he protested, sulkily.

'I miss the old days,' Cosimo sighed. 'I would have enjoyed this more.'

'We'll tell you all about it, don't worry,' Nic assured him.

Cosimo dipped his head in appreciation. 'I'd so love to see the Marino girl take down the Marino boss,' he said, pointing at me.

'What a coup,' agreed the lady next to him.

'Indeed,' said Elena.

I mustered a confident smile. I had been hurtling towards this moment ever since I came to *Evelina*, but now that we were almost on the eve of it, my stomach was constantly churning – fresh plumes of anxiety filling me up, threatening to choke the courage out of me. After Valentino's death, it had become unavoidably apparent just how close we all were to our own demise. Still, if I cowered behind closed doors, Donata would still come for me, for all of us, like she did that day in Holy Name Cathedral. We had to get them before they could get us. We would not underestimate them again.

I didn't realize Luca was looking at me until I turned my attention back to him. He caught himself, and refocused.

'The time?' asked Cosimo. 'Please, a little more clarity.'

The respect that Luca instantly commanded from the family had been a little jarring at first. It was as if the day he stepped into the role and vowed to avenge his twin brother's death, everyone saw him in a new light. They enveloped him gratefully, deferring to his authority without so much as a backward glance – even the older members, the ones who had survived many bosses by now. Luca was the one they were waiting for, and they weren't afraid to dip their heads in respect to him.

Luca took a step back until his head was framed by the three Marino photographs. He was sure and confident when he answered, and the ripple of his conviction travelled down the table and strengthened the family.

'One p.m., Christmas Day, at the Marino mansion.'

'Perfect,' said Nic.

The others murmured their agreement.

Luca smiled; it was small, and practised, and cold as ice. '*Buon Natale*, Donata Marino.'

The Falcone family laughed, echoes of '*Buon Natale*' rising up with their amusement.

I laughed too, but I don't know whether it came from my brain or my heart.

Merry Christmas indeed.

# CHAPTER THIRTY-SIX
## CHRISTMAS EVE

'Thanks for coming all the way out here, Mil.' I pulled my best friend into an embrace and tugged her across the threshold. Her hair smelt like apples and her face was perfectly made-up. She was tucked up to the chin in a goose-feathered cream coat. She looked like a snow queen. 'You look beautiful.'

'So do you!' she said brightly, the smile coming easily to her face. 'God, it's freezing. I nearly skidded off the road on my way in.' She shivered involuntarily. 'I think it's time I got a fancier car.'

'Well, it would match your coat,' I said.

'Do you like it?' She did a twirl. 'Cris got it for me. Turns out he's stinking rich.'

I arched a brow. 'He just gets better by the day.'

She shrugged. 'It compensates for his obsession with mindfulness colouring books.'

I shut the door behind her and she lowered her voice, the joviality seeping away. 'How has it been here?'

'Still the same,' I told her quietly. I ushered her upstairs towards my room, where we would have privacy.

'It must be especially hard at Christmas,' she said, following me up. 'Are you sure you're OK to stay here? You're still grieving for your mum. Maybe this place isn't the right home for you at the moment. You know you can always come to the cottage with me and my family, right? We're not leaving until later . . .'

'Mil, I really appreciate it—'

'But . . .' she cut in, sensing my hesitation.

'I need to be here with everyone. They're my family now.' I conveniently left out the second part of my reasoning: the Marino Massacre. By this time tomorrow, the death toll would have risen. Every time I thought about the potential casualties on our side, it made me feel sick, so I pushed it away.

'How is Luca coping?' Millie asked delicately. I shut the door to my room and we both dropped on to the bed.

*As a boss? Exceedingly good. As a normal guy grieving his brother? Terrible.* 'He'll be OK. We don't really talk about it.' The rest was too painful to admit. *We don't really talk about anything any more.*

'And you're staying out of trouble?' Millie asked. 'All that stuff in the newspaper about the blood war . . .'

'I told you, it's nonsense.' I waved away her concern. 'Zola had a grudge and tried to settle it. She's dead. So it's over now.'

'Are you safe?' She shuffled closer, studying me. 'Tell me you're safe.'

'I'm safe,' I lied. 'Safer than you, probably. You might get eaten by a bear at your cottage.'

She smiled grimly. 'Don't even joke about that. You know I have zero survival skills.'

*Unlike me*, I thought.

'I feel sad,' she said after a moment. 'Isn't that strange? I'm only leaving for a few days, but I feel sad that you'll be here and I'll be there. Why do I feel so sad?'

I grabbed her hand and squeezed it. 'It's a sad house, that's all. It's this atmosphere. Try not to let it get to you. It's Christmas. There's no reason for you to be sad.' I blinked away the threat of tears. The truth was, I didn't know for sure if I would see Millie again after today. I didn't know if I would end up in jail, or in the ground. I didn't know anything any more. I just knew I was walking into the Marino house with my family and helping to put an end to all the wrongdoing we had suffered at their hands.

'We'll be happy in the new year,' Millie said, the promise of it shimmering in her eyes. 'Just hang in there a little longer and then we'll get out of Chicago.'

'Yes.' The word was thick in my throat. 'Of course we will.'

'I got you this.' She reached inside her coat and pulled out a present. 'I hope you like it.'

I reached under the bed and fished her present out, too. 'It's not much,' I said sheepishly, handing it over. It was just a scarf and gloves, and some funny socks. She deserved better. 'I'm pretty broke and I've been confined to online shopping ever since Valentino passed away.'

307

Millie ripped open her present and buried her head in the scarf. 'I love it,' she whooped, wrapping it around her twice and then taking the gloves to try them on. 'These are beautiful. I hope you didn't overspend.'

I snorted. 'I appreciate the overenthusiasm.'

She swatted a glove at me. 'Open your gift.'

I opened the purple wrapping paper and a small Mason jar tumbled out. It had a purple cloth lid, and a heart hanging off the twine that encircled it.

'It's not honey,' she said quickly. 'Don't freak out.'

I picked it up and read the heart aloud. '*The Happy Jar,*' I said, glancing at her. '*To be used when you are feeling sad or when you are experiencing Millie withdrawal symptoms.*'

I shook it. There were loads of tiny folded-up pieces of paper inside.

'They're memories, mostly,' said Millie. 'But some are our dreams for the future. And other ones are just compliments that will cheer you up. Like "You have the hair of a fairytale mermaid princess." Stuff like that.'

I opened the lid, and shook one piece on to my hand.

'Just one!' she said, snatching the jar from me and closing it again. 'You can't read them all at once. They're supposed to last for a little while at least.'

Duly scolded, I unfolded the paper and read the memory scribbled across it.

'*Remember that time we snuck into an R-rated movie and when we got caught you told the usher we were twenty-seven because you thought overcompensating would throw him off? He kicked us out and you threatened to sue him for age discrimination.*'

I started giggling. 'I had forgotten about that.'

Millie was laughing too. 'You were so indignant, I almost believed you myself!'

'Can I read one more?' I asked hopefully.

'Are you feeling sad?'

'A little,' I admitted.

She handed the jar to me and I unfurled another piece of paper.

'*When my dad told us we were moving to Chicago I cried for six nights straight. If I had known you were waiting somewhere on the other end for me, I would have leapt on to the plane and never looked back. I thank the universe every day for giving me a friend as good and loyal and kind as you.*'

'Oh,' I said, wiping a rogue tear. 'That's so lovely. And now I'm crying.' I dived at her, wrapping her in a big hug that pushed us both backwards on the bed. 'Thank you,' I said, squeezing her tight. 'Thank you so much, Mil. I love it! It's so wonderful and thoughtful and perfect.'

'You're welcome.' She blew her hair out of her face. 'Sheesh, anyone would think you'd never got a gift before.'

'None like this.' I sat up and placed the Mason jar on my bedside table, smiling at all the loveliness inside it. All those tiny bright sparks for me. I would read them all tonight, just in case.

'It's about hope,' Millie said. 'It's about happiness. It won't always be like this,' she said quietly. 'I just wanted you to remember that.'

I couldn't look at her face any more. I was sitting beside my best friend and I was lying to her. Even by not saying anything, I was misleading her. 'Thank you.' I knitted my hands together, studying my fingernails. Tomorrow, one way or another, there would be blood on them.

She grabbed my hand, covering it with hers. 'We'll always have each other, Soph. And that's the most important thing of all.' Her smile held the promises of tomorrow.

'You're so sappy, Mil.' I pulled her in for another hug, keenly aware that it might be the last one I ever gave her. I was determined to make it count.

'Oh, you love it.' She hugged me back just as strongly, until my breath came out in laboured wheezes.

'I know,' I huffed, blinking back the tears.

# CHAPTER THIRTY-SEVEN
## STARLESS NIGHT

Christmas Eve passed mostly in silence. Gino made a snowman in the back garden and Dom kicked its head off before he could stick a carrot on for the nose. They ended up brawling on the ground, making an impressive, if inadvertent, pair of snow angels. Elena watched them from the window, a sad smile painted across her face.

CJ came along and demolished the rest of the snowman, and Dom chased him all the way to the barn before wrangling him into a headlock and smashing a snowball into his hair. Gino rolled to his feet and started rebuilding his snowman. Nic went outside with a carrot and helped him. I watched from the window, drinking hot chocolate and feeling a pinch of sympathy for Gino. Like Luca, he didn't belong here either, but he was too blissfully unaware to see it. At least,

I hoped he was.

'They're good boys,' Elena said quietly. It was the first thing she'd said all evening. 'They're like their father.'

I realized she wasn't talking to me.

Dinner wasn't exactly a joyful affair, but Elena and Paulie still managed to make an incredible spread for everyone. 'The Feast of the Seven Fishes,' Gino told me, 'is going to be unlike any eating experience you've had up until now.'

He was right.

It was my first Italian Christmas Eve, and despite the thundering fear of all that still lay ahead, I found my appetite was in surprisingly good shape, probably owing to the mouthwatering selection of food neatly arranged across the dining room table. There was salted cod and clams casino, deep-fried calamari, lobster salad, marinated eel, salmon rillettes with breadsticks for dipping, and my favourite dish – grilled shrimp with chilli, coriander and lime. There were salads and baked bread, a seafood stew, and bowls of freshly made tagliatelle in a creamy mushroom sauce. For dessert, Gino made rainbow cookies with gelato, and Elena made cannoli – pastry shells stuffed with sweetened ricotta cheese that melted in your mouth.

There was so much decadence and care in every dish that I found myself wishing that, just once, my father had embraced his roots so we could have experienced something like that when I was growing up.

We sat down to eat at nine p.m. Luca raised his glass – water – and we all followed suit, a mismatch of whiskies and red wine and vodka soaring towards the ceiling.

'*Salute,*' was all he said. He had been quiet all day, hidden in his office, going over plans and layouts.

'*Salute*,' we replied as one.

'The Last Supper,' said Gino. He smiled at his mother – it was the saddest smile I've ever seen. Elena shut her eyes tight, and when she opened them again they were clear.

No one answered him.

We picked up our forks and started eating.

After dinner, I stayed behind with Dom and Gino to clear up. Luca had arranged for a priest to come out to the house to celebrate midnight Mass – a Christmas tradition the Falcone family refused to miss, even if we weren't able to risk going to a church to experience it. After Mass, there was confession for those who wanted it. Every single Falcone availed themselves of it. The significance wasn't lost on me.

I was washing a pot in the sink when Luca appeared behind me, his hand light against my lower back. I jumped, and it fell from my hands. He grabbed it by the rim before it could clatter into the sink.

'Sorry,' he murmured, just above my ear.

It took everything in my power not to lean back into him and close my eyes. We hadn't been this close since Valentino passed away.

I turned to look up at him. 'Is everything OK?'

He moved his hand to the edge of the sink, his body so close we were almost touching. My breath caught in my throat. Dom and Gino were being suspiciously quiet somewhere behind me. Luca dropped his voice. 'Meet me on the roof after Mass?' he asked. 'I have something for you.'

I offered him a half-smile. 'I'll only come if it's a present.'

'It is. It's a unicorn.'

Then he turned and strode out of the kitchen without looking at Gino or Dom.

'So, that's still going on,' said Dom.

I was going to glare at him, but his tone was neutral and when I saw his face, I realized he wasn't teasing me.

He slotted the final plate into the dishwasher and straightened up. 'You know he's going to get himself killed tomorrow, don't you?'

I disregarded the pot I was halfway through cleaning. 'What?'

Gino had stopped wiping down the table. He turned to look at Dom.

'Luca isn't planning on making it out of the Marino mansion alive.'

'What are you talking about?' I could feel the anger flashing in my cheeks. 'Of course he'll make it out alive. We all will.'

Dom just shrugged. 'It's his final stand.'

'Why would you say that?' I tried to keep the panic at bay, but this didn't feel like one of Dom's stupid jokes.

'Look at him,' said Dom, his hand flying out to where Luca had just been standing. 'He's resigned. His thirst for retribution is going to outweigh his self-preservation. Valentino and Luca weren't made to be apart. They can't live without each other.'

'Why are you talking like this?' Gino sounded like a small child. 'You make it seem like suicide.'

'He's just different,' Dom said. 'He doesn't care any more.'

'He cares about getting rid of the Marinos,' Gino argued.

'And what else?'

'I don't know,' said Gino.

'Exactly,' Dom sighed. 'Exactly.'

I picked up my pan, scouring it until my fingers were red raw and the sting in Dom's words had passed.

When everyone had retired to bed, post-confession, with clean souls, I climbed through Luca's bedroom window. I crept across the roof, leaving my footprints and handprints in the thin layer of snow like the tracks of a giant toddler.

Luca was sitting at the edge, in the same place he had been on the night of the meteor shower. He turned to watch me crawl towards him.

'Ever cautious,' he said softly.

He reached his hand out to help me steady myself. After much manoeuvring, I managed to make camp beside him.

'Hi.' I tried to ignore the sinking feeling in my chest. Stupid Dom and his apocalyptic words.

'Are you cold?' he asked.

Strangely, I wasn't. I shook my head. 'There are no stars in the sky,' I pointed out. The night was cloudy – the moon just a nebulous smudge.

'Everything is different now.' I got the sense he wasn't just talking about the weather.

I nodded, the sense of glumness expanding inside me.

He tipped my chin up so I would look at him. 'But not how I feel about you, Sophie.' He brushed his hand against my cheek, his thumb lingering on my bottom lip.

I blinked away the surprise. I had been expecting his feelings to trickle away, like water, even though mine had blazed ever brighter with each passing day. Still, there was no joy in the way he said it, no whisper of something more – of a future unfurling before us. It was hard to feel the sense of possibility now, no matter how badly I wanted it.

Still, there was tonight.

'I bought you a Christmas present.' I reached into my coat pocket and pulled out a small wrapped parcel. 'It's not much, and you're probably going to think it's really silly, but I wanted to get you something you've never gotten before and I thought it might be something special, just for us . . .' I trailed off.

He raised his eyebrows, taking the package and rotating it in his hand. 'I have to be honest, Soph, I'm really hoping it's another poem.'

'That was a one-time deal,' I said.

He frowned. 'But I love your poetry.'

'No you don't.'

'I do,' he insisted. 'I mean, it's really *really* terrible, but that doesn't mean I don't love it.'

Before I could stop myself I shot forward and kissed him on the cheek. 'Open it, before I go out of my mind with suspense.'

He laughed a little, amusement turning to concentration as he unwrapped it piece by piece. Excruciatingly slowly, just to annoy me. I let him have his moment. At least he was being playful.

When he was done and the paper had been peeled away, he let it sit there on the palm of his hand, while he stared at it. This inconsequential-looking black stone with little thumb-print-shaped grooves inside it.

Embarrassment roared inside me.

He obviously had no idea what it was. He just kept looking

at it, like he was trying to figure it out.

Oh God. He thought I was giving him a rock for Christmas.

Well, technically I was.

But it was a special one.

I thought about just covering my face and rolling off the roof, but it was my stupid idea in the first place, so I figured I may as well just explain myself and get the mortification over with.

'It's not just a rock,' I said to the side of his face. 'It's more than that, I swear. See, it's a—'

'It's a Sikhote-Alin Meteorite,' he said, looking up at me. 'From Russia.'

'Yeah. It is . . .' I said, surprised.

He looked back at the rock in his hand. 'It's from a meteor crash site in Siberia in 1947. Is that what you were going to say?' He was looking at me again, and he was wearing the strangest expression on his face. I had never seen it before.

It was . . . wonder.

I smiled sheepishly at him. 'I was actually just going to say it's a fallen star.'

He held it between us, passing his thumb over the small ridges. 'These are coarsest octahedrites,' he murmured. 'Part of the surfaces of these meteorites were blasted off while they passed through the atmosphere on the way to earth. That's why it's not smooth. See.' He placed my thumb under his, so I could feel it.

'Do you, um, do you already have one?'

'No,' he said quietly. That look, still on his face. His eyes seemed bigger, his mouth fuller, his breathing quicker. 'I don't.'

'Good,' I said, relieved. 'Because I had to outbid an old lady from Kansas for it, and it got right down to the wire, but I'll be damned if I was going to let her play the age card on me. Like, what? I'm just going to let her steal it out from under me when—'

'I love it,' he said, cutting me off. 'I love that you went head-to-head with some sweet old lady and won. And I love that you have absolutely no remorse about it. I can't believe you did this for me.'

I moved a little closer. 'Why is that so hard to believe?'

He shook his head, his smile small and sad. 'Because I don't deserve it.'

'Yes, you do,' I said, willing him to look at me, but he was already disengaging, reaching into his jacket pocket.

'I have something for you, too, Sophie.' He pulled out a small box.

I took it from him, and held it in front of my face. 'OK, this looks a little small to be a unicorn, Luca.'

'Maybe I was just trying to throw you off the scent,' he said, leaning closer as I opened it.

It was a bracelet, delicate and silver, with a single, heart-shaped charm. I read the words engraved on it. *'Hope smiles from the threshold of the year to come, whispering, "It will be happier."'*

'It's a quote from Alfred Lord Tennyson,' he explained.

'It's beautiful.' I slipped it on to my wrist, trailing my finger around the heart-shaped charm. 'I love it, Luca.'

I wanted to say the rest: *I love you.* But the moment was so fragile and precious, I was afraid I might shatter it.

'It's about possibility,' he said quietly. 'All the possibility

318

in your life.'

'In *our lives*,' I amended.

He didn't say anything. I could feel the weight of every-thing pressing down on us, the sadness at the edges ready to swoop in and take him away from me.

He took my hand, and wound my fingers in his. 'Sophie,' he said, his voice calling to the space inside my heart. It beat faster as I looked at him. 'Please don't come tomorrow. Please stay here, where it's safe.'

'Don't,' I breathed. 'Please let's not talk about tomorrow.'

He laid his forehead against mine. 'I am begging you.'

'No,' I said firmly. 'I go where my family go. Where you go. This is our revenge. This is our destiny.'

He shut his eyes. It was too late. We were both going, and neither of us could stop the other. This was too big, it was too much of what we had been pushing towards. We owed it to Valentino, and to my mother. Luca wasn't going to back down, and neither was I. Dom's words from earlier skated through my mind.

'No more talk of tomorrow,' I said. 'Please. Let's just enjoy now. What will be will be.'

'Your teeth are chattering.'

'Are they?' I couldn't tell if it was from a sudden onslaught of nerves or the chill in the air. It wasn't enough – this moment, as perfect as it was. I wanted to be closer to him. I wanted to hold him tight, to wrap my legs in his, to fall asleep with my head on his chest. I wanted to stretch out the moment and live inside it for ever.

'Let's go inside,' he said.

'Can I stay with you?' I asked, suddenly feeling this

crushing sense of finality between us. The words fell out before I had time to temper them, but I didn't care. I wanted it so badly, it was clenching around my heart. This could be the last time we ever sat together or kissed or laughed with one another. This could be our last night. Dom's words had bound themselves to my consciousness. It was like Valentino had said: those who have the most to live for are the hardest to kill. 'I want to fall asleep next to you. I want to wake up in your arms . . .' I lifted my gaze to his, the meaning implicit. 'I want to be with you tonight.'

Luca swallowed hard. 'Are you sure?'

'Yes,' I said. 'I'm sure.' I was so sure it ached. 'Can I stay here with you tonight?'

'Yes,' he said, a little breathless. 'Yes, stay with me.'

There was something in his words that felt a little bit like goodbye. I could sense his grief in them. It broke my heart that I couldn't take it away, but I could be in it with him, at least for now, for tonight. We could be in it with each other. We could harness a little spark of happiness and keep it warm, just between us. Tomorrow was a different story. Tomorrow would change everything.

It was Christmas Eve, and I was spending it with the person I loved, and there was some small joy in that at least.

He pulled me up with him, anchoring me by the waist as we crossed the roof. We climbed back in the window and he shut it after him. He ran his hands along my arms, warming them up. I shuffled into his heat, and his arms came around me as I buried my face in his neck, inhaling his scent and the perfection of that one small moment.

I lifted my chin and opened my mouth to him, revelling in

the sudden softness of his lips, the warmth of his tongue against mine. He grabbed the back of my head, pulling me in, and I gave myself to the kiss, to us. His tongue moved with mine, growing more insistent as he kissed me like it was the last kiss he'd ever have. Heat rushed over us and we came together fiercely, his hands wrapped tightly around me, my fingers lost in his hair, every part of us moulded together until there wasn't an inch of space between us. Our breaths were short and ragged, the low groans in his throat spurring me on, making me forget every shred of sadness inside me. He was the remedy, and I never wanted to let him go. And then his shirt was off and I was tracing the scar across his chest, trailing my fingernails along his taut muscles, his smooth olive skin, and listening to him catch his breath. I slipped my sweater off, and he tugged it free gently, careful of the wound in my shoulder, of the scars between us, as we came together – skin on skin. And then we were in each other's arms, wholly, completely, the world around us forgotten, and all the pain inside us burning up in an intensity I had never known, in a love I had never felt.

It was perfect.

It was fleeting.

That night, I fell asleep with Luca's arms around me, my head against his chest, lulled by the steady sounds of his breathing. For the first time in forever, I had no nightmares. I dreamt happy things – of a life far away from us, from the words 'Marino' and 'Falcone', from newspaper headlines and funerals, from gunshots and bloodshed, where he and I were the people we were supposed to be – happy, ordinary, in love.

# CHAPTER THIRTY-EIGHT
## TASTE

Christmas morning was surprisingly calm. There was a sense of peace, of readiness. Murmurs of *Buon Natale* filled the corridors in the house, brought soft smiles to our faces as we ate breakfast together in the kitchen. There was no food in the oven, no gifts waiting to be unwrapped.

It was almost like we knew we wouldn't all be coming back.

We didn't utter the name Marino before we had to. We didn't acknowledge that we were even leaving the house until we broke up after breakfast, most of us pottering back to opposite ends of the house to shower, to get dressed properly, to arm ourselves.

I stayed in the shower for a long time, where the quiet rush of water drowned out all my thoughts. It quelled the pain in my chest – the ripple of anxiety that had been growing and growing. I sat down and pulled my knees into my chest, throwing my head back to the beads of water and letting them drip down my face and back into my hair. I let memories from last night run through my head, lighting me up, the lingering feeling of our closeness holding me together, keeping me strong. I would come home for him. He would come home for me.

Slowly, slowly, the darkness crept back in. The need for revenge, the thirst for completion. It was time. I was going to use my fear, my anger, my grief. I was going to sharpen them, use them as a weapon and point that weapon right at Donata Marino. I chanted the words to myself and like a cool balm, they eased the cloying sense of fear that was creeping up my spine.

When I got back to my room, there were two things laid out for me on the bed: new rounds of ammunition for my gun, and a bulletproof vest. I didn't give myself any time to dwell on just how badly I needed it or how relieved I was to have it, or how there are hundreds of other places on your body you can be shot that can cause you to bleed out.

I dressed in sneakers, dark jeans, my new vest, a sweater and a dark jacket. I wound my hair into a bun at the base of my neck, slipped my switchblade into my back pocket. I looked at myself in the mirror. I looked like a soldier. I felt like a soldier. I wore my mother's necklace and Luca's bracelet. For bravery. For courage.

I stashed the ammunition in my pocket, and loaded my gun with a fresh round. Dom had the automatic weapons packed up in the car. I had had trouble getting to grips with mine, so I had chosen the handgun. It felt flimsy to me now –

light and insubstantial compared to what the others had – but I could shoot it, and I was good.

I ran into Nic in the foyer. We hadn't said very much to each other since he had caught Luca and me kissing. Valentino had passed away so suddenly that the whole debacle had been swept aside, and what remained was a lingering strangeness between us.

He was dressed in black, his hair already covered by a rolled-up balaclava.

'Hi,' I offered.

'Hi.' He passed me a balaclava. 'Are you all set?'

I rolled it on to my head, tugging it down at the back and leaving it folded on to the front of my hair. 'Yeah,' I said. 'I'm ready.'

'You look ready now. It suits you.'

I offered him a grim smile. I supposed that was his idea of a compliment. 'Thanks.'

His smile was easy. A trickle of tension left my body. We were being cordial; we were getting back to the way we were. 'Look, Nic, I don't want there to be any hard feelings . . .' I trailed off. 'You know, with everything . . .'

He released an uneasy laugh, his feet shuffling slightly. 'It's fine,' he said, a little too breezily. 'I get it, you didn't want me.'

'It wasn't about that,' I said quietly. 'I didn't want anyone.'

'You wanted him.'

'In the end, yes,' I admitted.

Something flitted across his face – too quick to catch, but it twisted his lips. 'It's kind of messed-up,' he said. 'Because after today, he won't want you any more.' He gestured at me, his finger leaving an invisible trail of ice down my front. 'He only loves you because you're innocent. He's fascinated by it.'

'Nic, let's not do this.'

He held my gaze. 'I would have loved you either way.'

I ran my hand across the ridge of the balaclava, trying not to feel self-conscious. 'You always wanted me like this,' I pointed out.

'The way you're supposed to be.'

'Can we be civil?' I pushed away from the topic of Luca. I didn't want to be mad at Nic today. 'Can we put everything behind us?'

His laugh was sharp. 'Why? In case I die?'

'In case of anything.'

He stuck out his hand. 'OK. Friends,' he said, in a low voice. I slipped my hand into his and shook it. He tightened his grip on my wrist and pulled me into his chest – into the hotness of his breath, the smell of his aftershave. 'Let me promise you this, Sophie.' He was looking down on me, his eyes blazing with intensity. 'You and I are getting out of that house alive.'

I pushed against him, and he dropped my hand and stepped back, as if remembering himself. 'I'm not worried about how we get out,' I said, schooling my annoyance. 'I'm worried about how we go in.'

'We're fine,' he said. 'I promise.'

I took that kernel of forgiveness, and smothered my anger with it. Of course he was still bitter about Luca. Of course he would say those things about him. He didn't want us to be together. He would prefer me alone than with his brother.

Felice strode downstairs. He was dressed in a shiny silver suit, his balaclava clenched tightly in one hand. 'Lovers' tiff?' he called over the banister. 'Has she realized the error of her ways yet, Nicoli?'

Nic rolled his eyes.

Felice's shoes tapped the stairs on the way down. 'It was a joke,' he said, noticing my scowl.

'Next time you tell a joke you should try and make it funny, so there's no confusion.'

He reached the bottom and sniffed the air. 'It feels like a good day to kill a Marino, doesn't it?' he said, leering at me.

I sniffed the air, too, my fingers curling on the gun inside my jacket pocket. 'It feels like a good day to die, doesn't it, Felice?'

He arched one perfect silver brow. 'I'm sure our boss would agree with you.'

I narrowed my eyes at him. 'Your family loyalty needs a lot of work.'

His thin lips spread wide, his mouth curving into a shark's grin. 'Not as much as yours does, Marino.'

'It's Falcone,' I corrected him.

His smile was a cruel, twisting thing. 'For now.'

Like a swarm, the others began to assemble, until we were one big black mass, armed to the teeth, embracing in the hallway, whispering last words, offering careful smiles. And then we left, one by one, fingers unrolling balaclavas as we climbed into the fleet of cars poised to storm Donata Marino's mansion.

Luca and I were the last ones to leave. He turned around, one full 360-degree turn as he took in the empty foyer. He stopped, and regarded me in silence for a moment. A long, lingering look.

'What?' I asked, feeling my throat dry up.

'Would you stay?' he said, taking a step towards me. 'Would you stay here?'

I shook my head. 'Not a chance.'

He ran his hands from my shoulders down to my arms, his fingers trailing along my sleeves. He looked away, rueful.

'Don't be worried,' I said, shuffling closer. 'We'll go in together, we'll come out together.'

He opened his mouth, but the words caught on his tongue. He swallowed them with a sigh and before I could utter some other empty words of encouragement, he was pulling me towards him and kissing me.

It tasted of desperation, of loss.

It tasted like goodbye.

# CHAPTER THIRTY-NINE
## MILLIONAIRES' ROW

**D**onata lived in a gated community made up of eleven mansions. Perched on the top of a winding hill, they formed a sprawling semi-circle. Each one looked out on to a park full of exotic-looking trees and vibrant bursts of flowers. In the middle, waterfalls tumbled into a fresh lagoon. It was like something out of a fairytale, a haven nestled away from the dusty streets of the city, far removed from the bright lights of Eden.

It was called Millionaires' Row.

And every single house on Millionaires' Row belonged to a member of the Marino crime family.

The sixth house – the one right in the middle of the other houses – was the largest. It was more like a museum or a parliament building than a house. It was pure white, with balconies spilling out from every angle and huge floor-to-ceiling windows sucking in every possible fleck of sunlight.

It was the house my father and my uncle grew up in.

It was the house Donata Marino now lived in.

In a convoy of three cars – all black, identical, and unplated – we pulled up to the security booth. I had to crane my neck to see all the way to the front of the line. Felice got out and shot the security man once in the head. Dom dragged his body back inside the booth. Paulie destroyed the entrance cameras, and all within the space of twenty seconds, the black gates to Millionaires' Row swung open, and the Falcone family drove inside.

I didn't look back.

I didn't glance at the body – the edge of a shoe, the glint of a belt buckle in my periphery.

I swallowed the lump in my throat, and gripped my gun inside my jacket pocket.

There was no going back now.

# CHAPTER FORTY
## BUON NATALE

Luca and Paulie kicked in the front door on their third attempt. We ran in after them, double file, across a wide foyer that led to engraved wooden doors inlaid with glass panes.

Nic was out in front by then, his automatic gun nestled across his chest. He shot the glass out from the window and slammed the heel of his foot into the doors at the same time. They swung open to the sound of Donata Marino's screams.

They were sitting around a long narrow table. My uncle still had the carving knife in his hand. The turkey, huge and crispy brown, sat undivided in the middle, a gaping bullet hole inside it. A man was slumped forwards on the table, his blood dribbling across the white tablecloth, a wound in the back of his neck where Nic had shot him through the glass pane.

There was a painful split second of nothingness where the smell of blood rose up between us all, and the horror of the moment froze everyone in place. Then Marco Marino sprung to his feet at the end of the table and stumbled in front of his mother.

Felice shouted '*Buon Natale!*' and shot him right in the chest. By the time he fell backwards, clutching at his torso, Donata was scarpering past the pantry and out on to the patio, and the rest of the Marinos were closing rank, shooting right back at us.

They were armed, even at dinner.

They were no match for us.

Three of them fell in the first thirty seconds, and as many others scrambled towards the back of the house, and out into the fresh snow. The boys followed them, an army of bala-clava-ed assassins, shooting straight as they marched. Elena led the way, shouting her sister's name as she went. My gun was still cold in my hand, my finger poised on the trigger.

I sprinted past the pantry, following CJ. Felice and Luca were still behind me, casing the remainder of the kitchen. The sound of a grunt stopped me at the doorframe. I backed up, slipping into the pantry, my attention trained on the kitchen, the gun ready in my hand. Jack sprang up from under the table, and flung his carving knife right at Felice's head. Felice lunged to the side, and the blade sliced into Luca's shooting arm. He fell to his knees, and Jack sprinted across the kitchen and through the open patio door. I hopped out after him, but my bullet lodged in the doorframe a foot above his head.

*Move. Go after him.* But my feet had stopped working.

Luca was hurt. And if I left he would be alone with Felice. I wheeled around, watching Felice as he circled his nephew across the room.

The sound of shooting was at a distance now, the others trekking through the garden after the scattered Marinos, tracks of blood already soaking into the snow.

Luca was doubled over on one side of the table. He raised his head, his eyes glassy as he stared at Felice. The knife was two inches deep in his forearm. He held it out, supported by the other one. His gun was on the ground beside him.

'Pull the knife, Felice,' Luca heaved. 'I can't get it.'

Felice cocked his head. His gun was dangling by his side.

'Come on,' Luca urged, pain vibrating in his voice. 'Before the others get away.'

Felice didn't move.

'Felice!' Luca said.

Felice took a step backwards. 'No.'

I took a careful step forwards as horror twisted in my stomach.

'*No?*' Luca repeated.

'Why would I help you when I didn't bother to help your father?' Felice asked, as calmly as if they were discussing the weather. 'What makes *you* so special?'

There was a heavy beat of silence as understanding bloomed across Luca's face, drained the colour from his cheeks. 'You let him die,' he said. 'You stood there and did *nothing*.'

It was a statement, not a question.

I crept closer, my fingers shaking around my gun.

Felice shrugged. The movement was rigid and forced; here

332

was a man not made to shrug. 'Angelo let himself die. I just didn't get in the way of it. Much like how he didn't get in the way of my wife leaving me. Much like how he didn't get in the way of his incompetent offspring clambering to the top of this family.'

I froze, a breath bound up inside me. I could see it all unfolding in my mind, could hear the ticking of the clock in my head. Felice was unravelling, and Luca was going to suffer for it.

'You have no idea what you're talking about,' Luca gritted out.

Felice waved the interruption away. 'Valentino's demise was not unlike your father's, you know.' I could hear the smile in his voice, the slimy satisfaction of it, when he said, 'In the end, the Marinos did the hard work for me. There's a lot to be gained from simply looking the other way at the opportune moment.'

I swallowed the scream building inside me. So it was true. Felice was a traitor, all this time, vying for a position at the top and willing to crawl over the dead bodies of his family to get it.

Luca's expression turned feral, hatred twisting his mouth, pouring venom from his lips. 'You heartless son of a bitch.'

Felice raised his gun and pointed it at Luca's head. His laugh was low and hard. 'Beware the fury of a patient man, nephew.'

The shot seemed to suck all the air out of the room.

Felice collapsed in a heap, sliding against the table until he tumbled backwards, a collection of limbs all giving up at once. He crumpled right in front of Luca, unseeing eyes staring towards the underside of the table, the bullet wound in the back of his head, hidden. A pool of crimson spilt out beneath him, creeping underneath the table.

The gun was molten hot in my hand. Still raised, at the space where Felice had just been. Adrenalin surged up my arm – hammered in my heart, dissolved the moisture from my mouth. My breathing was quick and shallow, my cheeks uncomfortably warm.

Luca was staring at me.

I stared right back, my heart climbing up my throat. 'It was him or you.'

'Sophie.' One word. Surprise. Relief. And something else. Something I couldn't place.

I kept my chin up, tried to squash down the urge to vomit. My teeth were chattering. 'There was no redemption for him, Luca.'

His mouth twisted. He shook his head at me. 'You really are something else.'

I lowered my gun and came towards him. I knelt down and gripped the knife in his arm. 'Hold still.' He groaned as I pulled it out. I grabbed a cloth napkin from the table and wrapped it around his arm twice, tying it tight, just above the wound. I was kneeling in a pool of Felice Falcone's blood, a hair's breadth from his lifeless body and surrounded by a host of dead Marinos – most of whom I was related to – and I was entirely focused on Luca and that wound. On what needed to be done. On what was still left.

I was in soldier mode, and it had come upon me so quickly I hadn't even noticed. I was a *soldato*.

'Thank you,' he said, rotating his wrist, clenching and

unclenching his fingers. I could tell he was in pain – his face was twisted up and his breathing was ragged.

'You can't shoot like that,' I said. 'You have to see a doctor. You need to get to Vita.'

He shook his head. 'My family is here.'

I grabbed him by the shoulders. 'Don't be stupid.'

'I'm not leaving.'

'You'll get killed.' Desperation rose in my voice. 'Please, Luca. Don't be stubborn. Not now, not like this.'

He got up, half of him already bloodstained. He offered me his good hand and pulled me to my feet.

'It's almost over,' he said, sliding past me, and striding towards the open patio doors. 'I need to finish this.'

'Luca.' I ran after him. He pulled me against him, around the side of the house, as we tracked the sound of bullets – of shouts and faraway curses, our feet sinking into the snow. I could see Nic at the other end of the garden, standing over a lifeless body. A white shirt, blue jeans – a Marino. A pool of snowy blood halo-ing him. Dom and Gino were further on, moving into a cluster of trees. Two more bodies littered the lawn. I couldn't make out who they were. We kept moving towards the others, keeping our backs to the wall as we went, the purposeful crunch of our footsteps filling the silence.

Another gunshot pealed through the air, and in the distance, CJ went down. A shout rose up. 'Jack!' Luca hissed. I couldn't see well enough – they were too far away. 'Stay here,' he called over his shoulder as he took off running.

A thud from the kitchen startled me out of my pursuit. I turned around, my gun raised. A shadow slipped by the patio doors and around the side of the kitchen, away from view. I shuffled forward, suddenly conscious of just how alone I was.

The sound of a chair scraping backwards. They could see me through any of the windows. I had no cover, just snow and nothingness. I was a sitting duck out on the patio. I pressed myself against the wall of the house between the window and the door. 'Who's there?' I called over my shoulder. 'I'm armed. Show yourself!'

'Sophie?' I snapped my head forward, my attention splitting in two. Jack was coming around the side of the house. The left side of his shirt was covered in blood.

I pointed my gun at him. 'Don't. Move.'

He straightened, just a little, his gun still by his side. 'You wouldn't,' he said, cautious, afraid. Good.

I was not afraid any more.

A fresh surge of adrenalin bolted through me. My cheeks flooded with warmth. I tried to concentrate. I tried to press my finger against the trigger. *Come on. Do it. Do it or he'll kill you.*

'Wouldn't I?' I said, as coolly as I could make myself sound.

'I'm your blood.'

'You killed my mother,' I hissed.

His smile was patronizing, his gold filling glinting at me in the frigid sunlight. 'She was in my way. In fact, she was always in my way.'

'Any last words before I kill you?'

'Yeah,' he said, stepping towards me. 'I hope we meet in hell.'

I smiled at him. 'Save me a seat.'

I pulled the trigger.

It clicked, but the bullet jammed. I pulled it again. Nothing.

Jack started laughing. He looked at his gun, and then at me. 'Looks like you'll get there before me, Persephone.'

There was nowhere to run. He was going to kill me. I wouldn't give him the satisfaction of my fear. I would not cower before him. I was stronger than that. I was stronger than them.

I took a deep breath.

The snow crunched as he came towards me.

# CHAPTER FORTY-ONE

## BROTHER

'Jack.' That voice. Cautious. Near. 'Stop.'

I snapped my eyes open. My father stepped out of Donata Marino's kitchen, and my knees nearly went from under me.

Jack stopped walking. 'Mickey?' he said, the word sucked into an inhale. 'Where the fuck have you been? We've sent word out for you!'

My father stepped in front of me. I faltered backwards, using the shield, trying to calm myself. 'In hiding,' he told Jack.

'Just not with your family?' Jack replied, distrust starting to seep into his voice. His gun was still half-raised. I scanned my father. His hair was scruffy, his clothes a bit too big for him. He had a gun, too. 'You know we have the resources to hide you, Mickey. You should have come here first.'

'I'm coming to you now,' my father said evenly.

There was something between them – something cold and dark. It wasn't camaraderie.

'Good,' Jack grunted. 'It's about time.' He lowered his gun.

My father raised his, just a fraction. 'Were you about to shoot my daughter?'

'No!' Jack spluttered. 'She was about to shoot me! I was just going to immobilize her.'

'And what about my wife, Jack?' My father's words were acid on his tongue. I could feel his anger in my bloodstream. 'What about Celine?'

Understanding dawned across Jack's face. 'An accident,' he said quickly. But my father was already pointing the gun at him.

'Liar.'

'What are you doing?' Jack said, his voice frantic. 'Mickey, what the hell are you doing?'

My father took one final step towards his brother. 'Killing you.'

He shot him, right there on the Marino lawn, in the house they both grew up in another lifetime ago. Jack careened backwards, falling heavily, like a beached starfish, his face turned towards the afternoon sky. And my father, who I had once thought kind and gentle and good, didn't even flinch. He looked at the body of his dead brother for no more than three seconds, then he turned around to me.

His shoulders slumped, the gun dangling uselessly at his side.

I just stood there, a mixture of horror and relief, a half-painted grimace plastered across my face. 'Dad.'

He kept the distance. Perhaps he thought I was scared. Perhaps I *was* scared. 'It had to be me, Sophie. Do you understand?' he said. 'I had to do it.'

'That's why you came out,' I realized. 'To get to him.'

My father nodded. 'And now it's done.'

'I was going to do it.'

'Better me than you,' he said.

'He's gone.' I looked at Jack's lifeless body, half-sunk in the snow, and tried to process what that really meant. 'He's finally gone.'

My father was still looking at me, his eyes glassy now. 'And I'm sorry, Sophie. For not being there when you needed me. For not protecting you.'

I looked up at him. I couldn't think of anything to say. I was still struggling to understand it all, to resist the sadness filling me up.

'I'm so sorry,' he said again. 'For everything.'

The air exploded and he fell to his knees. He grasped at the space between us as another gunshot slammed into his side.

I whipped my head around. Nic was running and shooting.

'Nic!' I screamed. 'Nic, don't!'

Another gunshot. My father's face pressed towards the earth. I went to him, lifting his head in my hands, so I could look into his eyes as the life was leaving him.

'I'm sorry, too,' I said quickly. 'Dad, I'm sorry, too.'

His lids fluttered. He opened his mouth but no words came out, only blood.

'I love you,' I said, my voice growing shriller, the fear vibrating in it. 'I love you, Dad.'

A whisper of a smile, his lips wobbling as the blood painted them red, and then he closed his eyes and slumped forward, and I caught him, pressing my head against his and letting my tears soak into his hair.

I pulled myself out from underneath him, laying his body across the grass just a couple of yards away from his brother. Half red, half white. Bullet-riddled and pale as the snow around him. I got to my feet. Nic was standing there, his gun holstered, his expression unreadable.

I turned my face to his, all the things I wanted to say suddenly evaporating into nothingness. My legs were shaking. Luca was racing back up the garden towards us.

Nic held my gaze. 'He had to go, Sophie. I'm sorry, but he had to go.'

Luca was beside us. He slammed his fist into his brother's face, screaming at him as he went down. 'You fucking idiot! You *fucking* idiot!'

I stumbled backwards, across the bloodstained snow and into the kitchen. I couldn't see properly any more. My vision was blurring, my head was swimming. Everyone sounded impossibly far away. It had been less than ten minutes, surely, since we had arrived, but it felt like hours. Painful, slow hours. I must have dropped my gun somewhere. I was all wet now too, and my hands were dark red. I was freezing. My teeth were chattering and my legs were shaking so violently I could barely stand.

I reached the sink and anchored myself to it, my stained fingernails clawing at the metal. I bent over it and vomited until I couldn't stand any longer. Then I sank to my knees and waited for the shaking to stop.

# CHAPTER FORTY-TWO

## ESCAPE

Paulie lifted me to my feet. I grabbed his arm and pulled myself up. My face was prickling uncomfortably, and my mouth had run so dry my lips felt like they might crack open. My mind was a tornado of thoughts – too quick to grasp, too loud to shut off.

'We're going,' he said quietly. 'Donata and Romano got away. All the others are dead.'

I nodded at the ground, my fingers still clutching at his sleeve. All the others were dead. Now there was only Donata. Only Donata. I tried to focus on that one thought, but the others were roaring inside my head. My father's eyes, his last attempt to smile. Nic, standing there with gun in hand. Felice crumpling to the ground, that knife in Luca's arm. Jack, staring, unseeing, at the sky.

All the others were dead.

All the others were dead.

And I was alive.

Did I want to be alive?

'Come on now.' Paulie slipped his arm around my back. His voice was gentle but firm. We passed by the Marino casualties, and Felice in between them all. My kill. Paulie didn't look back. Did he know he was dead? Did he know why?

Did it matter?

The Falcones were swarming in behind us.

Behind me, Elena and Nic were arguing in Italian. Luca and Dom were holding CJ up between them. He was bleeding badly from his left leg.

I looked at my feet.

*One foot in front of the other.*

*One foot in front of the other.*

*Just keep going. Just keep going.*

*Walk it off.*

*Walk it off.*

I climbed into an SUV and laid my head back until my face was tilted towards the roof. I didn't want to look at anyone or anything. Someone climbed in beside me. I shut my brain off. I ignored my surroundings. I pictured a white, blank page.

We sped off, one car after another, away from the perfect row of houses, away from all those dead Marinos, away from Felice, away from my father and my uncle lying side by side on snow-tipped grass, and every last crimson shred of my old family.

# CHAPTER FORTY-THREE

## HOLLOW

The second I set foot in *Evelina*, I climbed the three flights of stairs to my bedroom, grabbed a towel and locked myself in the bathroom. I stood under the shower, and watched the steam rise up off my skin, the red smears fall away with the soap. I washed my hair so many times I lost count. I opened my mouth and swallowed the water. I sat down and curled my arms around my body, and let the beads slide down the back of my neck. I wanted to be clean.

I couldn't make myself clean.

After an eternity, I shut off the water, wrapped myself in a towel and padded back towards my room. The house was eerily quiet. Paulie had said there would be an immediate debriefing when we got home. I had shunned it.

I slipped into sweatpants and a hoodie and climbed into bed. I didn't know what time it was. The sky was beginning to dim outside. I tried not to think about what they were talking about downstairs. I tried not to think about my father, about Jack, about any of it.

I was bone-tired. Without triumph or contentment. There was no joy in watching Jack fall. There was no relief, as I had hoped. I just felt hollow; empty. I felt broken.

Irreparably broken.

Luca had been right. This wasn't the answer. But I was so wrapped up in it now, it didn't matter any more. I had cast my die. I had taken a life. I had lost every last tether to my old identity.

My mind slowed down, and the blackness crept in.

A quiet knock at the door. Luca. I peeked at him from underneath the covers. He had changed into a T-shirt. His arm was bandaged all the way up to the elbow. He was pale, his black hair stark against the rest of him.

He just stood there.

We watched each other, everything we might have said communicated in that one long look.

*I'm sorry.*

He sat down on the side of my bed, and brushed the hair from my face. 'You were brave today.'

I blinked up at him. I thought this would unite us, but I could feel the hollowness in him, just as I could feel my own. This was no victory. Even if we had gotten Donata too, the emptiness would have stretched on, devouring the rest of me, until I was nothing.

I was nothing.

I was worse than nothing.

I *had* nothing.

Luca traced his fingers along my hairline, waiting. Waiting.

I was so tired.

'I feel empty,' I told him.

'I know,' he said.

*You were right.* I wanted to tell him he was right, but of course he already knew. He was wearing the anguish of today on his face, too. It was deep in his eyes, in every careful breath. There was no respite from Valentino's passing, no feeling of a great wrong being righted. There was no relief in knowing my mother's betrayer was in the ground, in seeing my father fall the way I once believed he deserved to.

I pushed the covers back and moved over. Luca lay down beside me, his arm around me as I rested my head on his chest, and listened to the sound of his heartbeat thudding beneath me. He curled his hand around mine.

'Sleep,' he said. He pulled the covers over us, and pressed his lips against my hair. 'I'll be here.'

I drifted into the blackness, into oblivion, as exhaustion swept over me like a wave.

Hours dragged by, when evening turned to night, and slowly, dawn crept in, flashing streaks of orange and pink across the sky.

When I woke up, Luca was gone, and I was alone again.

# CHAPTER FORTY-FOUR

## BY THE SWORD

'Have you packed yet?' Dom was staring quizzically at me in the hallway. 'Also, why does your hair look like a bird's nest?'

I ran my fingers through it and felt the tangle. 'I just woke up,' I said defensively. 'What do you care, anyway?'

Dom whistled under his breath. 'Wow, killing really doesn't agree with you, Sophie.'

It was only then that I noticed the duffel bag in his hand. 'What's going on?'

'You obviously haven't checked your phone,' he surmised. 'We're moving to a safe house. The police are looking into the Marino murders and Luca wants us to lie low. Donata's still at large, so we could be in danger . . .' He trailed off, his brows lifting, the silver scar stretching to white.

'What?'

He shrugged. 'I suppose it seems kind of inappropriate to stay in this house . . . you know, what with you having shot its owner.'

I crossed my arms over my chest and held his stare. 'He was going to kill Luca.'

'I know,' said Dom. 'We had a debriefing.'

'There wasn't any other option,' I added, feeling like I had to defend myself, feeling like no matter what I said, it wouldn't wash the guilt from my hands.

Dom laid a hand on my shoulder and I faltered with surprise. 'You did the right thing, Sophie. We all know that.'

I clamped my mouth shut. I was afraid of what I would say next – of all the things still unsaid between us in that moment – Jack, my father . . . 'So, we're going into hiding?'

'Until New Year's Eve.' A glint had returned to Dom's eyes. 'Donata's expected at the mayor's yacht party for the count-down. If she shows up, we're going to take her head.'

I swallowed back my revulsion. 'Another coup.'

'We keep pressing forward,' said Dom, confidently. 'When you have the advantage, you run with it. We've almost won.'

'What a great feeling.' My voice was entirely hollow.

'You'll get used to it, Sophie. Although,' said Dom, gesturing at my face, 'a word of advice? You look like you've been dragged through a bush backwards, so I would suggest you spruce yourself up a little before we move out.' He twirled his finger around in the air, gesturing at my scowling face. 'Give us something pretty to look at.'

I swatted his hand away. 'Once a dick, always a dick, eh, Dom?' I stalked past him, making a beeline for the bathroom, my thoughts kicking into gear and whirring at a million miles a minute. Where were we going? And why had no one told me? There were no texts on my phone.

I got dressed and packed up all my things like Dom had told me to. I didn't have that much anyway, just one suitcase and a backpack. It was the day after Christmas, and I had never felt less cheerful. I still hadn't come face-to-face with *him* yet. And I would have to, because he was in this house, too, and wherever we were going now, we were going together.

I dragged my suitcase out into the upstairs hallway, pausing to take a breath. I hadn't eaten in twenty-four hours and even though I felt more nauseous than hungry, my body was feeling the lack of nutrients.

When I straightened up again, Nic was hovering at the top of the staircase. His hands were shoved into his pockets and he was leaning just a little on his right leg. His hair was coiffed and gelled in dark waves, and his eyes were bright. He looked incredible. Totally and utterly unaffected.

I wanted to claw his eyes out.

I reined my temper in, swallowed the threat of tears, and stood across from him with my chin raised.

He nodded at my suitcase. 'Do you need a hand with that?'

'No, I'm fine.'

'Are you sure? You don't look so good.'

*Say it*, I dared him with my eyes. *Address it.*

He hesitated, a word caught on his lips. He pursed them and swallowed. 'We're leaving in half an hour. The drive is pretty long, so you might want to eat first.'

'I'm fine,' I said.

He narrowed his eyes a fraction but didn't contradict me. *Coward*, I thought. His bedroom wasn't on this floor. There was no reason to come up here, except to talk to me, and now he was here, he wouldn't utter a word about it.

'Was there something else?' I said tightly.

He took a step forward.

'Don't,' I said warningly.

He stopped. His hands were still in his pockets. There were no circles under his eyes, no lines of exhaustion, nothing tugging at his features.

'I had to do it, Sophie.'

'Did you?' I asked.

'He was a threat. A Marino.'

'So am I.'

'No,' he said, more firmly. 'You're a Falcone.'

'He was my *dad*, Nic.' My voice cracked. 'We were just *talking*. *He* shot Jack.'

Nic frowned. 'He had to go. He was expecting it.'

Rage surged inside me. I pressed it down, down, calming myself. 'How could you possibly know that?'

He had the audacity to hold my gaze. 'You live by the sword, you die by the sword.'

'You're not sorry,' I said.

'I didn't want to hurt you.'

'Right.' I gritted my teeth. 'Well, that's it, then. I don't have anything else to say.'

'Are you dismissing me?' he asked, the ghost of a grin forming on his face.

'Yes,' I snapped. 'I don't want to look at you right now.'

'You killed Felice,' he pointed out.

'You know that was different.'

He didn't have an answer to that.

He turned around, and then paused, one foot on the stairs. He looked at me over his shoulder, his voice hard when he said, 'Do you forget sometimes, Sophie, that it was your father who murdered mine?'

I came towards him, until there was just a yard between us. With acid in my mouth and fury raging in my heart, I kept my voice as steady as I could. 'I suppose I forgot that your heart will always beat for revenge first, and love second.'

'Unrequited love,' he clarified.

I gaped at him. 'So you did it to punish me? You did it because I couldn't love you back – the way you love me?'

'I did it because Luca couldn't,' he said simply.

I stepped backwards, away from his smell, his face, his eyes. It would take a long time to conquer this feeling of betrayal – no matter what logic dictated, no matter any of it.

'We're not at war, Sophie, you and I,' Nic added. 'I'm on your side, but you're a Falcone now, remember?'

He turned and thudded back downstairs, taking the cold, hard truth of the matter with him.

My phone buzzed against my hip. It was a text from Millie.

I'm at Evelina. Come outside.

# CHAPTER FORTY-FIVE
## OUT OF THE DARKNESS

Millie was leaning against the door of her car, arms folded across her chest.

I jogged towards her. 'What is it?'

She slammed into me, and wrapped her arms around me so tightly I could barely breathe. 'Oh my God oh my God oh my God, Soph, oh my God.'

I held on tight, breathing in her Flowerbomb perfume. 'I'm sorry, Mil.'

She pulled back from me, a steadying hand on each shoulder. 'It's all over the papers.'

'My dad—' My voice broke off.

She pulled me into another hug. 'I know. I'm so sorry.'

I didn't realize how much I needed Millie until she was there, holding me up. All the pain and confusion and emptiness fissured, and the tears came freely.

'Did you see it?' she asked, pulling back from me. 'Did you see who killed your father?'

'Nic.'

'God,' Millie sighed. 'Oh God, Soph, I'm so sorry.'

'I'll never forgive him. I can't even look at him.'

Her frown deepened, crinkling her nose and pulling her brows together. Her freckles were darker in the harsh winter light. It was so early still, and yet she must have been driving for hours . . .

'How did you get here so fast?' I asked her. 'How did the paper come so early at the cottage? I thought you were in the middle of nowhere.'

She frowned at me. 'Don't you know?'

'Know what?'

'Soph, Luca called me.'

'L-Luca?' I couldn't grasp that sentence. 'What? Why? When?'

'Late last night,' she said. 'He told me everything.'

'Why?' I repeated. I had been busy trying to keep Millie in the dark and now she knew everything – and Luca had been the one to tell her. He had shattered *omertà*.

Millie was looking at me with equal confusion. 'Why?' she repeated. 'Because he wants me to take you away from here, Soph. He wants you out of the family.'

*He wants you out.*

The chasm in my chest peeled open again. 'I don't understand.'

'Yes, you do,' said Millie. 'You understand perfectly well.'

There was a hint of scolding in her voice. I knew that

beneath her sympathy and worry she was angry with me. I had been reckless. I had gone after something that was never going to cure me or make me feel better. I had lied to her. I had put myself in danger.

'It's a miracle that you're still alive,' she said. 'You realize that, don't you?'

I nodded, barely aware of the tears sliding soundlessly down my cheeks.

'Staying here is no longer an option.'

I stared at my own scuffed Converse.

'It's madness,' she said. 'I'm not leaving here without you.'

I looked at her again – I had never seen her so serious, so determined.

'I'm pulling you out, Soph,' she said. 'You can come willingly, or you can come by your hair, but this world you're living in is about to implode and this life is not for you. I know you know that. Choose to recognize it. Please.' Desperation broke into her last word. Her eyes were filling up. '*Please*,' she said again. 'Choose life. Choose happiness.'

'I don't know how, Mil,' I whispered. The tears were falling freely on to my neck, sliding inside my collar and turning to pinpricks of ice.

'Try,' she pleaded. 'Forgive yourself.'

'I can't.'

'You can,' she insisted. 'Forgive yourself.'

I shook my head.

She grabbed it in her hands. 'Look at me,' she demanded. 'There is no life here, Sophie. Only death. Only grief. You are more than your pain. You are more than your loss. You are more than your mindset.'

I grabbed her hands and kept them in mine.

'You know you have to go,' she told me. 'You know that, don't you?'

I did know. I knew the minute we left Donata Marino's house.

I nodded, slowly, reluctantly. 'But where?' I asked her. 'I can't stay with you, not while the Marino family are still active. The Falcones are moving to another safe house, and I don't have anyone else. No one who would be willing to hide me . . .' I trailed off, feeling nothing but despair. 'I'm lost.'

'You have to trust your father,' she said firmly.

'What?'

She reached into her pocket and pulled out an envelope. 'I stopped by my house on the way back from the cottage this morning. This was waiting for me. It's a letter from your father.' She thrust it towards me.

I took it with shaking hands. My father's last written words. And they were to my best friend. I opened the envelope and unfolded the letter.

Millie,

I'm sorry to have to put you in this position, but you're the only person I trust to deliver this message. With Celine gone, Sophie has tied herself to the wrong people. She is now an official Marino target.

I expect soon I will be caught or killed. I know what I have to do. I am going to take the threat away from Sophie. Today, on Christmas Day, I will go to Donata Marino's house and remove her from power. I will remove my brother too, and face whatever punishment comes with it.

*If I am unsuccessful, the Marino family will rebuild itself. In this case, I need you to send Sophie away. There is someone at the address below who will hide her until she is free to be herself again.*

*Sophie trusts you more than anyone. She will listen to you. Please, keep her safe. Do what I couldn't do. Take her out of this life, before it's too late. Give her this address, and when it's done, burn this letter and erase all traces of it from your memory.*

*If she will hear it, tell her I'm sorry. Tell her I love her.*

*You are the best thing that's ever happened to her, Millie. Please take care of my girl for me.*

*Be well,*

*Michael*

'Did he do it?' she asked, after I had read through the letter twice, the paper shaking in my hands. 'Did he kill Jack?'

'Yes,' I said, trying not to fixate on the image in my head, still staring at his words. 'I saw it.'

'Then you can trust him.' She tapped the piece of paper – the address of M Flores scrawled messily at the bottom. 'You can trust *this*.'

I took it from her, a frown twisting on my lips. 'And what? I'm just supposed to go?'

Millie nodded. 'Yes, that's exactly what you're supposed to do.'

'With what money?'

'Luca will sort it out.'

Bitterness swelled inside me. 'Wow, he must really want to get rid of me.'

'You know why he's doing it,' Millie said. 'Come on, Soph.'

I wiped a tear away before it could trace another line on my cheek. 'I have to go,' I whispered to myself. 'I have to go.'

'Yes,' said Millie softly. 'But I'll go with you. I'll take you as far as you want.'

'No,' I said firmly. 'You can't come with me. Not while there's so much heat on me.'

She grabbed my hand. 'I'll take you to the airport. I'll wait until you get on the plane. You'll call me when you get off. I'll be with you every step of the way. And then, in a month or so, when this has all died down, we'll sort something else out. You just have to lie low for a while.'

'By myself,' I said. 'With a complete stranger.'

'Better there than here,' Millie said. 'There will be no survivors from this, Sophie. You know that. Luca knows that.'

I heaved a shaky breath, the paper still clutched in my fist. Was I really going to pin all my hopes on my father's word? On someone I had never met before? Was I going to walk away from everyone I knew and loved?

*Yes.*

My mother's voice inside my head.

*Yes.*

My father's voice.

'OK,' I told Millie. 'OK.'

She reeled backwards. 'Thank God,' she said, passing a hand across her forehead. 'I'm so relieved, Soph.'

There were tears in her eyes now, too. She smiled – it was small and watery. She was pulling me out, and I could tell it was the only way. If I wanted to live – if I wanted to claw my way out of the darkness – I had to go with her. I had to crawl towards my light.

And Millie was my light.

'I want to say goodbye to him,' I said. 'I need to.'

'Of course you do,' she said gently. 'Of course you can say goodbye.'

I turned back towards the house. It felt bigger, colder, more remote. Inside, the assassins were swarming, ready to move again. I started walking towards it, towards the boy I loved. The boy who was locked up in the heart of this place. The boy who would go to his death with his family.

'I'll get your things,' Millie said, following me up the driveway. We entered together. She went one way, and I went another, pushing my feet towards the Don's office, towards Luca.

Towards goodbye.

# CHAPTER FORTY-SIX
## NO RETURN

I shut the door to the office behind me, and kept my back pressed against it. Luca was already standing up, his arms crossed over his chest as he leant against the desk. He had dark rims under his eyes, and his shoulders were slumped. Only one of us had slept last night.

Anger flared inside me, quashing the jarring need to cry, to reach out to him and beg him to think of some other way for us to be happy. My defences shot up, and I felt myself shutting down.

'Your plan's come off,' I told him. 'Millie's outside waiting for me.'

For a long moment, he just looked at me, his expression blank. Then he blinked, slow and heavy, and with a sigh, came his response. 'Good.'

'So you're happy?' I pressed. 'You're happy that I'm leaving? That you don't have to deal with me again?'

I knew I was being irrational but it hurt so badly, like a pinprick right in the centre of my heart, that he was choosing to send me away.

'Sophie . . .' Even his voice was tired. 'Don't twist this.'

'I'm not twisting it.'

He stood up, his hands dangling by his side. 'You are,' he said. 'You know this is the way it has to be.'

'We were supposed to do this together, Luca. For my mom, for Valentino.'

'And look where that got us,' he said, a spark of life flooding into him. He took a step towards me. 'Look what happened yesterday. How much you lost. How much it hurt. Did it help? Do you feel happier now?'

'It will take time,' I protested, feeling the lie char my tongue. 'I want to be in this with you. I want to.'

'No!' he said. 'You don't want any of this. You're lying to yourself, Sophie. You're lying to yourself and you're lying to me.'

My lip wobbled. I bit down hard on it. 'Don't tell me how I feel, Luca.'

He splayed his arms. 'Sophie, you're so mired in grief you can't possibly know what you want, or what's good for you. You scream in your sleep, did you know that? You have all the signs of post-traumatic stress disorder. Your behaviour is erratic. You lose focus easily. You don't even smile properly any more. Whenever you find yourself laughing you catch yourself or cover your mouth until it stops. I look at you and see sadness in your eyes. I feel it – this sense of wrongness, and it's because I brought you here and made you think this was the way forward.'

'You saved me, Luca. I had nowhere else to go.'

'I was selfish, Sophie. I wanted you near me, but it's destroying you, and I can't justify it any more. I want the light to come back to your eyes. I want you to laugh and not worry about who hears you, to smile because you feel real joy.' He chewed the inside of his cheek, pausing, and not quite looking at me when he said, 'I want you to love someone who is worthy of your love.'

'You are worthy,' I said.

'No, I'm not.' He shook his head. 'This is not the life for you. I'm only sorry it took me so long to do something about it. My grief made me weak. My love for you made me selfish. And I'm sorry.'

I took a step towards him, but I could never bridge the gap now. It was stretching out like a chasm between us. 'You wanted us to be together. I want that too.'

He clenched his jaw. 'No.'

'Yes,' I said, pushing myself closer to him. 'That's what we both want.'

'I don't want that any more. I don't want you here.'

'I can do it,' I said, hearing the desperation in my voice. 'I can do this.'

'*I* can't!' Luca said. 'Don't you understand that, Sophie? *I* can't do this. Not with you.'

I faltered, the words tumbling back into my mouth.

He raked his hands through his hair, pulling the black strands away from his face. His eyes were startlingly blue, his lips twisting as he spoke. 'I am not strong enough to lose you.

361

Not to this life. Not after Valentino.' His voice cracked. He kept going, ignoring the tears as they slid down his face. 'I won't risk a loss that great again knowing I have the power to prevent it.' He came towards me and I went to him, until we were right in front of each other, the truth between us. 'If I lose you Sophie, I'll lose my heart. There'll be nothing left. I won't survive it.'

I surged into him, wrapping my arms around him. He pulled me against him, his lips in my hair as I pressed my cheek against his chest and listened to the erratic rhythm of his heartbeat, knowing it would be the last time I ever heard it.

'I love you,' he whispered into my hair. 'I'll always love you.'

I pulled back, just enough so I could look up at him. The tears were drying on his face already. 'Come with me,' I pleaded.

He caught a breath. 'You know I can't do that. I can't leave the family.'

'You can,' I urged, pressing my palms against him. 'Of course you can.'

'No.'

'Come to Colorado. Come to—'

He raised his palm in the air. 'Don't tell me where you're going. Don't tell anyone.'

'But—'

'I don't need to know. As long as you're safe, I don't need to know. It's easier this way.'

He wouldn't find me. Not if he survived into the New Year, not if every fibre of him pushed him to look for me, he wouldn't know where to look. Panic surged inside me.

'Please come,' I begged. 'We'll make another life.'

'There is no other life for me, Sophie. There is no other future.'

'You'll die, Luca. You'll die in this place. I can see it in your eyes.'

He didn't look away; he didn't deny it.

'If you go to that yacht on New Year's Eve, you won't come back home. Please,' my voice wobbled, 'please, just come with me now. We'll go somewhere else.'

'Sophie.' I could see the walls coming down, the careful shift in his expression. He was slipping into commander mode, and I could feel him drifting from me already. 'I don't want to fight with you.'

'We're fighting because we're unhappy,' I said. 'But not with each other. We're stuck here in this world where we don't belong, trying to be something we can't mould ourselves into.'

'Exactly,' he said, nodding now. 'You don't belong here.'

'*We* don't belong here!' I half-shouted. My heart was racing. I took a shuddering breath and stepped away from him. I had one last-ditch attempt to save him, and he was already a million miles away. 'Luca, you once told me I was ruled by emotions – that I couldn't walk away from danger if those I loved were involved in it. You told me I was foolish – reckless. Now look.' I gestured at him, at that hideous Falcone ring on his finger, at the office, and all the planned bloodshed its walls had seen. 'You're anchored to this family because you love them, because you can't imagine walking away from them even though you know staying will kill you. First it will take your soul, and then it will take every shred of your beautiful humanity and burn it away, and after that it will take your body – and you'll be nothing in the end, Luca. You'll be nothing but a memory – nothing but the lives you've claimed and the hypocrisy you lived.' I blinked my vision clear so I could see him crumple underneath my words. He needed to hear this – and, more than that, I needed to say it. 'You don't want this life. You never did. You know it's wrong, you know you're better than it, and yet, here you are, sinking with the others. And you want *me* to walk away. Without you.'

His shoulders slumped, and his face fell. I could sense it rising between us – finality. He was done. Done with the conversation, with the dilemma. I was going. He was staying.

I took a step backwards. 'There's nothing else I can say, is there?'

He shook his head. 'It is what it is.'

I looked up at him, a smile dying on my lips. 'I would go into the darkness with you, but you won't come into the light with me.'

His smile was sad. 'That's very poetic.'

I took his hand, and pulled him towards me. 'I've been spending quite a bit of time with this super nerd lately.'

He wrapped his arms around my waist and gently pulled me in. 'I love you,' he said.

'Just not enough.'

'Too much, actually.' He kissed me. It was fierce and passionate and full of every fibre of love we had in our bodies. And when we came apart, our eyes were wet and our hearts were broken.

# CHAPTER FORTY-SEVEN
## COLORADO

**M**illie and I drove in silence, the tears streaming down my face, her hand in mine.

'It will be OK, Soph. I know it doesn't feel like it right now, but it will. You will survive this.'

How many ways can a heart break? A shard for my mother, a shard for my father, and a shard for Luca. And all the empty space in between for me.

It would be over come New Year's Day. Either the Marinos or the Falcones would be wiped out, and every last piece of my identity might be gone, too.

Millie's parents' cottage was several hours outside Chicago, nestled inside a pine forest on the edge of a small lake. Luca had warned Millie to lie low here for a few days, and not to move through O'Hare airport or anywhere near

Cedar Hill at least until New Year's Eve. So I waited, quietly, as the days dragged past. I pretended to care about things I never thought about. I watched movie after movie, nestled between Alex and Millie. I made polite conversation with Cris when he came to visit. I lost at Scrabble way too many times to count. I won at Monopoly and didn't care. Not nearly as much as I thought about Luca, about my father. About my uncle.

I cried myself to sleep at night, my switchblade closed inside my fist – the last reminder that I had belonged somewhere. I wasn't ready to let that go yet.

The waiting was excruciating. The not knowing was even worse, but we didn't get the newspapers at the cottage, so I could live, at least for a few days, in ignorant bliss. There was no internet, and I barely had two bars of coverage on my phone. The police called – eager to speak to me about my father's death. I had already seen it; I didn't need the specifics. I didn't need the faux sympathy. I wasn't ready to open that can of worms yet, so I let the calls go to voicemail. They didn't come for me. They didn't know where I was, and whatever Millie told her parents was enough. Because they didn't push it either.

I booked a one-way flight to Colorado with the money Luca gave to Millie.

On the morning of December 31st, we left the cottage. Millie's parents were heading to a New Year's party in the city.

Millie drove me to the airport, and walked me right up to the check-in desk, her fingers curled tightly in mine. The address was burning a hole in my pocket.

'I can come, you know. I can come with you for a while. I

**366**

know you won't be gone too long but you don't have to go alone.'

If hugs could kill, I would have smothered her. 'I'll be fine,' I said, trying to smile. The truth was, I didn't know where I was going and whether it might be some last-minute Marino trap. It might have been my only viable option, but I wasn't about to risk Millie's life for it. 'I'll call you the second I arrive there.'

She pulled me into a hug and I squeezed her so tight we lost our breaths.

'I love you, Soph.' She pulled back from me, her eyes wide and searching. 'I'll see you really soon.'

'I know,' I said, forcing my smile. 'And I love you too.'

She tapped my nose, and dropped her voice to a conspiratorial whisper. 'We're the real love story here. You know that, don't you?'

I wiped a tear from her cheek. 'I know that, Mil. I've always known that.'

'Good,' she said. 'Call me when you land.'

I left her waving after me as I boarded the plane, and pointed my life in the direction of someone I had never met before, in a town I'd never been to, everything now pinned to the last words of my father and the hope that he loved me still, despite everything. My fingers encircled the bracelet on my wrist, my mind chanting the words over and over again: *Hope smiles from the threshold of the year to come, whispering, 'It will be happier.'*

I thought of Luca, and felt my heart crease. How could I be happy, knowing he was trapped?

# CHAPTER FORTY-EIGHT
## THE GIRL

I sat back in the cab and watched the Rocky Mountains in the distance as we wound further up the hill. I had texted Millie to say I'd arrived safely. There was no one else to tell. I fogged the glass and traced a heart in it, feeling the chill through the windows.

Boulder was beautiful. It was like another world – away from the madness, the bloodshed, the feeling that I was being watched. The police might still look for me, but it would take them longer to find me. Maybe they never would. As for the Marinos, or what was left of them now, I didn't know. Perhaps they were waiting for me already. I tried not to think about it. I had already cast my die.

It was New Year's Eve. Tonight the Falcones would make their final strike in Chicago. The yacht party would be crawling with police. I knew in my heart that whoever stepped on to that boat wouldn't make it out alive. I knew in my heart that I would never see Luca Falcone again. Beyond the grief and the sadness, the guilt and the panic, there was a sense of calm. Of numbness.

Resignation.

I had hit rock bottom, and I could barely put one foot in front of the other. Only for Millie. Only for the memory of my mother. Only for the life that Luca wished for me – the one I would have to lead for both of us now.

I dragged my attention from the winding streets where red-brick buildings crowded side by side – hipster cafes, a string of restaurants and an Urban Outfitters welcomed me to Boulder.

I laid my head back and closed my eyes. A split second seemed to pass before the cab door was swinging open and the driver was nudging me awake. I paid him, grabbed my bags from the trunk and stood in front of a small three-storey townhouse. The door was bright purple. It was tall and narrow, like something out of a storybook. There were flowers in the garden, peeking out from the snow. A painted mailbox with golden lettering: *Miss Marla Flores*. At least the address matched the name. I guessed that was something.

I climbed the three wooden porch steps and paused to welcome a familiar rush of anxiety. There was nothing. Just dullness – a slight ache, a flicker of nerves, and then nothing. I rang the doorbell and a melodic chime rose up behind the door.

It was almost sundown. The birds were still singing. It was cold, but the sun was out, and everything looked brighter than it should have been. I was about to ring the doorbell again when a frantic shuffling of feet galloped behind the doorway, followed by the sound of a lock shifting. I stood straight, going over my introduction in my head. *Hi, my name is Sophie Gracewell. I think you knew my father . . .*

The door creaked open, and a little girl peeked her head around it. She had wide grey eyes and thick black hair that hung in ringlets around her face. She smiled at me. Her front teeth were missing. I tried not to be knocked off-kilter by the appearance of an objectively adorable little girl, but somewhere in my mind, I was thinking, *Is this my father's love child? And if it is, who or what am I going to punch?*

'Hallo,' said the little girl. She didn't open the door any further, so I couldn't see behind her.

'Hello there.' I smiled, but it was twitchy. She didn't look remotely like me, but I had been tricked out of a family before. 'What's your name?'

She blinked her big eyes. There was something so familiar about them. God. I could almost feel it coming like a freight train. 'Emilia.'

Emilia. Those eyes . . . that grin.

'Where's your mother, Emilia? Is she here with you?'

Emilia bit her bottom lip and made herself look very guilty. 'She's in the bathroom. I'm not supposed to answer the door, but I saw you in the window.' She gestured to the side window, where a lace curtain had been pulled away behind a potted plant. 'And I liked your hair, so I thought it would be OK. It's like the sun.'

She reached up to touch it, but a voice startled her back into the house. 'Emilia! What have I told you about answering the door? Come inside now.'

Emilia melted back into the house, and a heartbeat later, the front door swung open and I was standing face-to-face with Evelina Falcone.

# CHAPTER FORTY-NINE

## MARLA FLORES

I grabbed the side of the wooden awning and tried not to pass out.

I was staring so hard my eyes were vibrating. I had seen her photo a million times at *Evelina* – the one of her beaming on her wedding day, her head resting against Felice's. I had memorized her oil painting, felt her gaze on the back of my neck every time I went to the library. I had traced the sadness in her eyes a thousand times, and felt it reflected inside me.

She looked the same – just a few more lines around her eyes, a tightness to her mouth.

She was beautiful.

She was *alive*.

I wanted to reach out and touch her to be sure.

Evelina stood motionless, letting me take it all in.

That's how I knew she had been expecting me.

I rubbed the shock from my chest. 'You're alive,' I said, coming a little closer, as though she was an apparition. 'You're supposed to be dead. My—' I froze and felt the colour run from my face. My father was supposed to have killed her. But he hadn't killed her. He hadn't touched a hair on her head. And if she owed us a favour, that meant he had helped her.

'You're really alive.' And the relief was like ice in my bloodstream. My heart expanded, just a little. My father wasn't a monster. He wasn't irredeemable. He wasn't a stranger, after all.

And someone special, someone who had deserved to live, was still living. 'You're Evelina Falcone.'

She sprung into life, hushing me with her hands. 'I haven't been Evelina since before my daughter was born,' she whispered. She ushered me inside, and I went willingly, as though tied to a string. I had a million questions and more.

The hallway was brightly lit, and Emilia was jumping down it with a blue skipping rope.

Those big grey eyes.

Felice's eyes.

Felice's daughter.

Alive and well.

Unlike him.

Evelina led me into an airy kitchen with bright green cupboards. 'Lemonade? You must be thirsty after your journey.' She didn't wait for me to answer. She busied herself at the fridge, keeping her back to me. Her hands were shaking, just a little. Strands of hair were wisping out of her long dark braid. 'Your father said you would come soon,' she said over her shoulder. 'He was here with us before . . . until Christmas Eve, that is . . .' She trailed off, her voice dipping.

*Ah.*

He had stayed here. With her. He had bided his time far from Chicago, waiting for the perfect moment to strike against Jack, just as we had. We had all chosen Christmas Day.

Did she know what had become of him? Did she know her Marino ally was dead?

'I promised him I would take you in,' she continued. 'I promised him I would help you. I hoped you would come.' She turned around, her eyes large, her expression earnest. 'I hoped you wouldn't get swallowed up in it.'

'I thought you were gone.' I was still trying to process her aliveness. 'I thought my dad . . .' I trailed off, conscious of Emilia drifting around us, her skipping rope clapping off the wooden floors. 'I found your ring. Your ruby ring.'

She laughed, a little grimly. 'I told him to sell it. I wanted to thank him.'

'When? How?' I wasn't talking about the ring any more. I was talking about everything. Everything, and all at once, and there wasn't enough time in the world to get through it all but I wanted to try. I wanted to understand. This was a life raft, and I didn't want to sink.

Evelina glanced into the hallway, making sure Emilia was out of earshot. She dropped her voice, pouring the lemonade into two glasses. 'Your father came for me one night in the city many years ago. I was at dinner with my girlfriends. The Marinos had been tracking us – *he* had been tracking me. I suppose you know what Felice did to his parents. I suppose you know your father was out for revenge. I shouldn't have been unchaperoned at the time but I was so tired of Felice by then. I was tired of always feeling afraid, of feeling trapped . . .'

I nodded, feeling a shimmer of understanding.

She stopped busying herself, cleared her throat. 'He couldn't do it, you know, when the time came. Even when it was just the two of us in the parking lot. Even when he knew he would have gotten away with it. He saw the bruises around my jaw. He saw the fear in my eyes. I was eight months pregnant at the time.'

I tried to piece together the scene in my head. A deserted parking lot, doused in darkness. My father with a gun pointed at Evelina Falcone. Her hands covering her bump, her face marred by Felice's temper.

'He was broken by it all,' she said. 'The anger, the violence. And so was I. We could see that in each other. We were on different sides, but we were the same in that sense. I was worried for my baby. For myself.'

'Of course,' I murmured, trying to imagine that particular brand of fear, and failing.

'It was strange. So strange.' Evelina smiled sadly. 'He dropped his gun. I didn't run, and neither did he. We talked. I wasn't afraid. I was never afraid of him. Not in the way I feared my own husband. He wanted to punish Felice and I wanted to run. Our desires weren't exactly at odds. There was something about him. It felt like we already knew each other.'

'So, he helped you then?' I said, willing myself to understand, to believe. 'He helped you get away?'

She nodded. She was beautiful, lit up by the dying sun, her

long hair gathered into a loose braid, streaks of caramel among the chestnut brown. A ghost come to life before me, and I couldn't remember a time when I had felt so grateful for something. 'He helped me take my life back,' she said, simply.

'Did anyone else know?'

'Not a soul,' she said. 'Not until you.'

I pressed the back of my head against the wall and took a deep breath. The ceiling fan whirred above me. There were paper butterflies tied to it, whizzing around, their wings painted messily in different colours. Here was something; a kernel of light. I had to hold on to it. I had to keep it safe. But there was still so much to wade through.

'Evelina,' I said. Emilia had skipped into a different room. 'My father is dead.'

'I know,' she said, softly. 'I saw it on the news. I am sorry, Sophie. He was a good man.'

I swallowed the lump. 'And Felice, too,' I said, my voice turning to a rasp.

Her expression changed. 'Yes.'

'I was there,' I whispered. The guilt was flooding through me and the words were tumbling out before I could stop them. I couldn't stand in her kitchen and pretend to be innocent. I couldn't lie to her face, not while his child was one room away, humming and skipping, her paper butterflies flying around above me. 'He was going to kill Luca,' I said. 'He was going to kill him. He had the gun pointed at his head, and – and I had to do something. I didn't set out to do it. I didn't want to harm him, not really, but he was going to kill Luca, and I had to stop him.'

'You saved a life,' she said.

'I took a life.'

Evelina took a step closer, a glass of lemonade held out in offering. I took it from her, held it tight against my chest. It felt bigger than it was. Another life raft.

She took a sip of her lemonade, swallowed hard and then looked right at me when she said, 'I have known both Falcones, Sophie. You made the right choice.'

'I'm sorry,' I said, because there was nothing else to say, and I could still hear his daughter singing to herself in the other room.

Evelina nodded. 'It is a kindness to us,' she said, quietly. 'That we no longer have to live in fear of him. And a kindness to Luca, whose life you saved.'

'I love him.' My voice was wobbling. 'I couldn't lose him.'

Evelina's face creased, a whisper of empathy lowering her brows. 'I can see why. Luca is very easy to love.'

'And he loved you,' I said, remembering my conversation with Luca about the stars, about possibility, about all the things she made him believe he could be.

*And he'll never know*, I realized. *He'll never know you made it out alive.*

A rogue tear slid down my face.

Evelina rubbed my arm, her fingers grazing my bullet wound. 'It's OK,' she soothed. 'I once lived in that world. It is a cruel, unforgiving place, where good men suffer and bad men thrive. It is filled with loss and regret, and guilt. I understand what you've been through.' She waited until I raised my gaze again. 'It's been hard for you. For both of us. But you are all the better for being here right now, with us. Will you stay?

For a while?'

Emilia was laughing at something in the other room. It was such a beautiful, foreign sound. I found myself nodding. 'Yes.'

'A new year starts tomorrow,' she said gently. 'A new beginning.'

But first there was tonight. And I couldn't get tonight out of my head.

# CHAPTER FIFTY

## MIDNIGHT

I was sitting beside Evelina Falcone with a half-drunk glass of red wine in my hand, watching the New Year's Eve countdown on a local news station, when the massacre began back in Chicago.

The screen changed, and footage of fireworks in Colorado was replaced by a BREAKING NEWS bulletin. Bile gathered in my throat as the words flashed across the screen: 'DISTUR-BANCE AT CHICAGO MAYOR'S YACHT PARTY'. The cameras were zooming in on a huge white yacht on Lake Michigan, and several police boats were already racing towards it. The scene shifted, and a reporter flashed on-screen, the yacht behind her right shoulder, horror etched across her face.

Evelina and I fell into silence, and I tried my hardest not to rip the skin from the backs of my fingers as I stared, barely blinking, at the final scene of my worst nightmare.

'MASS SHOOTING ABOARD MAYOR'S YACHT PARTY' scrolled across the screen.

Evelina covered her mouth with her hands, her scream trapped inside her. I was gripping the seat so hard, my fingernails were ripping into the leather. I stayed like that, glued, as the headlines changed, and slowly, slowly, the death toll mounted. All of them nameless.

I was still staring at the screen when Evelina got to her feet aeons later.

'Sophie,' she said, a hand laid on my shoulder. I barely felt it. 'I think we should call it a night.'

'Seven,' I said, my mouth so dry the words croaked out of it. 'And bodies in the water, too, they think.'

'Sophie,' she said.

'And injured. Lots of injured.'

'Sophie,' she said again. 'Look at me.'

I tore my eyes away from the screen, stared up at her. She was wearing a long pink robe – she had pulled all the threads from the ends, and now they were frayed around her fingers. 'This is part of your new life, Sophie. Learning to walk away. You can't look back. *We* can't look back. No matter how much we want to.'

Her mouth was moving but all I could hear was the word 'seven'. *Seven.* Seven dead already. Seven was a big number. Too big. One was too big.

'I have to know.' I lurched forward, willing the screen to change. There were no names released, just faraway images of body bags and police in riot gear rushing to and fro. Ambulances on standby. Sirens blaring. 'I have to know how many of them are . . . I need to know who . . .'

Evelina stood in front of the TV, head tilted to one side as she looked down on me. 'No, you don't. Not now. Not tonight.'

Something was heaving inside me, clawing against my insides. 'He could be dead,' I told her, my pitch rising. 'Or in the water, and if he's one of the bodies in the water then he won't survive because it's almost below freezing over there right now and—'

'Sophie.' Evelina hunkered down until we were at eye level. Over her shoulder, a helicopter panned over the scene of the shooting – the distant sounds of screams filling up the background. Seven. That was all of them. All the ones I cared about. Luca, Nic, Dom, Gino, Paulie, Elena, CJ.

'There won't be much more news tonight, Sophie. A good night's sleep will do you a world of good. Tomorrow is a brand new day.' I knew she wasn't trying to sound like a song from a Disney musical.

Evelina's hand on mine – warm, firm. 'Do you understand that this is part of your journey? Part of your recovery? We need to turn off the television, and you need to turn off your mind, and get some sleep. You need to start looking forward, to the future. You need to start concentrating on yourself again.'

'I – I need to know.'

'It won't change anything now.'

And that was the awful truth. It didn't matter. Because I was here and he was there. We had made our choices. We had said our goodbyes.

'Tomorrow,' she said, quietly. 'There'll be nothing tonight.

You can't be in this with them. You can't do anything. You're out.'

I was a statue, barely breathing. 'I'm out.'

'You're out.'

She shut the TV off – all the disturbing images and squealing sirens disappearing in one sudden blink. 'You're out,' she said, standing up again. 'You're out now.'

'I'm out,' I repeated, hoping to harness some kind of relief. There was nothing, just horror and grief, and fear.

'Go to bed, Sophie. Tomorrow is a new day.' She swallowed the unsteadiness in her voice. 'Keep walking away.'

She left me in the dark, staring at a blank screen, all the images bound up inside my head. Seven – and maybe more to come. Dead, dying, freezing in Lake Michigan. All of them. My family.

And what of the Marinos? Had they won in the end with the mayor behind them? Would they come for me next – the final notch on the Falcone belt? Suddenly Colorado didn't feel like nearly far enough.

The blood war was coming to an end. My family, my identity was gone. And so was the boy I loved.

And me?

I was out.

There was no solace in that.

# CHAPTER FIFTY-ONE

## PURSUIT

I sank into the cavernous silence, waiting for my legs to move. I fiddled with the bracelet on my wrist. Hope. I didn't feel any hope. We hadn't even done the countdown. Was it even midnight in Colorado? All I could think about was that death toll, creeping up my throat, choking me.

Evelina pottered somewhere overhead, getting ready for bed. Emilia had been asleep for hours.

Outside, a headlamp bathed the street in a sudden flash of bright light. I curled my fingers in my lap, my breath catching in my throat. The light vanished as the car rounded the bend, headlamps shutting off as quickly as they had appeared. The engine rumbled towards the house.

I crossed towards the window, peeked through the curtains at the Mercedes sitting outside Evelina Falcone's house and felt my knees go weak.

Was this my father's final coup? Was it a trick all along? Or had fate come to punish me for Felice's death?

The engine cut out and silence descended once more. My pulse raged in my eardrums. My family was dying hundreds of miles away and a Marino was sitting less than twenty yards from me, ready to complete the final task.

I knew instantly what I had to do. I crept into the hallway and pressed my forehead against the front door. I had done a lot of stuff I wasn't proud of, committed acts that would haunt me for ever, but in this I could be brave. I could do the right thing.

I slipped outside and shut the front door behind me, hearing the lock shift into place. I marched towards the end of the driveway, until I was close enough to the car and the shadows inside it. Close enough so they could see their final target standing in front of them.

The driver's door swung open, and I did the only thing I could do. I turned on my heel and ran as fast and as far away from Evelina's secret as I could, forcing the air into my lungs, waiting for a bullet in the back of my head.

Just not here. Not outside Evelina's house. Not in their world.

Somewhere on a yacht in Chicago, the Falcones were dying, and somewhere in the middle of a snowy mountain town in Colorado, so was I.

Maybe this was how it was always meant to go down.

I sprinted hard, spurred on by the sound of footsteps behind me.

There was no room for fear, just intent.

I wasn't running for my life. I was running for Emilia's life. For Evelina's life.

And I wasn't afraid, not any more.

# CHAPTER FIFTY-TWO

## INTO THE LIGHT

'Sophie?' That voice, so familiar and ragged with exhaustion, cut through the night. 'Sophie, stop!'

Impossible! My mind was playing tricks on me.

I kept running, my heart climbing into my throat.

'Sophie!' he huffed, his footsteps almost in time with mine now. He was so close I could hear his breathing on the wind. 'Please! Sophie!'

I wheeled around in time to see him skidding to a halt, almost slamming into me. He stopped himself just in time.

I was screaming his name inside my head, but when the word formed on my tongue, it was a pathetic thing, huffed out with the last of my breath. 'Luca?'

Luca was standing right across from me, our footsteps side by side in the snow-tipped pavement behind him. His black hair was mussed across his forehead, his bright eyes shining in the darkness. We reached for each other at the same time. I tugged him towards me by the collar of his jacket, and he pulled me into him, wrapping his arms around my waist and burying his face in my neck.

I rose on to my tiptoes to get closer to him, pressing my cheek against his, as relief burst me open and I sobbed so hard my body shook. He was alive. He was here. He was *here*.

'I want this life.' Luca's words hummed against my skin, his tears sliding against my cheeks. I could feel him shaking. 'I want possibility.'

I clutched him harder, feeling the dull roar of his heartbeat against my own. 'I thought you were dead,' I said. 'You're supposed to be dead.'

He pulled back from me, his hands coming to my face, his thumbs wiping the tears from underneath my eyes. His laugh was shaky, his words wobbly. 'Gee, thanks.' He ignored his own tears. They glistened against his skin.

'The yacht party,' I said, trying to explain. 'I thought—'

He shook his head, his words tumbling out in short breaths. 'I walked away,' he said. 'I walked away, Sophie.'

I was crying so hard all I could do was nod until my neck hurt. 'I've been driving all day to get to you. I've been driving for fifteen hours,' he said. 'I couldn't take any chances. I couldn't lead them to you. I rented a car, and broke every speed limit in the country. And then I got here, and I didn't know what to do, whether you would be asleep, whether you were even still here, so I thought I would wait until the morning. And then you came out and you got scared and I thought I would have to chase you all the way to Denver because damn if you aren't abnormally fast, Sophie!'

My laugh was just as shaky as his, the tears still streaming down my face. I pushed the words out, garbled and half-formed. 'I was awake. I couldn't bear to sleep. The yacht party, Luca. There's been casualties. A lot . . .'

'I know,' he said, his face crumpling. 'I was listening to it on the radio.'

'Do you know who . . . ?'

He shook his head, heaved a breath. 'Not yet.' He shut his eyes, tight, and when he opened them, they were clear again. 'I made my choice, Sophie. I made my choice.'

I pressed my palm against his heart. 'The choice to live.'

'And I'll live with the consequences. All that I've lost.'

'All that you'll gain,' I whispered, raising my chin so I could meet his eyes. 'I'm here for you. Whatever happens, I'm here.'

He ran his hands up and down my arms, warming my skin. He was mired in grief; it was etched across the planes of his face. I could feel it between us. But there was something else there too – clear and bright and bold. It was shining in his eyes. Purpose, rightness.

'It's over,' he said. 'It's over, Sophie. There is nothing more we can do.'

'How did you know where I was?' I asked, suddenly struck by the impossibility of it.

'Millie,' he said, the intensity in his expression flickering into a small smile. 'She made me promise that I wouldn't go back if I came here. That neither of us would. She made me swear it was for real.'

'She gave you the address.' And she hadn't said anything. Maybe she was afraid he wouldn't come.

'Not without a lengthy interrogation,' he said.

'She must have been sure of you.'

Luca pressed his forehead against mine. 'I've never been so sure of anything.'

My fingers were curled inside his sweater, clutching at his chest, pulling him closer, closer. 'My head is spinning,' I said.

Luca pulled back so he could look me in the eyes. 'I couldn't do it, Sophie. I couldn't do it, knowing there was another life for me out here with you. I saw what Millie did for you, how she waded into the darkness and pulled you out, and you went because you love her, because you owe yourself a decent life, and the truth is I love you more than I've ever loved anyone. You're the last good thing in my life – all the hope and joy for a future that I actually want, and when I watched you leave that day, it felt like my heart was splitting in two. I was stuck, balancing on the brink of hell, and then you tumbled into my life and for the first time, I saw the possibility of a life outside those walls. A life with you. A life worth living.' He inhaled sharply, coming closer until our noses were touching. 'And once I knew that, I couldn't let go of it. I'll go anywhere for you, Sophie. I want to be the person you see when you look at me.'

'That's who you are,' I said, knowing in my heart that it was true.

He pressed his lips against mine. That feeling, familiar and strong, came over me again.

'When I'm with you, it feels like coming home,' he said. 'I feel like I finally belong somewhere. You're my somewhere, Sophie.'

I pressed his hand against my heart so he could feel it racing beneath his fingertips. 'I'm going to go into cardiac arrest if you're not careful.'

His laugh was low and breathy. He slid his hand into my hair, his thumb caressing my cheek as I smiled against it. 'Just imagine how I feel every time you smile at me.'

I stood in the heat of his gaze and let myself burn. 'So, what now, Luca?'

'We'll have to lie low for a while, until the dust settles, until we're safe to move on.' He tipped my chin up with his index finger, a slow smile tugging at his lips. 'But we'll figure it out. Whatever happens, it will be an adventure.'

'Can we lie low in Disneyland?'

Luca tried to force a frown, but his lips were still curving. 'Trust you to lower the severity of the situation.'

'I'm trying to be helpful,' I pointed out.

'Why don't you leave the planning to me? I'm ridiculously intelligent, remember.'

I tapped my chin. 'But I don't respect your authority, remember?'

He grinned. 'That's why I love you so much.'

'Because I don't respect you?'

'Because you infuriate me,' he said, tapping my nose.

'And I love you,' I said, brushing my lips against his. 'Because you're so easy to infuriate.'

'Mmm,' he murmured, his mouth against mine.

'Come with me.' I dragged him back towards the house. I pulled out my phone and composed a quick text to Millie as we made our way back through the darkness.

Got your gift. He's a little tired and unkempt, but I think I'll keep him.

Her response was lightning fast.

Glorious news. Enjoy your lover, but don't forget who your soulmate is ☺

Never ☺

We reached Evelina's house, and I pulled him with me on to the porch and rapped my knuckles against the door. 'I just want Millie to know that I'm OK. Especially if I won't be seeing her for a while.'

'I'll make sure to reunite you two,' he said, before adding, with much less confidence, 'Once we figure out how to bury our underworld connections once and for all.'

'Speaking of which . . .' I said, looking at the net curtains as they rippled, and waving to let her know everything was fine.

Evelina swung the door open and took a step backwards into the hallway. 'Sophie? Is everything OK?'

We stepped inside, out of the darkness, and I pushed Luca in front of me so he could see. So he could witness possibility made flesh before him. His grip in mine grew harder. '*Mio Dio.*'

Evelina gasped into her hands, her dark eyes wide with disbelief.

'Evelina,' Luca breathed, wonder trilling in his voice. 'You're alive.'

She dropped her hands, a smile lighting up her face. '*La mia star*, so are you.'

And then they were embracing each other, laughing and crying as they hugged, and when they finally broke apart, neither of them quite believing their eyes, I was crying, too. We huddled together in that hallway – three Mafia runaways escaping from the underworld, and coming to live inside the possibility of a better future.

The path was dark, but somewhere in the distance, there was a flicker of light.

We could see it now.

I could see it.

# MAFIA BLOOD WAR ERUPTS AT MAYOR'S YACHT PARTY, KILLING SEVEN, INJURING TWELVE

A star-studded New Year's Eve party ended in tragedy on Friday night as rival Mafia gangs went head-to-head in front of hundreds of terrified onlookers.

In a strike thought to be connected to the Christmas Day Marino Massacre, where eight men and two women lost their lives, Elena Genovese-Falcone, sister of Donata Marino and widow of deceased mob boss Angelo Falcone, confronted her sister aboard the mayor of Chicago's private yacht party. Armed with a switchblade, she attacked the current Marino mob boss in front of shocked bystanders. Donata Marino died from a single stab wound in the chest. Witnesses report that Donata's cousin, Romano Marino, immediately opened fire on the crowd, killing Elena Genovese-Falcone, her son Dominico Falcone, and nephew, Calvino Falcone Jr, a minor. Security guard Ronald Smythe and dental hygienist Dawn Fierri lost their lives in the shooting, while a further twelve partygoers were injured. Several witnesses reported seeing three men jumping from the upper deck of the yacht into the near-freezing Lake Michigan, but search and rescue missions have failed to recover any bodies, and have now been called off.

Gunman Romano Marino was shot and killed by an armed bodyguard as the mayor was rushed to safety. This latest shoot-out marks the culmination of a particularly bloody period in Chicago's underworld, while Donata Marino's death is believed to spell the end of the active Marino dynasty. Several members of the Falcone crime family remain at large, and are currently wanted by the police for questioning. Sources close to the family have claimed that Nicoli Falcone has recently assumed leadership of the infamous dynasty. Falcone is the younger brother of the recently deceased 'blue-eyed assassin' Valentino Falcone and son of the late Angelo 'Angelmaker' Falcone. He is purported to be the youngest boss in Falcone history. The identity of the underboss remains unknown.

The investigation continues.

# EPILOGUE

The music from the radio was vibrating against the car windows, our voices drowning out the lyrics as we sang shamelessly at the top of our lungs. Luca was tapping a rhythm on the steering wheel, side-glancing at me with mock outrage as I pealed into another fit of laughter. Our fingers were entwined on the armrest between us, our faces pressed to the city as it rose to meet us.

It was summertime in Chicago, and my heart was full of possibility.

'There it is,' I shouted over the music. 'My one true love. Chicago.'

Luca pressed a hand to his heart. 'That hurts.'

'Were the buildings always so sparkly?' I asked.

'Was the sky always this blue?' he replied.

I batted my eyelashes at him. 'Can I know what the surprise is now?'

'Nope,' he said sweetly. 'Absolutely not.'

We drove into the heart of the city, Luca constantly rebuffing my curiosity, me refusing to relinquish it. Finally, we parked our rented Camaro in a garage on West Washington Street, and by the time I got out, I was almost ready to throttle him.

'*Now* can I know?'

He strode on to the street, beckoning for me to follow him. 'Why do you have to be so incessantly curious all the time?'

'Why do you have to be so incessantly annoying?'

He grinned at me over his shoulder. 'Just am, I suppose.'

I glared at the back of his head. 'I don't like surprises, I'll have you know.'

'You liked it when Millie came to visit you last week, didn't you? *That* was a surprise.'

'That was different,' I said pointedly. 'My love for Millie outweighs my distrust of surprises.'

Luca shrugged. 'Well, fortunately for me, I quite enjoy them.'

'You do not,' I said, jogging to keep up with his purposeful strides. He was dressed in jeans and army boots, his blue T-shirt rippling in the light breeze, and I was really trying to stay focused but even from the back, he was unfairly dazzling. 'You hate surprises.'

'OK, I'll amend that. I really enjoy Sophie-directed surprises.' He paused, and then added, 'Specifically when I'm the one doing the surprising.'

He slowed his pace, as if remembering that some of us

weren't over six feet tall. 'Don't keel over on me now,' he said warningly. 'It will ruin everything.'

The further away we got from the car the more buoyant he became. He was practically bouncing with every step, and not for the first time over the last six months, I found myself marvelling at this version of him: unguarded, happy, *free*.

I hurried along beside him, my yellow summer dress whipping behind me. The sun rippled along my arms, and I raised my face to it, letting it splash freckles across my cheeks. 'I forgot how much I loved summer in the city,' I said.

Luca nodded his agreement, his blue eyes blazing in the brightness. 'Some day, we can come back here for good, Soph.' His voice changed, a shred of darkness creeping in. 'Just not yet.'

*Not yet*, I reminded myself. It was too soon to rebuild a life with permanence, a life without threat. For now, everything was *not yet*.

'But we have today,' he said, his lips curving as he looked down on me. 'We'll make the most of it.'

Then I saw it. In fact, I would have seen it way sooner if I hadn't been dissecting every square inch of perfection on Luca's face. By the time I realized where we were, we were almost inside the Cadillac Palace Theatre. And I was standing directly in front of a giant billboard.

Every word in the English language galloped into oblivion. I was reading the words *The Phantom of the Opera* and I was trying very hard not to burst into tears. I thought I had sorted that annoying little problem out in recent months, but my heart was hammering in my chest, and my breathing had turned to little spiky inhales and I could feel Luca watching me, waiting for my reaction. I clamped my mouth shut and waited for my emotions to stop bouncing around inside me.

*Calm down. Focus. It's just a musical. It's not a big deal.*

*Yes, thank you, rational Sophie.*

*No. It's not just a musical. It's the musical. He's taking you here because your mother never got a chance to bring you.*

'Sophie?' Luca was leaning against the wall, his head cocked to one side, watching me. Concern rippled across his forehead. 'You haven't said anything.'

Oh God. I could feel my lip quivering.

His hand came to the small of my back – a gentle touch, a current of warmth in my skin as he drew me towards him. The world faded away, until it was just the two of us.

'Are you happy?' he asked me quietly. 'If you're not happy, we can go.'

'I'm happy,' I said. 'I'm so happy I think I might cry.'

He swiped a renegade tear from my cheek. I averted my gaze, clenching my nails into my palms to stop another one from sneaking out.

'Are you crying because you have to endure this with me?' he asked, delicately. 'That's it, right?'

'Yeah,' I said. 'You're just the worst.'

He pulled two tickets out of his pocket and pressed them into my hand. I wrapped my arm around his back, and he kissed the top of my head, his breath ruffling my hair. 'Happy birthday, *Cuore mio*.'

If anyone would have told me twelve months ago that I would be in a theatre, watching a giant chandelier swinging towards the ceiling as epic music shook the walls around me and thudded right down inside my heart while sitting shoulder to shoulder with the former boss of the entire Falcone dynasty and actually *enjoying myself*, I would have called them a dirty liar.

How quickly the world can change.

Months after being shot in the shoulder – after staring death in the face and rolling out from underneath it, after burying my mother and my father, relinquishing every tie to an identity I never wanted and clawing my way out of an underworld that once threatened to consume me, Luca had ignited something I thought I'd lost for ever. The soaring music, the drama, the passion, the sense of being elsewhere and other, of feeling safe and happy and thoroughly content. I felt joy, sitting in that dark room, my arm laid on top of his, our fingers grazing, our heads bent together. When the last song hit its crescendo, my eyes filled with tears, and I let the music sweep me up, away from the badness of the last year, and all the darkness it had left behind. I felt it then – the keenest sense of possibility – surrounding me. This other life – with creativity and art and music and love.

We emerged feeling giddy and breathless. I had a thousand different *thank you*s waiting on my tongue but they all jumbled together, so instead I grabbed Luca's hand, pulled him around the side of the theatre and kissed him until I lost my breath.

'Well,' he murmured, his finger tracing a line along my bottom lip. 'I should take you to the theatre more often.'

'Let's go home.' Back to a small, inconsequential town on the edge of Wisconsin that would do for now. Back to *not yet.*

He wove his arm around my back, his fingers trailing along my waist as we walked. 'My thoughts exactly.'

We hopped out on to the sidewalk, our footsteps made quicker by desire, our words lost to the thoughts in our head. At the next crossing, we hovered inside a huddle of theatre-goers scattering into the evening, and I don't know quite how, but I sensed it before I saw it. I felt it in the hairs on the back of my neck, in the goosebumps rippling along my bare arms. This feeling that the world was dimming, just a little.

We watched as a familiar black SUV rolled to a stop on the street beside us, the traffic light reflecting bright crimson along the hood of the car.

'Luca.' The word lodged in my throat, my heart climbing up to meet it.

He bristled against me, his hand moving behind his back. We stayed frozen like that until the traffic light turned green.

Slowly, the SUV started to move, and I wondered whether it was all in my head – the feeling that we were being watched as it rolled away from us.

When the SUV had disappeared down another side street, Luca released his grip on the gun inside his waistband.

'Just a coincidence,' he breathed.

'A coincidence,' I echoed.

He took my hand, pulling me with him. We ran all the way back to the car, the dying sun hot on our backs, Nic's face seared into my mind.

We were safe.

We were together.

We were running.

Always running.

# ACKNOWLEDGEMENTS

Phew! We made it! Well . . . most of us.

Publishing this trilogy with Chicken House has been a dream come true. Thank you to everyone at base for being so magical and enthusiastic. To Barry, for being the wizard at the helm of the operation, for taking a chance on me and giving me the freedom to take this story to weird, wonderful (and dark) places. Rachel H, Jazz, Laura S and Laura M, thank you for getting behind Sophie (and Luca) from Day One and staying behind them all the way through. Rachel L and Kesia, I couldn't have asked for a better editorial team. I would have you guys in my mafia family any day!

Thank you to Claire Wilson, who might just be the best thing that ever happened to me. I will be forever grateful for your kindness and wisdom. Thanks to my fellow Coven members, who are some of the most supportive, talented and hilarious people I've ever met. I feel very lucky to get to hang out with you and even luckier to get to call you my friends.

Thanks to my mom who raised me on a steady diet of musicals, plays and books – and thanks to my dad, who she made pay for them. I could go on and on about how deep my gratitude to both of you runs but I already did that at the end of *Inferno* and I don't want either of you getting a big head! Colm and Conor, as always, thanks for all your enthusiasm, humour and kindness. You're a couple of real sweet kids.

Thank you to my entire family, all the many branches that stretch far and wide. You have become the hype-masters for these books around the country and beyond. A thousand thank yous to all my amazing friends, who are the funniest, coolest people I know. Most of you are SO weird. And I love it.

Thank you to the bloggers, booksellers and librarians who have supported this series so ardently, and finally, to the readers, who have championed Sophie every step of the way. Thank you. Thank you. Thank you. I hope this story is a fitting end to her journey.

P.S. Thank you to those of you who helped me plot all of these fictional murders. You know who you are . . . And now I know what you're capable of. ❤

## UNDER ROSE-TAINTED SKIES by LOUISE GORNALL

I'm Norah, and my life happens within the walls of my house, where I live with my mom, and this evil overlord called Agoraphobia.

Everything's under control. It's not rosy – I'm not going to win any prizes for Most Exciting Life or anything, but at least I'm safe from the outside world, right?

Wrong. This new boy, Luke, just moved in next door, and suddenly staying safe isn't enough. If I don't take risks, how will I ever get out – or let anyone in?

*. . . the most beautiful, yet unflinching, depiction of agoraphobia I've ever read.*

HOLLY BOURNE

Paperback, ISBN 978-1-910655-86-3, £7.99  •  ebook, ISBN 978-1-910655-87-0, £7.99

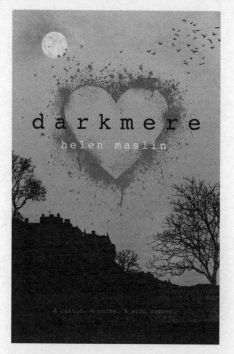

## DARKMERE by HELEN MASLIN

Outsider Kate has a crush on the coolest boy in school, Leo. He's inherited a castle, a menacing ruin on the rugged English coast. When he invites her along for the summer, she finally feels part of the gang.

But Darkmere's empty halls are haunted by dark ghosts. Two centuries ago, Elinor – the young wife of the castle's brooding master – uncovered a dreadful truth.

As past and present entwine, Kate and Elinor find themselves fighting for their lives – and for the ones they love.

Paperback, ISBN 978-1-910002-34-6, £7.99 • ebook, ISBN 978-1-910002-75-9, £7.99